NEW
PRIORITIES

Emmy's Story, Part 16

by
Kenneth Lee McGee

For Cousin Andy

He has been my biggest supporter
from the beginning.

For Cousin Andy

He has been my biggest supporter
from the beginning.

I would like to thank everyone who has

taken time to visit my website

kennethleemcgee.com

or my Amazon author page.

I appreciate the support

and kind words.

A special thanks to Dusty

for his insight and wisdom.

Prologue

South Hampshire officer Eric Sanders replied to the dispatch. "En route. Less than a minute out." He hit the lights and siren.

"Fire and rescue are on their way," the dispatcher said. "It doesn't look good according to a witness."

"Call for backup," Eric said as he turned onto Marlboro and mashed the accelerator to the floor.

"Will do."

Eric arrived on the scene and positioned his squad car behind the Civic. He jumped out and looked at the Chevy Suburban which had come to a stop fifty feet away as he approached the Honda. He peered into the car and saw the victim. Just then a man opened the driver's door of the large SUV and stumbled into the street.

"Stay right where you are!" Eric shouted. He heard squad cars and could see a firetruck and ambulance approaching. He looked into the Civic again and, even though he knew the victim could not hear him, whispered, "Hang on. Help will be here soon."

The firetruck and ambulance arrived and the paramedics rushed over to the Civic. As the first on the scene Officer Sanders issued directions to the other patrolmen. Very quickly the traffic was blocked and the driver of the Suburban, who didn't appear to have suffered any injuries, was placed in the back of one of the squad cars.

"He's a DUI," one of the officers told Eric. "He's oblivious to what happened."

Ten minutes later the paramedics loaded the victim from the Civic onto a gurney and into the ambulance. They immediately left for St. Bart's.

Officer Sanders took a deep breath and looked at the plates on the totaled car. "FAF1996. That plate looks familiar." He called it in and waited for a response. "Thanks, dispatch. I'll take it from here." He put a hand to his face and then rubbed his jaw. He walked back toward his car and retrieved his cell phone. *I can't do this over the network.* He took a deep breath and dialed a number.

1

"Hello, son. I thought you were working today," Police Chief Warren Sanders said. "Ray, could you check those steaks?" he shouted at his friend Ray Randich, the SoHam fire chief.

"I am on duty, and I'm at the scene of an accident," Eric replied.

Knowing his son would not call under most circumstances, Chief Sanders said, "Give me the details."

Officer Sanders did and then said, "You know them from the old neighborhood, right?"

"Yes, and I should handle the notification myself."

"That's why I called from my phone. I didn't want the media to catch it on the network."

"Smart thinking." Chief Sanders waved to his friend.

Ray Randich walked over carrying a set of tongs and saw the look on his friend's face. "This can't be good."

Sanders ended the call with his son and looked at Ray. "There's been an accident involving someone we both know, and I need to inform the family."

"I'll drive you since my car is blocking yours," Randich said.

"Thanks. Wayne, would you take care of the steaks, please?" Warren asked his brother. "We have to leave."

"Will do," Wayne replied without asking why.

"Let's go," Randich said. He led the way around the house to his official vehicle. They got in and he backed out of the driveway. "Where are we going?" he asked flipping on the lights.

"Bristol Ridge," Sanders answered. "The Colwell estate."

Ray looked at his friend and swore under his breath.

"Not him." Sanders shook his head. "It's Emmy. His wife." He used his cell phone to call dispatch and arranged for a squad car to meet them at Bristol Ridge.

Thirteen minutes later they arrived at the exclusive development. The security guard saw them approaching and raised the gate. Chief Randich roared past.

"It's the first driveway on the left. I hope the gate is open."

Fortunately, the gate was open and Randich killed the lights as he drove up the winding, hilly asphalt drive. He parked near the

2

front of the house, and the two men got out. They walked to the front porch, paused for a second and then slowly climbed the five steps.

"I doubt they ever use the front door," Sanders said. He took a deep breath and pressed the doorbell two times.

"What was that?" Kenny asked from the kitchen.

"Daddy! That was the front doorbell," Isabella said as she grabbed an apple from the island and raced away.

"Who would be ringing the front doorbell?" Kenny asked.

Rory, who had just entered the kitchen, turned and waved as he he walked down the hall. "I'll get it. It's probably Emmy trying to be funny." He laughed as he walked up to the double-door and opened it. The site of two men startled him for a split-second. "You're not..." He stared at the man on the right. "Oh, crap!" Rory muttered recognizing Warren Sanders.

Chief Sanders stared back for a moment, and then said, "Porter, right? Rory Porter from Raynor Park?"

"Yes, yes," Rory stammered. "Come in." Rory backed up and held the door open.

The men entered and waited just inside the door.

"We need to talk to Kenny," Sanders said without elaborating, but his serious expression spoke volumes.

"He's in the kitchen," Rory said. "I'll let him know you're here."

Rory turned and hurried back to the hallway dividing the house. Just as he turned the corner, he bumped into Kenny.

"Who is it, Rory?" Kenny asked.

"It's Warren Sanders and another man," Rory said quickly and then gulped.

Kenny walked around the corner and up to the entryway where Warren Sanders was staring at the floor while Ray Randich gazed at the high ceiling.

Kenny froze for a second before asking, "Chief Sanders, how can I help you?"

Sanders put an arm around Kenny's shoulders, squeezed and whispered, "I'm afraid I have bad news about Emmy."

Kenny clenched his jaw and nodded.

3

Rory and Rochelle stood in the hallway watching the scene unfold.

"Maybe you should watch the kids," Rory said. "I might need to take Kenny somewhere."

"There's been an accident, and she's on her way to St. Bart's. We're here to take you there," Sanders said.

Rory looked at Rochelle. "I'm going with him."

Rochelle nodded and said, "I will take care of the kids. Call me when you know anything."

"Do I need a coat or my wallet?" Kenny asked.

"No need," Chief Sanders said as Chief Randich walked outside. "We have his SUV and there is a squad car waiting."

"Should I say anything to the kids?" Rochelle asked.

Rory waved a hand and said, "Maybe you shouldn't until we know more, but you should find Father James' number and call him."

"What about her sister?" Rochelle asked.

"Shoot! I forgot about Diane. Could you call her, too?"

"I'll do that," Rochelle said. She kissed him.

Rory saw Kenny's cell phone and grabbed it.

The men hurried to the SUV. Sanders opened the rear door for Kenny. Rory jumped in on the other side. Randich turned the vehicle around and raced down the driveway. A waiting squad car escorted them out of the development.

Chapter One

Warren turned to look at Kenny, who had his eyes closed. "My son, Eric, was the first on the scene. He said she was alive."

Kenny opened his eyes and nodded.

"Do you know what happened?" Rory asked.

Sanders turned in his seat, placed one hand on the dash as Randich turned a corner fast enough to squeal the tires on the AWD vehicle and looked at Kenny and then Rory. "Her car was hit as she entered an intersection. The other driver ran a red light."

"Oh, that's bad." Rory nodded.

Kenny groaned, let his head fall back against the headrest but then turned and stared out the window.

The two vehicle convoy pulled into the horseshoe-shaped entryway of the Emergency section of St. Bart's and parked. The volunteer on duty stared as four men jumped out of the SUV.

"We're going to leave the vehicles here for the moment," the SoHam officer told the attendant.

"Yes, sir," he stammered in reply.

Ray Randich and Rory raced ahead of Kenny and Warren Sanders.

Eric Sanders, who had just arrived, saw them approaching and hurried down the hallway to meet them. "I can show you where they have Ms. Colasanti. Or does she go by Mrs. Colwell?"

"Both," Rory said and looked over his shoulder at Kenny. "Show us the way."

Chief Randich located the EMTs. "I want to talk to my people," he whispered and headed toward them.

"Please, follow me," Eric said holding a door open for the men.

Warren Sanders looked up at his son. His eyes asked the obvious question.

Eric shrugged and then shook his head. "I haven't heard anything yet," he whispered.

Eric led them past cubicles filled with patients. They turned a corner and saw two doctors rush into a cubicle and then a nurse drew the curtain closed. She saw the men and walked up to them.

"We're here about Emmy Colasanti," Sanders said. "I know you!" He waved a finger at the nurse trying to remember her name.

"Blair Wilewska," she answered. "We've met because I know your wife. We were in the same class at Roosevelt High."

Kenny and Rory stood behind Chief Sanders shifting their weight back and forth. Kenny clenched his jaw.

Sanders stepped aside and said, "This is Kenny Colwell. He is her husband."

Mrs. Wilewska stepped up to Kenny, looked at him and then Rory and said, "Your wife is alive and her vitals are stable, but she is still unconscious. The doctors are working as quickly as possible to assess her injuries, but this isn't TV. It will take time."

Kenny nodded. "I realize that."

Rory patted Kenny's back. "That's good to know."

"I want to see her," Kenny said.

"There's not much room in there, otherwise I would let you see her for a moment," Mrs. Wilewska said. "But I promise I will get you in there as soon as I can, okay?"

Kenny nodded and said, "Could you tell her I'm here and that I love her?"

"Of course, I will tell her right away."

"Is there a place we can wait without everyone... you know?" Sanders asked.

She nodded and said, "We will do everything possible to protect their privacy." She led them around a corner to a room with a door. "This is one of the old employee lounges, but no one uses it anymore. There is a vending machine, and I can get you water or coffee if you like."

"Thank you, Blair," the chief said. He glanced at Kenny and Rory. Neither of whom indicated a need for something to drink. "I think we're good for now."

"I will be here all night if need be," Mrs. Wilewska said. "As soon as the doctors know anything, I will let you know."

"Thank you. If you see Chief Randich, could you tell him where we are, please?" Sanders asked.

"Of course."

He led Kenny and Rory into the room and they took seats.

6

"Where are you living now, Rory?" Sanders asked.

"The Tampa area, Chief Sanders," Rory answered.

"Please, call me Warren. How is your mother?" Sanders thought about the day Mrs. Porter discovered her daughter shot to death in her apartment.

"She's doing all right. We see her several times a year."

Sanders looked at Kenny and thought about asking him something to keep his mind off Emmy, but decided against it.

The door opened and Father James entered. "I got here as fast as I could. How is she?"

Rory explained everything they knew.

Father James took a seat and started praying.

The men remained in the room for thirty minutes. At times they each got up and paced the small area.

"Sorry, Rory," Kenny said as he bumped into him. "I wasn't watching where I was going."

"No problem."

Rory's cell phone rang, and he stood in the corner to talk to Rochelle.

"Kevin was asking where his parents were, and he's hungry. Plus, I get the feeling they think it's weird that I'm the only adult here."

"Shoot! I didn't even think about that," Rory said. He looked at Kenny and then turned his back. "I didn't want him to be alone in case... you know. Father James is here now. I'll talk to him and see what he thinks. One of us should come back to the house, and since he's Emmy's brother, he should probably stay here."

"How will you get back?" Rochelle asked.

"I'll figure something out."

"Call me when you learn anything. I love you," she said.

"I will, and I love you more," Rory answered. He ended the call, looked at Kenny and sat beside Father James. He explained the situation at the house.

"You should go back. The kids know you," Father James said. "I just can't leave Emmy and Kenny right now."

Mrs. Wilewska knocked and entered the room.

"Do you have good news?" Chief Sanders asked.

7

"It is still early, but this is what we know. Does your wife go by Emily, or do you call her something else?" she asked Kenny with a practiced smile designed to help him relax and to talk.

"Everyone calls her Emmy," Kenny answered.

"Well, Emmy sustained a laceration to her scalp. That's why there was so much blood. That has been taken care of. The doctors do not think she broke any bones. They will do x-rays later. Of more concern is the fact she is still unconscious. Her vitals are stable. She is breathing on her own." Mrs. Wilewska glanced at her notes briefly. "At the moment she is undergoing a scan. The neurologist wants to check her brain for... issues. I've heard she is a very intelligent young woman. Is that true?"

Rory chuckled and said, "She's smarter than the three of us put together."

"I will let you know when we have more news. Can I get you anything for now?"

The men declined.

"I will return as soon as I know anything. One of the doctors will talk to you in a few minutes."

"That would be very much appreciated," Sanders said.

"Are you going to stay?" Rory asked the chief.

"I will stay a little longer. My son will be off duty in a couple of hours, but I told him to stay here to guard against any... uh... invaders of your privacy."

"I hate to ask, but could I get a ride back to Kenny's? My wife is alone with the kids, and they're asking questions."

"Not a problem as long as you don't mind riding in an unmarked unit. My SUV is back at my house."

"I should call Pastor Tyler and Tony and Diane and my parents," Kenny said. "Has anyone told the kids? I left without telling them where I was going." He reached into his pocket. "I don't have my phone."

"Shoot! I forgot to give it to you. I saw it on the island and grabbed it." Rory handed it to Kenny.

"Thanks, Rory. I will have to tell them soon, but I don't want to scare them. They are old enough to know something unusual is going on."

Ray Randich entered the room. "I talked to the paramedics, and they explained everything they did at the scene. They were able to extricate her quickly and that's in your wife's favor."

"We left the cars..."

"Taken care of," Randich said. "Unless you need me, I will head home. Your son or someone will drive you home whenever you're ready, Warren."

"Thanks for everything, Ray," He looked at Rory and then back at Ray. "Could I ask a favor?"

Randich agreed to take Rory back to the house. He looked up at Kenny and extended his hand. "I will pray your wife recovers quickly and completely."

"Thank you," Kenny whispered.

"Kenny, I'm going back to the house to help Rochelle with the kids. Call me as soon as you know anything."

"Thanks, Rory. I know you'd like to be here for Em, but someone needs to be at the house."

Five minutes later one of the doctors entered, introduced himself and reiterated everything Mrs. Wilewska had said. "I wish I knew more, but we have to wait for the results. We're doing an MRI now. The initial scan showed some brain swelling, but we did not see any sign of a bleed. Her brain activity is good. Her vitals are good, and we don't think she has any other significant injuries. She does have some cuts and bruises but no broken bones."

"Thank you, Dr. Bausch," Father James said.

Kenny saw the phone in his hand and slapped his forehead. "I forgot to make those calls, and I have to tell the kids."

"You can do it now, or I can call," Father James said.

"I'll call." He stared at the phone. "Maybe I should call Pastor Tyler first."

"Good idea. Maybe you should wait until Rory gets back to the house to tell the kids," Father James suggested.

Kenny nodded and called Tyler. "Hello, Pastor Tyler. This is Kenny Colwell." He explained the reason for the call.

"I just parked and will come to the ER," Tyler replied.

"Okay," Kenny said wondering why pastor Tyler would already be at St. Bart's.

9

"I will ask Mrs. Wilewska to show him where we are," Sanders said. He left the room, found her and explained the situation.

"I will wait for him," she said.

"I'm going to call the kids," Kenny said.

"Maybe you should call Tony and Sloane first," Father James said.

Kenny called Tony's cell phone, but it went straight to voicemail. He tried to remember Mama's number and dialed what he thought it was.

She answered after one ring.

"This is Kenny." He told Mama all he knew including the part about Rochelle being alone with the kids.

"I will stay with them. Ben is over there with Kevin."

"I appreciate that. Rory is heading back there. Maybe you should have him call my phone and I'll talk to the kids then."

"I will go right now," Mama said. "Kenny, God has everything under control. You have to trust Him."

"I know, Mama."

Five minutes later Pastor Tyler knocked and entered.

"That was quick," Father James said.

"How is she?" Tyler asked.

The guys sat down. Kenny told him what he knew and then asked, "Why were you already here?"

Tyler realized Kenny had not heard about Gideon. "I have more news, and it explains why Emmy was on her way to St. Bart's."

"What do you mean on her way to St. Bart's?" Kenny asked. "She was going to the grocery store."

"She was headed here because Gideon might have had another heart attack. I was coming down here to check on him."

"Not another one," Kenny said shaking his head and staring at the floor.

Father James put a hand on Kenny's back.

"I need to call Tony and my parents, " Kenny said looking up.

"I can make those calls," Tyler offered.

"Thanks, Pastor Tyler, but I should do it," Kenny said. He called his parents first and then called Tony.

"I'm almost there," Tony said. "I called Kristen and she called Diane and then I called Andy and Mr. Robertson. I called Pastor Tyler and I can't remember who else I called. Mama and Rochelle are watching the kids at your house, and I think Rory might be there. I saw an SUV fly past me earlier. I know I'm rambling, but I wanted everyone to know," Tony said talking faster than normal. "Where are you guys?"

"Come to the ER and ask for Mrs. Wilewska," Kenny said.

Sanders headed to the door and said, "I will watch for him. I'll show him where you are, but then I will go. I will make sure there is an officer on duty so no one bothers you. We are trying to keep this under wraps, but sooner or later, the news will leak out."

"Yes, there's nothing we can do about that. Thank you for everything, Warren." Kenny shook hands with him and thought about the days in Raynor Park where both families lived.

"I should see if I can find out anything about Gideon," Tyler said. "I'll be back as soon as I know."

Kenny's cell phone rang, and he saw it was the landline.

"I'm here with Mama, Rochelle and the kids," Rory said. "You better talk to them now."

"Can you put it on speaker?" Kenny asked.

"Sure thing," Rory said.

"Hi, kids," Kenny said as his voice cracked.

"Daddy! What's going on?" Heather asked. "Where are you and Mommy? Why did everyone rush off?"

Kenny took a deep breath and held it for a time before saying, "Your mother was in an accident, so she's at St. Bart's and the doctors are treating her."

"Is she okay?" Heather asked.

"Did she break her arm?" Kevin asked.

Isabella moved closer to the phone and asked, "Should Uncle Rory bring us to the hospital?"

"Not now. It would be better if you wait until later."

"Are you coming home soon? I'm hungry," Kevin said.

"Rory or Mama can make you something to eat," Kenny

said. "I might be here until you're in bed. I will call again after I know more."

"Give her a kiss from us, and tell her we will pray she gets better so she can come home tomorrow," Isabella said.

"I will tell her and kiss her for you," he said. "For now you better behave for Rory and Rochelle."

"I might spend the night here," Mama said.

"You don't need to," Kenny said.

"I will if needed, but let's see what happens."

"Thanks, Mama," Kenny said as Tony and Diane rushed into the room. Kenny noticed Tony's eyes were red and patted him on the back. "I've gotta go. Tony and Diane just got here."

"So what's going on?" Diane asked. "Don't tell me she's doing all right. I want the truth. Where is she? Why are you guys in here?"

"They're running some tests to check her brain," Father James said. "We're in here for some privacy."

Tony nodded without making his usual smart comment.

"Is she conscious? Have you talked to her?" Diane asked.

"We haven't seen her," Kenny said.

"Why the hell not?" Diane yelled. "She's your wife! You have a right to see her."

"Right now they're are running some tests," Father James said in a smoothing voice. "It's best we let the doctors do their jobs. We have to be patient and trust God."

Diane stared at him, shook her head and muttered, "That's easy for you to say."

"She might have a concussion, and the last we knew, she was still unconscious," Kenny added.

"You need to see her before they do anything else to her," Diane said sticking a finger in his chest. "You have to demand it."

"How should we tell your mother?" Kenny asked.

Diane laughed and said, "You can't be serious. You could tell her a thousand times, and she wouldn't remember it."

"So, we shouldn't tell her, right?"

"I don't see the point," Diane said.

Kenny and Diane sat down and Tony began pacing around

the room. Father James left to pray in the chapel.

Several minutes later everyone turned their attention to the door as Tyler returned.

"Sorry about the creaky door," Tyler said. "I hope it didn't spook anyone."

Kenny jumped up and asked, "Did you learn anything about Gideon?"

Tyler took a deep breath, looked at the men and Diane and shook his head. "They weren't going to tell me at first, but I explained I was his pastor and would need to call his mother." Tyler paused and stood up straight and looked at a spot on the opposite wall. "Gideon didn't make it," Tyler said with a clear and steady voice. "The paramedics worked on him and he was still... you know... when they arrived. They said he went into cardiac arrest and the doctors tried everything, but he didn't make it."

Kenny knew Tyler was not an emotional man and most often hid his feelings, but not this time. Kenny helped Tyler to a seat and sat beside him. Tyler leaned forward with his elbows on his knees and his head buried in his hands and sobbed quietly.

Diane looked up at Tony and mouthed, "Who is Gideon?"

Tony whispered the answer into her ear.

"Okay, I think Emmy's mentioned him," Diane said. "I wouldn't want to be the one to have to tell her about him."

"I hear ya," Tony said.

They looked at each other and realized they were assuming Emmy was going to be all right.

Dr. Peter Bausch returned with another doctor.

"Who are you and what do you know?" Diane jumped up and demanded.

"This is Dr. Powlus. He is the chief neurologist," Dr. Bausch answered.

"What can you tell us?" Kenny asked.

"I'm her sister, and I want to know what's happening," Diane added.

Dr. Powlus spoke using medical terms and then added, "What all that means is I believe the best thing for your wife would be to place her in a medically induced coma to allow the swelling to subside. It's similar to using anesthesia for an operation."

"How long will she be in a coma?" Diane asked.

"That depends on how soon the swelling is reduced. It varies among patients, but you can expect her to be in the coma for several days at least."

"If that's the best for Emmy, I will agree to what you said," Kenny replied. "But I want to see her before you do that."

"Yes! He needs to see her immediately!" Diane shouted.

"I will agree to that, but be prepared for how she looks," Dr. Powlus said. "Five minutes. No more."

Dr. Bausch led Kenny to the room. "You can talk to her for as long as you need."

"Thank you," Kenny said. He cautiously entered the room. He gasped when he saw her and didn't move for several seconds. He slid a chair next to the bed, sat down and took her hand in his. "Em, you look so tiny." He glanced at the bandage on her head. "I hope they didn't shave off all your hair. You will be mad if they did." He glanced at the IV line and at the monitor with its squiggly lines and ever-changing numbers. He closed his eyes, lowered his head, squeezed her hand and prayed, *Lord, I thank you for all You have given us. I don't make a habit of asking for things, but I am now.* He rested his head on the edge of the bed. *Please help the doctors find out what's wrong with Emmy. I know you can heal her, and that's what I would like.* His head jerked up and his eyes opened when he heard a beep. He stared at the monitor, but the beep did not repeat. He sniffled, wiped his eyes with his handkerchief and looked at her face. "I wish you could tell me if anything hurts. I would kiss it and make it well like we always have for the kids. I wonder what they did with your clothes." He looked around the room but didn't see them. "I guess I won't worry about that now." He took a deep breath and held it for a moment. "Just in case you're wondering, I've called everyone, and they are praying for you. Father James and Diane and Tony are here. Rory came with me, but he went back to the house to help Rochelle. The kids know some of what happened, and they said to tell you they love you and miss you already. I'm not sure how long you'll be here, but I'm going to stay until I know you're okay. The doctor said I shouldn't stay in here too long because you need your rest. If you wake up and don't see me, just holler and I'll come running." He stood up, leaned over, and tenderly kissed her mouth. "I love you, m'lady, and I know God is watching over you." He squeezed her hand one more time, turned and walked out.

Mrs. Wilewska saw him, handed him some tissues and said, "This is the plan. They are going to move her up to the NICU in about an hour. They will induce the coma and once everything is settled, you can stay in the room with her."

"Thank you, Mrs. Wilewska," Kenny said.

"You should call me Blair, and you are welcome. Your wife is going to get the best care possible."

Kenny returned to the waiting area, and everyone tried to talk at the same time.

He held up his hands. "Hang on." He explained what was going to happen and said, "There's really nothing you can do tonight. I'm going to stay here obviously..."

"So am I," Father James said.

"Me, too," Tony insisted.

"That won't help," Diane said. "Let's find something to eat and drink. Then we can talk about who's staying and who's not."

"Who is thirsty?" Tyler asked. "I will take orders."

"I could use something to drink," Diane said. "Kenny, you should get something because you haven't eaten since lunch."

Kenny took a deep breath and nodded. "I would like a Dr Pepper or a Coke."

"I'll see what I can find," Tyler said. "Tony?"

Tony turned away from the window and shook his head.

"You should sit for a while," Kenny said. "You've been standing for hours."

Tony waved. "I'm good. If I sit down, I might fall asleep."

"Tony, I appreciate you wanting to stay, but I think you should go home," Kenny said. "You have your own family to take care of."

"Are you sure? You will call if anything happens, right?"

"I promise," Kenny said.

Tyler returned with three cans of Dr Pepper. "I should go

15

home and help Liz with the kids. I'll be back early in the morning."

"Thank you for staying," Kenny said. "And thank you for making sure everyone knows about Emmy."

"I've been getting texts all night. People are concerned and praying, but they understand your need for privacy. Please call me immediately if anything changes," Tyler said. "Liz won't be able to sleep until she knows Emmy is all right."

"I will," Kenny said.

"I should go, too," Diane said. "Brady will have his hands full. Call me if anything changes."

Ten hours after arriving at St. Bart's, Emmy was moved into the NICU and placed in a coma. Kenny was able to sit with her an hour later.

"There's a waiting room at the end of the hall. I'm going to make that my base camp. Come and get me if you need a break," Father James said.

"I will, but I don't plan to leave the room. Oh, Mom and Dad called. They were at the house, too. They wanted to take the kids back to their house, but I thought it would be best if the kids stay at home. I told my parents to sleep in their own beds tonight because it could be a long week, and they will need the rest."

"Is Mama still at your house?" Father James asked.

"Rory said she stayed until the kids went to bed."

Father James headed to the waiting room, took a seat by the window and stretched out his legs.

"Is there anything I can get you, Father?" a nurse asked.

"Not at the moment. I'm going to take a nap. I'm staying here until we know she's going to be okay."

Chapter Two

Tyler Hammond walked into the NICU room with three Dr Peppers and a box of donuts. "I found these in the cafe."

"You found then?" Rory asked reaching for a Dr Pepper.

"I bought them because I'm hungry," Tyler replied. "I'll share." He glanced at Emmy and then at Kenny. "Did you get any sleep. You look rather haggard."

"I got a total of two hours. Ten minutes at a time," Kenny answered.

"Thanks, Pastor Tyler," Rory said. "I didn't realize anyone else would be up so early. I just got back a few minutes ago."

Tyler chuckled and said, "I'm an early riser. I like to get up before the kids. I take Derby for her walk and have time to pray and read the Bible."

"Speaking of kids, have you talked to them this morning?" Rory asked. "They were still asleep when I left the house."

Kenny shook his head. "No, but I texted them. They know Emmy was in an accident, but I didn't mention the coma thing yet."

"Who's watching them?" Tyler asked.

"Rory and Rochelle spent the night at the house," Kenny said.

"Are they going to school today?" Rory asked.

"I thought it would be best to try to maintain a normal day," Kenny said. "Diane will take them to school and pick them up. I said they could see their mother for a few minutes."

"Is that wise?" Tyler asked.

Kenny shrugged. "The nurse didn't recommend it, but she said she would look the other way as long as they were quiet."

Rory said, "Other than the tube in her mouth and the monitors and the lines attached to her, those bruises and that Foley thing, she looks like she's just sleeping."

"That makes it sound perfectly normal," Kenny said. "I told them the doctors had to cut her hair and use stitches on her. Kevin Michael wanted to know if she got a Superman Bandaid. I told him the whole top of her head was in a bandage."

17

"That sounds like Kevin," Tyler said and then chuckled.

"What do you imagine she's thinking about?" Kenny asked looking at Emmy and then the machines that glowed red and green.

"Who knows?" Rory shrugged.

"Do people dream when they're in a coma?" Kenny asked.

Rory shrugged and said, "I have no clue. We'll have to ask her when she wakes up."

"Suppose she is dreaming. She might not remember anything when she comes out of the coma," Rory said. "We don't remember most of our dreams when we wake up."

"But she might remember things she hasn't thought about for years," Kenny said and took a sip of Dr Pepper. He checked out the donuts and chose a chocolate glazed one.

"I'm going to talk to Father James and see if I can convince him to go home. He hasn't eaten anything and looks rather tired."

"Good luck with that," Kenny said. "He can be as stubborn as Emmy. I don't know for sure, but I think there's something wrong with him. He's losing weight when he shouldn't."

"I noticed that, too."

"He never complains about his own health. He thinks it's a sign of weakness."

"Tell me," Rory said and then chuckled. He drained his Dr Pepper and finished his donut. "The breakfast of champions. Caffeine and sugar."

Tyler returned and said, "I tried my best, but Father James won't budge. He vowed to stay here for the duration. I'm still getting texts from lots of people from church."

"I thought about calling Stephanie Grachan and having her prepare a press release, but I think I'll wait," Kenny said.

"Good idea," Rory said. "The whole world doesn't need to know about the accident."

Kenny looked at Emmy. "If she is dreaming, I hope they are good dreams."

"I hope she isn't having nightmares about the crash."

"I should talk to the guys about the tour," Kenny said. "There's a chance we might have to cancel or delay it."

"I'm sure she will all right before then," Rory said. "It

18

wouldn't surprise me if she wakes up tomorrow and asks for a chili dog from Darby's."

"Darby's sounds good now that you mention it."

"It's a little early but maybe later," Rory said.

"I could run over there and bring us back some food," Rory said later that morning. "Hospital food isn't all that good for you."

"Why do you say that?" Kenny asked.

"Because it's meant for sick people."

"You're sick, but it could be true. Are you sure you don't mind?"

"Not at all. We don't have anything as good as Darby's in Florida."

Kenny pulled out a twenty and handed it to Rory. "I'll take a chili cheese dog, fries and a root beer."

"So, the usual, huh?" Rory asked with a smile.

Kenny looked back at Emmy and sighed.

Rory touched his shoulder. "I'll let everyone know you need some time alone with her. They will understand."

"Thanks, Rory," Kenny said. "Who is here. I know my parents already left."

"Mr. and Mrs. Robertson are here. Tony and Mama were here, but they might have left. There was a couple from your church, or maybe a different one. Oh, the wife's name is Lynette."

"That's Paul and Lynette Jefferson. He's the pastor of SoHam First Nazarene. She and Emmy go back a long way. I should talk to them later," Kenny said. "Have you seen Father James lately?"

Rory chuckled and said, "Sister Ruth was here, and she demanded he leave and get some sleep."

"I don't think I know her," Kenny said.

"She's not much bigger than Emmy, but she sure made Father James cringe."

"Good! I'm glad there's someone who can order him around."

"I'll run to Darby's, but I need to get back to the house," Rory said.

19

"Oh, I forgot. Rochelle is there by herself. I'm sorry."

"She's been reading and listening to tunes. I promised I would bring her up here to see Emmy for a bit."

"You should take her out to dinner tonight," Kenny suggested. "You are on vacation. You should do something enjoyable."

"I might just take you up on that. I need a good pizza. We don't have a decent pizza place near us."

"Kerry Lynn's Pizza & Pasta is still our favorite."

"I know where it is." He glanced at Emmy. "She's gonna be all right," Rory said and then left the room. He stopped to tell everyone in the waiting room to give Kenny some privacy.

Kenny pulled a chair close to the bed, sat down and reached for her hand. He squeezed it and prayed silently for a moment. "I told the kids about the accident, and they want to see you after school. I know you would tell them to stay home, but they're coming. Don't worry about your hair or anything. You are still the most beautiful girl in the world to me. You wouldn't believe how many people have stopped by the hospital." He glanced at the ledge by the window. "You have a bunch of cards already. A couple plants, too. I'll read them to you later if you want." He let go of her hand and gently rubbed her arm. He looked across the bed at the IV lines in her other hand and arm. "Pastor Tyler sent out texts and emails, so probably everyone from church knows what happened. Oh, I'll have to make sure someone called Aunt Doris. She still doesn't have a computer or a smartphone." He closed his eyes for a moment and fought back the tears. "Warren Sanders and the fire chief brought me and Rory here yesterday. They came to the house and he told me about the accident. His son was the first officer on the scene. I guess I must have been in shock because I really didn't get emotional. I suppose I didn't want to cry in front of them, but now it's just you and me in the room, so please don't get mad at me if I get a bit emotional. I've never been able to be as transparent as you. The whole world can tell if you happy or sad or mad or whatever. You never hide your feelings. I guess it's a guy thing. Anyway, in case you're wondering why you can't wake up it's because the doctors are making you sleep to

20

allow your brain to get better. They don't know for sure how long it will take, but I'm going to be here until you wake up. I might have to run home once in a while to shower and change clothes so I don't reek too much. I'll have to sleep a little, but I'm sure someone will be here in case I'm not." He paused, took out his handkerchief and wiped his eyes. "Chief Sanders told me about the man who hit you. Apparently, he was drunk and walked away without a scratch. That figures. Rory and Tony were pretty upset about that, but I don't hate him. I don't like what he did, but I can't hate him. If he walked into the room right now, I don't think I would even yell at him. Of course, I have no idea what he looks like or even his name for that matter." He paused and took a deep breath. "I know God is looking out for you and I trust Him and the doctors with your life. We have to be patient, but I know you're going to get well. The kids will be your nurses after you get home." He paused and thought about Gideon for a moment. He decided that news could wait. "Rory ran to Darby's and is bringing back some food. He said hospital food isn't good for you. Maybe the smell of a chili dog and fries will help you get better. Too bad you can't eat one now because of that tube, but as soon as you can, I'll get you as many as you want."

"Knock, knock," a nurse said.

Kenny turned to look as the door opened.

"I'm sorry, but we have to check her vitals and do a little adjusting. Dr. Tillery and Dr. Powlus will be here shortly to examine her."

"Should I step out for a few minutes?" Kenny asked.

"It might be a good idea. You look like you could use a break. Is there anything I can get you?"

"Thanks, but I have some food coming."

"It won't take long, and I'll let you know when you can return."

Chapter Three

"Danny Darby was there, and he gave me a bunch of extra food," Rory said upon his return to the NICU.

"Was the twenty enough?" Kenny asked.

Rory laughed and said, "He wouldn't take any money." Rory set the food and drinks on the countertop on the far wall. "There are chili dogs, regular dogs, fries and a couple burgers."

"I'm not real hungry," Kenny said.

Rory pulled out a regular dog and handed it to Kenny. "That's understandable, but you need to eat something."

"I suppose you're right," Kenny replied. He turned and looked at Emmy. "Do you think she can smell the food?"

Rory took a bite of his chili dog and said with a full mouth, "She will be pissed if she can. She knows we went to Darby's and she can't eat anything."

"You're right about that."

"I'm going down the hall and see who's in the waiting room before I leave," Rory said a few minutes later.

"Could you take the food with you? I can't eat anything else, and I'd hate to waste it."

"Sure, and call me if you need anything," Rory said. He looked at Emmy and whispered, "It was his idea to get Darby's, Em. Don't be mad at me when you wake up."

"You can only see her for a few minutes, and you need to be very quiet," Kenny said Monday after school. "I should warn you about the machines."

"What machines?" Kevin asked. "Are there any robots?"

Kenny shook his head. "Sorry, Kevin, but there are no robots. There are monitors keeping track of Mommy's heart, and there's a machine helping her breathe." He made sure the kids would not be too shocked by her appearance. "Are you ready to see her?"

"Yes, and we will be real quiet," Isabella said.

Kenny opened the door and the kids followed him into the room. They slowly approached the bed.

Kevin pointed to the heart monitor. "I know what that does," he whispered.

"Can we hold her hand?" Isabella asked.

"Yes, but just one at a time. You can talk to her if you do it quietly. She won't be able to talk back because of the tube in her throat, but she can hear you."

One by one the kids took a turn.

"Okay, that's long enough," Kenny said after seeing Jewelle point to her watch.

"Goodbye, Mommy. We love you and will come back to see you later," Isabella said.

Kenny led them out of the room. He kept an eye on Heather, who had been very quiet the whole time.

"Are you okay, Heather?" he asked when they were back in the waiting area.

She looked up at him. "Is Mommy going to die?"

Kenny clenched his jaw, pulled Heather close and held her tightly. "No, she is going to be all right," he whispered. "It's going to take some time for the medicine to take effect. The doctors know what they're doing."

She wrapped her arms around her father. "I hate whoever caused the accident, and I wish they were dead!"

Kenny put his hand on the back of Heather's head and whispered, "That's not what Jesus would want. I know it's not easy to understand, but we are supposed to love him even though he hurt your mother."

"I won't hate him as much when Mommy gets well, but I will hit him as hard as I can if I ever see him."

Kenny met Jeff Rawlings, Dave Pershing, Paul Joseph and Adam Vicini Wednesday morning in the band's office.

"I'll try to make this brief because you're busy."

"We're not too busy to do whatever we can for you, Emmy and the kids," Jeff said after taking a sip of coffee.

"Any updates?" Dave asked.

"No, but the doctors are hopeful," Kenny said. He talked about Emmy's condition and then brought up the summer tour.

"I think we should cancel it," Jeff said. He set his coffee down and pointed a finger at Kenny and added, "You need to be here until Emmy is back home. That could take longer than we know."

"I'm not sure I agree with Jeff," Dave said. "But I will understand if we do cancel."

Kenny sat on the front edge of the desk. He faced the guys and gathered his thoughts. "I appreciate the concern about Emmy, but the doctors are extremely hopeful she will recover quickly. I would hate to cancel the tour today only to have Emmy be fully recovered by the end of the week."

"What do you suggest, Kenny?" P.J. asked. "It should be your call."

"I agree," Adam, the youngest member of the band said.

"Let's not make a decision until the weekend at least."

"Okay, but if we don't cancel, we will have to start rehearsing soon," Jeff said.

"I know, but I can't think about that at the moment. I'm going back to St. Bart's," Kenny said.

"Who is with Emmy now?" Adam asked.

"My parents came up this morning. They told me to go home and shower."

"Let us know when she wakes up," Jeff said.

"I will. Thanks for the positive thoughts."

He returned to her hospital room and sat beside the bed and touched her small hand. "I wonder what your dreams are about today, Em."

"You should go home and sleep in your own bed," Father James said as he entered Emmy's hospital room and saw Kenny struggling to stay awake in the recliner. "There's no reason for both of us to spend the night." He removed his light jacket, walked up to the bed and whispered, "I know you're faking it, little sister. Open your eyes and let me see that sparkle again."

"I could go home for a few hours, but I won't be able to get any sleep in our bed. I'm so used to her taking up two thirds of it." He looked at his wife, chuckled and said, "It's funny how such a

24

petite person can take up an entire king-size bed."

"You could always move her."

Kenny shook his head. "I'm used to sleeping with her right next to me."

"Any changes?" Father James asked. "Did they do another scan?"

"Yes, and the swelling is continuing to go down. They took an x-ray of her shoulder and there's nothing broken. It's pretty bruised, but that will heal quickly." He stood up and stretched his arms over his head. "Are you sure you want to stay again? You've been here every night so far."

"I don't mind. If I stay, I can get an early start on my visits. I now have three parishioners on the eighth floor, and a few more people I stop and talk to. They are happy for the company."

"Okay, you twisted my arm hard enough, but I'll be back early."

"Okay, you twisted my arm hard enough, but I'll be back early."

"Get a good night of sleep. She will still be here in the morning."

Chapter Four

"That is good news," Kenny said with a smile.

Dr. Tillery leaned over the bed and listened to Emmy's heart. "Nice and strong. I like that." He patted her hand, straightened up and faced Kenny. "We have started weaning her off the meds and the ventilator. By the morning she should be breathing entirely on her own."

"Do you know how soon she will wake up?" Kenny asked.

"That will depend on her. If I have to guess, I would say sometime in the morning," he answered while waving to a colleague. He looked back at Emmy. "She has recovered faster than expected. I wish I could take the credit, but I believe God has done the work."

"Will her memory be affected by the swelling?"

"She may be a bit fuzzy when she wakes up, but she shouldn't suffer from amnesia. I will stop in to see her in the morning. She will recover completely. I am very confident about that. The latest scan showed the swelling is almost gone." He patted Kenny's shoulder. "You should go home and get some rest. You're looking a bit haggard."

"I will, but I'll be back early."

Why do I keep walking along Fifth Street? Where am I going? I can smell hot dogs and fries. I have a taste for onion rings and root beer. I think that used to be our house, but I can't remember. Where is that ambulance going? My head feels sticky, and I keep hearing a loud noise. Why is everything covered in fog? That's where Rory used to live, and that's Kenny's house. Why are they next to each other. That can't be right. Where did my house go? It was just here between Kenny's and Rory's houses. Who is that girl riding a purple bike? Why won't that noise stop? Diane is that you? Why are you with Owen? Why do Kenny and Rory look like each other? I keep seeing flashing lights, and something smells funny. There's my house, but it looks bigger than it should. Who is that little boy? Why can I see two of me?

Emmy opened her eyes, blinked several times and looked around the room. She heard a beeping sound, turned her head to the left and saw a machine with squiggly lines and red numbers. She turned her head to the right and smiled.

"So you finally decided to wake up, huh?" Kenny asked with a straight face. "It's about time."

"Where am I?"

"St. Bart's," he answered. "You were in an accident."

She closed her eyes and fell back to sleep.

"Thank you, Lord," Kenny said letting his tears flow.

She woke up again an hour later.

"You're still here," she whispered.

Kenny leaned closer, took her hand and said, "I thought I'd stick around since I didn't have anywhere else to go. How do you feel?"

"My throat feels funny, and I'm thirsty. Could I have some ice water?"

"I might be able to get you some, but it will cost you. They charge you for everything little thing here." He sighed and added, "Sorry, that's a bad joke."

"What day is it? How long have I been here?"

Kenny squeezed her hand and answered, "Two years, seven months and three days. Give or take."

"No wonder I have to pee," she replied.

He looked at the Foley bag attached to the bed.

"How long really?"

"This is Friday morning. What do you remember?"

"Everything seems fuzzy."

"Do you remember what happened?"

She closed her eyes for a moment. "I think I was driving my car. I'm not sure, but I think I was going home."

"Anything else?"

She looked around the room again. "I think I was dreaming."

"Can you remember anything about the dreams?"

"Not really."

"Anything at all?"

27

She closed her eyes for a moment. "Yes, I was back in high school." She looked up as a nurse brought in some water with lots of ice chips.

"I thought you might need something cool," Jewelle Ellis said. "I'm going to give you a few minutes to talk. Then I will check your vitals. Are you warm enough?"

Emmy looked at the thin blanket and touched the hospital gown. "I'm okay."

"Take it easy with the ice water. I don't want you to choke," Jewelle said. "I will be right outside."

Emmy watched Jewelle waddle out of the room and heard her humming a tune she recognized as one of her own. She turned back to Kenny. "My dreams felt so real. I could swear I was really in high school." She paused for a time. Looked around the room again and said, "Was I in a car crash?" She touched the left side of her head and felt a bump and some stitches.

"You were on your way... here," Kenny said. "You were hit by a large SUV and it caused your brain to swell. The doctors decided it would be for the best to put you in a coma until your brain could recover. They said it might take a while, but you recovered quicker than expected. I fully believe all the prayers said in your behalf helped."

"What happened to my head?" She touched the area again.

"They had to shave part of it because you needed stitches and you might have some headaches, but nothing too severe. You might have a small scar on your forehead."

She stared at Kenny for at least fifteen seconds. "Who are you? You look familiar, but I don't remember your name. Are you a doctor?"

Kenny looked at her and waited for her to smile. She didn't.

"Are you serious?"

"Yes, I think so." She looked at her hands then at Kenny and asked, "Will I still be able to play the guitar?"

He laughed and squeezed her hand again. "You're a goof."

"I seem to remember some children. Do you know who I mean?" she asked and then grinned.

"They stopped by to see you everyday after school. I told

28

them you could hear, so they sat and told you about school. Heather thought she could pull a fast one. She confessed she likes a boy at school without knowing I heard her."

"I hope you grounded her," Emmy whispered. "Why does my voice sound so funny and weak?"

"You've had a tube down your throat all week," he explained. "You probably shouldn't try to sing for a while."

She grinned and asked, "Am I a famous rock star?"

"You're a real riot, Em. I'm the famous rock star."

"No, you're a dorky rock star. I remember that much."

"Kevin Michael asked when you were coming home. He said he was hungry and you need to make breakfast."

"Do I know how to cook?" Emmy asked and then took a sip of water.

Kenny tilted his hand back and forth. "So, so. You can cook the basics. Instant oatmeal, hot dogs, frozen pizza."

"Why was I coming to St. Bart's? That's where I am, right?"

"Yes, you're not at Mercy."

"Have you been here the whole time?"

"Just about. I did go home to change clothes, shower and sleep an hour or two most nights. Rory and Tony have been here a lot. Pastor Tyler and Liz have been in to see you everyday. Actually, you've had lots of visitors, but you might not remember since you were busy dreaming about Roosevelt High. Father James has spent every night with you so I could get some rest."

"He didn't need to do that, but I'm glad he did. I would stay with him if he was in the hospital," she said. "Did the kids come to see me? They probably shouldn't have. I probably look horrible."

Kenny ignored the fact she was asking the same question again. "They were here for a few minutes. Kevin was fascinated by the machines they had monitoring you. He said he wants to be a brain doctor now and a bug scientist on the side."

"He changes his mind every week." She glanced around the room, noticed lots of cards and a couple plants by the window. "I should read the cards now that I'm awake."

Kenny gathered the cards and handed them to her. She

smiled and even laughed at some of them.

"This is just like Tony to find a goofy card."

She continued to read and came across one from the worship team.

"What do they mean by 'sorry for your loss.'" She stared at Kenny and then closed her eyes. She opened them a moment later. "I remember where I was going now. I was coming here because of Gideon. How is he doing?"

Kenny blinked rapidly, then clenched his jaw. He took her hand and laced his fingers with hers. *Lord, should I tell her the truth? Is this one time when a lie would be better. Shoot! Why did you have to remember this now?* He closed his eyes and prayed. He opened them and saw tears streaming down her face.

"Tell me, Kenny. I'm strong enough to know."

"I'm sorry, Em, but he didn't make it. He passed away about an hour after he arrived."

She closed her eyes and Kenny could see her lips moving as she prayed. "Did I miss the funeral?"

"It's actually tomorrow, but it's in Los Angeles. That's what his mother and brother wanted."

"I can't believe he's gone. He was so young." She reached for Kenny and he held her while she cried.

That afternoon Emmy heard a knock on the door and a familiar voice asking if anyone was home.

"You can't come in unless you've got a chili dog, fries and a root beer," she said.

Father James walked into the room, up to the bed and handed her a bag. "I guess you're feeling better."

She opened the bag and took a fry. "They're still warm."

"I try to please," he said.

Kenny moved a chair next to the bed. "Have a seat. I need to use the little boy's room."

Emmy laughed and said, "Such a dork."

At that moment Kenny knew she would be all right.

"Where's my root beer?" she asked taking another fry.

"I've got the drinks," Rory said as he entered. "Did you

30

want root beer? I got you a Diet Coke."

"You better not have," she said pulling the blanket up higher.

"I know better." Rory handed her the root beer.

"Where's Rochelle?"

"She's doing laundry. We're leaving tomorrow," he said.

"Why? You just got here. I haven't had enough time to see you guys."

"Sweetie, we've been here too long. It's been almost a week. We need to get back to work," he explained. "Besides, I've been here everyday, and you wouldn't even talk to me."

"That's because you were so boring it put me in a coma," she said with a grin.

He smiled back. "I always thought if you were ever in an accident it would be because you were speeding, but you couldn't have been going very fast."

A different nurse entered, saw the chili dog and fries and frowned. "I suppose it's all right since you aren't on a restricted diet." She glared at the men and pointed to the clock.

"We won't stay long," Rory said.

Rory and Rochelle stopped in for a brief visit Saturday before flying home.

"You can come in," Emmy said when she saw Rory in the doorway. "Kenny brought some pajamas for me. I'm not wearing a hospital gown now."

Rory and Rochelle entered and stood beside the bed.

"You look a lot better today, Emmy," Rochelle said. "There's more color in your cheeks."

"That's just the bruises," Emmy replied. "I'm purple and yellow and red all over. You guys can pull up a chair."

"I'll let Rory talk to you. I want to read your cards. Do you mind?" Rochelle asked.

"Go ahead." Emmy pointed to the window. "I keep getting them by the handful."

Rory moved one of the smaller chairs next to the bed and looked at the monitor. "Your numbers look good."

31

"I feel pretty good. I get a bit woozy when I get up to pee."

Rory checked the bottom rail of the bed. "They removed the Foley, huh?"

Emmy giggled and said, "Now I can pee like a normal person again."

They talked about the kids, Rory's job and made small talk for a few minutes. Then they looked into each other's eyes.

Rory took a deep breath then whispered, "Maybe I shouldn't tell you this."

"You can tell me anything," she whispered back.

"You scared the crap out of me, Em. When Chief Sanders first told us about the accident, I thought we were going to lose you. I was so worried about Kenny and the kids. I didn't know how they would cope with that. I don't often pray for selfish things, but I did on the way here. I'm certainly not one who can pray in front of people or anything, but I prayed silently."

"God hears every prayer, Rory. It doesn't matter if you talk out loud or pray silently. There are some people who pray very eloquently and use all the fancy words Christians are supposed to say, and there are others like me who just kinda talk to God using normal language."

Rochelle walked up behind Rory and placed her hands on his shoulders. "You should say goodbye for now. We need to get to the airport. I will wait outside if you want."

Rory grabbed Rochelle's hand for a second. "You don't need to leave. We were through talking."

"Have a safe flight home," Emmy said. "Thank you for staying. I know you missed work."

"Send us an email when you feel up to it," Rory said. He squeezed Emmy's hand, stood up and turned to leave.

Later that day, Gideon T. Logan was laid to rest under sunny skies, and Emmy wept as she thought about him.

"Can we really see Mommy after church?" Kevin asked when they arrived Sunday morning.

"Yes, she might be moved to a different room today," Kenny answered.

"Does that mean she isn't hooked up to machines?"

"She might still be hooked up a heart monitor or something, but she will be able to talk to you."

"Uncle Tony said she will come home soon, but we still need to be quiet and help around the house," Isabella said.

"Who's ready to see Mommy?" Kenny asked after church.

"Dad! Do you have to ask? Of course we want to see her," Heather said.

"Is she still in the NICU?" Isabella asked.

Kenny pulled out of the parking lot and headed to St. Bart's. "She is in a regular room now, and she can talk to you."

Emmy was sitting in a recliner when Kenny and the kids arrived. She held out her arms and hugged each one.

"I am so glad to see you. I missed you so much."

"We missed you, too," Isabella said.

The kids stood in front of her and told stories about their week.

"When are you coming home?" Kevin asked.

"I'm hoping it will be real soon. They did another scan on my head this morning and the doctor said I was doing great. Have you been helping Daddy around the house?"

"Yes, and Mama came over to help us clean. She made us straighten up our rooms and she cleaned all the bathrooms," Kevin said.

Emmy stared at Kenny and frowned.

"You weren't supposed to know, Em. I tried to stop her, but you know how she is. She insisted on helping."

"Did she cook for you, too?" Emmy asked.

"She made meatballs in the Crock-pot with sauerkraut, and it was good. I ate three helpings and didn't get sick," Kevin said while rubbing his stomach.

"I can't wait to get home and eat real food," Emmy said.

"I have good news," Kenny said as he made pancakes for breakfast Tuesday.

"What is it?" Isabella asked as she poured orange juice into her glass. "Is Mommy coming home today?"

Kenny smiled and flipped over the last three pancakes. "There is a very good chance she will be released this afternoon. You might need to get a ride home with Aunt Diane."

"I hope Mommy gets to come home. She's been gone for so long," Isabella said.

He took the kids to school and drove to the Walker Management office building.

"Good morning, Gladys," Kenny said to Andy's longtime secretary, Mrs. Santos.

"Everybody is in the conference room," she replied without looking up. She tapped a pencil on the desk and muttered, "I hate being put on hold. Oh, I heard your wife might be released today. Is that true?"

"There's a very good chance," Kenny said. He headed to the conference room and updated everyone on Emmy's condition.

"That's good to hear," Jeff Rawlings said.

Andy Walker sat at the head of the large mahogany table and studied a printout of the upcoming Fridays At Five summer tour. "If everyone would take a seat, we can start."

The men sat and looked at Kenny.

"Now that Emmy is coming home, I believe we can go ahead with the tour," Kenny said glancing at each man.

"Now wait a second," Jeff said. "That is great news, but shouldn't you be home while she recovers?"

"That's a good point," Dave said.

"Thank you for your concern, but she is doing great. The doctors have assured me she will be back to normal in a few days."

"Has Emmy said anything about the tour?" Andy asked.

"We talked about it, and she told me to go ahead. I might see if I can hire someone to help around the house for the summer, but that might not even be needed."

After some discussion, the band voted not to cancel the tour.

Kenny left and drove to St. Bart's. He walked into her room and saw an empty bed. He checked the bathroom and then went back out into the hallway. He saw her walking toward him with one of the physical therapists and smiled.

34

"I am so ready to come home," she said.

Kenny looked at the therapist. "Is she ready?"

The therapist nodded. "She is ready to go as soon as Dr. Tillery signs the paperwork. It should be an hour or so."

"That means three hours," Emmy said. "Hospitals run on a different timescale."

This time was different and Emmy was released and on her way home just after two.

"If you get your car, I will stay with your wife," Jewelle said as she pushed Emmy in a wheelchair.

"Right! I need to get the car. Where did I park it?"

Jewelle laughed and said, "Is he always this way. He reminds me of an absentminded professor."

"He's always been a dork," Emmy said. "But I love him that way."

Kenny pulled up and Emmy hugged Jewelle before getting in the car.

"Do you want to hear more about my dreams?" she asked as he drove.

"You can tell me tonight if you want. The kids will be so excited to see you. Should I make something special for dinner?"

She looked out the window, sighed and said, "I have a taste for hamburger pie. Could you make that?"

"I believe I could handle it," he replied.

"Mom! Mom! Are you home?" Kevin shouted as he raced from the mudroom into the kitchen and then down the hall.

"I'm in the family room," she answered.

She smiled as the kids raced down the hall and skidded to a stop in front of the couch.

"You know you aren't supposed to run in the house, but I'll let it slide this time." She hugged all three kids at once and then wiped away the tears.

Chapter Five

"How are you feeling this morning, Em?" Kenny asked while sitting on the edge of the bed.

She sat up and pulled her knees up. "I'm okay, Kenny. You don't have to treat me like a baby." She glanced at the clock. "Why did you let me sleep so late? Did you take the kids to school?"

"Diane did, and I thought you might need the rest. It's only nine thirty."

"Half the morning is gone."

"I could make breakfast if you're hungry," he said standing up.

"I have a taste for pancakes. Could you make some while I shower, please?"

"You wish is my command, m'lady," he said with a grin.

Emmy got out of bed. "Such a dork," she said walking toward the bathroom. "If we don't have blueberries, you could use chocolate chips."

"As you wish," he replied.

Emmy came downstairs fifteen minutes later and sat at the kitchen island. Did you hear from Rory or Rochelle?"

"Got a text saying they arrived safely, and they wish you well," Kenny answered. He stacked three pancakes on a plate and set it in front of her. "I added butter already. Should I pour the syrup on them?"

She took the jug of maple syrup from him. "I can do that myself."

Kenny sat next to her and watched.

"Are you going to cut up my pancakes for me?" she asked with a glare.

"I can if you... Sorry, Em. I don't mean to be a pain in the butt. I'm still worried about you."

She reached up to the cut in her scalp. "I'm going to be all right. Most of my bruises are clearing up, and I didn't break any bones. My brain is functioning like before the accident. What did you say your name was?"

"Very funny, Em. Have you given any thought to replacing

your car?" he asked.

She shook her head. "I'll drive my BMW for now. I don't think I'll ever want a compact car again. I feel safer in a SUV."

"I can make more pancakes if you're still hungry."

"Three was enough," she said. She got up and placed her plate in the sink. She leaned against the counter and took a deep breath. "I had an idea for a new book."

"About what? Are you going to write about the accident?"

"Not exactly," she said and then bit her lip.

"What then?" He opened the fridge, grabbed a bottle of water and took a sip.

She took the water from him and handed it back after taking a long drink. "I have some scenes floating in my head about a girl in high school and some things that happen to her."

"Are these things based on anyone I know?"

"It's not things I did if that's what you mean," she answered walking away.

He followed her down the hallway and into the family room. She sat on the couch facing the TV, and he sat in his leather recliner. They stared at each other for a moment.

"While I was in my coma or whatever, I had some dreams about when I was in high school. I thought about things I hadn't thought of for years, and even recalled some times I might have never mentioned."

"Are you going to enlighten me now?"

"Maybe I should get some ideas on the computer before I let you read anything."

"How are you feeling, Em?" Kristen asked as she sat in the kitchen nook drinking coffee with Emmy Wednesday morning.

"I'm feeling better. I'm still weaker than before the accident, but I haven't had a headache for a couple days."

"That's good," Kristen said. She looked outside for a moment. "Where's Kenny?"

"The band is rehearsing for the summer tour. He dropped the kids at school and should be home by six. Diane will pick up the kids for me."

"Have you driven anywhere since the accident?" Kristen asked.

"I drove around the neighborhood but that's all."

"Has your doctor said anything about driving?"

"He said I should take it easy for now. No long road trips," Emmy answered.

They sipped their coffee in silence for a time.

"I don't know if you've heard this from anyone, but John moved out," Kristen said as calmly as if she was talking about a grocery list.

"What?" Emmy yelled spilling the last of her coffee. "What do you mean by that?"

"He took some stuff and is staying with a friend."

"Why? When did this happen? Are you yanking my chain?"

Kristen shook her head, looked out the window and sighed.

"You better tell me everything," Emmy ordered.

"I didn't want to mention it before..."

"I'm not in a coma now! I need to know what's going on with my friends."

"Settle down, Em, and I'll explain." Kristen stood up and took the coffee cups to the sink.

"I will not settle down," Emmy shouted using air quotes. "What's going on?"

Kristen returned to the nook and sat across from Emmy. "Things have not been going well for a while, and last Saturday we got into an argument and he left."

"Have you talked to him since then?"

"No, but I asked Tony if he knew anything."

Emmy rolled her eyes. "That creep wouldn't know anything if it hit him in the head with a boulder."

"That doesn't make any sense, Em," Kristen said.

"Has John been going to work? Did you ask Tony that?"

"Yes, and John didn't say anything about moving out to Tony. Tony was shocked when he found out."

"Does Mama know?" Emmy asked. "She will be really pissed if she finds out."

38

"I made Tony promise not to tell her for the time being, but I'm sure she will hear about it from the kids soon enough."

"Do your parents know?"

Kristen nodded. "They're on vacation right now. I told Mom Monday. That was difficult. She didn't take it well."

Emmy put her hands on the table and buried her face in them.

Kristen chuckled and said, "I always thought if any of us had trouble in our marriage it would be you."

Emmy raised up and stared at Kristen. "Why would you think that?"

"Because of your relationship with Rory," Kristen answered with a shrug.

Emmy sighed and buried her face in her hands again.

"John hasn't been as attentive the last couple of months," Kristen admitted.

"Are you saying you haven't had sex for that long?"

"Maybe longer."

"Jesus, Kristen! Why not?"

"We have been so busy," Kristen said.

"That's the lamest excuse I've ever heard. Kenny and I manage to have sex even when he's on tour."

Kristen stared at Emmy.

"Stop looking at me like that. I'm not talking about sex with other people," Emmy said. She looked directly at Kristen and asked, "Is John having an affair?"

"Not that I know of," Kristen answered.

"Maybe you should find out!" Emmy yelled. "If I thought Kenny was fooling around I would be furious, and you better believe I would get all over his case."

"I am not you," Kristen said. She got up and grabbed her purse and keys. "I'm going home. I'm glad you feel better, Em, but try not to get all upset about John and me."

"How can I not get upset? I feel like puking. We've been friends forever. Have you thought about counseling? My parents went to a counselor and she helped them."

"I don't know if he would even consider it, Em. Anyway,

39

this could all blow over, and he will come back this week."

"Ha! Even if he comes back, you guys have issues to work out. You can't go for months without having sex. That just ain't normal."

"Please don't tell anyone. I don't want anyone to worry about us," Kristen said as she left.

"I will pray for you guys. You can't stop me from doing that," Emmy whispered as she walked into the laundry room.

"Are you busy?" Father James asked over the phone Sunday afternoon.

"I don't have any plans other than doing laundry," Emmy said. "Kenny is down at the warehouse rehearsing with the band and the kids are playing outside."

"Should I stop at Darby's?" he asked.

Emmy thought about it. "I haven't had a chili dog in forever, but you don't have to stop if it's out of your way."

Father James laughed. "That means you want one. I'll stop and order dogs and fries, but you have to provide the beverages."

"Deal, but I'm not sure there's any beer left in the garage," Emmy answered while grinning.

"I'll take my chances."

Father James opened the mudroom door forty minutes later and walked into the kitchen. "I'm here. Where are you?"

Emmy walked out of the laundry room carrying a basket of folded clothes. "You walked right past me. What did you get? How much do I owe you?" She set the basket on the island and rolled her eyes. "Why do I even ask? Danny never makes you pay."

Father James set the bag of food on the counter. "FYI, Danny wasn't there, and I had to pay like any other customer. I grabbed the last two beers, too."

"Did you really have to pay? Must have been a new employee," Emmy said. "You can have both beers."

"Obviously a breakdown in communication." He opened one of the bottles and sat down on a barstool. "I didn't know how hungry you would be, so I bought three chili dogs and two large fries." He looked at his half-sister. "Are you eating at all? You

40

look like you've lost more weight, and you don't have many pounds to lose."

"I haven't been on a scale, but my jeans are looser." She looked at him. "I'm not the only one losing weight. You look like you've lost several pounds. Your face is a lot thinner."

"I've lost a few pounds. I haven't had much of an appetite lately."

"Did you bring ketchup, or do I need some from the fridge?"

"I assumed you would have a bottle here." He emptied the bag and set the food on the granite countertop.

Emmy grabbed the ketchup and a bottle of water from the fridge and sat next to him.

"I talked to the bishop yesterday," he said and then took a bite of his chili dog.

"And?"

"Since that young priest is doing pretty much all the work at St. John's, the bishop reassigned me."

"To do what? Where?"

"The hospital chaplain passed away last month, so I've been assigned to replace him."

"Does that mean you aren't a priest anymore?"

"I will always be a priest, but my duties have changed because of my health. Eat your food while it's hot, and I'll explain."

"Please do. Does this have anything to do with your father? You said he was doing better and the stroke wasn't very severe. You're not moving back to Kansas, are you?"

He waved a hand as he chewed and then swallowed a bite of his chili dog. "I'm not going back to Kansas."

"Does this have anything to do with your weight loss?"

"Maybe."

"If you can't keep living in the rectory at St. John's, you could stay with us," Emmy offered.

Father James smiled.

Emmy saw his smile. "Is that what you had in mind? Were you going to ask to stay here?"

"I thought I could help with the kids until you regain your

41

strength," he replied. "It would only be for a few days, and they aren't kicking me out of the rectory. I can live there until I'm eighty. Priests don't retire. It's a lifelong calling."

"I'm not an invalid, but I could use some help. If we do allow you to stay for a few days, you have to clean the nanny suite yourself. I'm not cleaning up after you."

"I can do that."

She bit her lip and moved her head back and forth. "You have to buy your own beer and those nuts you're always eating."

"They're called pistachios." He scratched his forehead. "My own beer, huh?"

"Yeah! No way I'm buying it."

"I suppose I could buy the cheap stuff. All right! It's a deal." He offered a hand and she shook it.

"How soon do you want to move in?"

"I am a simple man of few worldly possessions," he said folding his hands as if praying.

"Do you have your clothes in the car?" Emmy asked rolling her eyes.

"I might have packed a suitcase with essentials. Do you need to talk to Kenny first?"

"I'm sure he won't mind. You do realize we can close off the nanny suite from the rest of the house, right?" she asked.

"I do need some privacy for my devotional times," he said with a smile.

The kids raced into the house and saw Father James talking to their mother.

"Father James, I found a great place in the woods to build a new fort," Kevin Michael shouted.

Heather added, "We were riding our bikes behind Grandpa Robertson's house and found it."

Isabella nodded in agreement.

"You can't build a fort just anywhere you want," Emmy said. "It has to be on our property."

"But no one ever goes back there," Kevin protested.

Emmy shook her head.

"Okay, but can we still play there?"

42

"You can play, but you need to be careful," Emmy said. "Oh, Father James is going to stay in the nanny suite for a while."

"Are you going to be our nanny?" Isabella asked.

"No, but I'm going to help out while your father is away. Your mother needs to take it easy until she's back to full strength."

"That's because she hurt her brain in the crash," Kevin said. "Dad said she was in a coma and might have trouble remembering things. Grandma hurt her brain, too, and now she doesn't remember anything."

"I don't think your mother will forget everything, but you should be extra nice to her until she's better."

Kenny returned and heard the news.

"Is it all right with you if he stays for a few days?" Emmy asked.

Kenny smiled and answered, "This is even better than I was praying for, Em. He can stay all summer if he wants."

Father James waved a hand. "I'm talking about a few days. I cleared it with the big guy."

"You asked God?" Kevin asked.

"Father James chuckled and said, "No, I meant the bishop. He owes me some favors because of a golf match."

"Were you feeling guilty about being gone the whole summer?" Emmy asked Kenny.

"Not until the accident. This is another example of how God provides for our needs over and above what we deserve."

Emmy drove the kids to school Monday morning and found Father James sitting at the kitchen island when she returned.

"I could have taken them to school, Emmy."

"I know, but I wanted to do it. I needed to drive somewhere other than the neighborhood."

"Any trouble?" he asked.

She shook her head. "Not with the driving, but I did think about something on the way home."

"What was that?" he asked setting down his coffee cup.

"You might think I'm overreacting, but I want to trade in my BMW. The new models have more safety features."

"Such as?"

"A better frame. More driver assistance technology. Blind spot monitoring. Lots of stuff."

"Really? My old Civic doesn't have any of that stuff."

"Would you have time to run to the car dealership with me? I need to do some research first, but I want to do this as soon as I can."

"Do you need to ask Kenny first?"

"I called him on the way home, and he said to do what I think best."

"I better go inside to pick up the kids," Emmy told Father James later. "They won't be expecting me to show up in a white BMW."

"I'll wait in the car so no one steals it."

Emmy rolled her eyes as she jumped out. "No one will steal it at church. You can come in with me."

Ten minutes later the kids stared at the new SUV.

"Do you like the color?" Emmy asked.

"It's okay," Kevin said. "Does this mean we can't eat in the car since it's new?"

"I would like to keep it clean for a few days," Emmy replied.

Kenny got home later, pulled into the garage and noticed the new BMW. He went inside and found Emmy and Father James in the kitchen.

"I see you traded cars. Do you feel safer driving this one?"

"I do, and I'm heating up some chicken enchiladas for dinner." She checked the oven timer. "Should be ready in fifteen. Would you like a salad?"

Kenny patted Father James on his back. "I hope she got a good deal."

Father James laughed and said, "She nearly had the salesman in tears. She told him how much she wanted for her old one and what she was willing to pay for the new one. He tried to get her to go higher, but she wouldn't budge. She threatened to buy an Audi, and he caved."

"Do I have time to shower?" Kenny asked walking up to Emmy and kissing her cheek.

"Yes, and tell the kids we're about ready to eat. They were supposed to be cleaning their rooms."

Kenny headed upstairs.

Father James looked at Emmy and asked, "Are you going to inspect my room?"

"Well, I'm not going to clean it when you go back to work," she answered.

"I made some coffee," Father James said. "Are you supposed to drink anything that strong?"

"No, all I can drink is diluted water."

He stared at her.

"When you add ice cubes to water and they melt, it dilutes the water.

"You're nuts. Your brain must have swollen up again."

They sat at the island and drank their coffee.

"Since you are feeling better. I'm going back to work. I'm tired of going to the hospital in the morning and coming back here to take care of you during the day."

"I can manage on my own now."

"If you say so."

"Hey! I've been meaning to ask you about your parents."

"What about them?"

"They were born in Russia, right?"

"They were," he answered and then tilted his head.

"How did they get from Russia to Kansas?"

"Planes, trains and automobiles."

She smacked his arm. "I'm serious. Do you know?"

"Believe it or not, there is a rather large community of German-Russian people in the Topeka area. They started immigrating here in the late 1800s. My parents arrived in the 40s."

"Are you kidding me?"

"Nope! That's the absolute truth."

Chapter Six

"Kenny, do you have time to listen to something I recorded this morning?" Emmy asked as they cleared the dishes from dinner a week later.

"Sure, Em. By the way, the lasagna was really good. Don't be upset because Kevin didn't like it."

"He usually likes spinach, and I didn't put that much in it," Emmy said scraping Kevin's plate into the garbage disposal.

They headed downstairs to Kenny's recording studio a few minutes later.

"I wrote a new song, and recorded it just playing the keyboard. I kinda like it, and was thinking it should be added to the new CD. Let me know what you think." She handed him a piece of paper with the lyrics and played the three minute recording as they sat at the console. "What do you think? Be honest."

He read through the lyrics again, then looked at her and smiled. "If this is the title, I think it should also be the title for the CD."

"I'm calling the song 'Gideon's Heart' and it could be the title for the CD. I actually drew a simple picture for the cover. What do you think?" She reached for the drawing and handed it to Kenny. "It's pretty simple, but I'm sure the art department could come up with something."

He looked at the drawing. "Is this supposed to be an acorn? I can tell this is a heart."

"I'm not an artist. That's the best I could do."

"I really like the song. Do you want to leave it the way you recorded it, or should we add tracks?"

"Both," she answered. "I want to keep the demo as is, but I want to record it to fit with the rest of the tracks. Know what I mean?"

"Sure. We could add strings to it, too."

After getting the kids to bed Wednesday night, Kenny took Emmy downstairs and played the track from their two days of recording at Steward Music Group.

"That doesn't sound like a full string section," Emmy said after listening to the track.

Kenny shook his head. "It's not. I thought it would sound better using a string quartet."

"I like it, but what did you do with my vocal track?"

"I used the guide vocal from the demo and combined it with your studio track. I had to use some magic to get them to sync," he said, smiling and using air quotes. "No background vocals at all. I don't think it needs them."

"Play it again, please."

He did.

"I love it just the way it is," she said. "Don't change a thing."

"It has to be mastered, but other than that, it's done."

"Did you hear anything from the art department? I know this is last minute stuff, but I really want this to be the title and cover."

"If this was the old days before all of this could be done on a computer, it might push back the release date, but it should be ready to send to the manufacturer next week," he assured her.

"Thank you for meeting me for dinner," John said to Kristen Friday evening. "How are the kids doing?"

"They said to say hi, and they miss you. You can see them tomorrow if you want," she said picking up a menu.

"I would like that. Should I come over to pick them up around noon?"

"That will work. I need to do some shopping in the afternoon," Kristen answered. "I'm not real hungry, so I'll just have a house salad." Kristen said to the waitress. "Thousand island on the side, please."

John ordered a burger and a beer. They talked about mundane topics as they ate.

"Are you finished, ma'am?" the waitress asked later.

"Yes, thank you," Kristen replied.

The waitress cleared the table and left the check.

"Okay, you said you needed to talk about something. What

47

is it?" Kristen asked. "I hope it wasn't about that construction project along the river."

John finished his beer, set the glass down and stared at her.

"Come on, John. Just tell me. I know you don't love me anymore," she said with strength in her voice.

"I still love you..."

She rolled her eyes.

"Fine. I have met someone, and it's rather serious."

He confessed to having an affair with a lady he met at a conference.

"Well, at least you aren't fooling around with someone at work. Do I know this lady?" she asked.

"No, not likely. She's from Cincinnati and her name is..."

Kristen waved a hand and stood up. "I don't need to know her name. You can see the kids tomorrow, but only for the afternoon."

He stood up and watched as she left. He sat down and took a deep breath. *You know this is not all my fault, Kristen. You haven't exactly been there for me lately.*

After John picked up the kids the next day, Kristen called Emmy and they drove to Sainsbury's to do the grocery shopping.

"So tell me what John wanted to tell you. How was dinner? I've never been there," Emmy said as they pushed their carts through the produce section.

Kristen picked up a bag of red seedless grapes, set it in her cart and said rather matter-of-factly, "He confessed to having an affair with a lady from Cincinnati he met at a work conference."

"He what?" Emmy shouted as she broke a cucumber in half.

"You heard me and don't create a scene. We can talk about it on the way home."

Though Emmy tried, Kristen refused to discuss the matter until they were back at Emmy's new car.

"When did you buy this?" Kristen asked as they loaded the groceries into the back.

"A couple weeks ago and don't change the subject. Spill it,

or else I will... uh... I'll tell Mama about it."

"Don't you dare, Emmy."

"Does she even know he moved out?" Emmy asked as she got in and started the car.

"I don't think so," Kristen said buckling her seat belt.

"Why on earth would he have an affair? This woman can't be as pretty as you," Emmy said making 'woman' sound like a swear word.

"It's not a matter of who's prettier, Em."

Emmy slapped the steering wheel and frowned at Kristen. "How can you act like this is no big deal? I would be furious. I am furious," she said and threw the car into drive.

"I am upset, Emmy. I just hide my emotions better than you."

"Is he still seeing this... uh... this woman?"

"I didn't ask, but I know he hasn't been to Cincinnati lately."

"Ya think!"

"Will you slow down before you get into another accident," Kristen said.

"When he brings the kids back, you need to sit down and talk about stuff. Tell him you have to see a marriage counselor."

Kristen shook her head. "I doubt if he will agree to that. He doesn't like to talk about his issues."

"Duh! He's a man. None of them ever talk about their feelings. They have to act all macho with each other. They can't show any weaknesses."

"I can suggest counseling, and see what he says," Kristen said as she pointed to a traffic light.

"I can see it's red." Emmy came to a stop and waited a few seconds after the light turned green. "You have to get him to agree to counseling."

"And if he won't?"

"Then I will get after him," Emmy warned.

Kristen grinned and giggled.

"What is so funny?" Emmy asked.

"I was picturing you getting on his case."

"And?"

"You do realize he is much bigger than you, right?"

"Hey! I may be small in stature, but I'm not afraid of him."

"You aren't afraid of anything, Em," Kristen said.

"Was everyone glad to see you back at church, Mommy?" Isabella asked on the way home Sunday.

"They gave your mother a card and lots of hugs," Kenny said.

"Are you going to start singing again?" Heather asked.

"I will wait until next month," Emmy answered.

Emmy's cell phone rang Tuesday night just after she said good night to the kids. She checked to see who was calling and smiled.

"What's up?" she asked.

"Do you remember me telling you I wrote to my father?" Rory asked.

"Yeah. Did you get a reply?"

"Yup! He actually wrote me back and invited us to come to Australia for a visit. Can you believe it?"

"No way! You aren't actually going all that way to see him, are you? I mean he hasn't been a father to you for ages."

"We're thinking about it. We both have vacation time coming," he answered.

"You aren't going to think of him as your father, are you?"

"I've never had a real father, so I wouldn't know how to treat him like that."

"Do you know how much it would cost to fly to Australia?" Emmy asked.

"Not exactly, but I know it won't be cheap." He laughed and said, "We haven't made up our minds yet, Olivia."

"Good, and why do you still call me that? I'm not on tour right now."

"Even so, it is your middle name," he replied.

"Then should I call you Clarence?"

"Not if you still want to be my friend," he said.

"Does Rochelle ever call you that?" Emmy asked.

"Never! I told her how much I dislike it."

"Okay then, you don't need to get all riled up, Clarence," she teased. "If you decide to go, when will you leave? Do you know how long you'll be gone?"

"Probably in the summer," he answered.

Emmy laughed and said, "Do you realize when we have summer they are in the middle of winter?" She waited for an answer. "Are you still there?"

"I'm here. I was asking Rochelle if you were pulling my leg. I forgot about the difference in seasons."

"If you wait until December, you would miss part of our winter and get some extra summer."

"On the other hand it gets hot here in the summer. We could go to Australia to get away from the heat and humidity."

"Good point. Let me know what you decide. I hear Kenny calling. Say hi to Rochelle for me and take care, Rory."

"You too, Olivia," he replied and hung up before she could answer back.

"Hey, brat, did you join the gym, too?" Tony asked without saying hello.

"What gym? Who joined a gym. I certainly didn't," she replied. "And hello to you, too, creepozoid."

"Sloane didn't talk to you about joining a fitness center?" he asked.

"She never mentioned it to me. Why? Did she sign up for one?"

"You know that new place that opened down the road from the church?"

"I've seen it. Lifestyle Fitness, right?"

"I think so. Anyway, she found a deal for the summer and wants to start working out. She asked me to watch the kids."

"Yeah, so what? They are your kids, too."

"Why do you think she wants to start working out now? Why all of a sudden?" he asked while shrugging. "She's not going to play basketball again."

51

"I'm not saying this to be mean, but maybe she wants to lose a few pounds. She has given birth to all your babies."

"I've never said anything about her losing weight. I love her just the way she is. Everyone gains weight after they have kids," he said. "I take that back. Everyone except you that is. You don't look any different than when we were in high school."

"Thank you, Tony. That was almost like a compliment."

"You know what I mean." He paused and asked, "She hasn't said anything about me, has she?"

Emmy tilted her head and asked, "Are you worried she might leave you because of the trouble Kristen and John are going through? Have you not been sleeping together?"

"Of course we sleep together. You've seen our bedroom, brat," he answered.

"You know what I mean. When was the last time you had sex?"

He coughed twice then said, "I am not discussing my sex life with you."

Emmy laughed. "Men are such wimps. Talking about sex has always embarrassed you."

"I'm hanging up. So, you don't know anything about this fitness thing, huh?"

"Nope! Maybe you should start working out, too. It wouldn't hurt you to start running before work. I would offer to join you, but you wouldn't be able to keep up." She laughed again and realized he had ended the call. *Sloane could stand to lose a few pounds.* She patted her stomach. *I could probably fit into my jeans from high school.*

Chapter Seven

"Is that all you have?" Emmy asked as she looked in Father James' closet.

"This is everything I own in the world," he answered. "I have taken a vow of poverty, my child."

"Yeah, right. I bet you've got a grand in your wallet right now."

He smiled and they walked out to her Odyssey.

She got in, started the engine and pulled away from the rectory. "Will St. John's survive without you? Is the new guy any good?"

"I will still be working here occasionally in addition to my duties as the hospital chaplain," he replied. "I will always be a man of the cloth."

"So, the bishop replaced you because you're getting old and senile, huh?"

"Not exactly."

"You're not telling me everything about your health, are you?"

"A man needs some secrets."

"Yeah, right," she smirked. "You know in some ways I admire you."

He waited for a smart remark and when none came, he asked, "How is that?"

"You aren't materialistic at all. You rely on God to meet your needs. You don't need a big house or a fancy car. Where is your car, by the way?"

"In the shop. The brake lines are rusted, and I don't think I want to spend the money to get it fixed. Thank you for the lift. I didn't want to call a cab."

"Well, I suppose you can use one of our cars for the time being."

"What time did Kenny and the band leave?" Father James asked. "Is tonight the first night of the summer tour?"

"He left around ten. They're flying to Minneapolis. He will be gone all summer."

Father James stared at Emmy for a moment before looking out the window.

"What?" she asked while slowing down at an intersection.

"I didn't say anything," he replied.

"You were going to, and you had that look on your face."

He shrugged.

"Just because he won't be home doesn't mean I won't see him if you get my drift."

"I was just concerned about your well being," he said.

"He took care of my well being last night," she said using air quotes. "The kids and I plan to fly out to see him two or three times this summer. You don't have to worry about me."

"I don't worry about that, but I am concerned about your health. You were in a coma just a month ago."

She rolled her eyes and said, "Will you get over it? My doctor said I am completely recovered. My brain is just as good as ever, and don't you make a smart remark."

"Never," he said.

"Why did the bishop choose you for the hospital gig?"

"He thinks I have a gift to deal with sick people. Who's watching the kids? I know Friday was their last day of school."

"No one. I told them to behave until I got back. They are old enough to survive for an hour without supervision."

"You hope."

"I told them no swimming while I was gone. Kevin was playing over at Tony's, and the twins were texting with friends."

Emmy pulled up to the entrance of St. Bart's. "Do you need a ride back to the rectory?"

"No, I can bum a ride off someone."

"Call me if you need one. We'll work out a time for you to come and get one of our cars."

"You will never guess what happened, Em," Kristen said Wednesday morning.

"Uh! Did you win the lottery?" Emmy asked.

"No! I don't play the lottery," Kristen answered.

"Are you going to tell me, or do I have to keep guessing?"

54

"John agreed to try counseling!" Kristen exclaimed.

"For real? Are you kidding?"

"I am dead serious. We actually have an appointment with Dr. Tolliver for next Tuesday."

"Oh, Krissy, I'm so happy for you. I hope you guys can work things out."

"We're going to try," Kristen said.

Emmy asked, "Did he come home? Did you guys... you know?"

"No, but I did have dinner with him Saturday."

"Why didn't you tell me?" Emmy said as she plopped onto the couch and ended up on her back.

"It was a last minute thing, and I didn't make it to Sunday School."

"I wasn't sure if Dr. Tolliver was still taking clients, but I'm glad she is. She helped my parents when they were ready to get divorced."

"Are we supposed to bring any food?" Emmy asked Tony after church Sunday morning.

He shook his head. "Mama made some stuff, but she actually called Gina Tobin and ordered most of the food."

"I'm glad she did. Gina is one of the best caterers in the city, and she doesn't charge a small fortune, either."

"Uncle Carmen requested that chicken Gina makes. He said it was his favorite."

"We will be over as soon as we can change clothes. Will Carmen's kids be there?" Emmy asked.

"Bobby and Charlotte arrived Friday night. They still live in North Carolina. Brian is supposed to show up. He's living in Chicago somewhere."

"Did he ever get married?" Emmy asked.

"Not that I know of. He doesn't attend many family functions."

"I'm not sure if I've seen him since the trip to Colorado. That was forever ago."

Tony chuckled and said, "Yeah, I remember it. You turned

55

nineteen on that trip and thought everyone had forgotten your birthday. You moped around all day."

"Did not," Emmy replied smacking Tony's arm. "Do you remember the mountain bike race to the Maroon Bells?" she asked with a grin.

Tony shrugged and shook his head. "I don't remember anything about a race."

She smacked his arm again. "That's because I beat you up the mountain."

"If you did, it was because I let you," he said. "See you whenever you get there."

Two hours later Karla Keasling tapped on a glass to get everyone's attention. "Okay, I hope you all had enough to eat, but now it's time to cut the cake and sing. Maria, can you light the candles, please?"

Mama Bertucci followed her younger sister's direction and lit the two candles.

"Obviously, we couldn't light eighty candles because that would create a fire hazard, so I found an eight and a zero," Karla said.

Emmy nudged Kristen and whispered, "Is it my imagination, or does your mom look older."

"She has been under a lot of stress, and not just because John moved out," Kristen replied.

"What else is going on?" Emmy asked as Karla continued to talk.

"Daddy saw his doctor last week, and apparently his blood pressure medicine needs to be adjusted. He will be seventy-seven on his birthday, and his hip has been bothering him. He might need surgery."

"Hey, brat," Tony hollered at Emmy. "Aunt Karla wants you to start singing."

"Sorry," Emmy said and then led everyone as they sang "Happy Birthday" to Carmen Lombardi.

"Would you and Emmy cut the cake?" Karla asked as she rubbed her daughter's arm.

"Of course, Mom," Kristen answered.

As they were serving the cake, Emmy whispered, "How old is your mother now?"

"She's fifty-nine. I can't believe she will be sixty next year. That makes me feel old."

"I used to think of forty as being like ancient," Emmy said as she handed a slice of chocolate cake to someone. "You're welcome," she said with a smile and then asked Kristen, "Who was that?"

"That was my aunt Donna. She is married to Uncle Vincent. I'm not surprised you don't remember her. She looks a lot older now."

"Is your uncle Vincent here?" Emmy asked glancing around the large backyard deck.

He is over there with his sons," Kristen answered while pointing. "I was shocked when his kids showed up. I haven't seen either of them in probably fifteen years."

"He looks older than Uncle Carmen," Emmy whispered. "I don't think I've ever seen those cousins."

"You have because they were at Grandpa Howard's funeral. You probably weren't introduced to them."

"The one with the full beard reminds me of Marco," Emmy said referring to Tony's older brother.

Kristen stared at her cousin for a moment. "He does look like Marco now that you mention it. Did you know Marco is now a full professor at Johns Hopkins?"

"Tony told me about that. Do we have to call him Dr. Bertucci now?" Emmy asked shifting her gaze to the two Bertucci brothers. "If you met them on the street, you would never guess they're brothers."

"Auntie Em, may I have another piece of cake, please?" Peter Bertucci asked.

Emmy smiled, looked up at Peter and handed him another slice of cake. "There you go."

"Thank you," Peter said and walked away.

"Can you believe how tall he is now?" Kristen asked. "He grew about six inches in the last year. He will be as tall as his mother soon, and he doesn't turn fourteen until July."

"Which one?" Emmy asked. "Heather or Sloane?"

"Both really. Heather was almost six feet tall and Sloane is close to that."

Emmy bit her lip for a second thinking of Peter's birth mother, Heather Bertucci Khryzman. "How long has Heather been gone? She was so young when she died."

"It will be twelve years in the fall. It's sad, but I can't remember what day she died. I'm pretty sure it was in October."

"Would you ladies like a break?" Mama Bertucci asked.

Emmy giggled and Kristen looked at her.

"What is so funny?" Kristen asked as they took a slice of cake and walked away.

"Did you hear what Mama called us?"

"What?" Kristen asked.

"She called us ladies like we're old."

"You are a goof, Emmy. You still act like a kid at times even though you will be forty in a few years."

"Don't remind me." They walked around a corner and Emmy bumped into Carmen Lombardi.

He turned and peered down at her through eyes that commanded respect. "Excuse me, ladies. I should watch where I'm going."

Kristen put her hands on Emmy's shoulders and said, "It's all right, Uncle Carmen. Emmy should be more careful and happy birthday."

"Thank you, Kristen. I need to talk to your father."

Emmy leaned back into the wall as he walked away. "Did I ever tell you how intimidated I was when I first met your uncle?"

"From the look on your face, I would say he still intimidates you," Kristen said and then grinned.

"Remember how kids in school thought he was in organized crime? He was like the godfather character from those movies."

"Did you believe those rumors, Em?"

"Kinda," she answered.

"Do you want to know a secret?" Kristen whispered.

"What?" Emmy's eyes sparkled.

58

"It wasn't Uncle Carmen who was in the mob but someone else," Kristen said with a nod.

"Who?" Emmy asked looking around.

"Uncle Vincent had ties to some crime figures in New York. He used to work in entertainment as a talent scout and manager. I've heard stories about how he used to have thugs beat up promoters who refused to pay his clients."

Emmy peeked around the corner at the now frail man. She turned back to Kristen. "For real? Or are you yanking my chain?"

Kristen shrugged and walked away.

"Crap! You scared me," Emmy yelled when she felt two strong hands on her shoulders. She turned and smacked Tony in the stomach. "Don't sneak up on me like that."

"I thought you heard me. I said your name. What were you thinking about?" Tony asked.

"I was thinking about your uncles, and how scary I used to think they were," she admitted.

"I can see how some people would be afraid of them," Tony said. "Do you miss Kenny? How long has he been gone?"

"Twelve days, but I'm not counting, and I don't miss him yet."

"Yeah, I bet not," Tony laughed.

"Shut up! I can go without sex for more than a week." Emmy said and then put a hand to her face.

"I will pretend I didn't hear that," Mama Bertucci said.

Chapter Eight

"That wasn't all that bad, was it?" Stephanie Grachan asked after Emmy's press conference Tuesday morning announcing the release of *Gideon's Heart*, her latest CD.

"I should be used to these events by now, but I don't like talking about myself," Emmy said.

"Some of these so-called journalists should be banned from ever writing a single word," Stephanie said. "They ask the same stupid questions at every event."

"I'm glad it's over. How are your boys doing?" Emmy asked.

Stephanie chuckled and said, "They aren't exactly boys anymore, Emmy. They are all taller then either of us."

"Kids grow up so fast. My girls are almost teenagers, and you know what that means."

"I always wanted a daughter, but in a way I'm glad I have all boys. I have a friend who has five daughters. Can you imagine paying for five weddings?"

Emmy hugged Stephanie and said, "I should get home. Kenny is supposed to call at noon so we can Skype."

"I'll let you go. It was good to see you again," Stephanie said.

Just as Emmy was about to walk out the door, Klaus Kesson, now the person in charge of running Steward Music Group, waved and hurried in her direction. "Emmy, do you have a minute?"

"Sure, Mr. Kesson. What is it?"

"I talked to Nelson Grapella about booking a few shows to support the new project. He said he would get in touch with you, but since you're here now how do you feel about a short tour?"

"I'm already booked for the Fourth, but I suppose you would like a longer tour, huh?" Emmy asked with a grin.

"It wouldn't have to be a long tour," Klaus said ignoring Emmy's attempt at humor. "You could do three or four shows a week and be home with your family part of the time." He glanced at his watch. "Think about it, okay? I need to catch a flight to LA."

Emmy waited until he was out of the building and called her manger.

"Nelson, did you talk to Klaus?" she asked. "He just ambushed me and practically told me I had to do a tour to support the new CD."

"Hello, Emmy, I thought you had left."

"I was on my way. Are you still here?"

"I'm actually about to walk into my office."

Emmy looked out the window at the modern steel and glass Walker Management building across the parking lot. "We should get together to talk this week. I would now, but I have to Skype with Kenny in an hour."

"I'm free most of the week, Emmy. Call me and we can talk about setting up a tour."

"Thanks, Nelson. Say hi to Belinda and Nikolai for me. Oh, will he start preschool in the fall?"

"Yes, he will be five in December."

Emmy headed home, talked with Kenny using her laptop, made lunch for everyone, including Father James, and decided to go swimming with the kids. She spent thirty minutes in the pool before getting out.

"You didn't tell me how the press conference went," Father James said as Emmy wrapped a towel around her and sat at a table with him. He stood up and adjusted the umbrella. "How was it?"

She motioned with her hand. "It was okay. Same old boring questions from rookie journalists."

"Then why do you look so bummed out? Is it because you miss Kenny?"

"I miss him, but just before I left..." She explained the conversation with Klaus Kesson.

"I take it the son doesn't run the company the same way his father did, huh?"

"That's for sure. Klaus is more interested in making money. He doesn't care about the artists like his father did."

"You can't be too hard on him. The company needs to show a profit," Father James said while watching Kevin take a running start and cannonball into the pool.

"It's not that I mind touring. It's just that I don't like to miss church and school stuff with the kids."

"Would you rather take a whole month and do the tour all at once. Or would you like doing shows two or three days a week?"

"There are advantages to both. Kenny and the guys are working hard this summer, but by September, they will be finished. I've done tours that way, but I don't want to be away from the kids that long." She stood up and yelled, "Kevin Michael, do not dunk your sister under the water!"

"She started it," he shouted back.

"I don't care. You're bigger than Isa." She sat down. "Where were we?"

"The tour."

She thought about it while listening to some birds singing. "If we could set it up, I wouldn't mind doing Thursday and Friday shows as long as they weren't too far away."

"Does that mean you don't expect to fly?"

"That would be the best way to tour, but I hate to ask Mr. Robertson for his jet all the time."

Father James stood up, chuckled and said, "Somehow I don't think he minds one tiny bit."

"Nothing needs to be decided until I agree to tour at all."

"I need to go. I have five people to visit this afternoon."

"Are you loosened up and ready to go?" Emmy asked Tony early Wednesday morning.

He twisted back and forth a few more times and nodded. "I'll take it easy so you can keep up."

"Ha! No way you are gonna keep up with me, but I'll stop once in a while so you can catch up," she teased.

They took off along the trail used for mountain biking through the development. It wound around trees and up and down hills with an occasional section of straight, level trail. After a couple of minutes Tony slowed down to allow Emmy to catch up.

She looked at him and said, "Have you been running without me? I used to be able to keep up with you."

"I haven't been running, but I have been to the gym a few times."

"I must be getting old," she said.

They ran at a pace that kept their heart rates up, but didn't cause Emmy to get side stitches. They made it back to her house after walking to cool down. They sat on a bench on the deck, wiped off the sweat with towels, drank some water and looked at each other.

"Fine! You're in better shape than me, but it won't take me long to start leaving you in the dust."

"Yeah, whatever," Tony said. "Did you hear about Cam and Lindsey?"

Emmy wiped the sweat off of her face again and answered, "What about them?"

"They're moving back to Ohio."

"What? Get out! Why?"

"They resigned their teaching positions here, and got jobs in Troy."

"He never mentioned anything to the worship team."

"I think he told Pastor Tyler and Riordan after church last Sunday."

She placed the towel on her thighs and leaned back. "I guess I should be happy for them if that's what they want to do. How did Sloane take the news? She and Lindsey grew up together. I haven't been real close to them since they moved out of the guesthouse. I'll miss them, but you know how it is when friends move away, or you don't see each other that often."

"Sloane didn't get upset, but I think she will miss Lindsey. They've always lived in the same town. They went through school together, got teaching jobs together. You know the story."

"Did they sell their house?" Emmy asked.

"Sloane told me they're closing next Monday, and they are going to stay with her parents until they find a house."

"Doesn't Lindsey have sisters who live nearby?"

Tony shrugged and said, "I know she has a sister, and I think they still live close to their parents, but I couldn't tell you exactly where."

"You want something to drink?"

"Sure, I could use some water," he said.

She grinned, pointed to the garage and said, "Grab one for me, too."

He shoved her and stood up. "I will but only because you're still recovering from the accident."

She stuck out her tongue. "I feel like swimming. You wanna join me?"

"I didn't bring my trunks," he said walking toward the garage. He returned with two bottles of water but didn't see Emmy. He heard her in the pool and walked up to the wrought iron fence.

She saw him and yelled, "Are you gonna join me?"

He walked around to the gate, entered and walked up to the edge of the pool and looked at her. "I have your water if you want it." He sat down at one of the tables and took a long drink.

She swam for a few more minutes, exited the pool and joined him.

He handed her the water and stared.

"What?" she asked. "This is a sports bra, creep."

"At least you kept your shorts on."

"Oh, hush. You can swim in your shorts if you want. I'll just drain the pool after you finish," she teased.

"Have you decided when you're going to join Kenny on tour?" Tony asked and then finished his water.

"Not definitely. I want to go someplace where it won't be so hot. It's been so hot and muggy lately here. I get soaked just walking outside." She was quiet for a moment.

"What are you thinking?" he asked.

She laughed and said, "You don't want to know, and don't you dare come over here tonight after dark."

He looked at her and then rolled his eyes.

"Hey! It's our pool, and no one can see me if I decide to go swimming at night."

"Same time tomorrow?" he asked standing up.

"Unless you're too sore," she answered.

"See ya, brat. Thanks for the water and the workout."

A week later Bobby O'Connor tapped Emmy on the shoulder as she was talking to Liz Hammond after Family Night at church.

Emmy finished talking to Liz and turned around. "What's up, Bobby?"

He held up a CD. "This came out yesterday. Have you seen it or heard it?"

She took the CD from him. "I knew they were recording a second one. Have you listened to it?"

"Yes, but this one is for you. I have another copy."

"Did you like it?" she asked looking at the cover. "*Hill Country Boogie*, huh. That's a different title."

"It's an area in Texas," he said.

"I know that. Where did they record it? I know it wasn't at Steward Music, and they didn't use Kenny's studio."

"A studio in Memphis, and they produced it themselves. I've only played it once, but it didn't grab me like the first one."

"Is that because the new drummer sucks?" she asked and then laughed.

"The new drummer isn't the problem. I think the songs are weaker."

"If you don't have any plans for tonight, you could come over and go swimming. I'm going to stay in the pool all night. The heat never used to bother me this much. I guess I'm getting older."

"Can Shay come with me?" Bobby asked. He looked around for his girlfriend Shay Brennan.

"Of course. Any news about a wedding?"

"We aren't engaged, Emmy, but we have talked about it."

"Are you guys living together?" Emmy asked.

"No! But it would be cheaper than having two apartments," he confessed.

"I'm not gonna ask about..."

"Good! Because my love life is none of your business," he said. "I'll talk to Shay and let you know about tonight."

"I know it's late to get together, but it's still humid so I'm going to use the pool."

He left to find Shay and returned several minutes later.

"Shay can't tonight because she has to be at work early."

"How about Sunday after church?" Emmy asked. "Tony and his kids will probably come over, but Diane and Brady are on vacation again. Kristen doesn't like to let Zach and Grace swim unless she's with them."

"I'll see, but it sounds good."

"I knew you would be upset if I didn't call you right away," Jonah Galves said.

"Did Mary have the baby already?" Emmy asked. "I thought she wasn't due for a few days."

"Apparently, our son didn't want to wait any longer," Jonah said and then chuckled.

"Is Mary all right?" Emmy asked and then hollered for the twins. "Girls, come here."

Heather and Isabella raced out of their bedroom, scrambled down the hall, skid around the corner and dashed into their parents' bedroom.

"Did Mary have the baby?" Heather asked.

"Yes, and I'm talking to Pastor Jonah," she said and put a finger to her mouth. "I'm sorry. I was talking to the girls. What is his name again?"

"It's Ewan Josiah. E-W-A-N." He spelled the name. "He weighed seven pounds and five ounces. He has dark hair and a good set of lungs."

"Has Mary been able to nurse him?" Emmy asked.

"He's drinking formula for now," Jonah replied.

"Is she up to having visitors?"

Jonah looked at his wife, who had been the first nanny for Emmy and Kenny's kids. She nodded.

"She says yes. Her mother is here already."

"If I can get someone to stay with the kids, I will come down there, but I won't stay too long."

Emmy headed to St. Bart's for the first time since she was released after the accident. She got off the elevator and knew exactly where room 4012 was. She knocked on the door and without waiting for an answer, walked in.

"I want to see Ewan. Is that how you pronounce it. I assume it's an Irish name."

Mary smiled and said, "It is and you said it correctly. He's asleep now if you want to hold him."

Emmy nodded. "Hello, Mrs. Michaelis." She took the baby in her arms and cooed at him. "He looks like you, Mary."

"You're just saying that to make me feel better," Mary said.

"Did you have a rough delivery?"

"It took longer than with Erin," Mary said. "They are only thirteen months apart."

"Darian and Eli are only fourteen months apart," Mrs. Michaelis said.

Emmy looked at Jonah. "Maybe you better wait a bit longer if you want another baby."

He held up his hands in surrender. "Whatever you say, Emmy."

"Now if only Dany and Darian would give us some good news," Mrs. Michaelis said.

"Tell me," Emmy rolled her eyes. "They've been married for three years already. What are they waiting for?"

A few minutes later Dany Michaelis walked into the room.

"I thought you were working," Emmy said. "I would have picked you up if I knew you were home."

Dany, who was Liz Hammond's younger sister, and Darian Michaelis, the older of Mary's two brothers, lived in the guesthouse on Kenny and Emmy's property.

Dany shook her head. "I took the rest of the day off." She walked up to the bed and looked at her sister-in-law. "How do you feel?"

"Happy, but tired."

"Do you want to hold him?" Emmy asked.

"Yes, please," Dany answered.

Emmy handed Ewan to his aunt. "We were just talking about you."

"What did you say?" Dany asked. "He is so precious."

"We mentioned how long you and Darian have been married," Emmy said.

67

Dany laughed and said, "I know what you really mean, and we've been trying to get pregnant. It takes time."

"It only takes one time," Emmy said and then giggled. "I should go so you can get some rest." Emmy rubbed Mary's arm. "Get some sleep now because... ah, you already know."

Emmy said goodbye and decided to stop off at the third floor. She walked to the NICU where she had been earlier in the year. She walked around but didn't see anyone she recognized. She stopped by the waiting room, sat down and began to pray. "Lord, please be with the people on this floor. Be with their families and give them strength to get through whatever they are struggling with."

"Emmy, I though I saw you earlier. How are you?" Genna Ademilola asked. "I work in the CICU if you remember."

"I remember, and I'm doing great. I was on the fourth floor visiting the kids first nanny. She just had her second baby. Since I was here, I thought I would see if I saw anyone I knew."

"I heard you praying for the families," Genna said. "I do that too." Genna put her arm around Emmy's shoulders. "I'm sorry about your friend. He was so young."

"Thanks," Emmy said and then bit her lip. "I heard you talking to him in... I don't know what language they speak in the Philippines."

"Tagalog," Genna replied. "Gideon came from the same part of the country as my family. I should get back to work, but it was good to see you."

"You, too," Emmy said. She watched Genna leave, prayed a bit longer, then left.

"Are you coming over after church?" Emmy asked Bobby before Sunday School. "I made taco salad."

"We can come over, but it would be after lunch. Shay invited me to have lunch with her parents.

"That's weird," Emmy said.

"What's weird?' Bobby asked.

"Her parents have already met you, and they still want to eat lunch with you around. How strange is that?" she teased.

68

"Hey! Her parents like me. They think I'm a good influence on their daughter, and I agree with them."

Emmy coughed several times.

"Real funny, Em."

"Has Shay met your parents?" Emmy asked.

"Yes, and my parents are pushing for an engagement if you must know."

"Does Shay have any siblings?" Emmy asked as they walked down the second floor hallway.

"Two younger brothers. Aaron and Keenan. Her parents are younger than mine. Her father's name is Toby and her mother's is Rachel Joy."

"Rachel Joy. Is that like one name?" Emmy asked.

"No, but everyone calls her that and it fits. She is always smiling and has a bubbly personality. It's kinda strange at times. I'll see you later, Em."

"You can always come over earlier if you don't like what Rachel Joy makes for lunch."

"Yeah, Shay is not about to let that happen," he said.

By the time Bobby and Shay arrived, Emmy, Tony and most of the kids were in the pool.

"Hey, Em! Your security guard wasn't going to let us in. Aren't we on your list?" Bobby asked as he opened the gate and entered the pool area.

"I thought you were. It must be a new guy," Emmy answered. She climbed out of the pool and adjusted the back of her bikini bottoms as she walked up to Bobby and Shay.

"Will you make sure we're on the list?" Bobby asked as Shay watched Tony and the kids frolicking in the pool.

"No," Emmy said. "Did you eat?"

"Yes, my mother made tuna noodle casserole," Shay answered. "My brothers love it." Shay checked out the pool and the deck and then gazed up at the large house.

"I told you it was a nice place," Bobby said with a grin. "They own about twenty acres all together."

"Did you bring suits?" Emmy asked.

"We did," Bobby said as a beach ball flew toward him.

"A little help, Bobby," Tony hollered.

Bobby tossed it back.

"One of these days we should add a pool house, but until then you can use the house. You know your way around." Emmy waved in the direction of the house. "There are beverages in the fridge. Help yourself."

Bobby and Shay returned a few minutes later with bottles of water. Bobby dove right in and Shay sat on the edge with her feet in the water.

"Mom, can we play in the woods for a while. We're tired of swimming?" Kevin Michael asked.

"Okay, but you need to wear shoes. I don't want anyone to get a cut like Taylor did last week."

The younger boys left. Tony and Peter tossed a ball back and forth with Dotty, Noemi and the twins.

Shay watched Bobby and Emmy for a moment and then decided to join them.

"Bobby told me about your house, but it's different from what I envisioned," Shay said.

"How so?" Emmy asked and then splashed Bobby. "Did you tell her we lived in a dump?"

"No, he described it as more like a mansion, but it doesn't look extravagant at all. Sure, it's huge but I pictured something more modern like some of the homes on a Netflix show I watched."

Emmy moved to the edge of the pool and looked at the house. "Kenny didn't want anything flashy. He wanted something solid that could be enjoyed as a home even though we didn't know if we would ever have kids." She turned around and put her hands and arms on the ledge, stretched her legs out in front of her and floated.

"It does look substantial," Shay said.

"I can show you the rest of the inside later," Bobby said.

Tony whispered to the girls, "Watch this. I'm going to get your mother."

"You won't hurt her, will you?" Isabella asked quietly.

"I would never intentionally hurt her, Isa."

70

The girls watched as Tony swam underwater to where Emmy was relaxing. He came up from underneath, wrapped his arms around her and jumped to the middle of the pool.

Emmy didn't have time to yell until they popped back to the surface.

"Why did you do that?" she yelled. She tried to kick Tony but missed.

"I thought you needed it." He put his hands on her slim waist and tossed her straight up.

She landed close to Tony, and they began to splash each other. Soon Emmy and the girls were ganging up on Tony and laughing.

Shay sat on the edge of the pool next to Bobby and watched for a time. "Do they always carry on like that? You would think they were married or something. It's weird."

Bobby shifted his eyes from Emmy and Tony to Shay and shrugged. "It's just the way they treat each other. They're kinda like siblings in a way."

"I heard her girls calling him uncle. Are they really related?" Shay asked.

"Not technically," Bobby said though he had to think about it for a second. "Tony and Kristen are cousins, but Emmy isn't related by blood as far as I know. A lot of the families who live in this area are related somehow. Even if it's not by blood, they think of each other as family. The Robertson's live over that way, and all the kids think of them as grandparents. They are real grandparents to Brady and Diane's two youngest. They are Emmy and Diane's godparents, but that's another story."

"It still seems weird to me," Shay said. "It's like communal living in a way."

"I guess I'm used to it."

"Well, I'm not and I think they should stop."

Before they knew it, Shay and Bobby were having their first fight.

"Take me home now!" Shay yelled as she walked away.

Emmy and Tony heard her yell and stopped goofing around.

71

"We need to leave," Bobby said standing at the edge of the pool. "Thanks for the invite, Em." He turned and walked away.

"Don't forget your clothes," Emmy said just before Tony pulled her under the water again.

Later that night Emmy called Bobby and asked, "Did you guys have a fight?"

"We had a little disagreement about something."

Emmy made him tell her the details.

"So, she thought it was weird."

"I guess so," Bobby replied.

"We were just having fun," Emmy said. "You know he's like a big brother to me."

"I understand it, but she didn't."

"Is she still mad at you? Did you guys make up?"

Bobby hesitated.

"Tell me, you creep. I will feel guilty if something I did caused you and Shay to fight."

"We talked and made up. She's not mad at me anymore," he answered.

Emmy grinned and asked, "Did you have make up sex?"

"Good night, Emmy. I'll talk to you later." He ended the call without answering her question.

She looked at her phone and giggled.

Chapter Nine

"Who wants to go to the airport to pick up Daddy?" Emmy asked after breakfast.

"I'll go," Kevin said. "I want to see the planes landing and taking off."

"Does this mean Daddy is finished with the tour?" Isabella asked.

"No, the tour isn't over, but the band usually does a concert here on the Fourth of July. It's kinda like a tradition. He will only be home today."

"Can we stay here?" Heather asked. "I was going over to see Dotty and Noemi."

"You don't have to go," Emmy answered. "But I want to have lunch as a family."

"Will there be circus performers at the stadium?" Isabella asked. "There used to be."

"I don't think there will be any street performers, Isa. It won't be a day long festival like some of the previous years."

"Are we going to stay for the fireworks?" Kevin asked.

Emmy shook her head. "The fireworks were last night, buddy. I'm not sure why."

"That's okay. Ian Plant has some firecrackers and stuff. We're going to blow some things up."

"You are not going to blow up anything, young man," Emmy warned. "You can get hurt playing with that stuff."

"Mom! We know how to blow up stuff," Kevin argued.

They arrived at the SoHam airport and five minutes later the band landed.

Kenny saw Emmy waiting and hurried up to her, smiled and asked, "Are you waiting for someone in particular, pretty lady?"

"Not really. I like to hang out at the airport and pick up strange men," Emmy teased.

"Did any of the kids come with you?" he asked looking around.

"Kevin Michael is around here somewhere."

He leaned close and kissed her. "Did you miss me, Em?"

She smiled and answered, "Oh, were you gone?"

He kissed her again.

"Do we need to wait for your luggage?" Emmy asked noticing his backpack and briefcase.

"Nope! This is all I need for now," he said and then explained that his new assistant, Cole Milne, would take care of the luggage.

"I guess there's no need to unload everything since you'll only be home for one night," Emmy said.

"True, but you and the kids are still coming to Seattle, right?"

"That's the plan," she said with a grin.

They found Kevin staring out the windows of the terminal watching a plane pull up to the gate.

"Dad! I didn't see you land. I thought you might be on that plane."

Kenny handed the backpack to his son. "Did you miss me? Your mother didn't."

Kevin grinned at his father and said, "You weren't gone that long."

Emmy and her band took the stage at six thirty that evening. They played three songs without a break.

"Thank you for being here tonight," she said after catching her breath. She talked to the crowd for a minute while Paul Mahnari and Tommy Joseph were handed different guitars by the tech guys. "This is our first show in two years. We might be a bit rusty, but we'll do our best to entertain you tonight." She looked at Jeremy Lenhart and he began playing the introduction to "Gideon's Heart" in the background. "I want to dedicate tonight to a special friend who passed away on April 30 this year. His name was Gideon T. Logan." She looked back at Bobby O'Connor as she waited until the crowd stopped yelling. "For those of you who knew him, or might have heard of him, he was a dear friend and part of my band. This next song is called 'Gideon's Heart' and it's for my dear Gideon."

The band started the song, and Emmy noticed the cell phones and lighters being held aloft by the crowd. She finished the song and walked back to the drum kit to take a sip of water.

"Are you okay, Em?" Bobby asked.

"I'm fine. I made it through without crying," she answered.

An hour later Emmy waved to the crowd and left the stage.

"That wasn't too bad for our first gig in two years," Bobby said as he walked beside Emmy.

She looked up at him, grinned and teased, "Yeah, except when you counted off that song with the wrong tempo, you doofus."

"We recovered," he answered wiping the sweat off his face and then snapping the towel at her.

She jumped out of the way and snapped her towel at him. "It was more fun than I expected. You know I might tell Nelson to see if Prater-Saylor can book a few more shows for the fall tour. I've forgotten how much I like singing for people."

"They still seem to like hearing you sing and watching you run around the stage. I thought since you're a bit older, you might not dance around as much. Guess I was wrong," he said.

"I'm not that old," she answered with a frown. She spotted Frankie Hanna and walked up to the first crew member ever hired by Fridays At Five. Frankie happened to be Kenny's cousin. "Hi, Frankie. How's the tour going?"

"Good," he answered.

"Do you know where he is?" she asked.

"Interview," Frankie answered pointing to his left.

"Thank you, Frankie," she said with a grin. "You're still a man of few words."

Emmy spotted Kenny talking to Lexi Gabriel, who managed the local rock station WSHO, and waited until she finished.

"Em, I'm sorry I didn't get to listen to your set. How was it?"

She beamed and answered, "Fantastic! I can't wait to get back on the road."

His eyebrows shot up. "Really?"

"Well, I'm not looking forward to all the hours on a bus, but it will be good to sing for people again."

"What are you doing, Mommy?" Isabella asked a few days later.

"I absolutely have to finish my book today, Isa." Emmy held up her laptop as she finished a cup of coffee. "I have to send it to Denise tonight, so we can fly to Seattle in the morning."

"Does that mean we shouldn't disturb you all day?"

"I hope it doesn't take all day, but if you could fix your own lunch, I would appreciate it."

"Mommy, we aren't babies anymore," Isabella said. "We won't starve, and we can entertain ourselves."

"I know. You are growing up so fast. I'll be in the den if anyone needs me."

Emmy finished the book, and emailed it to Denise Bartell, who edited all Emmy's books. She walked out of the den and down the hall to the kitchen.

"Are you finished, Mommy?" Isabella asked.

"I am," Emmy said walking up to the island. "You're making a taco salad for dinner, I see."

"Yes, and I added the ingredients just the way Daddy does," Isabella said with a grin. "See! I'm even using the slotted spoon."

"Did you brown the hamburger all by yourself?" Emmy asked.

"Father James is here. He helped with that."

He walked out of the pantry just in time to catch the last part of the conversation. "I only supervised. Isa did it by herself for the most part. Here is the last bag of Doritos." He handed the bag to Isabella.

"I didn't know the first thing about cooking when I was their age," she said taking a seat on one of the barstools. "I could make sandwiches but that's about it. My mother never let Diane or me do any cooking. She made us do dishes all the time though. Mama Bertucci taught me how to cook."

"She did an excellent job," he said.

76

"Are you teasing? Your face looks fuller. Have you been eating more?"

"I'm not teasing, and I've gained five pounds since the bishop reassigned me," he said patting his stomach. "I might have to start walking to St. Bart's to get in shape."

"You could join Tony and me for a run. We are running almost every morning."

He shook his head. "Not a chance. You two race each other, and I would never be able to keep up. Walking is more my speed."

"Kevin Michael! We need to leave for the airport in ten minutes!" Emmy shouted the next morning. "Stop playing and bring your bag downstairs."

"Do we have to bring him?" Heather asked. "He could stay home, and Father James could check on him every few days."

"Believe me, Heather, I've thought about it, but your father wants to see all of you," Emmy said as she checked her purse for the third time. "Have you seen my phone?"

"It's on the desk," Heather answered.

"Thank you." Emmy found her cell phone under some junk mail.

Kevin tromped down the stairs and into the kitchen dragging his backpack. "I'm ready to go," he announced.

"How much underwear did you pack?" Emmy asked.

"Two pairs plus what I'm wearing," he answered. "We're coming back on Tuesday."

"You are so gross," Heather said with her hands on her hips.

They landed in Seattle in time to be taken to the hotel.

"We are on our way," Emmy said on her phone to Kenny. "How soon do you have to leave for the venue?"

"Not for a couple of hours," he answered. "Cole will meet you in the lobby and bring you up to our suite."

Cole was waiting and immediately took Emmy and the kids to Kenny's suite on the top floor.

"How are my precious kids doing?" he asked when the kids

rushed inside. He hugged them briefly, smiled at Emmy and kissed her.

Kevin ran to the window and looked out. "Is that the Space Needle? Can we go there?"

Cole walked to the window. "It is the Space Needle, and I believe there will be time for a visit tomorrow."

"How was your flight?" Kenny asked Emmy.

"Uneventful," she answered. "Does Cole always dress so sharp? He looks more like a banker than your assistant."

Kenny looked at Cole, shrugged and said, "I don't think I've ever seen him without a tie while he was working."

"At least he doesn't carry a briefcase," Emmy teased.

There was a knock on the door, and Cole opened it after looking through the peephole. One of the hotel employees brought Emmy's bags upstairs.

"Just set them there for now," Cole said. He tipped the employee and turned to Kenny. "I will let you have some time alone. We need to leave for the venue in ninety minutes."

"Thanks, Cole," Kenny said.

"Do you have plans for tomorrow?" Emmy asked after Cole left.

"Do we have to go to church?" Heather asked.

Kenny shook his head. "There won't be time."

Isabella walked out of one of the bedrooms and pointed at her brother. "Where is he going to sleep? He is not sharing our room."

"He won't," Kenny said. "I wanted to stay at this hotel because of the view, but they don't have suites with three bedrooms. But!" He walked over to the couch and sat down. "This turns into a bed and Kevin can sleep here."

"Cool!" Kevin shouted. "I can watch TV all night long."

"That's not going to happen," Emmy ordered. "You will be going to bed as soon as we get back from the show."

Emmy and the kids returned to the hotel thirty minutes after the last encore.

"You can have some time to unwind, but no longer than an hour," Emmy said. "No TV, Kevin."

"I'm ready to fall asleep now," Isabella said. "I'm still on Illinois time, and we never stay up this late on a Saturday night because of church."

"You don't have to stay up, Isa. It might be very late when your father gets back."

It was just after two when Kenny slipped into the bed beside Emmy. He put an arm on her hip.

"What took so long?" she asked without opening her eyes.

"I tried to get back as soon as I could," he answered. "At least we can sleep late."

Kevin knocked on his parents' bedroom door just after seven the next morning.

"Go away," Emmy hollered.

"I'm hungry, and we need to see the Space Needle." Kevin knocked again and then opened the door. "Can we order room service?"

"No! We are not ordering room service," Emmy shouted. "It's too expensive. We can get dressed and go down to the restaurant."

"Em, it might be better if we eat up here. More privacy for the kids," Kenny said. "And it doesn't cost that much."

"Yeah, and we can eat in our pajamas," Kevin said. He ran to his sisters' room to wake them up.

After breakfast Kenny took Emmy and the kids out to do some sightseeing. The kids didn't pay any attention to the security detail that accompanied them. They arrived at the concert venue around four and didn't return to the hotel until midnight.

"What time are you leaving?" Kenny asked as he snuggled closer to Emmy.

"Our plane is supposed to depart at ten. What time are you guys flying to San Francisco?"

"Cole said we need to be at the airport by eleven," Kenny answered.

She kissed him and ran a hand along his jaw. "You need to shave."

"I will tomorrow."

"Were you happy to see me?"

He answered twenty minutes later.

She grinned and said, "I could leave the kids home and spend another weekend with you."

"I thought you were going to bring them to Tampa. Did you change your mind?"

"No, I'm still planning to bring them to that show. Rory invited us to stay a couple nights. He wants to take the kids to Orlando."

"They're old enough to enjoy the other parks now. No more Mickey Mouse and Cinderella stuff."

"No, they would be more interested in a Harry Potter theme park if there is such a place."

Emmy checked her email Friday afternoon and opened one from Denise. She quickly read through the email. *I wonder how many changes you've made to my story.* She opened the file containing Denise's comments. *Wow! Over three hundred comments. I should get started on them tonight. I won't have time over the weekend.* She looked at the third comment. *I knew there should have been a comma there.* She read the email a final time and tapped her jaw. *I like that title suggestion. I can change it. Reminisces of a Rough Rider. There. Done.*

Chapter Ten

"Have you got a minute?" Darren Eaton asked as he entered Pastor Tyler's office and closed the door.

Tyler looked up from his laptop, noticed the look on Darren's face and said, "Sure. Have a seat. I take it you have an answer."

"Yes, and we have decided to take the position," Darren answered.

"I can't say this is a surprise. You've always expressed a desire to become a senior pastor, and when the opening in Columbus popped up, I thought you might take it. It appears God has opened the door for you and Jody to return home at last. How many years has it been?"

"We were hired in November of 2011. You know exactly how long it's been," Darren said.

Tyler stared at his friend for a moment. "We've seen quite a few changes in the church the last six years."

"You've been on the staff since... when did you first come here?" Darren asked.

"It was September of 2005," Tyler answered. "Liz and I were engaged, and I was an intern on the staff." Tyler chuckled and said, "I can't believe we've been here almost twelve years. The time has gone by so fast."

"I know it's always a possibility, but can you ever see yourself leaving Crest Ridge?"

"I will go where God tells me, but I'm hoping He won't send me anywhere else. I've always hoped to retire from here someday. I have had offers, but we never thought God wanted us to leave."

"I did write out my resignation. I can send an email or print it out."

"I suppose I need it to read to the board," Tyler said.

"Have you talked to your friend about the position?" Darren asked. "You do need to replace me, and I don't mean that in an egotistical way."

"That's for sure. I've never been very good at the

administrative side of things. I have learned how to delegate over the years."

"There's no way any senior pastor could survive in a church of this size without the ability to delegate. There's way too much going on."

"Once it became apparent you and Jody were seriously considering this offer, I did reach out to Wyatt. I explained the situation, and he is interested. He has already resigned his position and is willing to relocate."

"Did he ever get remarried?" Darren asked.

Tyler shook his head. "He always says he hasn't found the right woman to replace Evie."

"There are plenty of single women in this church," Darren said. "Will you tell everyone tonight, or will you wait until Sunday?"

"I will email the board today, but I won't make a formal announcement until Sunday. Unless you want to announce it."

Darren waved a hand. "You can tell everyone."

"Hey, Wyatt, did I call at a bad time?" Tyler asked Saturday morning.

"No, I was running the garbage disposal and accidentally dropped a spoon down the drain."

"I thought it sounded like a train," Tyler chuckled.

Wyatt Pearson flipped the switch and shut off the faucet. "That's better. What's on your mind?"

"Darren took the position in Columbus."

"He did, huh? That doesn't surprise me. I visited the Harvest Avenue church a couple of years ago. It's a nice facility. Not as big as Grove City or Crest Ridge, but it's a thriving church."

"I don't have anyone else in mind for Darren's spot. Have you thought about it anymore?"

"It's funny, but last night as I was getting ready for bed, I thought about you and felt the need to pray about Crest Ridge. I do believe the Lord is opening a door."

"That's good because I would like to fill the position quickly. None of the current staff members really qualify."

Tyler and Wyatt talked for several minutes.

"So, it's settled. You can stay with us for the weekend and the board will have a chance to meet you and ask a few questions. I like to have the board's approval before I hire someone even though it's not really necessary."

"Sounds like a plan. It will give me a chance to spoil your kids some more."

"Before class starts Dany and I would like to make an announcement," Darian said Sunday morning.

"By all means, please do," Pastor Williams said with a smile.

Emmy put a hand to her mouth and stared at Dany. Dany didn't change her expression.

Darian stood up. "Dany is pregnant," he said quickly.

"It's about time," Emmy shouted as she stood up, pulled Dany to her feet and hugged her.

The men in the room congratulated Darian and shook his hand.

"I see Emmy is thrilled by the news," Tony said. "She loves babies."

Emmy finally released Dany and let other people offer congratulations.

After everyone had taken their seats, Dany leaned close to Emmy and asked, "Will you let us stay in the guesthouse after the baby is born?"

"I wouldn't dare let you move. I want to be close enough to spoil the baby."

During the second service Pastor Tyler again announced Darren's resignation.

Emmy whispered to Kristen, "Liz told me they were leaving. He's going to be the senior pastor at the church where I first met him. Liz said Tyler already has someone in mind to replace Darren."

"Really? That's rather quick," Kristen said. "Did Tony say anything about the board interviewing him?"

"He only said the new guy would be here for an interview

next week. I need to talk to Liz and find out more about him. All I know for sure is that he and Tyler are old friends."

Emmy found Liz after the service and asked, "What can you tell me about Tyler's friend?"

Liz explained how they met in college and where Wyatt was born.

"I've done a couple shows in Ann Arbor, but I don't know much about the city," Emmy said. "Is he married?"

"He's a widow," Liz answered.

"Oh, no. What happened?" Emmy asked and then bit her lip.

"He married Evie Bobak while they were still at Olivet. She lived in my dorm one year, but I didn't really know her until she married Wyatt. After college they moved to Pennsylvania, and we didn't see them very often. Tyler and Wyatt kept in touch though." Liz paused for a moment. "I guess it was five years ago that Evie was diagnosed with breast cancer. She went through all the usual treatments, but it was too far advanced and she passed away in May of 2013."

"That is so sad," Emmy whispered. "Did they have any children?"

"No, they had planned to start a family, but then she got sick. I should go, Em. I need to round up the kids. We're supposed to have lunch with Rebecca and Ryan."

"I'll talk to you later, Liz. I need to gather up my gang, too." She looked around and spotted them talking to Tony and his kids.

"The boys want to go swimming. Would you mind?" Tony asked.

"Not at all. I plan to use the pool this afternoon. You could bring them over and tell me about Wyatt."

"Who?"

"Don't give me that. You know who I mean," Emmy said. "Come over after lunch."

Tony brought the kids over later and joined Emmy at a table to watch the kids swim.

"What's Sloane doing this afternoon?" Emmy asked while

84

adding more sunscreen to her arms and legs.

"She went to the gym," he answered. "She hasn't told me a number, but I know she's lost weight."

"Good for her. I can tell. Her face is slimmer," Emmy said.

"I give her credit for sticking to it."

"So, what do you know about Wyatt Pearson?"

"Tyler emailed his resume. Are you aware he was once married?" Tony asked.

"I know about his wife, and that he and Tyler became friends at Olivet." Emmy shook her head because Ben and Kevin were playing dodgeball with Taylor and Coby in the pool. "Are you watching the boys?"

"They can't hurt each other with that beach ball," Tony said.

"Will the board approve him to replace Pastor Darren?" Emmy asked as her cell phone rang. She saw it was Father James, put it in speaker mode and asked, "Are you at St. Bart's?"

"Yes, but I'm going to meet a few friends to play cards. I need some spending money."

"Don't take them for all they've got and no cheating," Emmy warned. "Did you see your doctor this morning?"

"Yes, but I'm not going to discuss my health with you." Father James hung up.

"Was he joking?" Tony asked.

"Pfffft!" Emmy rolled her eyes. "He gets together with other priests and they play for pennies, but no one ever collects any money."

"I'm pretty sure the board will go along with Pastor Tyler. Wyatt's resume is pretty good. He's going to be here next Monday."

"Now that we've got everything settled about the new vehicle, I would like to allow you time to interview Wyatt," Pastor Tyler said to the church board Monday evening. "Has everyone read his resume?"

All twenty board members replied in the affirmative.

Tyler brought Wyatt to the conference room.

"Wyatt, please take a few minutes to tell everyone about yourself. They've read the resume, so you don't have to go over that again."

Wyatt nodded and looked around the large conference table. "Before I start, I would like to pray." He closed his eyes and began. "Lord, I pray for all the people around this table, and if this is where you want me, please open all the doors."

He quickly covered some basic biographical information and then smiled. "I accepted Jesus as my Savior when I was ten. It was at Nottawaseppi Lake Nazarene Camp."

Tony looked up from Wyatt's resume and recognized the name of the camp. He tapped Mr. Michaelis on the arm and whispered, "That's where our kids go."

Wyatt continued, "I was a sophomore in high school in Ann Arbor when I felt the call to enter the ministry." He glanced at Tyler for a moment. "Like Tyler, I fought the call for a time, but came to the realization I needed to do what the Holy Spirit was telling me."

After Wyatt finished the board members asked questions for a half hour.

"If there are no more questions, we can let Wyatt go and determine if we want to take any action tonight," Tyler said.

Wyatt left the room and five minutes later the board voted to hire him at a salary similar to what Darren Eaton earned.

"I will tell Wyatt and bring him back," Tyler said.

Before the board adjourned, Wyatt accepted the offer and gave Tyler a date to start his new position.

Chapter Eleven

"Can I at least give my birthday girl a hug? I know you're too big to sit on my lap like you used to do," Tony said.

Dotty gave him a hug. "Oh, Papa, I remember when I used to fall asleep on you, and you would pretend to be asleep so you could hold me."

"You might be a teenager now, but you will always be my little girl."

"Little my butt," Emmy said. "I want a hug when you're finished."

Tony released Dotty and she turned around.

"You're bigger than me, and it won't be too long before Noemi and my girls are taller then me." Emmy hugged Dotty. "Heather was almost as tall as your papa and Sloane is tall, too."

"Auntie Em, I didn't get my genes from Mom if you know what I mean," Dotty said watching Sloane talk to Mama Bertucci.

"Sometimes I forget about that," Emmy whispered. "You do look a lot like Heather, and I can see the Bertucci side of the family in you. If you ever want to hear some stories about your birth mother, I have a few."

"Mama has told me a lot about her, but I've never had the courage to ask about the day she died. I don't want to make Mama sad," Dotty said.

"One of these days I will tell you everything I know." Emmy hugged Dotty again.

"What about my father?" Dotty asked.

Emmy bit her lip for a second. "I can tell you about him, too."

"It's okay, Auntie Em. Peter has told me how he didn't want to take care of us and that he drank a lot."

"I know how it feels to live with a father who has issues with alcohol," Emmy said. She looked at Tony and added, "It's pretty amazing how your papa gave up beer to become more involved in the church, but he never had the same problems as our real fathers."

"Are you ready for some cake?" Peter asked his sister.

"I'm ready," Dotty answered. "Why are you looking at me like that? Get rid of that silly grin."

"Papa told me about a surprise party for Aunt Emmy."

Emmy shook a finger at Peter. "You are not going to smash cake into your sister's face. You might be a lot bigger than me, but I can still take you out."

Peter smiled at Emmy. "Should I smash the cake on you instead?"

"Just try it, buster," Emmy warned poking him in the stomach.

"It's time to sing," Sloane said. "Emmy, will you get us started?"

Emmy started the song, but then stopped and listened to all the kids. *I am so blessed to live with my friends and family in such a wonderful place.*

"You have to make a wish before you blow out the candles," Ben told his older sister.

"I think she knows that," Peter said while ruffling Ben's hair.

Dotty smiled and then blew out the candles.

"Is Uncle Rory supposed to pick us up?" Kevin asked as he walked through the terminal at the Peter O'Malley Airport just outside of Tampa.

"He texted a few minutes ago," Emmy answered looking around.

"There he is!" Isabella shouted. "Come on, Heather. Let's get out of the airport so we can go swimming."

"No running!" Emmy shouted in vain.

"Hi, Uncle Rory. Where's Rochelle?" Heather asked handing him her backpack. "Will you carry it for me, please? It's heavy."

"What do you have in here?" he asked. "It must weigh a ton."

"She packed some books," Isabella said."

"I should have known, and Rochelle is at work. She won't be home until around midnight."

"Are you going swimming with us?" Isabella asked. "Mom said we could swim before Daddy's concert. Are you coming to the show with us?"

"I took the day off just so I could go, but I don't have a ticket."

Heather grinned and said, "Don't worry. We'll tell the security people you are in the band and sneak you in. You might have to show them your tambourine."

Rory took Isabella's backpack and waited for Emmy and Kevin Michael.

"How was the flight?" Rory asked.

"Okay. This is the first time I've ever flown into this airport. Is it new?" Emmy asked looking around. "It looks new."

"It opened last year. Do you want me to take your luggage?"

She saw he was carrying the girls' backpacks and shook her head. "It has wheels. Where did you park?"

"Just outside. One of the perks of a small airport is not having to park a mile away."

They headed outside and Kevin saw a corporate jet coming in for a landing. Rory loaded the luggage in the back of his CR-V.

"Is this new?" Emmy asked.

"Yeah, the other one needed some work, so I traded it in on this. It's a 2017 EX-L with navigation. Do you like the color?"

"Blue looks good on this SUV. Did you get a good deal?"

"I did my research online, so I didn't get shafted," he said.

"Did you get all-wheel-drive?"

"Why?" he said then shrugged. "It doesn't snow here, Em."

She smacked his arm. "Don't rub it in. I would never buy one without it."

"Did you let Kenny know you're here?"

"I texted him when we landed, but he will be busy doing radio interviews all afternoon. You're stuck with me and the kids today," she said getting into the front seat.

"How am I suppose to deal with that," he teased.

"Oh, hush. You know you love seeing us."

"I do like seeing the kids and how much they've grown.

89

The girls are older than you were when we first met. How does that make you feel?" Rory asked. "Is everyone buckled in?"

"How far away do you live from here?" Kevin asked.

"Twenty minutes if the traffic's not too bad," he answered looking in the rearview mirror. He turned and looked at Emmy. "Are you gonna answer my question?"

"I'm trying to remember if we did anything I wouldn't want my kids to do when I was that age."

"I can't think of anything unless you count playing football with the guys." Rory turned onto the main road leading out of the airport.

"I don't have to worry about the girls doing that. The only sport they like is playing soccer and riding their bikes around the neighborhood."

"You used to ride that old bike of yours around Raynor Park."

"I'm glad they can ride through Bristol Ridge. There's not much traffic."

Rory chuckled and added, "True, but they can't ride to Darby's and hang out like we did."

"When did you ever ride a bicycle? Did you even have one?"

"Owen had one that I would ride occasionally until my friends started driving. Do you remember going places with me and my gang?"

Emmy laughed.

"What?" Rory asked.

"Your idea of a gang is so different than today's definition of a gang. You were just a bunch of delinquents who liked to drink beer and smoke pot. You never got into real trouble like teens do today."

Rory eased to a stop at a red light. "There were some guys in the neighborhood who ended up in jail, and I remember at least two who were killed in gang fights."

"Who?" Emmy asked.

"Do you remember Bill Layne or Rich Dalpiaz? They were my age or maybe a year younger. I can't remember."

"I vaguely remember them from junior high, but I haven't thought of them in many years. They were shot, right?"

"Yeah, about a month apart. I don't think they ever caught the people who did it, but they knew it was a rival gang."

"Do you think Raynor Park is worse now than when we grew up there?" Emmy asked. She looked over her shoulder and noticed the kids were listening to their iPods. "I wonder if Kenny's parents will ever move. They've talked about living in Florida during the winter."

"It's changed a lot over the years. The last time I drove through there I didn't recognize it. Your house looks a lot different, and the place I lived was painted a hideous green color. The bushes in front were overgrown, and the front steps looked ready to collapse if you put any weight on them."

"The Colwell house is the only one on that block left from the early days."

"There are still a lot of big houses along Western, but that's at the upper end of Raynor Park. Those are gigantic two-story places that must cost a fortune to heat. The cathedral area to the north is thriving. Lots of young families are moving into that neighborhood. If we ever moved back to SoHam, I would check out that area."

She tilted her head and stared at him for a moment. "Are you thinking of moving back?"

"We've discussed it, but Rochelle's family wouldn't like it," he answered. "But that could change. Her brothers are living all over the country now. My in-laws like to travel, so they're hardly ever home anymore."

"The kids would like it if you moved back," she said.

Rory looked at Emmy and asked, "What about you?"

"I would learn to live with having you around."

"Mom!" Kevin hollered.

Emmy turned to face him. "What?"

"Are we going to the hotel or to Rory's apartment?"

She looked at Rory.

"I thought you wanted to go to the hotel so the kids could swim."

91

"Yeah! I want to go swimming," Kevin said.

After eating a light lunch and spending time at the pool, Rory drove everyone to the James Raymond Arena, parked in a VIP lot and they cleared security and entered through a back door.

Emmy looked around, spotted Cole and waved.

He rushed up to her. "Mr. Colwell just asked if you were here yet."

Emmy grinned and asked, "Does he know you call him that? Oh, this is Rory, or better known as Tim Burine. He's a famous tambourine player."

Cole and Rory shook hands.

"I've heard the story," Cole said. "The band just finished their soundcheck and are doing more interviews at the moment. I'm sorry, but this has been the most hectic day of the tour. All the guys are tired."

"I bet they're all cranky," Emmy said. "I know what it's like to deal with all the crap that goes along with being in a band on the road. We will hang out backstage and see Kenny back at the hotel at least."

Later, Emmy was able to see Kenny for a few minutes before the show.

"I'm sorry today was so crazy," Kenny said. "Will you be awake when I get to the hotel?"

"I might be, but the kids will be asleep. You will have to wait until the morning to see them."

"At least there's less than a month left for this tour." Kenny turned to Rory and offered a hand. "Please tell Rochelle hello and thanks for putting up with Em for the day."

"I will and it wasn't too much of a sacrifice. It was good to see the kids again," Rory said and then grinned at Emmy.

She made a face at him and poked him in the side. "Next time I'll make sure you're working so I can spend the day with Rochelle."

"What's up with Dotty?" Tony asked when Sloane sat next to him on the couch in the family room Sunday afternoon. "She didn't eat anything for lunch and barely spoke to me."

"I'm not supposed to tell you, but she started her period yesterday. Please don't mention it, okay?"

"Are you kidding me? She's only thirteen," Tony said.

"Some girls start even earlier. You have to accept she's growing up," Sloane said picking up her book. "She is not a child."

"I know that." He took a deep breath. "We only have two daughters. Can you imagine what it must be like at the Vinson house. They have six daughters living at home."

While taking Scout out for a walk that evening, Tony stopped at Emmy's house to return a Tupperware bowl. He sat at the island and sighed.

"What's wrong with you? You look like a sad puppy. Did you leave Scout outside?" Emmy asked while inspecting the yellow bowl.

"I tied her up. I didn't want to bring her inside because the last time I did, Kevin's allergies kicked in."

Emmy leaned on the granite countertop opposite Tony. "What's up? You look downcast."

"I'm not supposed to say anything," he whispered.

She laughed and said, "But I know you will. Spill it."

He took a deep breath before saying, "Dotty started her period."

Emmy waited for more.

Tony shrugged.

"Is that all? She is growing up, you doofus. Did you think it wouldn't happen?"

"I thought it might be a ways off. Maybe a few years away."

She walked around the island, sat on the barstool next to Tony and put a hand on his back. "Did I ever tell you what happened when I got my first period?"

"No, and I don't want to hear about it now." He shrank away from her.

"Did you know when Heather started hers?"

"Of course not," he said.

"Yeah, I can see that. She was several years older than you."

93

"Female stuff was not a topic of discussion in our house."

"We didn't discuss it at the dinner table at our house, but Daddy always said he could tell when it was happening."

"Do we have to talk about this?"

Emmy grinned because Tony was looking paler than normal. "You aren't going to be sick, are you?"

"I'm not going to puke, but can we change the subject, please?"

"I told Kenny when it happened to me."

Tony stood up, walked around the island to the fridge, got a bottle of water and took a long drink. "How did he react?"

"He didn't make a big deal about it. I think he asked if it hurt."

"Does it?" Tony asked as he sat beside her again.

"Some women suffer from cramps and bloating when the flow is heavy."

Tony stood up and turned away. "Please don't tell me anything else or I will be sick."

"Can you tell when Sloane is having hers?"

"Not usually. John always said he could tell when Kristen was going to start hers. Can Kenny... never mind."

Emmy grinned and said, "He can usually tell if he's home, but not always. Sometimes he doesn't know until we're in bed."

"Gross! I'm going home, and don't you tell Sloane I said anything. Don't tell Dotty either."

"I won't. Thanks for bringing back my bowl and don't freak out so much. It's just a part of growing up."

"I'm glad we have four boys."

"Boys have to deal with puberty, too," Emmy said walking Tony outside. "Hi, Scout girl. Did you have a good walk?"

Scout barked and tried to lick Emmy's face.

"At least boys... never mind. Come on, Scout. Let's go for a long walk."

Chapter Twelve

Dahlia Michaelis carried the blue plastic basket to the checkout counter hoping the assorted toiletry items would hide the two home pregnancy tests. Fortunately, the high-school-age cashier didn't comment on Dahlia's purchases.

"Thank you and have a pleasant afternoon," the cashier said monotonously.

Dahlia smiled and walked out of the Runyon Pharmacy and muttered, "I would have died if that cashier said anything to me. Thank God she was too bored to pay attention." Dahlia tossed the bags in the back of her 2012 Toyota Corolla and drove home. "I'm glad Ma and Da are on vacation and Eli is at work," she whispered as she set the toiletries on the counter in her bathroom. She sat on the toilet, picked up one of the pregnancy test packages and read the instructions. "Maybe I should wait until I go to bed." The sound of the landline ringing startled her. "I better get that because it's probably Ma."

"We arrived and didn't have any trouble finding the cabin," Cora Michaelis said.

Mother and daughter talked for several minutes.

"Call Mary or Darian if you need anything, and please don't fight with Eli."

"Ma! I'm twenty years old. I can take care of myself and I won't have any trouble getting along with Eli. He will be at work all day. Why does he insist on working construction all summer. You'd think he would want a summer vacation like other teachers."

"He's saving money and gaining the experience needed to build a house."

"He's never going to move out, and his job at Jamie McGee Junior High pays more than enough to buy a house," Dahlia said.

"You know your brother likes to be independent. He wants to build a house and not have a mortgage," Mrs. Michaelis said. "We should return home Saturday afternoon. Do you have enough money?"

Dahlia rolled her eyes. "If I run out of cash, I'll use your Visa card."

"Try not to charge too much."

"Really, Ma, I will be fine. You guys have a good time and don't worry about us. We will be all right," Dahlia said.

Dahlia ended the call and walked back to her bathroom. She stared at the two packages on the vanity. "I should suck it up and get this over with. It could be I just skipped a month."

After the second test confirmed the positive result, Dahlia sat on the toilet with her head in her hands and wept. She raised her head, wiped her eyes with a hand towel, stood up and looked in the mirror. "I am responsible for my actions, and I will deal with this as a mature adult." She marched out of the bathroom, entered her bedroom and threw herself on her bed. "Who am I kidding? How am I ever going to tell Ma and Da? They will be so disappointed in me." She grabbed her cell phone and turned onto her back. She hesitated for a moment but then dialed her older sister's number.

"Mary, could you stop by the house. I really need to talk to you," Dahlia said.

"Hang on a second." Mary Galves checked Ewan's diaper. "Good! You aren't poopy. That must have been gas. Jonah isn't back from church yet. He probably won't return until after five thirty."

"Could I come over there?" Dahlia asked.

"Of course. Erin loves to see her aunt Dolly."

"Did she call me that?"

"She's trying to talk and she can almost say daddy."

"I'll be there in a little bit," Dahlia said.

Mary left the front door open for Dahlia. After allowing Aunt Dahlia to hold her niece and nephew for a few minutes, Mary put them down for a nap and returned to the living room.

"What is on your mind? You have been acting rather nervously," Mary said as she sat next to Dahlia on the couch.

Dahlia took a deep breath, exhaled and said, "I'm pregnant."

"Come again," Mary said as her eyes opened wide.

"I am pregnant," Dahlia repeated slowly.

"Don't be daft. How can you be pregnant?" Mary asked.

96

Dahlia turned her head toward her sister. "Do I have to explain it?"

Mary stared at Dahlia for what felt like an eternity to her sister. "Who? Why? Are you sure?"

"I'm not going to answer the first two questions, but I took two tests. I peed on the sticks, and they were both positive. I am late, and I am never this late."

"But who? I didn't know you were serious about anyone."

"Mary, I am not telling you who the father is, and it wasn't a serious relationship."

"You were sleeping with someone, Dahlia. That makes it serious whether you like it or not. Have you told this man he is going to be a father? How are you planning to tell Ma and Da?"

"I don't know, and I haven't told anyone except you," Dahlia answered.

"What are you going to do about school? Are you going to take time off to have the baby?" Mary asked putting a hand to her forehead. "I can't believe this. Are you absolutely sure you're expecting?"

"These tests are pretty reliable now."

"You need to see your doctor," Mary insisted.

"Will she have to tell Ma and Da?"

Mary shook her head. "You are legally an adult so she will keep it confidential for now."

"That's a relief," Dahlia sighed. "I thought I would stay in school for the fall semester. If I wear loose-fitting clothes, no one will know I'm expecting."

"I think you are being rather naive if you think you can hide this pregnancy, and you are going to have to tell Ma and Da as soon as they get back," Mary ordered.

Dahlia leaned forward with her elbows on her knees and said, "Maybe I should move to Canada and change my name."

Mary rubbed Dahlia's back and whispered, "Don't be silly. They love you no matter what. After they get over the shock, they will be supportive."

"If the shock doesn't kill them."

"What time they are getting back?" Dahlia asked again.

Mary looked up from her book. "They said before five."

Dahlia looked at the clock next to a family photo.

Mary set her book down. "Time will not go any faster because you are pacing back and forth. You should sit down and try to relax."

"Right! I should relax," Dahlia huffed. "Easy for you to say. You were married when you got pregnant. What I should do is move to South America and change my name."

"That is an option," Mary said with a grin. "But you would miss Erin and Ewan too much."

Dahlia plopped on the couch next to her sister and put a hand to her forehead. "What should I do? How should I tell them?"

Mary sighed and said, "First, you need to stop being a drama queen. I know that's the way you've always dealt with issues, but it's time to grow up. You are going to be a mother in a few months."

At exactly 4:27 Mary and Dahlia heard the garage door opening.

"I do believe Ma and Da are home," Mary said. She set the book down, stood up and faced Dahlia. "Are you going to sit there like a lump?"

"No, I'm going to go to my room and hide in the closet."

"Anyone home?" Dylan Michaelis shouted a moment later from the kitchen. "We are back."

Mary headed to the kitchen and hugged her parents.

"Where are my precious grandchildren?" Cora Michaelis asked.

"I'm afraid it's just me. The children are with Jonah," Mary replied. "How was your trip?"

"Let me put on a kettle and we can have tea while I tell you all about it," Cora said.

Dylan carried the luggage upstairs. Mary fixed the tea and Cora sorted through the mail.

"Dahlia, come and have some tea while Ma and Da tell us about their trip," Mary said.

"I'm not thirsty," Dahlia replied.

"Then you can sit and listen," Mary insisted.

Everyone gathered around the dining room table and talked for thirty minutes. Dahlia listened and only replied when asked a direct question.

"Have you and Eli been getting along?" Ma asked. "You look rather blue."

"He's been working so many hours I haven't seen him much," Dahlia answered.

"Has anything happened around here I should know about?" Da asked as he took the last cookie.

Mary looked at Dahlia. Dahlia looked at the buffet. Da looked at Ma after an eternity of silence.

"Well, I guess that's good," Da said.

Mary nudged Dahlia's foot, tilted her head and stared at her sister.

Dahlia clenched her jaw, frowned and tried to kick Mary's foot but hit the chair instead.

Ma noticed the looks. "What is going on? Why are you upset with each other?"

Mary shrugged and said, "I'm not upset."

Dahlia took a deep breath, looked at her parents and allowed tears to begin cascading down her cheeks.

"Dahlia, honey, what is the matter?" Ma asked.

"Drama queen," Mary muttered under her breath so only Dahlia could hear.

"Tell me, honey," Ma whispered.

"I have bad news, and I'm afraid you will hate me forever," Dahlia said as she sobbed.

Ma stood up, walked around the table and put her hands on Dahlia's shoulders. "We could never hate you. Please tell me what is troubling you, child."

Dahlia sobbed again. Da took out his handkerchief and passed it to Mary. Mary used it to wipe Dahlia's tears away.

"Tell us, sweetheart."

Dahlia avoided looking at her parents, stared out the window, cleared her throat and said, "Please don't hate me, but I am going to have a baby."

Da's expression froze. Ma squeezed Dahlia's shoulder harder. Mary closed her eyes and prayed.

"Hey! You guys are home earlier than I thought," Eli said walking into the room. "How was your trip? Do anything exciting?"

Mary looked at her brother and put a finger to her mouth.

Eli scanned everyone's expressions. "What happened? Did someone die? Why does everyone look so weird?"

"Your timing could not be any worse," Dahlia said. "I just told Ma and Da that I'm pregnant."

"You mean Mary is pregnant," Eli said looking at his older sister. "Tell Jonah congrats for me."

Mary shook her head. "You better sit down, Eli."

He took his usual seat across from Dahlia. "Will someone tell me what's happening?"

"I just did," Dahlia said. "I am expecting a baby."

"That's not possible," Eli said. "You're just a kid."

Mary's eyes bored a hole through Eli. He shut up.

"Maybe we should let Dahlia explain what happened?" Ma said as she walked back to her seat in a daze.

"Ma! I'm not going to tell you how it happened. It happened the way all babies are made."

Da made a clicking sound with his tongue, Pushed back his chair, stood up and looked at Cora. "Perhaps Eli and I should go for a walk to let you talk to our daughters."

"I knew you would hate me," Dahlia burst into sobs again and lay her head on her arms on the table. "I never should have told anyone."

"I think we would know eventually," Mary said rubbing Dahlia's back.

Eli stood up, stared at his sisters and, after a moment, followed his father out of the room.

"I didn't know she was interested in anyone," Eli said. "She's never mentioned a boyfriend."

"I don't think that makes the situation any better," Da said as they walked outside.

"Yeah, I guess not," Eli said.

Ma took a deep breath. She let it out slowly and said, "Let's not worry about things we cannot change or control. What has happened has happened."

"Do you hate me, Ma?" Dahlia asked. "I know I screwed up."

"Dahlia! We do not use such language in this house."

"I'm sorry."

Ma looked at Mary. "Who is the father?"

Mary looked at Dahlia and shrugged. "I don't know. She will not tell me his name."

"Dahlia, tell me who he is," Ma insisted.

Dahlia shook her head. "I can't." She saw the horrified expression on her mother's face. "No! I mean I know who the father is, but I can't tell you who he is."

"Have you told him about this?" Ma asked.

"No, and I'm not going to until I absolutely have to," Dahlia insisted.

Nothing Ma or Mary said could change Dahlia's mind.

"I must say this is quite unexpected, Dahlia Kathleen," Ma said. "I need more tea."

"I will fix it," Mary offered.

"No, I can make my own tea. You should talk to Dahlia. I feel like I don't know her right now."

Eli and his father returned from their walk in time to see Darian and Dany pull into the driveway.

"How was vacation, Da?" Darian asked.

"Vacation was great, but coming home has been a bit rough."

Dany touched Darian's arm and said, "I'll meet you inside. I need to talk to Mary."

"We will be in shortly," Darian said.

Dany headed into the house, found the ladies in the kitchen, sat down and said, "I got your text, Mary. What's going on?"

Mary and her mother looked at Dahlia.

Dahlia rolled her eyes. "I am pregnant, and everyone is making a big deal about it."

Dany's feet froze to the floor as her jaw dropped.

Standing in the driveway Darian stared at his father with clenched fists. "She has to tell us who did this to her. Eli and I will take care of him."

Eli nodded.

"This is not the 1800s. You are not going to do anything rash," Da said.

The men joined the ladies in the kitchen. Darian put an arm around Dany's shoulders and frowned at his younger sister.

Dahlia sighed. "So, you know, too. Don't even ask about the father."

"You have to tell us," Darian insisted.

"Not going to happen," Dahlia said. She shook a finger at both brothers. "Don't think you are avenging my honor or some chivalrous thing that is so archaic."

"Were you a willing participant?" Eli asked which earned stares and frowns from everyone else.

"I knew what I was doing," Dahlia replied. "Now that everyone knows the news, can we get on with our normal lives?"

Mary shook her head and whispered, "Life will never be normal around here."

"Emmy, I need to talk to you," Mary said in the hallway outside of their Sunday School room after class. "Do you have a moment?"

"Sure," Emmy answered. "I'm not singing today. What's up? Did your parents get home?"

"They did. Could we wait until everyone leaves and use the classroom?"

Emmy stared at the kids former nanny. "This is something serious, huh? Your eyes give it away."

A few minutes later Emmy took a deep breath then asked, "Why won't she tell you about the father? Do you have any idea?"

Mary shook her head. "None of us knew she was seeing anyone. We certainly didn't expect this out of the blue. She should have known better."

"She should have been using precautions," Emmy muttered.

102

"Emmy!"

Emmy looked at Mary. "She shouldn't have been having sex in the first place, but it happens. Even good Christian girls are tempted. I was."

"But you never... never mind," Mary said. "It's driving us mad because she is acting like this is no big deal."

"Do you want me to talk to her?" Emmy asked. "She might tell me about the father, and I promise not to tell anyone about this. I won't even tell Kenny."

"You can try, but Dahlia can be rather stubborn," Mary said.

Emmy grinned and touched her heart. "I am an expert when it comes to stubbornness."

"Can I help you, young lady?" Pastor Tyler asked. "Are you a new student?"

Emmy stopped walking before she ran into Tyler and looked up from the computer printouts in her hand. "Hi, Tyler."

"Good morning, Emmy," he answered. "Are you getting the kids' class schedule?"

Emmy glanced at the schedules in her hand and then at Tyler. "Yes, but I know their teachers already." She shifted her gaze to the man standing next to Tyler.

"Have you met Wyatt?" Tyler asked.

Emmy shook her head without answering.

"We have never met, but I do know who you are," Wyatt said offering a hand. "I've been to a few of your concerts."

Emmy shook his hand and bit her lip. *Should I say anything about his wife? Maybe I better not. Why bring up bad memories?* "I hope you enjoyed them."

"I did and I have to admit I was surprised to hear such an amazing voice out of such a petite young lady."

Tyler shuddered and said, "He means that in a good way, Emmy. Please don't hurt him. We need him to work around here."

"Why would I hurt him?" Emmy asked. *Are your eyes green or are they gray? It's hard to tell, but I love your smile. It shows confidence.*

103

Tyler shrugged and said, "Because he made a reference to your stature."

Emmy peered at Wyatt again. *You're not exactly tall, but probably close to six feet. You're definitely not as skinny as Tyler but you're not big like Tony.* "Is this your first day here?"

"This is my first official day on the job. I'm trying to get the lay of the land and not get lost. This is a much larger facility than where I was."

"It's pretty big for a church and private school," she replied. "Are you sure you want to work with Tyler?"

Wyatt laughed and said, "It will take me a while to understand my role. I know Tyler doesn't like the administrative side of the church."

"It's not that I don't like it," Tyler said.

"Yeah! You've got more important things to occupy your time," Emmy said with a grin. "Tell Liz I said hi and will call her later."

"Will do," Tyler answered.

"It was nice to meet you," Wyatt said. "I'm sure we will be seeing more of each other."

Emmy watched Tyler and Wyatt walk away. *I shouldn't even be thinking about this, but I should introduce you to Kristen.* Emmy shook her head, sighed and continued walking. *No! I'm sure Kristen and John will work out their issues. They just have to.*

Chapter Thirteen

"Since you're here, will you watch the kids while I meet with Denise?" Emmy asked.

Father James finished his coffee and set the cup in the sink. "I can because I don't have to be back to St. Bart's until this afternoon, but I'm not going to follow the boys through the woods. I'm getting too old for that."

"They should be all right. Heather and Isa have to clean their room before they can go swimming." Emmy grabbed her purse, keys and laptop. "If I'm not back before lunch, will you feed them?"

"I can make sandwiches and open a can of soup," Father James replied. He waved a hand. "Go. The kids and I will survive for one morning."

"Call me if you need." Emmy left the house and drove to Starbucks to meet her editor, Denise Bartell. She entered the coffee shop and saw Denise sitting at a table in the back corner. She walked past the counter, heard the sound of the espresso machine and inhaled the aroma of coffee.

Denise stood, waved her floppy hat and smiled.

Emmy sat across the table from Denise. "Have you been waiting long?"

Denise sat down. "I got here thirty minutes ago so I could get some work done. The office is so hectic with everyone working on stories about the bridge collapse."

"I heard about that," Emmy said. "Thank God no traffic was on the bridge at the time."

"It was a miracle, but the people responsible for its maintenance have known it was unsafe. Would you like something to drink? My treat."

"Maybe later. I read through your suggestions for the book, and I agree with most of them."

"Most of them?" Denise asked sipping her coffee.

"I changed everything that dealt with grammar, and I didn't realize how often I use the words that and just. I understand what filtering means now."

"They are usually unnecessary," Denise said.

"There are three suggestions I don't agree with. Let me turn on my computer, and I'll show you."

Emmy moved around the table and sat next to Denise.

"The scene about the main characters at the pool party is true, and I don't want to cut it," Emmy said.

"You need to decide if you want this to be based on true events, or total fiction. Readers will know the main character is you even if you change the name to Molly Malone. This book is different than the collection of stories in *Adventures in Raynor Park* and the book about your life on the road with your band. The Raynor Park stories are pretty innocent compared to this."

"Those stories are set before I was a teenager," Emmy said.

"This book is about you in high school, right?" Denise asked though she knew the answer.

"Yes."

"Is it safe to assume nothing in the book will come as a surprise to Kenny?"

Emmy nodded.

"Even so, do you really want everyone to know what you and the Dexter character did?" Denise asked and took a sip of her coffee.

"The Dexter O'Keefe character is really a combination of three different people and two of them are dead."

"I want you to give some serious thought about this. I think you could turn this into a fictional series and not draw entirely on your life experiences. I can see Molly and Dexter as a couple through high school and even into college. Not everything that happens to them needs to be based on real events."

Emmy leaned on her elbows. "I should decide who my target audience will be, huh?"

"That would be wise. If you intend this to be a series for a secular audience, you need to make it more realistic."

"What do you mean by that?"

A secular audience will accept crude language and swearing among other things. You might need to write about situations outside of your comfort zone."

106

Emmy grinned and whispered, "You mean it needs more sex, right?"

"Exactly!" Denise slapped the table and laughed. "I doubt Molly would remain a virgin for very long if she sneaks around with Dexter all the time."

"That's probably true," Emmy replied. *If Rory hadn't moved away when he did, I doubt if I would have waited until I got married.*

"If you decide to turn this into a series, I suggest you change the names. I'm not totally sold on Molly and even less of a fan of Dexter. To me Dexter suggests a rather weird character and not one your readers will think of positively."

"To be honest, I don't like that name either. I'll think of something better."

"Are you sure you don't want something to drink?" Denise asked. "I need a refill."

Emmy shook her head. "Thanks, but I'm good."

Denise returned a moment later. "I don't normally read books in this genre, but I do like your writing style. Your characters are multi-dimensional."

"I don't do that on purpose," Emmy replied.

Denise chuckled and said, "That's a good thing. Even your minor characters are visible. For instance, in chapter five there is a character who only appears in one scene yet you describe him so vividly in just one sentence."

"Which one is that?" Emmy asked.

"Let me find the page." Denise found the line and read it. "Without responding to the insult Stanley replaced the pen in his pocket protector and touched the tape on his thick glasses." Denise smiled at Emmy and held up a hand. "First, I know he's a nerd." She touched one finger. "Second, I can feel his insecurity and lack of confidence." Denise pointed out two other things she knew about this character. "Do you follow what I mean? I know this person."

"That character is based on a boy who lived across the street for a year or so. I don't even remember his real name," Emmy said.

"Doesn't matter." Denise waved a hand. "Your readers all know a Stanley. Everyone knows a Stanley." She took a sip of coffee. "I bet Stanley either works in a computer store or owns it."

Emmy sat back in her chair and stared absently at the people in line at the counter. "I did like creating the characters and their world."

"That is one of your strengths as a writer. I would suggest you take some time to decide where you want to go with this story. I think it would make a good series."

"If I decide to expand it, I would want to make some changes in the characters and probably their names," Emmy said.

"You can do that. It is your creation," Denise replied. "I need to get back to the office. I am supposed to interview the mayor this afternoon, and I need to prepare some questions."

"Are you going to ask him about the bridge and how long it will take to repair it?"

"You better believe it," Denise said and then laughed. "He won't get any easy questions from me."

"I'll make a decision and get back to you." Emmy watched Denise leave. *I could turn this into a story about what my life might have been if I chose to ignore God.*

"Mom, you don't have to walk us to our classroom," Heather said as Emmy parked her BMW in the church lot. "We are in sixth grade. We're not babies. We know where to go."

Emmy turned in the driver's seat to look at the kids. "I know you're not babies, but don't you want me to meet your teacher."

"You know Mr. Starks is our teacher this year."

"Are you ready to have a man be your teacher?" Emmy asked.

"He's really nice. Carson, Peter and Dotty were in his class, and they all liked him," Isabella said. She grabbed her backpack and climbed down.

Kevin Michael opened the door on the other side and jumped out. "Ms. Dalton is my teacher, and I know what room is mine. See you after school, Mom."

108

"I won't go inside today, but one of these days I will."

"Whatever," Heather said.

Emmy watched her children walk into the school. "I can't believe the girls will be in junior high next year." She was startled by a rap on the window.

"Hey! Aren't you going to go inside?" Tony asked.

Emmy lowered the window. "I was but they didn't want me to. They said they're not babies anymore."

"Tell me about it," Tony said watching Dotty and Ben walking toward the school. He glanced down at Taylor and Coby. "At least these two still allow me to walk them to their classes."

"Did Sloane drive separately?" Emmy asked.

"Yeah, all the teachers had to be here early for the first day. Most of the time she will bring the kids with her."

"At least Carson and Peter can catch a bus to St. Raymond's."

"Only because there are four other kids from Bristol Ridge attending St. Ray's. Otherwise, they would need a ride."

"Have you and Sloane decided where Dotty will go to high school?" Emmy asked.

"Talked about it, yeah, but we haven't decided."

"Dad, we need to go," Taylor said tugging on Tony's arm.

"Talk to you later, Emmy. I need to get these guys inside. Oh, Mama wants to talk to you about something. Give her a call."

Emmy decided to stop by the house instead of calling. She parked in front of the garage and used the code to enter. "Mama! Are you home? Tony said you needed to talk to me."

"I'm in the kitchen," Mama said. "Come on in."

Emmy found Mama doing the breakfast dishes. "You should use the dishwasher."

"I hate to run it unless it's full."

"What are you going to do now that all the kids are in school all day?" Emmy asked while leaning against the countertop. "You need something to keep from getting bored."

Mama rinsed the last bowl and set it in the strainer to dry. "Let's sit in my room, and I'll tell you."

Emmy followed Mama to her private in-law suite. Mama

109

sat in her favorite rocking chair and Emmy sat across from her.

"What are you planning?"

Mama took a deep breath, let it out slowly and smiled. "Peter and I always talked about taking a trip to Italy to visit family. We never got the chance because he was so busy with the construction company."

"And then he passed away before you had the chance to go," Emmy said. "You didn't want to go without him, and you had the kids to take care of. You are so unselfish. You never think about yourself."

"Yes, but now that the kids are getting older, I want to go," Mama said. "If I wait much longer, I might not have the health to travel."

"By yourself?" Emmy asked. "You've never gone on vacation by yourself that I know of. You go on senior citizen trips but always with a group."

"I talked to Karla about it, and she is willing to go with me. She and Daniel have been to Europe several times. She suggested we hire a driver and let him, or her, be our guide."

"I think that's a great idea. When would you go?" Emmy asked.

"Karla wants to take some time to plan the trip, so I think it wouldn't be until October. Certainly no sooner than late September. It would have to be in the fall while the kids are in school and before the weather gets too cold."

"Let me know if I can help plan it. One of these days I want to take the kids on a real European vacation."

"My mother used to describe the small town where she lived as the most beautiful place in the world. I'm sure it wasn't, but I would like to see it."

Chapter Fourteen

"Did I wake you up?" Kenny asked.

"Of course not," Emmy answered sleepily and tried to focus on the alarm clock. "I'm always awake at two in the morning."

"I'm sorry I woke you up, but I wanted to tell you this tour is officially over. We left the building five minutes ago and are on our way to the airport. I will see you shortly. Go back to sleep, Em."

"I'll see you in the morning. I'm taking the kids to church. You're welcome to come with if you wake up in time."

"Make sure I get up," he answered.

Emmy checked the clock on the nightstand and shrugged. *He did say to wake him up.* She nudged Kenny's shoulder and he grunted. She leaned close and whispered, "It's almost nine and you need to wake up."

He turned onto his back and opened his eyes. "I didn't try to wake you when I got home."

"And I appreciate that, but you did say you wanted to go to church. You haven't been there all summer."

"How long do I have to get ready?"

She looked at the clock, tilted her head and answered, "Fifteen minutes at the most."

He grinned and tried to pull her on top of him.

She scooted away. "I'm already dressed, and there's no time for that. I need to find out if the kids are ready. I'll be back in a few minutes to make sure you're dressed."

She headed downstairs and heard the kids in the kitchen.

"Mom! I made breakfast all by myself," Kevin shouted.

"What did you make?" Emmy asked looking at the stove.

"I used the microwave to heat up an egg sandwich." He held it up for her to see.

"Where are your sisters?"

Kevin pointed to the powder room. "In there. They already ate."

111

"Finish your sandwich and wash your face and hands. We need to leave soon."

Heather and Isabella walked out of the powder room.

"Is Daddy going with us?" Isabella asked.

"He is unless he fell back asleep," Emmy answered.

"Should we check on him?" Heather asked.

"I should do that because he might be in the shower. I will be back in a minute."

Kenny had finished showering and was shaving when Emmy walked into the bathroom.

"I'm going as fast as I can," he said.

She leaned against the vanity and snapped the elastic on his bright red boxers. "Try not to cut yourself."

"I'm always careful." He swatted her hand away.

"How was Los Angeles?" she asked while walking into his closet and grabbing a clean shirt. "You can wear your black jeans with this."

"The concerts were all right. LA can be a tough crowd, but that's not what you're asking, is it?"

She tossed his shirt on the bed, walked back into the bathroom and leaned against the vanity again. "Did you have a chance to see her?"

Kenny wiped away the remaining shaving cream and asked with a straight face, "Who do you mean?"

She swatted his arm and frowned. "You know who."

"If you are referring to Becky and Taylor Claussen, the answer is no," he answered placing emphasis on Taylor. "I did not see or speak to her or any member of her family. Would you be jealous if I had?"

"Did you communicate via email or any other form of social media?" Emmy asked.

"I did not post anything on her Facebook page or text her." He squeezed toothpaste onto his brush and pointed it at Emmy. "No images on Instagram or FaceTime or whatever people use these days."

"How many kids does she have now? How old are they?" Emmy asked. "I can't remember their names."

112

"They have two boys and a girl. Josiah, Eve and Joshua." He held up a finger and quickly began brushing his teeth. "Josiah was born the same year as the twins, and Eve is the same age as Kevin Michael. Joshua is a couple years younger, I think," he said and then resumed brushing.

"You remember their names, huh? Do you have pictures of them in your wallet?"

He tilted his head as he stared at her. "Why would I do that? They aren't my kids."

She shrugged and then grinned. "No reason. I'm just yanking your chain. Hurry up and get dressed. Try to wear matching socks." She left the bathroom and headed downstairs.

A week later Tony caught up to Emmy in the church foyer after the second service. He waited until she finished talking to Liz and Dany.

"Do you need to talk to me?" Emmy asked.

"Did I tell you Dwight made the final roster for the Browns?"

"No! Did he really? That's great. What position does he play?" Emmy asked.

"Mostly right tackle, but he can play the other offensive line positions, too. Marco send me a photo of him in his uniform. Wanna see it? It's on my phone."

"Do I have a choice?" Emmy teased.

Tony rubbed his jaw and scoffed, "You don't have to pretend to be interested."

"Show me," Emmy said.

Tony found the photo and handed his phone to Emmy.

She stared at it. "Is that really Dwight?"

"Yeah," Tony said. "You don't recognize him, huh?"

Emmy shook her head. "Not with that bushy beard and long hair. He looks pretty big."

"He's six eight and weighs over three hundred pounds. He makes me look small."

"Who does he get his size from? His mother is taller than Marco, but not as tall as you. Is his real father very big?"

"Marco said his birth father is a couple inches taller than me, so I guess Dwight takes after him."

"Did he graduate from Notre Dame?"

"Dwight or his birth father?" Tony asked.

"Dwight, you goof. Why would I care... never mind."

"Dwight got a degree in business and will get a master's degree after he finishes playing football."

"I hope he has a long and successful career. Maybe the Browns will win a Super Bowl one of these years."

Tony grinned and said, "I'd be thrilled if they make the playoffs."

"Hey, Emmy, got a minute to talk?" Bobby O'Connor asked.

"I suppose," Emmy answered. "I'm on my way home from dropping the kids at school. Where are you?"

"Home. I don't have to work until noon."

"I was going to stop and grab some coffee. Wanna meet me?"

"Where?"

"I'm close to the Donut Den on Hudson Street. Know where that is?" she asked.

"Sure. Will you buy me a chocolate muffin?" Bobby asked.

"Fine, but I can't stay too long. I promised Diane I would stop and see Mom for a few minutes."

"And a large black coffee?" Bobby asked.

"You're pushing your luck. I'll grab a table."

Bobby arrived a few minutes after Emmy and spotted her at a table by the front window. He sat across from her and took a sip of his coffee. "I didn't know it was supposed to rain this hard."

"Are you afraid of melting?"

"No. Drowning. Thanks for the coffee and muffin. I have news you might be interested in."

Emmy took a bite of her blueberry muffin and waved a hand. "Go ahead. Tell me."

"Boyd and Christian left the Bender Brothers Band. Boyd called me last Thursday to tell me."

114

"Why?" Emmy asked. "I thought they wanted to be rock stars."

"Apparently not. Christian is moving back to LA, but Boyd is coming back to SoHam."

"What is the band going to do? Have they already replaced them?"

"Boyd said the band is relocating to Texas and will hire replacements from there. Boyd sounded pretty bummed out. He realizes he really messed up his life," Bobby said.

"His and Bailey's," Emmy said. "Is he going to try to patch things up with her?"

Bobby shook his head and took a large sip of coffee.

"Why not?"

"Bailey is in a relationship and doesn't have any interest in Boyd now. He could use a job."

"I'm starting my tour on Wednesday. I don't need another guitar player, and he wouldn't have time to learn the new material even if I did," Emmy said and then took a bite of her muffin.

"I think he realizes that, Em. Would you consider hiring him as a crew member?"

She looked out the window at the rain for a moment. "He would have to give up drinking. Do you think he would be willing to do that?"

"I can pretty much guarantee he would. He's really repentant about what he did."

"Let me think about it, Bobby. Nelson would have to hire him," Emmy said. "I'll talk to him and get back to you."

"I'll let Boyd know. Thanks, Em. I'm sure he would appreciate the job."

Emmy talked to Bobby Tuesday afternoon after their final rehearsal before her tour started.

"So, Nelson agreed to hire Boyd, huh?" Bobby asked.

"Yes, but it will be with the understanding he has to stay clean and sober. He can start tomorrow," Emmy said. "If this works out, I might be able to use him in the band. Teresa is pushing Tommy to go to college."

"I will text him and let him know. I will keep an eye on him, Emmy."

"He's not your responsibility, Bobby. He will have to want to do this for himself."

"It won't hurt to have someone watching his back," Bobby said.

"I suppose so." Emmy leaned forward and let her hair fall down her face. "I should have got it cut, but it's too late now."

"How was your visit with your mother?"

Emmy sighed and rolled her eyes.

"She is your mother, Em."

"I know. I stayed a half hour, but spent most of the time cleaning her apartment. I found some of her clothes under the sink, and an empty box of crackers hidden behind the couch. She's not supposed to have snacks in her room."

"Sounds like cruel and unusual punishment," Bobby said.

"She doesn't like any disruptions to her routine. That can really set her off."

"Does she know who you are?" Bobby asked.

Emmy shrugged. "I think she knows I'm family, but she can't remember my name. I tell her I'm Emmy, but she forgets it five minutes later."

Bobby hugged Emmy and whispered, "I'm sorry. It can't be easy to deal with that."

"I know God has everything under control, but sometimes I wonder if Diane or I will end up like Mom or Aunt Betty."

"Maybe researchers will find a cure by the time you get that old," Bobby said.

Chapter Fifteen

"Emmy, we're ready for you," Nelson Grapella told her backstage Thursday night in St. Louis.

"I'll be right there. Do I look all right?"

Brenda Grapella straightened the shoulders of Emmy's top. "You look as pretty as ever."

"I hope I can remember the words to some of the older songs. I haven't played some of them for several years," Emmy said.

Nelson led her to the side of the stage. She waved to Bobby and the other band members as they started playing. The emcee introduced her, and she closed her eyes, took a deep breath, exhaled and walked to the center of the stage. She grabbed her wireless microphone, waved to some fans she knew and began singing.

"I feel so much better now," she said ninety minutes later as she headed backstage with Bobby.

"Don't tell me you were nervous about tonight," he teased.

"I was. I haven't played outside of SoHam in an eternity," she said while nudging him with her elbow.

"Were you afraid people wouldn't remember you?"

"I wasn't sure anyone would like the new songs. *Gideon's Heart* hasn't been selling as well as Klaus hoped." She smiled and waved at some friends. "Save me some food. I need to talk to my friends."

"I'll try but Tommy and Tariq told me they were starving," Bobby replied as he headed to the catering area. "There might not be much left, Em."

Emmy walked up to her friends.

"Emmy, it's so good to see you," Jackie Wainwright held out her arms as Emmy approached. "Let me give you a hug."

Emmy allowed Jackie to envelop her as she looked at the two children standing with their father.

"We heard about your accident, and the whole church prayed for you," Jackie said.

"Thank you. I needed those prayers."

"Let me look at you, girl." Jackie took a step back and inspected Emmy. "My! My! My! How do you do it? You don't look any different than the first time I saw you and that had to be fifteen years ago."

"That's nice of you to say," Emmy said. *I wish I could say the same about you, but that would be a lie.*

"It's been three years since you were in St. Louis," Jackie said as she hugged Emmy again. "We're so thrilled to see you again."

"I can't believe how much your kids have grown," Emmy said. She shook hands with Isaiah and smiled. "Are you still pastoring at the same church?" *I hope that was a tactful way of asking because I don't remember the name of the church.*

"I am," he replied.

"Girls, don't be so shy," Jackie said because her daughters were being unusually silent. "This is Abriana and this is Calneshia. They've never been this quiet since they learned how to talk." Jackie laughed and put an arm around each child.

"Mom! Do you have to embarrass us?" Abriana said.

After letting Emmy talk for a few minutes, Nelson broke up the reunion.

"Emmy, there is someone from KLJY who would like a couple minutes of your time. I think you should talk to her," Nelson said.

"I'll be right there," Emmy replied. She allowed Jackie to hug her again and said goodbye.

"Should I know that family?" Nelson asked while leading Emmy away.

"That's Jackie. She came to a concert years ago, and we've kinda kept in touch over the years. Her daughters are close to Heather and Isabella's age. Who am I meeting?"

"Justine Rivers. You've met her before."

Emmy smiled at Justine and recognized her because of the tattoo of a cross on her arm. "How are you? It's good to see you again," Emmy said.

They talked for a minute and then Justine mentioned, "I wanted to let you know that a friend of mine at KRCH has started

118

playing 'Gideon's Heart' as part of their regular rotation."

"That's nice," Emmy said. "I appreciate it."

"Em, KRCH is the top station in the area for adult contemporary music. That could break 'Gideon's Heart' to a wider audience," Nelson explained.

"Oh, I understand." She smiled and said, "Then I really appreciate it."

Two weeks later Klaus Kesson attended Emmy's concert in Dallas and joined her backstage after the show.

"I was impressed, Emmy. I didn't see an empty seat in the auditorium," he said.

"This isn't all that big a venue," she replied. *What's going on? You've never been to one of my concerts.*

"Are you aware stations all across the country are now playing 'Gideon's Heart?'" he asked.

"Nelson told me a few stations were adding it to their rotation."

"The downloads are growing by the day. More people are streaming it than any of your other songs. I do believe we have a hit on our hands," Klaus said with a smile. "I would appreciate it if you would consider adding some more dates to your tour. Possibly adding Saturday nights and a few Wednesdays."

"I'd rather not be away from home on the weekends," she replied.

"It wouldn't be for long, Emmy, but it would be a way to make money for both of us. Just think about it. I'll talk to Nelson more in the next few days. Congratulations on a great show. I have to get back to LA tonight."

Emmy watched Klaus and his entourage leave. Nelson walked over and stood beside her.

"Did you hear what he was asking?"

"He talked to me earlier, Emmy. You don't have to decide anything right away," Nelson assured her.

"Things have sure changed at Steward Music since his father retired."

Nelson chuckled and added, "And not for the better."

119

"Tell me about it," Emmy said and then sighed.

She called Kenny later that night and passed along the request from Klaus.

"I know you don't like the travel, Em, but I can see his point," Kenny said while getting ready for bed. "More concerts equal more opportunities for the company to generate revenue from CD sales, downloads and whatever technology they come up with next."

"Would you miss me if I was gone more nights?" she asked.

"You know the answer. Don't put this on me. You have to decide. It's your career."

"You're no help," she said. "I could look at it as a way to reach more people."

"People might come to your concerts because of 'Gideon's Heart' who would never attend a church," he said.

"That's what I thought when Nelson first told me about it getting some rotation on secular stations."

"I know this doesn't matter, but it will mean more income for you and the band."

"If I want my music to reach unsaved people, I need to take it to where they are."

"Jesus sought out the poor and sinners."

Emmy laughed and replied, "I can't always be singing to the choir, huh?"

"Not if you want to reach new people for the Kingdom."

"I guess it won't kill me to add a few more dates, but you better miss me if I do."

Chapter Sixteen

"Mama, you do realize you and Mom will be gone for a month, right?" Kristen asked. "You are allowed to check in two suitcases and still have your carry on bags."

Mama Bertucci looked at the two suitcases on her bed and shrugged. "It seems like a lot to take. I'm sure I will be able to do laundry over there."

"Mom told me she is taking an extra suitcases, and she doesn't care how much the airline charges her."

"I'm not paying extra. Can I really take two suitcases?" Mama asked.

Tony heard what was said as he walked into the room. "This isn't the first time you've been on a plane."

"No, but it's the first time I've been back to Italy in thirty years," Mama said as she closed the suitcases.

"Do you have your passport and driver's license?" Tony asked.

"I don't plan to do any driving," Mama answered.

"You still need to have it with you," Kristen said.

"How soon do we need to leave?" Mama asked. "Do I have time to say goodbye to all the kids?"

Tony checked the time. "We need to leave in thirty minutes. Kristen, is your father bringing your mother here, or do we have to pick her up?"

"Dad is dropping her off here. Are these ready to go?" Kristen asked pointing to Mama's suitcases.

"Yes, and my carry on bags are ready, but I need to find a book to take," Mama said.

"Tony, will you take these to the van?" Kristen asked walking out of the room.

While Tony carried the luggage to the minivan, Mama kissed and hugged all the kids.

"We will miss you," Peter said.

"Make sure you behave for your parents," Mama instructed. "I don't want to hear about any mischievousness."

Tony walked back into the kitchen.

"Where are Mom and Dad?" Kristen asked. "They should have been here by now. Should I text her?"

"No need. They arrived just as I finished loading Mama's stuff. Uncle Daniel and I loaded your mother's luggage, and they were saying goodbye."

"Let's get going," Kristen said. "Who knows what traffic will be like? I don't want them to miss the flight."

"Where are you today?" Peter asked.

"We're still in Rome," Mama answered. "We've been sightseeing at other towns around here, but we're staying at a hotel in Rome."

The six Bertucci children sat in the family room and stared at Tony's laptop.

"Did you go to the Colosseum?" Ben asked.

"Yes, and Aunt Karla took lots of pictures. Have you been behaving?" Mama asked.

Noemi Claire pointed to her three younger brothers. "They were wrestling and broke one of Mom's vases."

"When are you coming home?" Coby, the youngest sibling, asked.

"Not for three more weeks," Mama answered.

"Are you going to stay in Venice and ride one of those gondolas?" Dotty asked. "If I ever go there, I want to do that."

"We will be there toward the end of the month. We are taking a train to Milan Tuesday. We are going to stay with some of our cousins and other relatives."

"Are you going to see the tower that looks like it's ready to fall over?" Taylor asked.

"He means the Leaning Tower of Pisa," Peter said.

"I figured that," Mama said with a laugh. "I hope we can see it, but there are so many different places to go. We might not have time to see everything."

"Can you understand how people talk?" Ben asked.

"I can understand Italian if they don't talk too fast," Mama said. "My parents used Italian most of the time at home, so I grew up speaking two languages."

"I know some Spanish, but not enough to understand everything," Peter said.

"Okay, we better let Mama go," Sloane said. "Say good night and don't take forever."

One by one the children said good night.

"I miss all of you, and I will be home before you know it," Mama said.

"Hi, Mary. How are you and the babies?" Emmy asked. "I've been meaning to call you."

"We're doing all right. Ewan is sleeping most of the night, and Erin is trying to get him to play with her."

"I remember when we brought Kevin Michael home. The twins treated him like their toy," Emmy said.

"Emmy, I have bad news," Mary said.

"Tell me." Emmy turned off the TV.

"Dahlia is in the hospital. She lost the baby," Mary said.

"Oh no! When did it happen?"

"Last night. She was complaining about pain and started bleeding. I drove her to St. Bart's, but it was too late."

"How is she doing?" Emmy jumped up from the couch and headed to the kitchen. "Are you still there?"

"Yes, but I need to go home to take care of the kids. Mom is here."

"Should I come to the hospital?" Emmy asked.

Mary glanced over her shoulder at her sister. "Dahlia's sleeping now, and she hasn't been in a vary talkative mood."

"That's understandable," Emmy said and then sighed.

"What, Emmy?"

"Do you think she will tell you about the father now? Who he is, I mean."

Mary turned away from her mother and whispered, "Maybe, but I don't want to upset her more than she already is."

"I don't know why she has been so secretive about it. Don't any of her friends at school know?" Emmy asked.

"If they do, they are keeping it to themselves," Mary replied. "But I don't think Dahlia told anyone about the baby."

123

"Couldn't they tell?" Emmy asked. "She was a couple months along."

"She always wore loose-fitting clothes," Mary replied. "If you have time later, you could come up to see her, but please don't upset her."

"I know how to be supportive," Emmy replied. "I will come up later and give your mother a break. I promise I won't ask about the father. If she wants to talk, I will just listen."

A week later Dahlia returned to her classes at North Park College. She came home after her classes Monday evening to do some laundry.

"How was your first day back?" Mom Michaelis asked. "Did everyone wonder where you'd been?"

Dahlia answered, "I told them I had a bad case of the flu."

"Are you ever going to tell your friends the truth?"

Dahlia shook her head. "It's none of their business, Ma."

"I'm sure you have a lot of work to catch up on. My students do if they miss a week."

"Ma, you teach third grade. It won't take me long to get caught up."

The doorbell rang.

"Are you expecting company?" Dahlia asked. She stared at her mother and frowned.

"I thought you might need someone to talk to, so I called Liz and Emmy."

"I'm not telling them anything," Dahlia insisted.

Mr. Michaelis got up from his recliner. "I'll get the door." He let Emmy and Liz in. "Dahlia is doing some laundry, and her mother and I are going out for ice cream."

"Did Dahlia know we're coming over?" Emmy asked. "Her mother asked if we would talk to her and try to cheer her up."

"I think Cora just told her."

Dahlia and her mother walked into the room.

"Thank you for stopping by. I know you are both busy," Mrs. Michaelis said. She turned to Dahlia and whispered, "Be nice. They are concerned about you."

124

Dahlia's parents left and Dahlia led Emmy and Liz into the family room. Liz and Emmy sat on the couch, and Dahlia sat across from them on the love seat.

"Would you like something to drink?"

"We're good, Dahlia," Emmy answered. "I know this must feel weird to you, but we just want to talk and make sure you're all right. Losing a baby has to hurt emotionally."

"It hurt physically, too."

Liz looked around the room. "I love the family photos."

"Haven't you ever been here before?" Emmy asked.

Liz shook her head.

Dahlia glanced over her shoulder at the photos. "We need to take another one with Jonah and Dany."

"Is Eli dating anyone now?" Emmy asked.

"Not that I know of, but he wouldn't tell me if he was. I don't see him that often except once in a while at church," Dahlia replied.

"I know he's still teaching at McGee Junior High, but didn't he buy a house last year?" Emmy asked.

"He thought about it and looked a several fixer-uppers, but decided to wait until he has enough money to build his own," Dahlia said.

"Have you talked to Dany and Darian lately?" Liz asked.

"They came to see me at the hospital, but didn't stay too long. I think Dany felt uncomfortable about being pregnant and me losing my baby."

"She has been a little under the weather," Liz said about her younger sister.

They talked about families, the church, Emmy's tour and school for a few more minutes, but then the conversation lagged.

"We should go," Emmy said. "You probably don't feel like having company. Would you let us pray for you before we go?"

"You don't have to leave, but I would like you to pray for me. I haven't been too faithful about my prayer life lately. I guess you know that since I got pregnant."

"We aren't here to judge you, Dahlia," Emmy said. "No one is perfect. We all make mistakes."

"I sure made a big one," Dahlia said. She clenched her jaw and began to sob.

Emmy and Liz moved to the love seat, sat on either side of Dahlia and hugged her.

"We should pray now," Emmy said after Dahlia stopped crying.

Emmy and Liz held Dahlia's hands and prayed for several minutes.

"Do you feel better now?" Emmy asked as she wiped tears from Dahlia's face.

"I do and I prayed silently. I can't pray out loud like you guys."

"Kenny is like that," Emmy said. "He used to pray with the kids at bedtime, but he would get so flustered if someone at church asked him to even pray for a meal."

"I remember one time when Tyler asked someone from the church to pray to close a Sunday School class and the man just couldn't. Tyler learned from that experience."

"What did he learn?" Dahlia asked.

"He learned not to ask someone to pray publicly unless he had heard him pray before," Liz answered.

"Could I have some water now, please?" Emmy asked.

Dahlia brought bottled water from the kitchen for everyone and sat back down.

"Can I talk to you about what happened?" Dahlia asked while staring at the ceiling.

"You can talk about anything and trust us to maintain your secrecy," Emmy said.

"You won't tell anyone, will you?"

Emmy crossed her heart and Liz nodded.

"His name is Te'von Treadway, and I met him in one of my classes. He plays basketball, and he's been to our church a few times."

"I think I remember him," Liz said.

Emmy tried to recall him but couldn't. Then she remembered seeing Dahlia and other girls talking to a tall African American and wondered if that could be Te'von.

"He hasn't been to church for several months."

"Were you guys dating seriously?" Emmy asked and then rolled her eyes. "Sorry. I guess it was serious if you were intimate with him."

"I wouldn't say we were dating. We saw each other quite often at school. We had a couple classes together and would study at the library or sometimes at Howe Hall."

"In your room?" Emmy asked.

"I should have known better, but one thing led to another and we ended up in bed a couple times."

"Didn't he use protection?" Emmy asked. *Please tell me you didn't have unprotected sex.*

"One time he didn't," Dahlia said.

Liz squeezed Dahlia's hand, but didn't say anything.

Emmy stared at Dahlia for a moment and then asked, "Was he your first?"

"Emmy!" Liz exclaimed. "That's none of our business."

"Sorry, Dahlia. You don't need to answer that."

"It's okay. I don't mind. Te'von wasn't my first. I was involved with someone my first year, but it didn't last long, and he left North Park later that year."

"Do any of your friends from school know about Te'von?" Liz asked.

Dahlia shook her head. "I don't really have a friend I feel close enough to confide in. I can't talk to Mary because she still thinks of me as a child."

"There are times when I feel lonely even though I have four kids and Tyler around," Liz admitted. "I had a best friend at Olivet, but we don't see each other very often. We talk once in a while, but." Liz stopped and shrugged.

"You can always talk to me, Liz," Emmy said. "I understand how you feel though. I'm thirty-seven and Diane still treats me like a teenager at times." Emmy rolled her eyes. "Don't even get me started on my mother. Even before she lost her mind, she treated me like a kid."

"Dany and I used to be closer, but now that she's married and expecting, we don't talk as much as we should," Liz said and then put a hand to her mouth. "I'm sorry if that was insensitive."

Dahlia smiled and patted Liz's arm. "I'm not going to get emotional and shatter every time I see an expectant mother. I made a mistake. I'm not ready to be a mother. I have to finish college first."

"Just because you've been with a couple men, doesn't mean you can't stop. I know it's difficult to remain celibate once you've started having sex," Emmy said.

Liz and Dahlia stared at her.

"What? Why are you looking at me like that?"

"Are you speaking from personal experience?" Dahlia asked.

Emmy realized how they took her statement. "No! I did not fool around before I married Kenny. Not enough to get pregnant anyway."

Liz grinned and Dahlia laughed.

Emmy made a face, pulled her knees to her chest and wrapped her arms around them. "I wasn't always an angel, but... never mind."

Liz stood up. "We should go. Dahlia, you can always talk to me if you need a friend."

"What about me?" Emmy asked as she jumped up.

"You're too immature," Dahlia teased. "I need an adult friend."

Chapter Seventeen

"What's up?" Emmy asked using her free hand to pull three dresses from her closet.

"I just got home," Kristen answered.

Emmy set the dresses on the bed and then punched the button to put her cell phone on speaker mode. "Where were you?" Emmy asked setting the phone on the bed and picking up one of the dresses.

"At my attorney's office," Kristen said, took a deep breath and then continued, "I signed the papers so she could file for divorce."

Emmy grabbed her phone, hit the button again and held it to her ear. "Oh, Krissy, I'm so sorry."

"I've done everything I can think of. We tried the counseling, but it just didn't help."

"Does he know you're filing?"

"Yes, and he's not going to contest it. We've sort of worked out a settlement."

"You are keeping the house, right? You can't move away. I won't allow it."

Kristen chuckled and said, "I get to keep the house, Em. You're not getting rid of me."

"Is he going to pay alimony? He better pay child support."

"I'm not making him pay alimony, but he did set up trust funds for the kids. He will be paying child support until they're out of college."

"He has to be insane for doing this."

"Not everyone has a perfect marriage, Em."

"Ha! You know our marriage isn't perfect. Never has been and never will be. We struggle at times just like everyone else, but we manage to make it work."

"That's because one of you is always gone. You can always get away from the mundane, tedious part of life."

"That's so not true. I'm coming over to talk to you. Don't go anywhere," Emmy ordered.

"Don't you have to leave today?"

"Not until later."

"Come on over. We can have lunch."

Emmy came to a stop at the end of her driveway and cautiously inched out into the street. She looked both ways twice before turning left and making a quick right. She parked in front of John and Kristen's garage and jumped out. She rang the doorbell after finding the door locked.

"Come on in," Kristen said opening the door.

"When did you start locking the door?" Emmy followed Kristen through the garage and into the house.

"A few years ago. Don't you lock yours?"

"Not always."

"You should because of the kids."

Emmy sat at the island and stared at the photos on the fridge. "Tell me what happened at your lawyer's office."

Kristen leaned against the counter and flipped her long, blonde hair over her shoulder. "I signed the papers. I told you that."

"You're giving up so easily. Why? Isn't John worth fighting for?"

"He is, but it takes two to make a couple, and he isn't interested anymore. He says he loves the kids, but not me."

"Did you do something I don't know about?" Emmy asked and bit her lip.

"What are you insinuating, Emily?" Kristen replied crossing her arms over her chest.

"You know."

"I'm not going to dignify that with an answer. I'm not like you. I don't fool around," Kristen said turning her back to Emmy.

"I don't fool around," Emmy said getting down and walked around the island to stand next to Kristen.

"Ha! What about Rory? I know there's more to your relationship than you let on."

"Rory is my friend. I've never slept with him. He's not like Ryan or whatever his name was." Emmy poked Kristen's arm with enough force to move Kristen back. "And what about that model from Brazil. Don't tell me you and he never..."

130

"His name was Joaquim, and he was married. You wanted to sleep with him. Not me."

"So, you've never... you know." Emmy said staring into Kristen's eyes.

"Ryan was a long time ago, and it was only the one time. You know that. There hasn't been anyone else."

Emmy hugged Kristen. "I'm sorry I doubted you."

"It's all right, but it's a good thing Rory moved away and got married. Do you still think about him? Do you miss him?"

"I think about him and Rochelle, but I don't miss him as much now," Emmy admitted.

Kristen backed up and looked at Emmy. "Why are you grinning like that?"

"Joaquim was pretty hot, huh? He had the sexiest body I've ever seen."

"You are so bad, Emmy. I'm going to tell Father James to make you do a bunch of penance for even thinking about him like that."

"I bet he's gained fifty pounds and has gray hair," Emmy said.

Kristen smiled and shook her head. "No chance. I saw him on a magazine cover recently, and he still looks great."

"Do you still have his number?"

"Maybe, but I'm not giving it to you."

Emmy's shoulders slumped and she stared at the floor. "I can't believe you guys are splitting up."

"The statistics show that over half of all marriages end in divorce," Kristen said.

Emmy looked up at Kristen. "I never thought yours would. I can't picture you without John. I can't imagine Tony and Sloane breaking up, or Derrick and Amber either."

"Diane went through a divorce. Did you think that would happen?" Kristen opened the fridge and took out a bottle of water. "Want one?"

"I'm good," Emmy said shaking her head. "That was a no-brainer. She never should have been with him in the first place, but I love Carson and Caden."

"I have some chicken salad for sandwiches. Are you hungry?" Kristen asked.

"You didn't make it yourself, did you?" Emmy asked as she walked around the island and sat down.

Kristen made a face at Emmy. "It's safe. I bought it at Sainsbury's."

"Then I'll take a sandwich."

"What are you smiling about?" Tony asked as Sloane sat on the edge of the bed.

"I weighed myself and guess what?"

"What?"

"I've reached my goal. I've lost exactly fifty pounds. I weigh about the same as my last year in college."

"Good. Does that mean you're going to stop working out so much?" he asked slipping an arm around her waist.

She stood up and faced him. "I want to keep using the gym. I'd like to drop another ten pounds."

"You look great the way you are." Tony got out of bed, pulled her close and kissed her.

"You're just saying that because you want something."

"You are so smart," he said.

"Maybe tonight. I need to make breakfast and get the kids to school. You need to head to the office and earn your salary."

"Are you going to make me lose weight?"

She paused in the bedroom doorway and looked back. "You've lost weight since you retired from football. Most guys gain weight."

"I don't eat as much, and I still run. That keeps the pounds off. Oh, speaking of running. Emmy wants to resume running before the kids get up. She claims that's the only time she has to work out."

"Are you sure you can keep up with her?" Sloane asked with a grin.

"She's not as fast as she used to be, and it would only be two or three days a week. She has to leave on Wednesdays for her tour."

"I don't mind if you run with her again," Sloane said. "Just make sure you don't turn it into some kind of competition."

"I won't, but she probably will."

Tony sat on the edge of his bed Monday morning and checked his phone.

"Is that Emmy texting you?" Sloane asked.

Tony looked over his shoulder and nodded. "She's ready to run." He leaned over and kissed his wife. "I won't be gone too long."

He got dressed and met Emmy in his driveway.

"Are you awake enough to keep up with me?" she asked.

"I could outrun you in my sleep, brat. Why isn't Kenny running with you?" Tony asked while stretching his legs.

"Because he's too lazy to get out of bed this early."

Tony laughed and said, "It is barely light enough to see where we're going."

"If we stick to the street, we won't need to worry."

"What about cars?"

Emmy laughed and shook her head. "No one who lives here is ever up this early. We will be finished before we see a car."

Forty minutes later they sat on the steps of Tony's front porch.

"I'm glad you were able to keep up," Tony said.

Emmy punched his arm and said, "Ha! I had to keep slowing down on the hills so you wouldn't fall behind. How far did we go?"

"That loop is about five miles," he answered.

Emmy turned to listen to some ducks flying overhead. "Sloane told me how much weight she's lost. Do you like how she looks now?"

Tony didn't reply.

Emmy turned and looked at him. "I know what that silly grin means."

"What?" he said with a shrug.

"It means you're taking advantage of Sloane."

"Never!"

133

"How do you guys find the time with six kids and Mama in the house? I never have the time."

"Mama is still in Italy, and we have this thing called a lock on our bedroom door. You should buy one."

"Do you put a 'do-not-disturb' sign on the door?" Emmy teased and leaned closer to him.

He pushed her away. "No, but maybe we should."

"Do you make Sloane be quiet when you're... you know?"

"What do you mean?"

Emmy rolled her eyes, looked up at the ducks again and then laughed.

"What is so funny, brat?"

"I remember one time when Isabella walked into the bedroom because she thought something was wrong. Has that ever happened to you guys?"

Tony waved his hands and stood up. "I don't want to hear about what you and Kenny were doing."

"I had to explain to Isa that I was okay."

"I'm not talking about what happens in our bedroom with you. Don't you need to go home and get the kids ready for school?"

Emmy stood up, faced him and poked him in the chest. "You guys are all the same. You like making love, but the minute any of us says anything about sex, you get all flustered and change the subject."

"Go home, brat. I have to get ready for work."

"Same time tomorrow?" Emmy asked as she headed down the sidewalk.

"As long as you don't slow me down and don't talk about... you know."

"I'm going to tell Kristen and Diane you guys are fooling around like newlyweds."

Tony sighed and shook his head.

"Why do I need to sign the title to the Odyssey?" Emmy asked the next morning. "Are you going to get rid of it? It still runs okay."

134

"I've been doing some research online, and I think we need a new one," Kenny said.

"How much are they?" she asked as she signed the title.

"It depends," he said softly.

"I know there are different trim levels. Which one are you looking at, and how much are they?" Emmy asked while staring at him.

"Em, you shouldn't look at how much it costs initially. Think of it as a long-term investment."

"Vehicles are not an investment unless they're a Ferrari or some exotic car like that," she said. "How much?"

"The list price is close to fifty grand after taxes and stuff."

No way, buster!" She shook her head. "Either find a used one, or else a cheaper trim. No way any sane person would spend fifty grand for a minivan."

"But, Em, the new ones have so many new features and the technology is way better now. Don't you want the kids to be able to take advantage of it?"

"I know the newer vans are supposed to be safer, but it's a lot of money." She sat on a barstool with her arms folded across her chest.

"They will like the rear entertainment screens."

"Fine, but you better get a good deal. Tell Mr. D'Antoni he has to knock off at least five grand or no deal."

"Do you have a color preference?"

"No black or white one. I don't like silver that much. Nothing weird like green or yellow." She tilted her hands back and forth. "Gray would be okay."

"How about blue?"

"Fine."

Three hours later Kenny returned, and Emmy and the kids ran outside to see the new Odyssey.

"Do you like the color, Em?" Kenny asked.

"It's okay. How much?"

"Less than I expected," he answered.

"Such a dork. You paid too much. It's just a minivan."

Chapter Eighteen

"Please tell me what is so important it requires an emergency meeting?" Derrick Keasling asked as he walked into the large conference room at Bertucci and Keasling Construction's headquarters building. He sat across the table from his sister, Kristen, and Tony.

Marco Bertucci entered the room with a large container of coffee and sat next to Derrick. "Howdy, everyone. Has anyone heard from Mama lately?"

"I talked to her yesterday," Tony answered. "How was your flight?"

Marco ran a hand through his bushy beard and motioned with his hand. "So, so. I got in late last night and stayed in a hotel."

"Why didn't you stay with us?" Tony asked. "We have room."

"I was tired and didn't think I would get much sleep with six kids in the house."

"My house is quieter," Kristen said. "You can stay with us tonight."

"Thanks, Kristen, but I need to fly back this afternoon. I have classes to teach."

Kristen smiled at her cousin and noticed the remaining hair on his head was mostly gray.

Derrick glanced through the folder in front of him and then looked up at Tony. "Is this for real? Is it serious?"

Tony nodded. "This is the third offer, and they have increased their offer by fifteen percent."

Kristen and Marco opened their folders and scanned the single document.

"What does this mean as far as our taxes go?" Kristen asked.

"You would have to talk to your accountant and whoever does your taxes," Derrick said.

"What about the management team? How will this affect them?" Marco asked. "I am assuming the new owners would want to install their own people."

136

Tony shrugged. "Too early to tell. I know Uncle Daniel looked into selling the company to the employees years ago. That might still be a possibility."

"Does Daddy know about this offer?" Kristen asked.

"He does, but he said it was our decision to make. He said not to worry about him or the history of the company."

"What do you think, Tony? You're the only one of us who actually works here."

Tony glanced at the number at the bottom of the page. "It is very tempting."

Kristen laughed and said, "What would you do for a job? Who wants to hire an ex-football player?"

"I haven't thought about it, but I'm sure I could find a job doing something. I could coach football or mow yards."

"How much time do we have to make up our minds?" Marco asked.

"They would like an answer before the end of the month," Tony answered.

"Will that give us enough time to see if the employees can put together an offer?" Derrick asked.

"It might be tight, but I'll get started on that right away," Tony said.

"I'm okay with this offer if it comes to that," Marco said. "I know I haven't been involved with the company."

"You do get a vote. According to the company's legal team, this is a good offer," Tony said. "I could survive on my share for a few years."

"Ha! We could all retire and never work another day in our lives," Kristen said.

"You don't have a real job, Krissy," Derrick teased his younger sister.

"I am a mother and that's a real job. Did Amber come with you?"

Derrick shook his head. "She couldn't leave her parents. Their health is declining faster than she had hoped."

Parkinson's ran in Amber's family and both parents suffered from the disease.

"Can we do lunch and talk about this more?" Kristen asked.

"I would join you, but I have tons of work to do," Tony said.

"Poor boy," Kristen teased. "Should we order something from Darby's for you?"

"I like that idea," Tony said with a smile.

Tony paced back and forth at O'Hare while waiting for his mother and her sister to return from their trip Saturday afternoon.

"How long will it take to go through customs?" Peter asked.

"Not sure," Tony answered. He pointed to the arrival board. "According to that their flight landed on time."

Twenty minutes later, Peter hollered, "There they are!" He waved and ran toward his grandmother. "How was your trip, Mama? I can push the cart for you."

"I enjoyed it, but I am so glad to be home. I missed everyone so much."

Tony took over for the man pushing the cart with his aunt Karla's mountain of luggage.

"Do you need help?" Karla asked.

"Did you buy extra suitcases while you were gone?" Tony asked as one of the smaller ones fell to the ground.

"I bought souvenirs for all the kids."

Peter helped Tony load the van and claimed the front passenger seat for the ride home. He pestered his grandmother with questions.

"I'm sure your brothers and sisters will want to know about my trip, Peter. Why don't we save the questions until we get home?"

"Okay, Mama," he said.

Tony dropped Aunt Karla at her house and carried all the luggage inside.

"I feel I should offer you a tip," she teased.

"If you ever decide to go back to Europe, I'm going to hire the entire Fridays At Five road crew to load everything and pick you up."

138

When Mama entered the kitchen, all the kids raced to hug her.

"Did you miss us?" Coby asked.

"I missed all of you so much. You look so much bigger than when I left."

"Let Mama rest for a while before you ask her a thousand questions," Sloane said. "She must be exhausted from the flight."

"I got some sleep on the plane, and now that I'm home I feel full of energy," Mama said. "Give me a few minutes to change clothes and then I will tell you all about my trip."

"Did you see the Leaning Tower?" Taylor asked. "Did it already fall over?"

"Mama will explain everything in a few minutes." Sloane pointed to the family room. "Read a book or something until she is ready." Sloane turned to her mother-in-law and asked, "Do you have any requests for dinner?"

Mama smiled and said, "Anything as long as it's not pasta."

The next Friday Tony and Kristen talked to Derrick and Marco via a video conference call.

"So, the plan to offer the company to the employees fell through, huh?" Marco asked.

Tony shook his head. "They couldn't come close to matching the offer. I hate to say it, but I think we should sell to the group from New York."

"I agree," Derrick said. "Now is the perfect time to sell. We might never get another chance like this."

Kristen and Marco agreed.

"Do you have any idea how long it will take to get all the legal stuff done?" Kristen asked.

"The lawyers told me it might be next April or May before the sale is finalized and the money dispersed," Tony said. "Do you think you can survive until then?"

"I might not have enough money to buy groceries, but I'll forgo a new wardrobe if need be," Kristen replied while making a face. "What are you going to do for now?"

"I will be working here until the transfer is completed. I

might be able to hire you as a temp if you have any skills."

"I'd rather starve to death than work for you," Kristen replied with a laugh.

Emmy waved to the crowd and left the stage with Bobby O'Connor at her side.

"Are you relieved to be finished with the tour, Em, or are you wishing you could do more shows?" Bobby asked.

"A little of both. It felt good to sing for people again, but I hate to be away from the kids."

"And Kenny?"

"Who?" she teased.

"I'll tell him you have forgotten him."

"He called me earlier today and we talked for thirty minutes or so."

"What did you talk about?" Bobby asked.

Emmy stopped walking and grinned.

Bobby saw the look on her face and shook his head. "I know what that look means. You guys had phone sex."

"We did not!" Emmy exclaimed.

"Then why the silly grin?"

She put a finger to her mouth. "I might have mentioned a few things I wanted to do to him when I get home."

"You are so wicked. No wonder Heather is boy-crazy."

Emmy smacked Bobby's arm. "She is not. Why would you say that?"

"Because I know how to push your buttons. I think those people want to talk to you. Smile and be nice."

"I'm always nice," she said and then whispered, "Except when I'm really bad."

Nelson approached and waved at Emmy. "The plane has been delayed."

"Why?" Bobby asked.

"Some kind of mechanical issue. They are grounded until it can be fixed," Nelson explained. "We are going to be stuck here until morning."

Emmy let her shoulders sag. "That's all right. I'd rather get

140

home safely than die in a plane crash."

"Emmy! How can you say that? Are you forgetting about getting creamed by that drunk driver?" Bobby asked.

"Shoot! I wasn't thinking. Are we going back to the hotel?"

"Yes," Nelson answered. "I've already made arrangements for the band to stay."

"What about the crew?" Emmy asked.

"They will take the bus home. Why? Do you want to ride the bus? I'm sure the plane will be ready in the morning."

Bobby grinned and was about to say something when Emmy cut him off with an elbow to the ribs.

"I can wait until tomorrow," she said.

Nelson walked away and she turned to Bobby.

"Hey! I wasn't going to say anything about your plans to ravage Kenny," Bobby said while still grinning.

"Why do I even like you? I should get a different drummer for the next tour."

"You might find a better drummer, but you'll never replace my charm and charisma."

Emmy rolled her eyes. "You are such a punk, and don't you dare say anything about phone sex to a soul."

He raised a hand. "I swear the words phone sex will never leave my lips. Are you going to call Kenny and tell him the bad news?"

"I should. He will worry if I don't come home tonight."

Bobby smiled. "Can I listen to your call?"

"No, why?"

"I want to hear you guys having foreplay over the phone."

"You swore you wouldn't mention... "

He shook his head. "I said phone sex, and I didn't say that. I said foreplay. It's different."

She sighed and took her phone from the back pocket of her jeans. "You are such a punk, and don't you dare listen. Not that I have anything to hide."

"I see some adoring fans over there. I will leave you to your own devices," he said and then walked away.

Emmy called home and explained the situation.

141

"I suppose I can wait one more day. Did they say how soon the plane will be cleared to fly?"

"Nelson was pretty sure we can leave in the morning. Kiss the kids for me, and I'll be home as soon as I can."

"I might kiss the girls, but Kevin Michael doesn't like me to kiss him anymore. He claims he is too old for that."

"He's still my baby. Tell him I will always kiss him no matter how old he is. See you tomorrow."

"Good night, m'lady," Kenny said.

Emmy put her phone away and looked around the room. She spotted Bobby and the four younger members of her band.

"Nelson informed me about the plane," Jeremy said as he walked next to her.

"I was looking forward to sleeping in my own bed tonight," Emmy said. "Have I thanked you for helping out on this tour? I really appreciate having you around. These young people make me feel old at times."

"It was my pleasure, Emmy. It made me realize how much I miss performing on stage."

"Have you ever thought about rejoining the band?"

"Occasionally, now that Jennifer is doing better. But I can't see Fridays At Five with two keyboard players."

"I can. The worship team often has two keyboard players."

"I'm going back to the hotel with Paul and Nelson. Are you going to hang out here?" he asked.

"For a little while," Emmy answered. "I want to make sure the kids behave."

Jeremy glanced at Tariq and Mason, who were showing off their dancing moves to a group of teenage girls. "They don't ever run out of energy."

"So true. I'll see you in the morning."

An hour later Emmy and Bobby rode the hotel elevator to the sixth floor.

"Did you call Kenny?" Bobby asked.

"Yeah, and he was disappointed."

The door opened. They stepped out, turned to the right and paused outside of their rooms.

"Did you tell him you would make it up when you see him?"

She pushed him against the wall. "Oh, stop it. We don't act like newlyweds anymore."

"If you say so," he replied. "Have you thought anymore about touring Europe in the spring? Klaus Kesson is pushing for it."

"I haven't decided. It would mean being away for one or two months without the kids or Kenny." She frowned at him. "Don't say a word about you know what."

"Have you told Kenny it might happen?"

"Not yet. I've been waiting for the right time to discuss it. I might refuse to go," she said and then shrugged. "What can Klaus do? He could drop me from the label, but that wouldn't make him any money."

"He's all about the bottom line."

"You got that right. See you in the morning. Want to do breakfast around eight?"

"Sounds good."

"Call me to make sure I'm awake," Emmy said as she opened the door to her room.

"What if you answer the phone in your sleep? Should I pound on your door instead?"

"Whatever. Good night, punk."

Emmy woke from a sound sleep. "What is that noise?" She realized someone was knocking on her door. She glanced at the clock on the nightstand, threw back the covers and jumped out of bed. She ran to the door and peeked through the peephole.

"Em, it's me. Are you up?" Bobby asked knocking again.

"Give me five minutes to get dressed," Emmy said after opening her door.

"I called you twice," Bobby said. "Didn't you hear your phone?"

"I guess not. I was completely zonked."

"Take ten minutes. I'll meet you downstairs in the restaurant. Should I order coffee and blueberry pancakes?"

"Yes, please."

Bobby smiled. "Late night, huh?"

"Hush, I had trouble falling asleep, punk."

Emmy made it downstairs fifteen minutes later and joined Bobby, Jeremy, Nelson and Paul Mahnari at the large booth in the back corner.

"How did you sleep, Emmy?" Nelson asked.

"Don't ask," she answered and took a sip of her coffee and looked at Bobby.

"We already ordered and they have blueberry pancakes. Here comes our waitress now."

"I timed it perfectly," Emmy said and smiled as the waitress set a plate of pancakes in front of her. "Thank you."

The waitress left after making sure everyone was happy.

Emmy prayed and asked Nelson, "Have you heard anything about the plane?"

He poured ketchup on his scrambled eggs and hash browns. "We are scheduled to fly out at noon."

"Is that soon enough for you, Em?" Bobby asked.

She leaned closer and poked him in the ribs. "It's fine."

"Were you needing to get home sooner?" Nelson asked.

Bobby chuckled.

Emmy frowned at Bobby. "Don't you dare say anything about why I want to get home."

"Why on earth would I say anything, Em?"

"Because you are a creep who likes to tease me."

Jeremy, Nelson and Paul smiled at each other.

"What was Bobby teasing you about?" Jeremy asked with a straight face.

"You guys are all so mean to me. I can't help it if I miss my family." Emmy replied while buttering her pancakes.

"We'll get you home as soon as possible," Nelson said.

Kenny was waiting at the airport in SoHam when Emmy landed. He waved and started walking toward her.

"You made it home safely. I'm glad." He took the small suitcase from her and rolled it along as they walked.

144

"It was some small sensor that had to be replaced. I'm glad to be home. Did the bus make it back yet?"

"It did and one of the guys dropped off your luggage."

She stopped and turned back to the other guys. "I should say goodbye."

Kenny waited while she talked to the band members for a moment.

"Let us know about Europe," Boyd said.

"I will. Make sure you stay clean."

"Does anyone need a ride?" Bobby asked.

"Is Shay picking you up?" Emmy asked.

"She should be here in a few minutes."

Everyone had rides coming or already waiting.

"I'll talk to you later, Em. It was a fun tour," Bobby said.

"I'll talk to Kenny about Europe this weekend. I'm not sure if I want him to say yes or forbid me to go."

"Maybe you should pray about it."

She poked his arm. "Hush. You know we will."

"Make sure you guys go straight home," Bobby said.

"Why wouldn't we?"

"You might be tempted to stop somewhere first."

She realized his meaning and blushed.

Chapter Nineteen

"Kenny, I need to talk to you about something kinda important," Emmy said after lunch Sunday.

"Does it concern the kids, or is this about John and Kristen?" Kenny asked while watching football in the family room. "The Bears suck this year. They're losing to the Lions."

She sat next to him on the couch and pulled her knees up to her chest. "It's not about Krissy, but is does concern the kids." She ran a hand through his thick hair. "And you."

"Do I need to turn off the TV? Did Heather do something again?"

"Just mute the sound."

He did.

"Heather didn't do anything."

Kenny looked at the old sweatshirt Emmy wore. "You might need to replace this one. The collar is worn out.

"I like it. It's comfortable, and I only wear it at home." She took a deep breath and said, "Klaus wants me to tour Europe this spring. I'm not sure if I want to go."

"Why not? You've never toured overseas before. You might like it."

"Because it would mean being gone for a month or two during the school year. That's why," she answered poking his side. "Wouldn't you miss me?"

He looked at her, realized what she really meant and grinned. "I get it now."

"You are such a dork. You wouldn't be able to see me for two whole months."

Kevin ran into the room and sat next to Kenny. "Why is the sound muted? Aren't you watching the game?"

"I was, but your mother and I were having a serious talk."

Kevin grinned and asked, "Is Heather in trouble again? Are you going to ground her?"

"Did she do something?" Kenny asked.

Kevin shrugged. "She's always doing something. Can I go play with Ben? He wants to explore the woods by the creek."

146

"Okay, but try not to get too muddy," Kenny said.

"Take a warm coat and gloves. It's sunny, but still cold," Emmy said. "It's not about either of your sisters doing anything bad," Emmy said. "What would you say if I went to Europe for two months in the spring?"

"Cool! Can we ditch school for that long?"

"No," Kenny said. "It would just be your mother going. Her boss wants her to tour Europe."

"So, I would be stuck here with Heather, Isa and Dad?" Kevin asked looking at Emmy.

"Yes."

Kevin put a finger to his chin for a moment and then stood up. "I can deal with that, but you have to bring me back something special. Not just a t-shirt that says Europe on it."

"Deal," Emmy said.

"Heather is texting Ian Plant again," Kevin shouted as he ran out of the room.

"Does that answer your question, Em?" Kenny asked.

"There would be no flying over on a weekend for a quick visit," Emmy said.

Kenny raised his eyebrows up and down.

"Stop that. I said a quick visit."

"How soon do you need to let him know?"

"He would like an answer by the end of the month. Should we pray about it?"

"Haven't you already?"

"Yes," she whispered.

Kenny put an arm around her. "What was the answer?"

"I probably need to go."

"We can work out a plan. Maybe the kids and I could fly over to see Charles for a long weekend. If not, we will survive. We've been apart for longer than that before."

"Yes, but that doesn't mean I want to do it again," she said leaning against him.

"If you're worried about the kids, don't forget that James is around. His chaplain job allows him some flexibility, and he's taking advantage of it," Kenny said.

147

Emmy snorted. "Big help he is. The other day I heard him teaching Kevin Michael how to swear in Polish or something."

"Polish, huh?"

"It might have been Russian. I don't know." She waved her hands around. "So, you don't mind if I say yes."

"It's only two months, Em. We will survive."

"Is there any pumpkin pie left?" Kenny asked as he looked in the fridge.

Emmy walked into the kitchen and emptied her coffee cup into the sink. "If there's none in there, I know there's one in the garage fridge. How can you be hungry again? You stuffed yourself at dinner, and you and Tony ate leftovers just a couple hours ago."

"Yeah, but I didn't eat any pumpkin pie. I was waiting until now."

Emmy pushed him out of the way and moved a couple Tupperware containers. "Here's some pie. Do you want whipped cream?"

"Of course. Thank you, Emmy."

She handed him the pie and the can of whipped cream. "You can fix it yourself."

The landline rang, and Emmy checked the caller ID. "It's Bobby. Why would he be calling the landline instead of texting me?"

"Maybe you should pick it up and talk to him. It might be important," Kenny said and he got a plate from the cabinet.

Emmy made a face at Kenny, walked away and picked up the phone. "What's up, punk?"

"And happy Thanksgiving to you, too."

"Happy Thanksgiving, Bobby. How was your day?"

"Good. Shay's mother cooked dinner, and I stuffed myself."

She boosted herself onto the countertop. "Kenny is eating again. I'm surprised he doesn't weigh a thousand pounds. What's up?"

"Did you tell him about Europe yet?"

"Yes, and he told me it was all right to go." She stared as Kenny added too much whipped cream to his piece of pie.

"Does he realize all he will get will be phone sex for two months?"

"I'm not sure. He said something about showing up one weekend with the kids. That would cost a fortune, so I don't think it will happen."

"Where are the clean forks?" Kenny asked.

"If there aren't any in the drawer, look in the dishwasher."

He found one in the dishwasher and walked out of the room.

"Have you told Klaus or Nelson?" Bobby asked.

"I emailed both of them. Prater-Saylor is going to set up the dates, and Charles La Rosse will coordinate things."

"Two months, Em," Bobby said slowly.

"Don't remind me, punk. But that means you won't see Shay either."

"We will have to be miserable together."

"Very funny. I better go. See you Sunday."

She replaced the phone, jumped down and walked down the hall and into the family room. She sat next to Kenny on the couch and used a finger to swipe some of his whipped cream. "What are you looking at?"

"I'm using my laptop to check local news."

A few minutes later he finished his pie.

"Would you like me to take that to the kitchen for you, m'lord?" Emmy asked as she stood up.

"Thank you, Em." He handed her the plate and his fork.

"No biggie. I was going to make more coffee anyway." She left the room.

Seconds later Kenny hollered, "Holy smoke! I don't believe it. Em! Come here quick."

She dashed out of the kitchen, raced down the hallway and slid into the family in her thick, woolen socks. "What is it?"

"Do you remember the guy who crashed into you?" Kenny asked looking up at her.

"How do you mean? I don't really remember what he looks like, but I kinda remember his name. Why?"

He patted the space next to him. "Check this out."

She sat down and he angled the laptop so she could see it, too.

"Read this," he said.

She scanned the article. "Someone was killed in an accident. They hit a tree."

"Check the name."

She did and bit her lip. "Was that him?"

Kenny nodded. "It says he was alone and hit the tree at over seventy miles an hour. Blood tests show he was above the legal limit by a ton."

She closed her eyes for a moment. "I don't know if I should feel sorry for him, or be pleased that he won't ever drive and hurt anyone again."

Kenny put an arm around her and pulled her close. "Maybe a little of both."

"This kinda reminds me of Alex Khryzman and the way he died."

"I suppose it does," Kenny said. "It doesn't say if this man had any kids though."

"Why was he even driving? Didn't he lose his license after he hit me?"

"I think so. Apparently, losing his license didn't stop him. The state should have taken away his SUV, too."

"Hey, Em, have you watched any games today?" Tony asked Sunday evening.

"I watched the Bears for a few minutes. They were getting crushed by the Eagles. Why?" She threw a packet of detergent in the washer, closed the lid and pushed a button to start the load of towels.

"I bought this package where I can watch any game I want," Tony said.

"Yeah, you told me. I think you wasted your money."

"I was watching the Browns against the Bengals." He opened the fridge, grabbed a bottled water and headed to the family room. "The Browns almost pulled it out but lost in the last minute."

"Did you see your nephew playing? Isn't he a starting tackle?"

"He is, and I saw him on TV a few times. He got called for holding once, but it wasn't that much of a hold. Anyway, later in the game he got hurt."

"Shoot! What happened? Is he all right?" she asked.

"He got hit down low. They had to take him off on a cart. Marco and Nancy talked to him later. He blew out a knee."

"Is he going to need surgery?"

"Probably. They will take him back to Cleveland and the doctors will examine him tomorrow. It looks like his season is over."

"I'm so sorry to hear that. Does Mama know? She always worried about you getting hurt."

"I told her. Did you worry about me getting hurt, brat?"

"No way! I always figured you were too tough to get hurt. Look at how many times you got hit in the head. It never bothered you because you don't have a brain."

"Such a riot."

"Seriously, I wonder how many other players have whatever the doctors call that thing where you have brain disease because of too many concussions."

"Chronic Traumatic Encephalopathy."

"How do you know that name?"

"Because I'm smarter than I look," he answered. "Don't say anything you might regret."

"A stump would be smarter than you look," she teased. "You better not have that. I would hate for Sloane to have to take care of you when you get older because you can't do anything for yourself."

"Thanks for your concern."

"Let me know whenever you hear more about Dwight. I'll pray for him and the doctors."

"Pray for the whole team. The Browns haven't won a game all year, and it doesn't look good for the rest of the season," he said.

Emmy grabbed the phone Wednesday evening on the third ring.

"Hey, it's me again," Tony said. "I have news about Dwight."

"Is he going to be okay?" Emmy asked.

"Marco said the surgery went better than expected. He told me the details about..."

"I don't need specifics about which ligament he tore or tendon or whatever those things are. Just tell me if he's going to be okay."

"Yes. He will be better than ever after he does the rehab stuff. He will probably miss next year, but it's possible he could return partway through the season if all goes well."

"Maybe he should wait until the 2019 season."

"He might have to," Tony replied.

"Do the Browns play the Bears this year?" she asked.

"They do. The next to last week of the year. Why?"

"They might beat the Bears because they suck big-time this year."

"They are struggling."

"Ya think! Who would you root for in that game?"

"I can't root against the Bears."

"Who would you cheer for if Ben or one of the boys was playing against the Bears?"

"Not likely to happen, but I would root for my kids."

"You better. Talk to you later."

Chapter Twenty

Emmy entered the Starbucks, looked around but didn't see Denise. She checked the time. *I am early, but she's always here before me. I wonder if she got stuck at the office.* Emmy ordered a White Chocolate Mocha Frappuccino, and sat at her preferred table. She opened her laptop and read through the story again. A few minutes later she spotted Denise at the counter. *I love that long black coat, and I should ask where you found that floppy, burgundy hat.*

Denise paid for her coffee and waved to Emmy. She walked over and set her heavy bag on the floor. "Have you been waiting long? I had to wait for a ride."

"I've been here about five minutes. How are you?"

"A bit flustered. I was up past midnight trying to finish a chapter of my new book. I could not get a scene to work until," she raised a finger and her voice rose in pitch, "I changed the setting to a dark room in an old library. That made all the difference." She laughed for several seconds. "I even added another sinister character to complement the antagonist. How have you been? How are the kids?"

"The kids are fine. I finished my tour the week before Thanksgiving and have been working on the book."

"Have you decided whether or not you will make it a series?" Denise asked and then took a sip of her coffee. "Oooh, that's hot."

"I want to make it a series, and I have new names for my main characters."

"What were the original names again?" Denise asked. "Molly something, right?"

"Molly Malone and Dexter O'Keefe."

"Right!" Denise threw a hand into the air. "I never liked the Dexter name." She waved the hand back and forth. "Molly was marginally okay but too common in my opinion. What are the new names?"

"Chelsea Duncan and Troy Farrell," Emmy answered. "What do you think?"

"Troy Farrell is definitely better. I'm not sure about Chelsea."

"I thought about using Claire Duncan or maybe Ruby."

Denise tapped a finger on the table as she gazed at the ceiling. "Chelsea makes me think of a ditzy character. Ruby would work, but I like Claire best."

Emmy grinned. "So do I! I want to use Ruby as Claire's little sister."

"Is that a new character? I don't remember a sister in your first draft."

"She's new. I thought my character needed a sibling."

"For what purpose?" Denise leaned back and waited for Emmy's answer.

"What do you mean?" Emmy asked.

Denise turned to face Emmy squarely and put a hand on the table. "What is the role of the younger sister? Is she a nuisance? Does she foil her older sister's plans? How does she fit into the story?" Denise waved her hands and then blew on her coffee.

Emmy laughed before answering, "Probably all of those. I picture Claire and Ruby fighting at times and being best friends at all times."

"Did you deliberately switch the roles of the sisters?" Denise asked. "In real life you are the younger sister. Is Ruby going to take on your personality?"

"Some of the time. I thought my Claire character would take on my good qualities, and Ruby would be a bit devious at times. Devious and naive."

Denise laughed, took another sip of coffee and said, "That sounds like you. You are basically a good person, but you can be devious at times and you are, or were, certainly naive about certain parts of life."

"I don't know if I should be embarrassed or thank you," Emmy said.

"Have you thought about how many books there might be in this series? How many pages would the books contain? Who is your target audience? You don't need to have all the answers yet, but you should have a rough idea."

"I actually have plot lines for ten books. They start in Claire's first year of high school."

"Did you change the name of the school?" Denise asked while checking her phone. "I need to answer this."

Emmy waited while Denise responded.

"Where were we?"

"The name of the high school," Emmy answered.

"Yes! What name are you using?"

"I've flipped back and forth between Steven Robinson High School and Henry Sherman. Sherman was an early mayor of SoHam and Robinson was a wealthy businessman."

"*Reminisces of a Rough Rider* doesn't have the same meaning without the Roosevelt name," Denise said.

"Yeah, that's what I figured," Emmy said and then tapped her mouth with a finger. "I thought about calling the series *Reminisces of Claire and Ruby* and using a unique title for each book. What do you think of that idea?"

"Obviously, you would use a different title for each book. However, the series title doesn't do anything for me. But we can work on that later."

"I thought it was kinda weak," Emmy admitted.

"Do you have a revised first draft of the first book?"

"I do and I emailed it to you. Your private email not the one you use for work."

"I haven't had time to check it today, but I will later. What title are you using?"

Emmy bit her lip for just a second before answering, "*Get Out of the Way, Kid*. That's something one of the older boys says to Claire on her first day of high school."

Denise tilted her head back. "It works for now. Give me a quick synopsis of the story. Take two minutes to sell the story to me."

Emmy did.

"I like it," Denise said with a smile. "All of this happens in the first two months of school, right?"

"Yes."

"How many words in your draft?"

"Just over 60,000. I want to keep the books under 200 pages if possible."

"You could make them a little longer but I would suggest no more than 250 pages."

"Heather and Isabella are reading books even longer than that, but I want to keep them short and have more books."

"Tell me your ideas for each book."

Emmy spent ten minutes explaining her ideas.

"I love the fact you aren't trying to make your characters flawless." Denise waved a hand. "There are no flawless people."

"Except Jesus," Emmy added.

"Yes, but you didn't mention church in your descriptions."

"I think Claire and Ruby will go to church occasionally, but I don't think it will be a big part of their lives. This series won't be like my other stories."

"That's fine. Can I ask a personal question?"

"Sure," Emmy replied.

"What book was it. The fourth or fifth one, I think. Claire comes to Ruby's rescue when she is with the bad boy." Denise laughed as she made air quotes. "Did that really happen to you?"

"Kinda, but Ruby was in a little deeper than me."

"Interesting. I will read the revised version this weekend and get back to you by the end of next week. I want your characters to make me laugh, make me sad and make me furious when they make bad decisions."

"Sounds like a lot to achieve," Emmy said. "I cried when I wrote some of the scenes, but that's easy for me."

"You can do it. You've done it in your other books. I expect this series to be even better. I need to get back to the office."

"Would you like a ride?" Emmy asked.

"Do you mind? It's not too far out of the way."

"Not at all."

Emmy wandered around the first floor the next morning and found Kenny in the library. She stood in the doorway and asked, "What are you doing in here? We never use this room. The kids think it's haunted. They only play in here to scare each other."

He turned with a book in each hand. "I was looking for a book. I couldn't find it in the den, so I thought it might be in here."

"Why would we keep a book in the library?"

"It is a logical place," he answered. "Oh, you're yanking my chain, huh?"

She rolled her eyes. *Ya think.* She walked into the room and ran a finger along one of the bookshelves. "I should remind the maid to dust in here."

"What maid?" he asked.

"Exactly!"

"You can hire someone to help clean the house if you want, Em."

She looked out the large window and watched two squirrels chasing each other. "We should have put a fireplace in here. We would use it more if we had."

"If we ever add on a first floor master bedroom, we can do something different with this room. Maybe it could be... I don't know. We hardly ever use the front part of this floor."

"Maybe we could put in a wall to separate the house and rent out this half. We could use the rent money to pay the real estate taxes," Emmy suggested.

"Or I could get a part-time job selling encyclopedias door-to-door."

"Good luck with that," she said. "I talked to Charles this afternoon. He said to say hi."

"Hi back. How's he doing?"

"Good. We talked about the itinerary. He is familiar with most of the venues."

"He's always done a great job for us. I'm sure he will take care of you, Em."

"I know. It will be great to have him along. He speaks so many languages."

Kenny chuckled and said, "I always found that most people we dealt with spoke English as a second language, and I know a little German and French."

"I don't want to hear about your European groupies," she said.

He waved a hand. "No, I meant the languages. "He looked at her. "Oh, you were kidding."

"Ya think. Did I tell you that I'll only be gone for six weeks?"

"You did mention that a few days ago. Are you glad you don't have to be gone for two months?" he asked.

"It's still going to seem like a long time," she said. "There are times when we have a concert in one country and move to a different country the next day. That seems so weird."

"You will find that traveling in Europe is different than here. You could almost think of the different countries as the different states in one big country," he said while searching the shelves for the book. "Ah! Here it is. I started reading this last year and never finished. I wonder who put it back in here."

"Probably the maid," Emmy said. "Tell me more about traveling in Europe. Do they have electricity in most countries."

"Sorry. What did you say?"

"Never mind. I'm going to call Kristen. I need to start Christmas shopping and could use some ideas."

"I'm going to read."

"Try not to stir up too much dust," she said waving a hand. "It isn't good for your lungs."

"Do you want me to drive?" Kristen asked over the phone two days later. "I want to go to the mall to start our shopping."

"You can drive, Krissy," Emmy said. "I forgot to put gas in my car. Why the mall? I haven't been there in years."

"There are several new stores. The whole place has been remodeled."

"I've been doing almost all my Christmas shopping online lately. No crowds to fight," Emmy said. "Pick me up whenever you want. I'm ready to go."

Kristen walked into Emmy's kitchen thirty minutes later.

"Give me a second to grab my purse and a jacket," Emmy said and then drained the last of her coffee.

"It's in the thirties and windy, so wear a winter coat," Kristen said.

158

"Yes, Mom."

They walked outside and Emmy stared at the SUV for a moment. "Is this new?"

"I've had it for a month. Haven't you seen it before?"

Emmy got in the front passenger seat and looked around the vehicle. "It smells like a new car."

"Doesn't yours still smell new. When did you buy it?" Kristen asked as she started the car.

"Back in May, and I guess it still smells new. I'm not letting the kids eat in it."

They parked, walked inside and Emmy looked around.

"I told you it was remodeled," Kristen said. "Bertucci and Keasling did the work."

"It looks a lot better than I remember."

"We even helped some of the shops , but that was more just refreshing than major remodels."

Two hours later they returned to Kristen's SUV carrying several bags each.

"Do you remember the last time we actually went Christmas shopping together?" Emmy asked as they loaded the bags into the back.

"Not exactly, but I would venture to say it has been many years."

"I think it was while we were still living together. That was before either of us was married."

"I feel as though I have been married for fifty years," Kristen said and then sighed.

"It hasn't been that long," Emmy said and then looked at Kristen. "Oh, I'm sorry, Krissy. Maybe just the last year feels like a long time."

Chapter Twenty-One

"Got a second, Emmy?" Bobby O'Connor asked after church Christmas Eve morning.

Emmy walked down the steps from the platform and joined him on the floor of the sanctuary. "Sure. What's up? Are you going to get on my case for screwing up that last song?"

"I wasn't going to, but did you make a mistake?"

"We were only supposed to do the bridge three times, but I did it four. I added the tag at the end, but most of the guys dropped out." Emmy saw Kenny and the kids walking out of the sanctuary.

Bobby turned to see who she was watching and asked, "Are Riordan and Sadie going to be back next week?"

"Probably."

"Didn't they go to California because one of their parents is sick or something?"

"Sadie's father was in the hospital. I think he had an issue with his heart, but nothing super serious," she answered. "As far as I know they will be back next week. Pastor Tyler didn't ask me to lead worship again." Emmy kept watching the crowd.

"Okay, you're busy. We should talk soon about the tour and who all is going."

"I'm sorry, Bobby. I'm a little distracted now because of the holidays and all."

"Who are you looking for?" Bobby asked as he scanned the crowd.

"Kenny's parents were supposed to be here this morning, but I didn't see them in either service."

"Don't they usually go to a different church?"

"Yes, but they have been talking about switching. They've also been talking about buying a place in Florida and spending winters down there. The cold is starting to get to Kenny's father."

"But all the grandkids live here. Wouldn't they miss them?"

"Now that the kids are older, they don't see Gra and Me-maw as much."

Bobby laughed and asked, "Do they still call them that?"

"Not as much as when they were younger. They use

160

Grandma and Grandpa a lot more now." Emmy put a hand to her ear. "Call me this week. We can do lunch and talk about the tour. You can bring Shay if you want."

"To Europe?"

"No, silly. Bring her to lunch. If Kenny can't go to Europe with me, then you can't bring your girlfriend."

"So, if you can't have sex, no one can, huh?"

She poked his side. "Go away, punk. We all have to make some sacrifices in this life."

Emmy talked to more people as she left the sanctuary. She saw Kenny and the kids waiting by the large Christmas tree in the foyer and headed toward him.

"Great job this morning, Emmy. Thanks for filling in," Wyatt said. "I haven't seen the numbers, but this might have come close to setting a new record for attendance."

"I didn't see too many empty seats in either service," Emmy said.

Wyatt greeted more people as Emmy waved at Tony and Sloane.

"See you next week, Wyatt. Merry Christmas."

"You, too, Emmy. Have a Merry Christmas."

Heather and Isabella saw their mother and dodged through the crowd to her side.

"Did Gra and Me-maw make it to church?" Emmy asked.

Heather shrugged and answered, "We didn't see them. What are we doing for lunch? Can we stop and get something?"

"Ask your father. I don't have any money with me."

"Merry Christmas, Emmy," Tony said.

"Merry Christmas to you guys, too. What are your plans for the holiday?" Emmy asked.

"I'll meet you by the van," Sloane said to Tony. "The kids are anxious to get home and pack."

"Pack? Are you guys going somewhere?" Emmy asked looking up at Tony.

"Didn't you know we're taking the whole family on vacation? We're flying to Florida tomorrow afternoon. I got great deals. It's only costing both arms up to the elbows."

161

"Ha! Ha! When did you plan this? I didn't hear anything about it."

"Since the kids and Sloane are off school for two weeks, we thought it would be the perfect time to get out of SoHam and find somewhere warmer to stay."

"Is Mama going?"

"Yes."

"Any extra room on the plane?" Emmy asked with a grin.

"No way! You're not coming with us, brat."

"You're no fun. I better go. Have fun and try not to get sunburned. Oh, who's watching the house for you?"

"Kristen said she would get the mail and check the house."

"Okay, see you when you get back."

On the way home Kenny stopped at Burger Bob's and bought lunch for everyone.

"Do we have more ketchup?" Kevin grabbed his chair in the breakfast nook.

"In the fridge," Kenny answered. "Unless your mother used it all on her fries."

"There's more," Emmy said. "Why weren't Mom and Dad at the service. When I talked to her a couple days ago, she said they would be there."

"I don't think Dad felt good. And he said it was too cold," Kenny replied.

"It's in the twenties," Emmy said.

"Mom said the cold bothers him more now than it used to."

"How soon will Gra and Me-maw be here? I want to open presents," Kevin complained.

"They will be here in a half hour or so," Emmy answered checking the time.

"I'm hungry. Do I have to wait until later to eat. Can't I have something now?"

"You can eat now. What would you like?" Emmy asked.

"Hash browns."

"I'm making stuff like that after we open gifts. You can have cereal or fruit."

Kevin inspected the bowl of fruit on the island. He made a face and went into the pantry. He came back out with Rice Krispies.

"You can add a banana to your cereal," Emmy suggested.

Kevin got a bowl from the cabinet and the milk from the fridge. "Will you cut it up for me?"

"What do you say?"

"Mom! I'm not a baby."

"Then why do I have to cut your banana?" Emmy stared at him. "Do not spill the milk."

"Please. Will you cut my banana, please?"

She cut half the banana into slices and ate the rest herself.

Later, everyone gathered in the family room.

"Gra, I helped Uncle Tony cut down the Christmas tree. I picked it out all by myself," Kevin said pointing the the tree which reached to the ceiling.

"It looks like an amazing tree," Gra said.

"Mom, do we have to hear the Christmas story again this year? You read it to us every year. We know the story by heart," Heather said.

"Than let's do something different this year," Emmy suggested.

"Yeah! Like what?" Heather asked.

"I think either you or Isabella should read the story," Emmy said.

Heather rolled her eyes and sighed. She crossed her arms over her chest and slumped back on the couch.

"Heather! That is not a proper attitude," Father James scolded.

Heather frowned as she stared at him but she didn't say another word.

"I can read it, Mommy," Isabella said. "Will you find it for me. I know it's in Luke something."

Emmy turned to the passage and handed the Bible to Isabella. She read it without rushing.

"Can we open our presents now?" Kevin asked.

"Who's going to be Santa?" Emmy asked.

"I will," Kevin said. "I do know how to read now."

This year it only took an hour to open all the gifts from under the tree.

"Make sure you thank everyone for your gifts," Kenny said.

"Thank you for the books, Uncle James," Isabella said.

"Thank you, Uncle James, and I'm sorry I was acting like a brat earlier," Heather said.

"Apology accepted, and you are both welcome." He hugged both girls and kissed the top of their heads.

"I got one from Uncle Andy. Where is he?" Kevin asked.

"He's spending the holidays in South Carolina with his brother and family. He won't be back until sometime in January," Kenny explained. "I've been getting the mail for him."

"I wish I was in Carolina, or somewhere with warmer weather," Gra whispered.

"Who's hungry?" Kenny asked after all the wrapping paper and empty boxes had been taken to the garage.

"Emmy, do you need help in the kitchen?" Elly Colwell asked.

"Most of it is done, Mom. I cooked earlier and put everything in the warmer. It will only take a few minutes to get everything ready."

"I can set the table for you, dear. Are we going to eat in the dining room or the breakfast area?"

"It would be easier to eat in here," Emmy answered pointing to the breakfast nook. "You should make the girls set the table. That's one of their regular chores."

"It's Christmas. They are busy reading their new books. I can do it."

"You spoil them too much," Emmy said.

"I know but we don't get to see them as often now that they're older. They have busy lives." Elly said as she grabbed silverware from the drawer.

"Is that why you guys are thinking about spending the winters in Florida?" Emmy asked. She put the sausage patties in the microwave and pushed a button. "It will be even harder to see them if you move."

"That's why we're even considering the move. Carter has trouble in the winter. He stays at home and doesn't like to go out at all. His back hurts if he tries to shovel snow. He's getting too old for the cold."

"He's only sixty-five, Mom. That's not so old."

"He's old enough for Medicare," Elly said with a chuckle. "We wouldn't consider moving at all, but now that you're back to normal. Well, you understand."

"Have you looked at real estate down there?" Emmy asked as she removed the plate of sausage and set it on the countertop. "I'm assuming you can afford to buy a nice place."

"We can. We looked at some condos. We don't want a big place, but it needs at least three bedroom, and it would have to be something that doesn't require any maintenance. Some place where we don't have to be there year-round. We would like to rent it out for half the year."

Emmy pulled the rest of the food from the warmer. "I think we're ready to eat. I'll let everyone know."

"If we find a place, you and Kenny could use it, too. When the kids are older, they could spend Christmas breaks with us."

Emmy walked down the hallway to the family room.

"Are we ready to eat?" Kenny asked when he saw her.

"It's ready." She stood in front of the fireplace and warmed her hands.

"Emmy, you're blocking the heat," Carter said.

"Sorry, Dad. Brunch is ready."

He stood up, smiled and hugged her. "Have I told you lately how much we love you?"

"You tell me every chance you get, and I love you even more."

Chapter Twenty-Two

"Can you believe that a year from now the girls will be teenagers," Emmy said as she and Liz Hammond were putting candles on the birthday cake. "I told them next year we could have a big party at the church, but I didn't want to this year."

"Your home is big enough for a party, Emmy," Liz said. "That's twenty-four candles."

"Can I help with anything," Dany Michaelis asked.

"No, and don't you be lifting anything," Emmy warned. "Let me look at you." Emmy put her hands on Dany's shoulders and stared at her stomach. "You look a lot like I did with Kevin Michael. I wore regular clothes as long as I could. Have you been feeling okay?"

"Sometimes I get tired and need to take a break. Darian is so sweet. He looks after me. I could get used to that."

"Mom! When do we get to eat the cake and ice cream?" Kevin asked. "You said we could after they opened their presents. We finished that hours ago."

"They only finished fifteen minutes ago. Is the family room cleaned up?" Emmy asked.

"Why do I have to pick up all the wrapping paper and stuff? It's their birthday. They made the mess."

"You can make a mess on your birthday and they can clean up after you."

"All right! I'm gonna make the biggest mess in history," he said and raced out of the kitchen and down the hallway.

"He's going to be taller than you pretty soon, Emmy," Liz said.

"Don't remind me. Soon I will be the shortest one in the family. Lily and Conor will be taller than me in a couple years."

"I doubt that," Liz said. "David might be taller though. He's only seventeen months and is taller than most of the two-year-old kids at church."

Father James walked into the room with a bag of garbage.

Emmy saw him and hollered, "What are you doing? Kevin Michael was supposed to clean up the family room."

166

"It needed to be done, so I did it," he replied.

"No! No! No!" Emmy raised her voice as she waved her hands. "That was his responsibility. You better stop spoiling the kids or else."

"Or else what?" he asked dropping the bag.

"You won't be allowed to visit!" Emmy sighed and let out her breath. "Sorry. I didn't mean to yell at you."

"It's all right. I'll make him take it out to the garage."

After Father James left the kitchen, Liz asked, "Are you getting along all right?"

"Most of the time, but he comes over here a lot. I love him to pieces, but you know how it can be."

Dany nodded and said, "Sometimes Eli and Darian set up the PlayStation and play games for hours. They act like teenagers instead of grown men."

"All men do that," Emmy said.

"Tyler and Jason play ping pong when they're together. They play like it's life or death."

"I remember how competitive they were," Emmy said. "I like it when Tyler mentions playing tennis in his sermons. He says he was arrogant and stuff. I can't picture him like that. He's totally different now."

"Jesus certainly changed his life. I can't imagine him being a physical therapist or a pharmacist now."

"He would make more money," Emmy said.

Liz laughed. "He makes a good salary from the church. His sister and her husband make lots of money, but they always say Tyler and I are happier."

"Money doesn't solve everything. Sometimes it can be a pain in the butt." Emmy waved her hands again. "Don't get me wrong. I'm grateful that Kenny and I have been blessed way beyond what we deserve."

"That's called grace," Liz said.

"Are you okay, Emmy? You look pale," Dany said.

"My head hurts a little. That's all."

Liz and Dany stared at her.

"Should we do something?" Liz asked.

Emmy realized what they were thinking and shook her head. "No, it's not anything serious. I haven't had any caffeine for a couple days. No biggie."

Kevin stomped into the kitchen, grabbed the garbage bag and tromped into the garage. He stomped his feet as he returned and didn't look at his mother.

"Thank you, Kevin Michael," Emmy said.

"You're welcome," he muttered.

"I think it's time to sing and eat cake and ice cream."

Soon everyone gathered in the kitchen to sing.

"Blow out the candles before the house burns down," Kevin shouted to his sisters.

Heather and Isabella looked at each other, then turned and blew out the candles in perfect synchronization.

"Good job!" Kenny said as he kissed his daughters.

"Oh, Daddy, we're not babies anymore," Heather said. "We can blow out candles without any help."

"Me-maw! Gra! We're here," Kevin shouted as he walked in the back door.

"Kevin Michael, you do not have to yell," Emmy scolded. "They know we're coming."

Kenny's parents walked into the kitchen.

Kevin ran to them and hugged his grandmother and then his grandfather. "Mom said I have to be extra nice to you today because we won't see you for months."

Heather and Isabella waited and hugged their grandparents after Kevin got out of the way.

"Do you want some help making lunch?" Isabella asked. "I have been making my own lunch at home."

"Thank you, dear. Would soup and sandwiches be okay. We need to eat the deli meat because it won't be any good when we get back. I started a chicken soup earlier. Maybe we can cut up these vegetables and add it to the mix."

"How long will you be gone, Grandma?" Heather asked.

"We plan to stay until the middle of April. We will miss Easter, but we want to avoid the cold weather."

After lunch, Kenny loaded his parents' luggage into the van. The kids and Emmy said goodbye and hugged Grandpa and Grandma.

"We will Skype with you when we get settled," Grandma promised.

While Kenny took them to the airport, Emmy and the kids went out to the carriage house.

"Grandma showed us some photos of the way it looked when you were a little girl," Isabella said.

"It was full of junk and cobwebs and everything was covered in dust," Emmy said as she opened the fridge to make sure it was clean.

"That would have been cool. Eddie Howser from school lives on a farm and they have an old barn that's full of junk. We explored it when I was at his birthday party," Kevin said.

"I like the pictures of how it looked when Daddy's band practiced in here," Isabella said.

"I like how it looks now," Heather said while standing in the bedroom doorway. "It looks so romantic. I want to stay here when I get married like Mommy and Daddy did."

"How do you know we stayed here?" Emmy asked.

"Everyone knows."

"I wish it was still full of junk," Kevin said looking into the closet.

"Mom, do you think Heather and I could sleep out here in the summer?" Isabella asked.

"Yeah, that would be fun," Heather said. "Maybe we could spend a month with Grandma and Grandpa."

"I like that idea," Kevin said with a big grin. "You guys could live here all the time."

"We would have to ask your grandparents," Emmy said as she wiped off the countertop. "If you stayed here, you would have to help with chores. You could be responsible for keeping this place clean."

"Mom, we're just kids. You can't make us work like that. It's against the law," Heather said with hands on hips.

Eight days later everyone gathered around Emmy's laptop waiting for Grandma and Grandpa to Skype.

"Hello, it's so good to see your faces," Grandma said.

The kids started talking and got louder and louder trying to be heard.

Grandma put a finger to her mouth. "I can't hear anything if you all talk at once. Try going one at a time, please."

The kids did and they talked for close to thirty minutes.

"Grandpa and I need to talk to your parents," Grandma said. "We will call you soon. We love you."

"We love you, too, Me-maw," Kevin said.

After the kids had left the room, Kenny asked," How do you like the condo?"

"It's perfect for us. We like it so much we put an offer on it this morning."

Grandma described the condo and even walked around with the laptop to give Kenny and Emmy a tour.

"It looks good," Kenny said.

"The furniture is brand new. It is being sold totally furnished. We are relatively close to the clubhouse. There are two pools and tennis courts. The people are friendly. Some of them live here all year, but about half are snowbirds."

"Where is Dad?" Kenny asked.

"On the phone."

He returned to view with a broad smile and said, "I have good news. The sellers accepted our offer. The place is ours, or it will be in a month or so."

"Did you pay cash?" Emmy asked. "How much are the monthly dues?"

"We paid cash, and the monthly dues are only three hundred. We checked and other buildings in this area can be a lot higher."

"I'm happy for you guys," Kenny said. "We might have to look at buying a place to stay in the winter one of these years."

"I don't think we will need to do that for a long time," Emmy said. "I like having four seasons."

170

Chapter Twenty-Three

Diane called Emmy Friday morning just after ten.

"What's up? Do I need to pick up the kids from school?"

"You need to sit down, Em. I have bad news."

Emmy sat on one of the barstools. "Okay, I'm sitting at the island. Is it Mom?" she whispered.

"I'm sorry, but I got a call from the nursing home earlier."

"What happened? I mean how did it happen?" Emmy asked.

"She didn't wake up this morning. Her care partner checked on her at seven and she was gone. Should I come over and stay with you? Is Kenny home?"

"He's at the band office. You don't need to come over. I will be all right. I'm not even crying right now."

"You will be later, Em. It's all right to cry."

"Did you cry when they called?"

"Not really, but that's just the way I'm wired."

"What do we have to do?" Emmy asked and then sniffled.

"Nothing right now. You know everything has been arranged and paid for. The funeral home will pick her up. I already talked to them. I'm going to take them some clothes later today. We need to go down there tomorrow just to make sure of everything."

"Like what?"

"We need to schedule the day and time for the service. We need to go over the obituary again."

"Is it still going to be like we discussed?" Emmy asked and then wiped her nose.

"Unless you want to change something, Em. You can if you want. I would rather just have a service at the cemetery."

"No! I want Mom to have a funeral at the church. Please?" Emmy asked. "It's important to me."

Diane sighed and stretched out a kink in her neck. "Yes, you can have it your way, but there won't be many people who come. Most of her friends think she passed away years ago."

"How can you say that, Diane?"

171

"It's the way it is with older people. They lose friends all the time."

"There will be some people from the church who show up," Emmy said. "You can take care of it like we talked about. We will still have a small service at the cemetery for just the family, right?"

"Yes, we can do that after the service at the church."

"People will expect to eat."

"Of course, baby. We can have a dinner if you would like."

"Should we get the kids and bring them home?"

"I think it will be okay if we tell them after school. I'll pick the younger ones up. Brady will get Carson."

"Can we invite Mr. Robertson and Mona to the service at the cemetery?"

"Sure. They are family, Em."

"How about Tony and Kristen?"

"We will see. There won't be a lot of room at the cemetery. We might have to hold the service in the chapel if it's too cold."

"Can they even bury her if it's too cold?"

"I'm not sure, but I will ask. Are you sure you don't want me to come over? Mona can watch the kids."

Emmy managed to say yes before she began sobbing.

Diane arrived five minutes later and found Emmy sitting in the kitchen. She rubbed her back and whispered, "I'm here, Em."

Emmy turned and let Diane hold her while she cried.

"Let it go, baby." Diane kissed Emmy's head and ran a hand through her hair.

Emmy eventually stopped and looked up at Diane.

Diane used a tissue to dry Emmy's face. "I just realized that it's been almost ten years since Daddy passed away. It doesn't seem like that long, but it is."

Emmy nodded.

"Do you want me to call Kenny for you?"

Emmy nodded again.

Diane called Kenny's cell phone and relayed the news.

"I will be home right away," he said and ended the call.

"He's coming home. Where is Father James? Is Andy still in South Carolina?"

"James is helping at the church this morning. You should call him, and Andy is still with Matt and Nina. He should know. He was planning to stay longer, but he will probably come back."

"Do you feel up to calling some of your friends from church? Pastor Tyler should be informed. We will have to schedule a day for the funeral service."

"I will call Liz in a little bit. She will pass it along."

Diane called Father James. He and Kenny arrived at the house twenty minutes later.

Kenny hugged Emmy while they both cried. Father James talked to Diane and got the details.

"I can go with you tomorrow if you want. I've been through this many times."

"It would be nice to have you along," Diane said.

Emmy called Liz, and she passed the news to Tyler and Dany.

An hour later the house was filling up with family and friends. Emmy sat on the couch next to Mama Bertucci. Tony volunteered to pick up the kids from school.

"Sloane always drives our kids to and from school," Tony said. "Should I tell them what happened, or do you want to do that, Em?"

"If they ask, you can tell them. They are old enough to understand. We have talked to them and told them this could happen at any time."

Kenny called his parents.

"We can get a flight home tonight if you want us to," his mother said.

"You guys just got there. You don't need to fly back. I'm sure Emmy will understand."

"No, son, we are coming home and no arguing about it," she said.

Father James sat in the backseat of Brady and Diane's 2017 Mercedes E-Class and listened to Diane and Emmy on the way to the Dames-Blackburn funeral home Saturday morning.

"I'm glad that's over," Emmy said ninety minutes later.

"These places creep me out. Why do the men always wear black suits?"

"To look professional," Diane said.

"The casket will be open on Tuesday, right? I will get to see her again, right?" Emmy asked.

"Yes, Em. You and I will get to see her one more time. We could do that here." Diane pointed to the funeral home.

"Could we do it at the church instead? I don't want to come back here if I can avoid it," Emmy said.

"Okay, but we will have to be there early," Diane said. "You can decide if you want anyone else to see her. Immediate family, I mean. Or if it will just be us."

"Do I have to decide right now?" Emmy asked getting into the car.

"No, but you should decide before Tuesday morning," Father James said.

When they got back to Emmy's house, Andy Walker greeted them in the kitchen.

"How did you get back so fast?" Emmy asked.

"Hey! I have some experience flying people around the world. I chartered a plane." He hugged Emmy and fought back the tears.

Kenny made a run to the airport to pick up his parents. People from church started delivering food. The kids were happy to be home for the weekend and stayed in their rooms most of the day.

Kevin came downstairs around two and looked in the fridge.

"Are you hungry?" Father James asked.

"I'm starving. Aren't we gonna eat today? There's a bunch of stuff in here."

"What would you like? Mama Bertucci brought over some lasagna and mostaccioli."

"Can I have some of that?" He pointed to the mostaccioli.

"Sure. Can you get it out for me?"

Emmy walked into the kitchen and hugged Kevin from behind. "That smells good. Will you share with me?"

"Sure, Mom. There's enough for an army."

Father James fixed plates for Emmy and Kevin, and they sat in the breakfast nook to eat.

"Are we going to church tomorrow, or do we get to stay home?" he asked with a mouthful of food.

"I'm not sure, but I think we might stay home. I don't feel like seeing a lot of people and answering the same questions over and over."

"We don't have to go to school Monday or Tuesday, do we?"

Emmy shook her head. "Maybe Monday, but not Tuesday. That's the day of the service." She looked out the window and felt the warm sun on her face. "All the snow has melted. It feels warmer than last week."

"Can I go play with Ben at his house, or do I have to stay here and be sad all day?" Kevin asked as he finished his mostaccioli.

"You can go play, and you don't have to feel sad."

"Thanks, Mom. I know you feel bad, but maybe Grandma is doing better now. Maybe she got her memory back," he said and then hugged his mother. "I'll come home for dinner."

"Diane, have you talked to Brady and the kids about tomorrow morning?" Emmy asked Monday night.

"I did," Diane replied.

"What did they say?"

"Brady has no opinion. He will do whatever we decide. Carson and Caden don't really want to see her in the casket. I didn't ask Lily or Conor. Did you talk to Kenny?"

"Yes, and he and the kids think it should be a time for the two of us. You and me, I mean. Kevin seemed a little spooked by the idea of seeing her like that."

"Then I'll drive us to the church in the morning, and everyone else won't need to be there until nine thirty," Diane said.

"We should be there by eight to get everything set up," Emmy said.

"That's plenty early. Won't there be someone from the

church to help us?"

"Tyler might be there, but he has to finish his message."

"Fine! I'll pick you up by a quarter to eight."

Emmy and Diane arrived at Crest Ridge United Nazarene at eight o'clock Tuesday morning. They headed to the old sanctuary where the memorial service would be held and saw Tyler tapping a thermostat.

"You're here early," Emmy said.

Tyler turned, chuckled and said, "It's a good thing. The furnaces on the roof are not working and it's a bit chilly in here. Reed Shafer is out of town today, and I haven't been able to get hold of anyone else. If I can't get them started soon, I suggest we move to the new sanctuary."

Emmy looked at Diane.

"It will feel so empty. We don't expect a lot of people to come," Diane said.

"True, but I'd rather have them be comfortable," Emmy said. "It is cold in here."

After all attempts failed to start the furnaces, the decision was made to hold the service in the new building.

"I forgot how big this place is," Diane said walking from the foyer into the sanctuary.

Just before nine Tyler walked up to Diane and Emmy and said, "The people from Dames-Blackburn are here. I told them about the change in plans. They are bringing the casket in now."

"Thanks, Tyler," Diane said.

Fifteen minutes later Clement Armstrong nodded to his three assistants, ran a hand through his white hair, adjusted his tie, smoothed out his black suit jacket and walked out of the sanctuary. He approached Diane and Emmy with his hands folded in respect. "Everything is ready for you now. We will close the doors, and you may take all the time you need."

"Thank you, Mr. Armstrong," Diane said. She waved at Emmy, who was talking to Tyler and Liz. "It's time, Emmy."

Liz squeezed Emmy's hand and whispered, "We will make sure no one disturbs you." She handed Emmy a box of tissues.

"You might need these."

"You know I will," Emmy said.

Mr. Armstrong closed the doors behind Diane and Emmy, and his assistants stood in front of the other sets of doors.

Diane and Emmy stood at the back of the large auditorium for a moment and looked at the floral arrangements lining the front on either side of the casket.

"I didn't think there would be so many flowers," Diane said.

"Me, either," Emmy added.

Diane began walking toward the front, but stopped and turned. "Are you coming, Em?"

"Will the rest of the lights be on later?"

"I think so. Why?" Diane asked looking at the ceiling.

"It's kinda spooky now. I'll tell Pastor Tyler to have them turn the lights up about fifty percent. The tech guys can do that."

"That's good, but tell them not to have a light show like you do on Sunday morning."

Emmy walked up to her sister and poked her arm. "We don't put on a light show. We use the lighting, but it's not flashy."

They walked up slowly and stood in front of the open casket. When Emmy set the tissues down and tried to hold her hand, Diane placed an arm around her shoulders.

"I'm sorry for being a baby," Emmy whispered.

"It's all right. You are the baby of the family."

"Have you ever wondered how our lives would have been if Mom hadn't lost the other babies?"

Diane shook her head. "Not for a long, long time. I've always been happy to just have a little sister. Those other kids would have been a lot older than us, anyway."

Emmy leaned against Diane. "You didn't want me around when we were kids."

Diane laughed and said, "That's because you were a brat and a tomboy."

"That's a nice dress," Emmy said moving away from Diane. "She always looked good in green. Is it new?"

Diane glanced at the small floral arrangement on top of the

casket. "It's not brand new, but I don't think she wore it more than once. This is from the grandkids."

Emmy nodded. "It looks pretty."

"Do you have any idea what Pastor Tyler will say? He didn't know Mom until after she lost her mind."

"I don't know, but we talked about when she and Aunt Betty were kids. Grandma Isabel used to tell us stories. Do you remember them?"

Diane shook her head. "I didn't pay much attention. I should have, but I thought they were boring." Diane placed an arm around Emmy's waist when she heard a quiet sob. "It's okay, Em. Mom is in a better place."

Emmy turned to face her sister and looked up into Diane's eyes. "Will you promise to take care of me if I ever get like Mom?"

Diane placed her hands on Emmy's shoulders, rested her forehead against Emmy's and whispered, "It's more likely that I will lose my mind, but I promise to always be there for you, little sister."

Emmy wrapped her arms around Diane and rested her head on Diane's chest.

Diane patted Emmy's back a moment later. "Are you ready to go?"

"Can I ask you something first?" Emmy took a step back and wiped her nose on a tissue.

"Sure. What?" Diane asked.

"Have you cried at all since Mom died?"

Diane shook her head. "You know I'm not wired like that."

"Do you remember the last time you actually cried?"

Diane froze for a second, but then nodded.

"When?" Emmy asked.

"It was the end of last April if you must know," Diane said.

Emmy bit her lip when she realized what Diane meant.

"We should go so the funeral guys can do whatever they have to," Diane said. "Say goodbye, or pray, or whatever you want to do."

Emmy moved close and touched her mother's hands. She

178

prayed for a moment then whispered, "I love you, Mommy." She took another tissue, wiped her eyes, handed the box to Diane and took a few steps back.

"Give me a second, and I'll walk out with you," Diane said.

Emmy turned and walked along inspecting the flowers and reading the cards. She reached the end and turned around just in time to see Diane take several tissues from the box and wipe her eyes.

"We used most of these photos for Daddy's service," Emmy said as she and Diane set up the stands of photos they had prepared the night before. She held up a photo of her parents on their wedding day. "Do you remember this one? You can't tell Mom is expecting."

"I remember it."

"We could have had several more brothers and sisters," Emmy said.

"Yeah. They might not have had you if... "

Emmy bit her lip and Diane saw it.

"I'm sorry, Em. That was mean. I can't imagine life without my little sister."

"I know I was an accident," Emmy said. "Mom used to say that when she was mad at me."

Diane put an arm around Emmy, smiled and said, "You weren't an accident. You were a miracle."

"Very funny, Diane."

By nine forty-five all the immediate family had arrived.

"Mom, do I have to wear this tie all day?" Kevin asked. "I bet Ben doesn't have to get so dressed up."

"It won't hurt you to wear a tie for a few hours. It makes you look handsome."

"I'll do it because the old people will expect it," Kevin said.

By ten, people were lined up waiting to pay their respects.

Kenny whispered, "Em, did you expect this many people to show up?"

"No way," she whispered back and then greeted another friend from church. "I thought a few people would stop by, but this

179

is crazy." She looked at the line of people along the outer aisle reaching to the back of the sanctuary.

"I hope there's enough food," Kenny said. "Tony's here."

"I will tell him to wait until last to eat."

Tony and Sloane reached Kenny and Emmy ten minutes later. He shook Kenny's hand and then hugged Emmy.

"Look at all these people," she whispered into his ear.

"I know. Amazing, huh? Don't worry. Mama brought a lot of food."

"We might need it. We didn't know how much to order from the caterers."

"I'm sorry about your mom, Em. At least... I don't know what to say. Sorry."

She hugged him tighter. "At least I still have Mama and Mom Colwell."

"Thank you for singing," Emmy told Liz after the service. "There was no way I was going to. You sounded as beautiful as ever."

"I did my best," Liz said. "I did a quick head count and would guess there were over four hundred people here. Even more if you count the kids in childcare."

"What if they all stay for lunch? Will we have enough?" Emmy asked.

Liz grinned and said, "You haven't been in the gym or kitchen, huh? The caterers delivered their food, and ladies from the church made their specialties. Genna and the hospitality team have been busy getting everything ready. No one will go hungry, Em."

"I need to thank Tyler for the service. He did a great job of making Mom sound like a better person than she really was."

"I wish I had known her earlier," Liz said.

"I'm glad Tyler told everyone they were welcome to stay for the meal but that the service at the cemetery would be just for close family."

"I'm sure everyone will respect your privacy," Liz said.

An hour later Tony tapped on Emmy's shoulder as she sat at a table eating.

"What?" she turned her head and asked.

"I'm pretty sure everyone has been through the line. Is it all right if I get some food now?"

Emmy pushed back her chair and stood up. "Don't tell me you haven't eaten yet."

"I was waiting."

"Come with me, and I'll fix you a plate."

"I can fill my own plate, Em. Been doing it for years," he said with a smile.

"I'll help you. I know Genna held some of Mama's lasagna back for an emergency."

She led Tony into the kitchen and they found the lasagna.

"Is that all you want?" Emmy asked. "There's still an empty spot on your plate right there," she teased.

"I thought I would grab some green beans with the onion rings and some of that corn souffle if there's any left."

"Naomi makes the souffle, and it always goes fast, but I'll see if there's any left. I'm pretty sure Lil made the green beans."

"Who is Lil?" he asked. "Do I know her?"

"She's the lady who checks the kids in on Wednesdays. You've seen her lots of times."

"I guess I never really knew her name."

Emmy found a couple scoops of corn souffle for Tony and added it to his plate.

"Thanks, Em."

"You're welcome, creep," she said with a grin.

"It's good to see you smile, brat," he whispered.

Later, Genna walked up to Emmy and whispered, "Emmy, you need to come with me. The caterers picked up their stuff already, but Tony's mother insists on helping clean up. I told her the ladies from church will do it, but she won't listen."

Emmy followed Genna to the kitchen. "Mama! What are you doing?" Emmy said sternly with hands on her hips. "You don't have to clean up. There are volunteers to do that. We have to leave for Rose Hill soon."

Mama finished drying a casserole dish and set it on the counter. "I just wanted to help."

Emmy took Mama's arm and pulled her out of the kitchen.

"Come and sit down. You should socialize with people."

"But I don't know everyone."

"Then I will introduce you," Emmy said. "I'm not going to let you work."

Mr. Robertson walked up to Emmy later and asked, "Is there anything you need?"

"I can't think of anything. Kenny and Brady loaded the photos in the van already. Diane said she would stop by Sunrise Garden and do something with Mom's clothes and whatever else she had. She will have to talk to the attorney about Mom's estate."

"Diane made sure your mother didn't leave much in the way of an estate."

"The advise you gave her helped with that."

"She made some wise decisions. Diane has always made good choices with her investments and your mother's money. Call us if you need anything, Emmy."

"I will," she said and then hugged him. "Thank you for coming. It means a lot to us."

Kenny stood next to Emmy as more guests began to leave. She said goodbye and thanked everyone for coming. She felt a hand on her shoulder and turned around.

"We need to leave for the cemetery," Diane said. "Mr. Armstrong has the cars organized. It will be just immediate family. There are squad cars waiting at Rose Hill to keep it private."

Emmy nodded and blinked her eyes several times.

"It will be over soon, Em," Diane whispered.

Emmy held Kenny's hand as they walked away from the gravesite later that afternoon. She looked up and let the sun warm her face.

"I thought Tyler did a good job considering he didn't know your mother all that well," Kenny said.

"He did." Emmy looked behind her and saw the kids walking with Kenny's parents. "I'm glad it's not freezing cold. Your father wouldn't have been able to be here."

"This is the warmest I can ever remember the end of January being," Kenny added.

"Mom, can you carry me?" Conor Robertson held up his arms.

Diane looked at her son and frowned. "You are four, Conor. You are big enough to walk."

"Come here, Conor," Carson said. "You can hop on my back, and I'll carry you."

Conor ran to his oldest brother and beamed. "Help me up, Carson."

Carson Garrett, who would turn sixteen in ten days, was a sophomore at St. Raymond's. He easily lifted his little brother onto his back.

"Go fast!" Conor yelled.

Carson picked up his pace and passed everyone.

"Where are you going in such a hurry?" Kenny asked.

Carson turned around. "Conor wants me to run, but I don't want to drop him."

Emmy looked at her parents' oldest and youngest grandchild and smiled. "You are looking more like your grandfather the older you get, Carson."

"Who do I look like, Aunt Emmy?" Conor asked.

"You look like Grandpa Robertson." Emmy glanced to her right and saw Mr. Robertson and Mona talking to Tyler and Liz. She let go of Kenny's hand and walked up to Diane. "You guys are coming to the house, right? We need to eat all the food before it goes to waste."

"We are coming, but I want to stop at home first. I want Lily and Conor to change clothes," Diane said. She looked at her husband, Brady, for a response.

"It's okay with me if they wear what they have on," Brady said.

Emmy looked at the new dress Lily wore and at the suit Conor was wearing. "They should change. You might want to save those clothes for another occasion."

Brady shrugged. "Whatever you decide is okay with me."

"We will be over as soon as we can, Emmy," Diane replied.

"I need to make sure Liz and Tyler know they're supposed to come to the house," Emmy said and headed toward them.

Mona Robertson saw Emmy coming, waited and hugged her. "I'm so sorry about your mother, dear. It was a special service. Your pastor did a good job."

"Thanks, Mona. I need to make sure he and Liz are coming to the house. I know you are coming over."

"We are, dear," Mona said.

Emmy walked to where Liz and Tyler were waiting.

"Are you all right, Emmy?" Liz asked.

"I'm okay. I wanted to make sure you guys are coming back to the house. You are, right?"

"We are. Dany is watching the kids."

Emmy thought about the guesthouse on their property where Dany and Darian lived and how small it would be with Liz and Tyler's four kids running around and smiled.

"I hope you liked the service," Tyler said.

"I don't remember every word, but I thought you did a great job. It can't be easy when you don't know if the person was a believer or not."

"I don't like to play the game of who's in and who's not," Tyler added.

"I like to think Mom and Dad are together somewhere," Emmy said. "I'll see you in a bit. You can bring Dany and the kids over if you want. There's lots of food and plenty of room."

"It will depend on how they're acting. I don't want them to bother you."

"Don't be silly. The house will be full of kids running around," Emmy said.

By the time Kenny and Emmy made it home, Kristen and Mama had all the food warmed up and sitting out on the kitchen island.

"You didn't have to do all this," Emmy said as she hugged Kristen and then Mama.

"It was no problem," Mama said. "We set out plastic plates and silverware. That way there won't be any dishes to do."

"What should I do with all the containers?" Emmy asked. "Some of them are labeled but not all."

"If people didn't put their names on them, I doubt if they

want them back, Em," Kristen said. "I wouldn't worry about it either way."

Pastor Tyler prayed and Emmy told everyone to eat.

"Where do we have to sit?" Kevin asked.

"Would you use the breakfast nook, please. The adults can eat in the dining room or the family room. Wherever there's room," Emmy said and then shrugged. She looked at Kristen and asked, "Where are Grace and Zachary?"

"John picked them up after school," Kristen answered. "He was taking them to a movie."

"I forgot this is Tuesday and the kids should be in school," Emmy said.

"No one expected them to be in school today." Kristen said.

Some people ended up eating in the formal, and seldom used, living room. Most of the men gathered in the family room, and the ladies used the dining room.

"Mama, you need to sit down and eat with us," Emmy said.

"I will. I wanted to make sure everyone else had something first."

"You've always done that. You should start thinking of yourself more. You deserve it."

Mama shook her head and whispered, "It's not in my nature, dear. I don't think that will ever change."

Emmy was able to fit everything back into the fridge after everyone finished eating.

"We're going to take the kids home," Mama said. "Tomorrow is a school day."

Emmy hugged Mama again. "Thank you for coming."

"Let me know if you need anything, sweetie. I'm just across the road."

"I will."

"Are you still coming over Sunday, Em?" Tony asked.

"What's happening Sunday?" she asked.

"The Super Bowl. You were going to watch at my house."

"I suppose so."

"See you then," he said.

Chapter Twenty-Four

Emmy sat next to Mama to watch the Super Bowl several days later.

"Who are you rooting for, brat?" Tony asked from his recliner.

"Who's playing? I don't even know," she said.

"For real?" Tony asked staring at her.

"It's not the Patriots again, is it?"

"Unfortunately, it is. They're playing the Eagles."

"Then I'm pulling for the Eagles."

"Me, too," Mama said.

"How about a little wager, brat?"

"Show me the money, creep," Emmy replied.

"I got five that says Brady smokes them."

"I'll take your money. I think the Eagles are going to run them out of the building. Who's their quarterback, anyway?"

"Have you followed this season at all?" Tony asked.

"Not much," Emmy admitted.

"The Eagles starting quarterback got hurt. They've been using a backup. Nick Foster. He's the tall skinny guy who's been with several teams. Brady will crush him."

Emmy made a face at Tony. "I don't care. I still pick the Eagles."

At halftime Tony and Kenny went to the kitchen to grab more snacks and pop. Mama put an arm around Emmy. Emmy scooted closer to Mama.

"Do you know it's been over twenty years that I've known you," Mama said. "I remember the day Tony brought you home as clear as if it were yesterday."

"And Heather thought I was a boy," Emmy whispered. "I remember that day. You made me feel like a part of the family right away. It always felt like home when I came to your house."

"I still think of you as part of my family," Mama whispered and kissed the top of Emmy's head.

"I have been blessed with two mamas beside my own. You and Mom Colwell, I mean."

"I know who you mean, sweetie."

Tony and Kenny returned and sat down.

"Did you bring anything for us to drink?" Emmy asked.

"Are you thirsty, Em?" Tony asked.

"I would like some pop."

"They're in the fridge." Tony pointed toward the kitchen. "While you're up, could you see if Mama wants something."

"You're such a creep." Emmy stuck out her tongue at Tony and stood up. "Would you like something, Mama?"

"Water would be fine, dear."

Between the third and fourth quarter, Mama whispered to Emmy, "I think you're going to win the five dollars."

"What are you whispering about?" Tony asked.

"We still think the Eagles are going to win. That tall skinny quarterback is outplaying the old guy on the Patriots."

"The games not over until the whistle bows or something like that. Let's see what happens."

On the third play of the fourth quarter one of the Eagles' offensive linemen went down with an injury.

Emmy saw Tony cringe during the replay. "Are you glad you retired without ever having a serious injury?"

"Yeah, after seeing Dwight get hurt, I have a hard time watching the games. The players are bigger and stronger now."

The Patriots lined up for the final play with a slim chance to score and possibly tie the game.

"I can sense a miracle happening," Tony said. "Can you say 'Hail Mary' for a touchdown?"

"No way," Emmy said as she gripped Mama's hand.

"Brady's fading back," Tony said. "He's going to try to get it to his tight end, Grabowski. He's the tallest guy on the field.

Emmy high-fived Mama when the pass fell incomplete to end the game. She jumped up, stood in front of Tony and held out a hand. "You owe me five bucks, creep!"

Tony shook his head as he reached into his wallet.

She grabbed the money out of his hand and did a victory dance.

187

"Are you asleep?" Emmy asked as she nudged Kenny's side.

"I was. I take it you're not."

She turned onto her back and said, "I'm having trouble falling asleep."

He raised up on his side. "What's wrong? What are you thinking about?"

"Should I cancel the tour? After all that's happened, I'm not sure if I can focus on doing a good job."

"I can understand that. When you were in that accident and decided to hang out at St. Bart's..."

"I was in a coma," she said kicking his shin. "I was not hanging out."

He grinned and said, "You took your time getting better. Anyway, my first thought was to cancel the summer tour. Maybe it was Jeff who suggested it first, but I was thinking about it."

"But that was different. You weren't leaving right away."

"True, but we waited to make a decision. Then you got better and... Hey!"

"What?"

He put a hand on her belly. "You were the one who actually convinced us not to cancel."

"I was improving."

"There's no reason for you to stay home, Em. You can grieve for your mother anywhere. Think about all the people who are depending on this tour. There's the band and the crew." He counted on his fingers. "The promoters and the people who work at the venues. Two or three people have already bought tickets," he teased.

She kicked him again harder this time. "You're a dork."

"Ow! I think you broke my leg," he said rubbing his shin. "It's up to you, but I would advise against canceling."

"Fine."

"Do you think you can get to sleep now?"

She scooted closer, grinned and said, "I might need some help."

"Say goodbye to your mother," Kenny instructed the kids. "We're leaving for the airport in two minutes."

"Bye, Mom," Kevin said. "Make sure you bring back some souvenirs."

"I will find something special for you." She hugged and kissed the kids. "Diane will be here soon. Are you ready for school? Did you brush your teeth?"

"Mom! We know how to get ready," Heather said.

Eleven hours later Emmy and her band landed at Heathrow to begin the six week tour of Europe.

"Are you excited, Emmy?" Bobby O'Connor asked as they shuffled along with everyone waiting to enter the United Kingdom.

"I miss the kids already," she whispered.

"What about Kenny?" he asked and then grinned.

"Hush. I won't miss him until I go to bed."

They made it through customs and Emmy spotted Charles La Rosse.

He waved and walked up to her. "I'm sorry about your mother, Emmy." He hugged her with his good arm and then shook hands with Bobby. "How was the flight?"

"It took an eternity, and I ended up sitting next to her," he said.

"Hush, punk. You slept half the time," Emmy said making a face.

"I have transportation waiting to take everyone to the hotel," Charles said. "You may not be ready to fall asleep, but we have a full schedule tomorrow."

"Did the crew get here all right?" Emmy asked.

"They arrived yesterday and started working this morning. Your tour manager had them check out the gear."

"I know I have a tour manager and a production manager and some other people on the payroll," she said tapping a finger against her chin. "What exactly am I paying you for?"

Charles grinned and answered, "You're paying me to be your friend."

"You're an expensive friend."

"Mommy, are you in England now?" Kevin asked.

Emmy adjusted the angle of her laptop. "I am. The plane didn't get lost."

"How many concerts do you have in England?" Isabella asked. "Will you get a chance to visit the Queen?"

The kids giggled and Emmy shook her head.

"Did it take long to get through customs?" Kenny asked.

"I don't know exactly how long, but it went pretty quickly."

"Mommy, are you going to see any castles?" Kevin asked.

"I will have time to do some sightseeing. Do you think I should visit a haunted castle?"

"Yeah! That would be so cool. Maybe you will see a real ghost."

"Are you going to Paris?" Heather asked.

"I think we're going to be in Paris for a couple days. Why?"

"We saw a program about the Eiffel Tower and Notre Dame Cathedral. Are you going to see them?"

"I hope so."

"Make sure you take a photo from the top of the tower," Kevin said.

Emmy turned her head because she heard Charles and Nelson talking. "I think I have to go. I will try to Skype again tomorrow or the next day. There's a difference in time between here and home," she explained.

"Mom, we know that," Heather said. "Put some pictures on Instagram."

"How about Facebook?" Emmy asked.

Heather grunted. "That's for old people."

Bobby walked off the stage with Emmy later that night. "Are you okay, Em?"

"I'm hungry. I didn't have time to eat beforehand."

"There's still food downstairs. Were you disappointed that there were a bunch of empty seats?"

She shrugged and said, "Not really. I didn't even notice to be honest. I could barely see the crowd at times."

"The lights were bright."

"I'm happy some people showed up at all. No one has heard of me over here."

"I beg to differ," Charles said as he handed Emmy her phone. "Tomorrow you have three radio interviews, and tickets are selling briskly for all the shows. It seems that 'Gideon's Heart' is on the charts in several countries."

Adam Vicini approached with Boyd Goldman.

"Great job, you guys," Emmy said. "I was hoping you would follow me on that one song."

Adam smiled. "It was like old times, Emmy. I looked at Boyd and he smiled. We thought you might go back to the bridge."

"This is almost like having the old band back together," Bobby said.

"We're just missing Perry and Ryan," Emmy said.

"And Sean," Boyd added.

"We do have Bruce doing the FOH mix and Josh running the lights," Adam said referring to Bruce Sutherland and Josh Morrissey, who had worked with Emmy for years.

"Rutger Sebastian did a good job with the monitor mix," Emmy said. "Is that his last name?"

"I think so," Adam said. "Charles said he's done monitors for Fridays At Five before. My mix was almost perfect."

"Remember the days when we all used wedges?" Bobby asked. "The sound level on stage would be a killer."

"I can't imagine not using my in-ears," Emmy said. "Let's find some food. I'm starving. I hope they have fish and chips and ketchup that has vinegar mixed in."

Emmy stifled a yawn as she talked to the radio personality conducting the interview the next morning. She filled in some background information about her recording career.

"According to my sources, you have a mix of veteran and new musicians on this tour," he said. "Could you tell our listeners about your band?"

"Sure," she said nudging Bobby, who sat next to her. "This guy is my drummer, Bobby O'Connor, and we've been together since he was in high school."

191

"She means we've worked together in a band," Bobby said.

"Right," Emmy said. "I borrowed Adam Vicini from my husband's band since he wasn't doing anything."

"You are referring to Fridays At Five, correct?"

"Yes. Adam was in my band before joining Fridays. Boyd Goldman plays guitar and he was part of my band. They were called The Only Hope, and they did two albums on their own."

"Who else is there, Em?" Bobby asked after she paused.

"Oh, let's see. Paul Mahnari plays guitar, and so does Tommy Joseph. I've known Tommy since he was born, I think. His father is Paul Joseph, who's in Fridays, too."

"This is like a family band, huh?"

"In many ways," Emmy said. "Mason Williams plays bass, and I have two other singers with me. Susan Lemmert and Tariq Jones. They're younger like Mason, and this is their first time in Europe. Then I have the crew..."

"How long will you be touring?" the interviewer asked.

"Six weeks..."

"I thought that went well," Bobby said later.

Emmy poked him in the arm. "You let me ramble too much. I should have given him shorter answers. Did you get the feeling he had never heard of us?"

"Maybe a little," Bobby answered.

"I wonder if anyone will show up for the shows in Italy or France."

"There might be a few people show up," Bobby teased.

"You're so supportive," she said and rolled her eyes.

"Are you coming with us, Charles?" Emmy asked.

"Where are you going?" he asked.

"We thought we'd check out the Brahms Museum in the Composers Quarter. You recommended it. I'm dragging Bobby and Adam along for company, but none of us speak German."

"You won't have any trouble communicating. Most people in Hamburg speak a little English, and I've been there several times."

"Be that way," Emmy said. "Andy would go with me."

192

Charles laughed. "He wouldn't be caught dead going to the Composers Quarter. If you give me ten minutes, I'll go with you."

They visited all six museums and headed back to the hotel.

"That was exciting," Bobby said while yawning.

"Oh, it wasn't that bad," Emmy said. "You would be more bored if you stayed at the hotel."

"I suppose." He checked the time. "We have two hours to kill. What should we do?"

"I'm going to see if I can Skype with Kenny. The kids will be at school."

She tried, but he wasn't on his computer. She walked across the hall and knocked on Bobby's room.

He let her in. "Any luck?"

"No." She saw Adam and Boyd in the room. "What are you guys doing?"

"Talking about the old days. Want to join us?"

"Maybe I should to make sure you aren't talking about certain stuff." She entered the room, sat on the bed beside Bobby and looked around. "How come your room is nicer than mine? My room isn't as big and doesn't have the same view."

"Shows who's more important," Bobby teased.

"Nelson said tonight's venue was close to being sold out," Adam said.

"We haven't sold out a place yet," Boyd said.

"Do you guys remember the night we played that college town in Arkansas?" Emmy asked. "I don't remember the name."

"It was a Bible college in some little town," Bobby said.

None of them could remember the name of the town.

"Anyway, we set up and about twenty people showed up. We played for an hour and then took requests for another hour. It ended up being fun."

"Did we get paid?" Boyd asked.

Bobby answered, "The promoter offered to pay us what he was supposed to, Emmy, but you told him to keep his money. You felt sorry for him."

"I think it was the first time he promoted a show. I didn't want him to lose his shirt," Emmy said.

"We had fun on those early tours," Adam said. "We never knew what kind of crowd would be there."

"We had fun because Emmy was a lot younger then. She liked to goof around and do stuff," Bobby said.

"We were all younger," Boyd added.

"We had fun, but we got serious when we needed to," Emmy said.

"I remember some of those nights in the bus. We would be wound up after the concert," Boyd said.

"I remember one night when you got after us for flirting with some of the young ladies," Bobby said looking at Emmy.

"You flirted with all the girls," she said.

"Hey! There were times when you would point out the cute girls to me."

"We were pretty naive back then," Emmy said.

"Says who?" Bobby teased.

"We never did the stuff that rock bands do. I was so shocked when I went to that Bender Brothers show in Chicago."

"Those guys kinda went off the deep end," Adam said looking at Boyd."

Boyd shrugged and added, "I learned my lesson, but it cost me my marriage."

"Should we fix you up with a young lady tonight?" Emmy asked.

The guys stared at her.

"I was kidding. Geez! Don't you know when I'm yanking your chain?"

"How are you getting by without the kids?" Adam asked.

"And Kenny," Bobby added.

She punched his arm. "I'm doing okay. We've only been gone two weeks."

"And you have another month to go," Boyd said.

"Don't remind me." She plopped onto her back and stared at the ceiling. "I can survive a month without seeing Kenny."

"Is that a question, or are you trying to convince yourself?" Bobby asked.

"What are you guys doing here?" Emmy yelled as she saw Kenny and the kids backstage three days later.

"It's the weekend, and we were kinda bored, so we thought we would check out Big Ben. We didn't know you were in town," Kevin said.

"Did your father tell you to say that?" Emmy asked as she hugged everyone.

"Daddy wanted to surprise you," Isabella said. "Did we?"

"You certainly did," she answered and then kissed Kenny. "This is a most pleasant surprise."

"Uncle Charles picked us up at the airport," Heather said. "They drive on the wrong side of the road here."

"It is different," Emmy said. "Wait until I see Charles. I'm going to get after him for not telling me you were coming."

"It wouldn't be a surprise if you knew, Mom," Kevin said.

Bobby walked up and shook hands with Kenny and high-fived the kids.

"Did you know they were coming?" Emmy asked.

Bobby shrugged. "I was sworn to secrecy."

"It was probably your idea for them to visit."

"I might have sent a text, but I can't be sure," he said.

"How soon does your show start?" Heather asked.

"We have about thirty minutes," Emmy answered. "Are you checked into the hotel?"

"We are, but we're staying a a different one," Kenny said with a straight face. "The place you're staying is too expensive."

Emmy kissed him again. "I know you're kidding. That must be why I got a suite for tonight and tomorrow."

Chapter Twenty-Five

"So you didn't even have a press conference, huh?" Emmy asked as she talked to Kenny Tuesday afternoon. "That's rather unusual."

"We didn't see the point," Kenny answered. "It's not new songs or anything. It's a live recording. There's a DVD and two CDs, but we kept the price pretty low. Who knows if it will sell or not, but Klaus insisted on new product even though *New Priorities* came out last year."

"I might have to pick up a copy before I get home. I could watch the DVD while we travel."

"Just remember the DVD you buy in Europe won't play back home," he said.

"Because of that region coding or whatever, right?"

"Yes."

"Do the kids remember me?" she asked. "I didn't get a chance to call them yesterday."

"I think they have an idea of who you are," he teased.

"I feel so bad that I won't be home for Kevin Michael's birthday. I will make sure I Skype with him that day."

"Oh, James called and asked about you the other day."

"What did he say?"

"Something about hiring someone to cook if you ever go on tour again."

"Have you been eating fast food every day?" she asked and rolled her eyes.

"Not every day. Sometimes we order pizza or Chinese."

"I better go. They're ready for our soundcheck."

"Talk to you soon, Em. I love you, m'lady."

"Love you too, my dork," she teased.

"Happy birthday, Kevin Michael," Emmy said ten days later. "I'm so sorry I'm not there. I've never missed any birthdays before."

Kevin shrugged and tilted the laptop screen back a bit. "It's okay. I know you have to work."

"I'll be back on Tuesday, and I'll make it up to you. We can do something special."

"Just the two of us?" he asked.

"Just you and me, buddy."

"Three days, huh? I better clean my room and change my underwear."

"I hope you're joking about the underwear."

"Mom! You know I am."

"Sometimes I wonder about you."

"Does anyone want to go to the airport with me later?" Kenny asked.

"Does that mean we get to skip school?" Kevin asked.

"Just for today, you can play hooky," he answered.

"Which one?" Heather asked.

"O'Hare."

"Okay, but can we stop and get some lunch on the way home?"

"I suppose so. Your mother will probably want a chili dog or something."

They waited over forty minutes in the terminal before Kevin spotted Bobby O'Connor walking with Adam Vicini.

Kevin waved and hollered, "Where's my mom?"

Bobby hooked a thumb over his shoulder. "She was right behind us. I think maybe the customs people think she's a spy."

"For real?" Kevin asked.

Adam laughed and shook his head. "No, Kevin. A couple of the customs officers wanted an autograph and some photos with her. She should be right here."

Emmy appeared a moment later and hurried to her family.

"Mom! Are you really a spy?" Kevin asked.

Emmy looked at Bobby. "What did you tell him?"

"Nothing, 009."

Kenny pulled up the van while Emmy waited with the kids.

"Did you bring back any souvenirs?" Kevin asked.

"I found something special for each one of my babies," she answered.

197

"Mom! We're not babies," Heather said.

They made a special trip to Darby's because Emmy craved a chili cheese dog with onions.

"I tried a hot dog in Germany, but it was awful compared to this," Emmy said with a mouthful of food.

"Why did Bobby say you were a spy?" Isabella asked.

Emmy held up a finger and finished chewing. "Let me tell you what happened. We were in France and the police came to the venue."

"Why?" Kevin asked. "Were they chasing bad guys?"

Emmy shook her head. "They got a tip that someone in the band or maybe the crew had a bunch of illegal drugs with them."

"Did they?" Heather asked.

"Of course not, but they searched through our gear. I told them why we were there."

"Did you tell them about God and Jesus," Isabella asked.

"I did. They said they didn't go to church and one of them said he didn't believe in God at all."

"Why?" Kevin asked.

"I guess his parents never took him to Sunday School," Emmy said. "Anyway, they did a search and didn't find anything. I offered to pray for them, and one of them actually let me. He said his wife was in the hospital, so I prayed for her."

"What was wrong with her?" Kevin asked.

"He didn't say specifically. He just said she was sick." Emmy took a long drink of her root beer. "I missed this, and I missed you guys."

They arrived home and Kevin asked, "Mom, when can we do our something special?"

"Would you mind if we wait until tomorrow, buddy?" Emmy asked. "I am suffering from jet lag and need a nap in the worst way."

"I can wait until then," he said. "Do you need Daddy to take a nap with you?"

Heather and Isabella looked at each other and giggled. Emmy saw their look and stuck out her tongue.

198

"Where do you want to go, Kevin Michael?" Emmy asked after school the next day.

"Is Robbins Old Fashioned Ice Cream Parlor still open?"

"Sorry, buddy, but it closes during the winter. Darby's has ice cream. We could go there."

"You just want another chili dog," Kevin said. "It's okay. Can I have one of their root beer floats?"

"Whatever you want."

They ordered root beer floats and sat in one of the booths around the corner from the "Fridays At Five" booth that tourists came to see.

"These are better than what Daddy makes at home," Kevin said.

"Did I ever tell you I worked here when I was sixteen?"

"Yeah, did you get to eat as many chili dogs as you wanted?"

"Yes and no. Mr. Darby didn't make his employees pay for food while they were working. I used to stop here after school with your father a lot."

"Did you and Uncle Rory come here, too?"

"Yes, but not as often. I even came here with Barry Newton a few times."

Kevin finished his float. "I think I still have room for something else."

"What would you like?" Emmy asked as she took some money out of her purse.

"We could split some fries."

"Okay," Emmy said and handed him a five.

Kevin returned with two orders of fries, sat down and handed the five back to his mother. "The man behind the counter wouldn't take my money."

Emmy looked and spotted Danny Darby waving to her.

"That's the man," Kevin said.

"That's Danny," Emmy said and explained who he was.

"Was he nice to you when you worked here? Did you get free food even if you weren't working?" Kevin asked.

Emmy poured ketchup on her fries and took one.

"Danny and his father were always extra nice to me. Mr. Darby said I worked harder than any other employee, and I never stole any food like some of the others would."

"Why would they steal food if he gave them some for free?"

Emmy shrugged and ate another fry.

"Is it because they didn't know Jesus and had sin in their hearts?" he asked with a serious expression.

"I suppose it was."

Kevin was quiet for a moment before saying, "I have Jesus in my heart because I said a prayer at church. Does that mean I won't do anything wrong anymore?"

"Not exactly. We all make some mistakes once in a while, but you can always ask Jesus to forgive you and He will. Then you should try not to make the same mistake again."

"Good because I got mad at Heather the other day and pushed her."

"Did you tell her you were sorry?"

"Yeah, but she was still mad at me."

"You can't control how other people act. Not even your sisters. Heather is responsible for her attitude and how she treats you and other people."

"Is that why the church's motto is 'Loving God, Loving Others'? I saw it on the wall."

"Yes. Do you understand what it means?"

He thought about it for a time. "It means we need to love God more than our stuff and should be nice to everyone, right?"

"That's pretty much right on the money," she said with a smile.

"I like having lots of toys and my electronics, but I don't mind sharing."

"That's a good way to be."

"Are you going to be gone when we get home from school?" Isabella asked Kenny the next morning at breakfast.

"Yes, I'm afraid so. I have to fly to Dallas this morning."

"How long will you be gone?" Kevin asked.

200

Kenny sat down and took a sip of coffee. "I won't be gone for six weeks like your mother was. We aren't traveling overseas this time. In fact, most weeks I will leave on Wednesday and be home before you wake up on Saturday. There are a few times when I won't get home until Sunday, but not every week."

"Are you going to fly everywhere?" Heather asked.

"Yes," Kenny answered. "It's safer than driving, and doesn't take as long."

"Then why do the guys who do all the work have to travel in a bus?"

"Because it would be too expensive to fly all the gear from place to place," Emmy said. She massaged Kenny's shoulders. "The people who work on the crew make good money for doing their jobs."

"But what if they get in a wreck?" Heather asked.

"We've been very fortunate because other than a few minor accidents, no one has ever been hurt while they're traveling," Kenny said.

"Are you going to be working all year?" Kevin asked.

"We are going to work until close to Thanksgiving, but there will be a few times I will be home all week."

"Will we get to see you play sometime?" Isabella asked.

"Maybe not until the summer because you have missed enough school this year," Emmy said.

"Mom! Did Dany have the baby?" Heather asked. "I just got a text from Natalie. She said her mother went to the hospital in a big rush."

"I haven't heard anything," Emmy said. "Let me check my phone. I talked to her Sunday at church, and she said she was ready to pop."

Kevin laughed and said, "Will she pop like the thing in the movie about that alien creature?" He used his hands to illustrate.

"You are so gross, Kevin," Heather said. "Babies don't just pop out. It takes a long time and it hurts the mother a lot."

"Did it hurt when I was born?" Kevin asked. "I don't remember."

"Not as much as when your sisters were born," Emmy answered.

Kevin made a face at his sisters.

"I just got another text!" Heather yelled just as Emmy's phone rang.

Emmy answered, "Liz! Are you at St. Bart's? Did Dany have the baby?"

"How did you know?" Liz asked.

"Heather and Natalie have been texting. I didn't know Dany was in the hospital."

"She went into labor around midnight, and Darian took her to St. Bart's around one."

"What did she have? She wouldn't ever tell me. Are they okay? Dany and the baby, I mean."

"They are doing great, and he has dark hair. Oh, I guess I just gave it away," Liz said.

"Kenny!" Emmy hollered.

He ran into the kitchen from the laundry room. "What is it?"

"Dany and Darian have a baby boy. Liz is there," Emmy said waving her hands and talking faster than normal.

"Do you want the details?" Liz asked.

"Yes, please."

"Okay, he weighed just over seven pounds. He's twenty inches long, and he can be pretty loud."

"What are they going to name him, Liz?" Emmy asked. "That's the important thing."

"Dany, do you guys have a name yet?" Liz asked her sister. "Emmy wants to know."

Dany looked at Darian and he shrugged.

"I don't think they've decided yet, Em. I know they were considering Derry and Declan, but..." Liz looked at Dany, who was shaking her head. "Nope! It won't be either of those. I know Darian would like an Irish name." She looked at her brother-in-law. "He nodded. They have some time to decide."

"Let me know as soon as they decide," Emmy said.

"Are you coming to St. Bart's?" Liz asked.

"I'll head there as soon as I drop the kids off at school."

Liz took a breath before answering, "Take your time, Emmy. Dany and the baby aren't going anywhere."

"I will be careful," Emmy said. *I've learned my lesson.*

"Can we see Dany and the baby?" Isabella asked on the way to school.

"Let me ask Dany first. If she says it's okay, then maybe we can go after school."

Emmy arrived safely at St. Bart's, got a pass and headed to room 4012. She knocked on the open door and peeked inside.

"Emmy! Come on in," Liz said. "Your timing is perfect."

"How's that?" Emmy asked. She smiled at Karen Kimmerle, stood at the foot of the bed and cooed at Dany and the baby.

"They just now decided on a name," Liz said.

Emmy looked at Liz, then Dany and then back at Liz. "Well, is anyone gonna tell me his name?"

"Dany, you can do the honors," Darian said.

"His name will be Patrick Cullen Michaelis, and we aren't going to allow anyone to call him Paddy."

"Wow! That sounds really Irish," Emmy said. "Can I see him, or is he asleep?"

"He's sleeping, but you can hold him," Dany said.

Emmy scooted around the bed and took Patrick in her arms. "He's so tiny, but he has hair."

Darian stood behind Emmy and whispered, "Did you expect him to be a giant like me?"

Emmy leaned against Darian, looked over her shoulder and said, "No, and I hope he looks more like Dany than you."

"I think he has our chin," Karen said.

"Mom, you can't tell who he looks like yet," Liz said.

Emmy stayed for a few more minutes and, just as she was leaving, asked, "Would you mind if I brought the girls up after school? Just for a quick peek. We wouldn't stay long."

"I don't mind," Dany said.

"I was going to bring Natalie and Phoebe up, too," Liz said. "Grayson and David didn't seem interested."

"Who's watching them now?" Emmy asked.

"Natty and Grayson are at school, and Bumpa is watching Phoebe and David," Liz answered.

"I love how the kids call your father 'Bumpa.' It's so cute," Emmy said.

"Gra is cute, too," Liz said.

Later, Emmy called Kristen and asked for a favor.

"Of course. I can bring Kevin home. I'm sure he doesn't want to see the baby."

"I could take Gracie with me if she would like to go."

"Thanks, Emmy, but she made plans for Brienna Plant to come over after school."

"Mom, what if he's sleeping when we get there? Can we stay until he wakes up?" Isabella asked on the way to St. Bart's.

"We are only going to stay a couple minutes. You can see him even if he's asleep," Emmy said.

"Hurry up, Mom! You're driving like Daddy now," Heather said.

"I can't go any faster because of the traffic," Emmy said even though several cars had passed her.

They made it to the hospital and room 4012.

"Can we come in?" Emmy whispered.

"Of course," Dany's mother said. "You just missed Darian's parents. Come on in, girls."

Heather and Isabella quietly walked up to the bed.

"He just finished eating," Dany said.

"Did you burp him?" Isabella asked.

"I did and he fell right to sleep. If you move closer, you can see him."

They walked right up to the bed, leaned over and stared.

"Some babies have funny heads, but he looks normal," Heather said.

Emmy sighed and rolled her eyes just as Liz entered with Natalie and Phoebe.

"Miss Liz, he's so cute."

"Girls, step back so Natty and Phoebe can see their little cousin," Emmy said.

204

"We can see him from this side," Natalie said.

The four girls stared at little Patrick.

"He's your real cousin, Phoebe," Isabella said. "We call all the kids who live by us cousins even though they're not real cousins except for Aunt Diane's kids."

Phoebe, who just turned four in December, climbed on the bed and sat next to Dany.

"Can you see him, Phoebe?" Dany asked as she shifted him a bit.

"Mommy needs a new baby," Phoebe said grinning at her mother.

Emmy jerked her head and stared at Liz.

Liz waved her hands. "Don't look at me. I'm not expecting again."

"You would tell me if you were, right?" Emmy asked.

Liz smiled but didn't answer.

Chapter Twenty-Six

"Before we do lunch, I should call home and make sure Father James is okay," Emmy said as she unpacked her suitcase. "Is this a new hotel?"

Kenny turned away from the window of the seventh floor of the recently opened Cambridge Hill Suites Hotel. "It wasn't here the last time we were in Denver, so I guess it's new."

"It's pretty fancy. I hope you got a deal since you rented out the whole floor."

He sat down in a plush leather chair. "I'm sure we did. They can use it for publicity."

"The kids signed a card for us. They picked it out themselves," she said. "I haven't seen it, and they made me swear we would open it together." She pulled it out of her suitcase, sat down and held it up. "Ready?"

He walked over and sat on the bed next to her. "You can do the honors."

She opened the envelope and pulled out the card. They looked at the front and laughed.

"If that's supposed to be us, we look like we're a hundred years old," Kenny said. "What does it say on the inside?"

Emmy opened the card, read the interior and handed it to Kenny. "I'm going to ground all of them when I get home."

He read it and laughed. "I guess we better be careful if we try to make love. Where did they find this card?"

"I took them to the mall, and they insisted I not follow them," she answered.

"They must see us as being really ancient." He stared at the front of the card again. "These people look familiar."

"Can you believe we've been married fifteen years?" Emmy asked.

"Fifteen? I thought it was more like thirty," he teased.

She stuck out her tongue at him. "You just blew it, buster. I was going to be extra nice to you tonight, but you can forget it now."

"We're ready to do a soundcheck," Ty Dalicandro, the tour manager for Fridays At Five, said to the band members. He looked at Emmy, who was holding Kenny's hand. "I hear today is your anniversary. Are you doing anything special tonight to celebrate, or is that none of my business?"

Kenny grinned and answered, "We already did something to celebrate."

Emmy let go of his hand and punched his side. Jeff and Dave laughed. Adam and P.J. grinned at Emmy and high-fived Kenny.

"Why did you tell them that?" Emmy asked. "They will think we're like newlyweds who... never mind." She stuck out her tongue, walked to the side of the stage and stood there with her arms over her chest.

"Let's get this done," Will Consoli said from his position behind the FOH mixer.

The guys moved into position and Kenny waved at Will, who had been mixing their shows almost from the very beginning of the band. "We're ready." He turned and looked at Dave Persching.

Dave banged his drumsticks together and the soundcheck began.

They finished in less than thirty minutes.

Kenny handed his guitar to Frankie Hanna, his longtime guitar tech and the first member of the Fridays crew. "I thought I heard some buzzing from one of the amps."

"I heard it. I'll fix it," Frankie answered.

Kenny saw Emmy talking to his personal assistant, Cole Milne and Sara White, who managed the wardrobe for the guys, and walked over.

"They will hate me if I even suggest it," Sara said.

"Hate what?" Kenny asked.

Emmy grinned and said, "I told Sara you guys should wear those matching suits tonight. The dark gray ones you wore back in the early 2000s for the Johnny March Tour. You could wear those skinny black ties, too."

Kenny looked at Sara. "Do we still have those?"

207

"I don't know why I brought them along this time, but I did. If you remember, I did some alterations on them a couple of years ago. Adam is roughly the same size as Jeremy, so his suit fits."

"You mean they actually still fit? They aren't as skinny as they used to be," Emmy teased.

The rest of the band wandered over and joined in the conversation. They thought it would be fun to wear the suits again.

"I can't wear this coat for the whole show," Kenny said after three songs. He removed it and handed it to Frankie. "Tell Emmy I'm going to make her pay for this. I'm going to make her come onstage and sing."

Frankie nodded and left to tell Emmy.

"No way!" she said shaking her head. "I'm wearing these old jeans and an even older t-shirt. If he wants me to sing, he will have to drag me out there."

Kenny waited until the final encore and pulled Emmy to center stage with him.

"Do we have to share a mic?" she asked as the band started playing "Sea Sick." One of their early hits and a longtime closing number.

"Just for the choruses," he answered.

"I hope you brushed your teeth before the show," she whispered.

Kenny surprised her by backing away from the mic for the second verse. She sang it by herself without missing a beat, or forgetting any of the words and having to look at the teleprompter.

Five minutes later they waved to the crowd and left the stage.

"Great job, Emmy!" Adam said. "Maybe we should bring you along for all the shows."

"Why did you guys keep playing the chorus and bridge so many times?" she asked. "I was ready to end the song. I could barely breath."

"We wanted to test your stamina," Jeff said accepting a bottle of water and a fresh towel from Denny Longenfeldt, his guitar tech.

Everyone headed backstage to the green room to wind

down before returning to the hotel.

Emmy rode in the back of a black Suburban with Kenny and said, "That place looked smaller than the other venues I remember in Denver."

"It is smaller," Kenny said.

"I even noticed some empty seats."

"Yeah, that's been happening more and more on this tour. We aren't selling as many tickets as in the past. We probably sold eight thousand for tonight."

"Are you worried about that?"

He shrugged and said, "Yes and no. We understand that no band remains popular forever."

"The Stones still sellout, and they're really old."

"Yeah, but they only tour once a decade," Cole said from the front seat.

"We still like playing for people," Kenny said. "As long as we can make enough money to support the crew and everyone, I guess we'll keep touring."

"You might have to forgo the jet and ride a bus for your next tour," she said.

"I hope we never have to use a van again like for the first one. That was pretty rough even though we were young."

Father James and the kids picked Emmy up late Saturday afternoon.

"Did you miss me?" Emmy turned in her seat and asked as Father James left the airport.

The kids looked at each other and giggled.

"Oh, were you gone?" Heather asked. "That's what you always ask Daddy."

"I missed you, and Daddy liked your card." She looked at her brother and asked, "Did they behave for you?"

"Yes, but they did complain about eating what I cooked a few times."

"Mom, he made tuna sandwiches and put onions and hot peppers in it," Kevin said. "They were great!"

Heather and Isabella made faces.

"Should we stop somewhere to get dinner?" Emmy asked.

"Burger Bob's! I need real fast food immediately," Heather said.

"We are not eating in the new van," Emmy said.

"Can we order pizza and have it delivered?" Kevin asked from the back row.

"Can you wait that long, Heather?" Emmy asked.

"I suppose," she answered.

The kids insisted on two pizzas because they could not agree on the toppings.

"Fine! I will let you order two tonight, but only because I'm too tired to argue."

She paid the delivery man and tipped him ten dollars.

"I'll say the prayer," Isabella volunteered.

Later, Emmy put the leftover pizza in the fridge, told the kids she was going to work in the den and closed the door behind her. She booted up her laptop and opened the folder containing their household budget.

"We definitely need to cut back on utilities and the cable bill. We don't watch that much TV, and we never watch the premium channels."

A few minutes later her cell phone rang. She checked the caller ID and answered.

"What time did you get home?" Diane asked.

"Around five," Emmy said. "Why?"

"What are you doing now? Do you want some company, or are you too tired from your little trip to Denver?"

"It was our anniversary," Emmy said and explained what she was doing.

Diane laughed. "Are you serious?"

"Yeah. The band is playing smaller venues. We might need to cut back on expenses."

"Give me a break. You guys are the most frugal people in history, and that means I think you are the cheapest people I know."

"Ha! Do you know how much we're paying for cable? It's outrageous."

Diane laughed again. "No, but it shouldn't be any higher than ours."

"We pay over two hundred a month and watch the same few channels if we even watch anything at all," Emmy said. "I'm going to get rid of it if they won't give us a better deal."

"Em, if times get really tough, you guys could always move in with us. We have room."

"Ha! Ha!" Emmy said making a face.

"You could sell the big house and live in the guesthouse," Diane suggested.

"We can't because Dany and Darian live there, and I could never ask them to leave."

"Well, I guess you might need to go back to work. Maybe Danny Darby will hire you."

"Yeah! I could work part-time and bring home enough food to feed everyone. The hot dogs might be cold and the fries a bit soggy, but Kenny and the kids will get used to it."

"You are such a riot."

"Why are you really calling?"

"I just wanted to make sure you got home all right," Diane said. "Geez! Is it a crime to be concerned about my little sister?"

"Why wouldn't I make it home okay? And thank you for your concern," Emmy said. *Why does everyone think I'm so fragile? My health is better now than before the accident.*

Chapter Twenty-Seven

"Why were you talking to Gracie so much?" Heather asked on the way home from Grace's tenth birthday party at Crest Ridge United Nazarene. "You even helped her open some of her presents."

"I wasn't talking to her that much, and I only helped because she couldn't open some of the boxes because of all the tape," he answered.

Heather and Isabella turned in their second row seats to stare at their brother.

"What? Stop looking at me like that," he warned.

"You like Gracie," Heather said. "Is she going to be your girlfriend?"

"No!" he hollered. "Mom! Make them stop teasing me." He made a face at his sisters. "She can't be my girlfriend because we're cousins."

Father James hit the button on the dashboard that enabled him to talk to the kids over the van's speaker system. "Kevin, you shouldn't let your sisters get under your skin. They are just teasing you."

Isabella whispered, "You do know she's not a real cousin, right? Diane's kids are real cousins. Everyone else in Bristol Ridge we call a cousin is pretend family."

"I know that," he said. "I still don't like her as a girlfriend. We're just friends because we're the same age."

"Mom, when is Daddy getting home?" Isabella asked. "He missed Gracie's party."

Emmy eased through the intersection after the light turned green. "He texted me during the party. He got home about an hour ago. He was going to come to the party, but I told him it was almost over."

"Why didn't he come home last night?" Heather asked.

"They had to film a TV show this morning," Emmy answered. "They have to do something to generate interest in the band."

After dinner everyone got ready for another birthday party.

"Are there going to be other kids at Mama's party?" Kevin asked as Emmy tried to comb his unruly hair.

"You will be there, and so will Tony and Sloane's kids."

"What about Zach and Grace?"

"They will be there, too. I can't think of any other kids who are coming. It's more of a party for adults."

"Do we have to listen to all the old people talking about boring stuff?" he asked.

"There! You hair looks better, and I'm sure you will be allowed to play in the basement or upstairs," Emmy said.

"Is there going to be ice cream and cake? Will Mama have to blow out candles?" he asked and then tilted his head for a moment. "How many candles will there be?"

"Probably two," Emmy said. "A seven and a four."

"Mama, are you ready to open your presents," Tony asked as he and Emmy entered the kitchen.

"I didn't want anything," she answered.

Emmy took Mama's arm and guided her out of the room. "Don't worry. There are only a few cards and one gift to open."

"I didn't want anyone to make a fuss about my birthday."

"Just wait till next year. We will have a big party and invite everyone you've ever met," Emmy said.

"You better not."

"Try and stop us," Emmy said. "You can sit between me and Krissy, and we will hand you the cards. Some of them are from the kids."

"Is it time for cake and ice cream now?" Ben asked his mother. "Me and Kevin were outside hiding from Taylor and Coby."

"Yes, but Mama wants to see all the kids first," Sloane said and then pointed. "She's in the family room."

Eleven children stood in front of Mama Bertucci, who sat on the couch holding some of the cards.

"I want to thank each of you for the cards you picked out or made yourself. I love you all very much, and I need a hug."

Coby Bertucci was the last to hug his grandmother.

"Thank you for the card, sweetie," Mama said. "I liked how you drew your whole family."

"I wrote my name without any help," he said.

"You did a great job. Now it's time for ice cream and cake."

"Are you sure your parents are all right?" Emmy asked again while watching Father James load his suitcases into his 2016 Civic. "Are you up to the drive? You look pale."

"For the last time, Emmy, I feel fine. If they were in bad shape I would be flying home. I just want to take a trip and see them for a few days. I will be back by next Sunday." He closed the trunk and took the small cooler from Emmy. "What's in here?"

"I made some egg salad sandwiches with bacon, chopped peppers and onions for you. I know you like them, and there's some coffee in the thermos. I know you won't stop unless you have to. Did you tell the kids you're leaving?"

"Yes, I sent them a text and told them to behave while I'm gone." He touched the tip of her nose. "You better behave, too."

"Call me when you get there, or if you have car trouble. I don't want you to be stranded along the road somewhere in the middle of nowhere."

"Yes, Emily," he said rolling his eyes the way she often did.

Emmy pushed her shopping cart around the corner of the bread aisle while staring at her grocery list and nearly bumped into another shopper. "I'm sorry," she said moving out of the way.

"Emmy! How are you?"

Emmy looked up and smiled. "Annie! How are you? I didn't know it was you."

"Would you have rammed me harder if you had known?" Annie O'Dell asked with a grin.

"No, but I should have been looking where I was going. Are you alone? Is Matt with you?"

"No, he's at work. I came here right from school." Annie moved out of the way of another shopper.

"Are you still living in your father's house? You grew up there, right?" Emmy asked.

Annie shook her head as she added a bouquet of cut flowers to her cart. "We decided to sell it after Alanna came along. I loved that house because of all the memories, but it only had two bedrooms. We talked about adding on, but the neighborhood has changed over the years."

"Where are you guys living now?"

"We actually bought a place in the Barclay Estates," Annie said.

"That's where Kristen and Derrick grew up. Those are really nice houses."

Annie chuckled and said, "Look who's talking, Emmy. We bought one of the smaller if not the smallest house in the development. We bought it because it's close to school."

"How are things at the Hungry Lion? We haven't been there in months," Emmy said.

"Oh, you haven't heard, huh?"

"Heard what?" Emmy asked grabbing a box of donuts and tossing them into her cart.

"He sold the restaurant," Annie said.

"When? I didn't know that. Why did he sell it? I thought business was good."

"Business was good, but he was tired of working seventy to eighty hours a week. He wanted to spend more time with me and the kids. He took a job with Cohen & Kliegman. That's an accounting firm."

"Oh, that's right. He got a degree in accounting at North Park." Emmy followed Annie and checked the peanut butter for something on sale.

"Now he's able to use it. He won't make as much money this year, but he made some good money selling the Lion."

"How about you? Are you still at The Barclay Academy? Have you written anymore books?"

"Still teaching, and I have been writing. In fact, my third book is available today."

"Good for you. What's it about? Do you have time to talk?"

215

"We can talk as we shop," Annie said. "The new book is part of the same series, and it's a murder mystery."

"Really? I could never write one of those. They are way too complicated."

"It's based on a true story, so I didn't have to create everything. Do you remember the coed who was murdered at North Park? It happened early in my sophomore year."

Emmy shook her head. "I don't really remember it. Kristen probably told me, but I must have forgotten."

"It happened in September of 1998, and the campus was shocked."

"Did the police ever solve the case?" Emmy asked. She loaded two cans of coffee into her cart.

"It took them about a month, but they caught the guy." Annie picked out some herbal tea and placed it in her cart. "How is your career going, Emmy? I know you still sing with your band. Are you still writing?"

"I did a tour around Europe in February and March. It was my first tour over there, and it was all right. "I'm finished with another book, and it should be coming out in a week or so. It's actually going to be a series about these two kids who live in SoHam except I'm not calling it SoHam."

"How do you find the time to take care of Kenny and the kids, write books, record CDs and travel around the world?"

Emmy sighed and answered, "I'm not sure sometimes. I'm still involved with my church, too. Father James helps a lot. He got reassigned and has more time to stop by the house."

"Are your characters based on you and Kenny?" Annie asked.

"Not really, but I did use some things that actually happened. Not necessarily to me and Kenny though." Emmy thought about telling Annie that some of the events involved Rory, but she didn't.

"I'm glad to see you've recovered from your accident," Annie said.

"How did you know about that?" Emmy asked.

"For real?" Annie asked. "It was all over the news, Emmy.

Everyone knows about it."

"I didn't realize it would make the news."

"You still don't understand people think of you and Kenny as celebrities, do you?"

"No, because celebrities are movie stars and pro athletes."

They finished shopping, checked out and walked outside.

"I'm over there," Annie said pointing to her 2015 red Honda CR-V.

"I'm over there," Emmy said. "We should get together again for dinner."

"I'd like that," Annie said.

"Is anyone home?" Father James hollered as he walked out of the mudroom.

Kevin ran down the hallway and slid to a stop beside Father James. "What took you so long? Mom was ready to call the police and report you as missing."

"I was not," Emmy said as she approached. "You should have called because I thought you would be here for dinner. How are your parents?"

He hung up his keys and said, "They are doing good, and they said to tell everyone hi."

Emmy stared at him and tilted her head.

"Hey!" Father James shrugged. "They are fine, Emmy. No one is sick, I promise. I survived the trip and feel pretty good"

"Ben and I found this big hole in the woods," Kevin said. "We think a fox dug it, or maybe a wild dog."

"Did you stop at the rectory?" Emmy asked.

"No, I came here first. That way the bishop doesn't know I'm back in town."

"You're so bad. Don't you feel guilty taking money from the church for hanging out at hospitals?"

"I provide comfort and companionship for those in need," he said.

Emmy turned and walked away. "I bet you play cards and take their money."

Kenny returned, walked up to Emmy, who was emptying the dishwasher, and coughed to get her attention.

She straightened up and set two plates on the countertop. "Thanks for taking the kids to school. Why are you looking at me like that, and what do you have in your hands?"

"I'm grinning at you because I love you."

"Seriously, what do you have behind your back?"

He handed her a dozen red roses.

She tilted her head. "And what are these for? It's not my birthday or our anniversary. What did you do? Are you guys going to tour all summer, and this is your way of breaking it to me?"

"No, Em. Don't you remember what today is?"

"It's Monday the last day of April." She took the roses and smelled them. "Are these because my book is coming out tomorrow?"

"No, I kinda forgot about that. Don't you remember what happened on this day?"

"Oh, crap!" she said and then bit her lip. "Has it been that long?"

"The accident was one year ago today."

"That means it was a year ago that Gideon passed away," she said as tears welled in her eyes.

"I'm sorry, Em. I didn't even think about that. I bought the roses because you're still here." He slapped his forehead. "What a dork! I didn't even think that you would... never mind. Should I throw them away?"

"Don't be silly." She kissed his cheek. "I appreciate the thought, and it's not your fault. I guess I haven't thought about Gideon lately since the tour is over, and I feel guilty. After he died, I would think about him every day. Every hour. I thought about him every night we played his song."

"It's normal to do that, Em. As time passes, things change."

"I'm surprised I stopped thinking about him so much so soon after the tour ended."

"I'm glad I don't have to take these to Rose Hill," he said as he hugged her and lifted her off of her feet.

"You can't put roses on... Oh, I get it now."

Chapter Twenty-Eight

"Where are the kids?" Emmy asked as she stood up and stretched out. "My hand is sore from signing my name."

"I told the kids they could look for some books," Kenny said.

"Did you set a limit of how many they could buy?"

"I told them no more than five apiece. Is that too many?"

Emmy shook her head. "I don't mind if they buy books."

Paul Tockstein, the owner of Paul's Bookstore, approached with a smile. "I was smarter this time."

"How so?" Emmy asked.

"I ordered twice as many books as your last book signing. Are there any left?"

Emmy quickly counted the stack of books on the table. "Ten of the new one."

"Not bad since I ordered two hundred copies," he said. He picked up one of the books and handed it to her. "Do you think you could sign one more?"

"Who should I make it out to?"

"How about to Paul?"

Emmy grinned at him. "You are my best fan." She signed the copy and handed it back.

They turned as someone came running down the stairs.

"Mom, can we buy these books?" Kevin asked trying to catch his breath. "I don't have any of these, and they're about football and basketball and baseball."

Emmy looked at Kenny and then back at Kevin. "Since when are you interested in sports?"

"Since I decided not to become a bug doctor." He handed the books to his father.

Kenny looked at the first one. "*Touchdown Pass* by Clair Bee."

"And this is *Championship Ball* and I really want *Strike Three!*," he said hopping up and down.

"How much are they?" Emmy asked. "This is the book series Kristen bought for John years ago."

Kevin shrugged and said, "I don't know." He handed a book to Emmy.

She looked at the price and raised her eyebrows. "I'm sorry, buddy, but they're too expensive," she said handing the book back. She looked at Kenny and asked, "Did you ever read these when you were a kid?"

"I'm pretty sure I did. I think my dad had a complete set, and I probably read them."

"Please! Can I buy one at least?" Kevin begged.

Paul walked up to Kevin. "Could I see that one?"

Kevin handed him both books.

Paul inspected the covers for a moment. He opened the book and checked the title page. "Ah! I see why these are rather expensive." He tapped his jaw for a moment. "If your mother wouldn't mind, I am pretty sure I have some less expensive versions in a box in the back. They are the same editions with the same photos on the cover, but they are a lot cheaper." He looked at Emmy for an answer.

She looked at Kenny, who was reading *Touchdown Pass*. "Kenny, what do you think?"

"Huh?" he asked looking up from the book.

"Can Kevin buy them if Mr. Tockstein can find cheaper ones?"

"Sure!" Kenny said.

Emmy shook her head. "Such a dork. You want to read them as much as Kevin." She looked at Mr. Tockstein and nodded.

"Come with me, Kevin, and I'll see if I can find that box."

Emmy looked at Kenny and pointed upstairs. "You better find the girls and see how many books they want to buy."

Kenny headed upstairs and Emmy sat back down.

Paul and Kevin returned a few minutes later.

"Mom! Mr. Tockstein found cheap books. They're only five dollars each. Can I buy some, please?"

"Five dollars, huh?" Emmy asked looking at Mr. Tockstein, who was carrying a large box.

"Yes," he answered. "I found these in a closet. They're not in mint condition, but he can read them."

"Please, Mom?" Kevin asked.

"Okay," Emmy said and held up a hand. "Only five."

Mr. Tockstein helped Kevin find the first five books in the series, and he sat at a table and started reading.

Emmy shook her head at Mr. Tockstein. "They would be worth more than five dollars even if the covers were missing."

He shrugged and said, "I suppose, but he looks so thrilled about them. I have hundreds of these books around somewhere. I can afford to sell them under their value since I probably only paid a few dollars for the whole box."

Kenny and the twins walked down the stairs. Emmy looked at the girls and sighed because they each carried an armful of books.

"Fine!" Emmy said after the girls gave their reason for buying each book. "It's a good thing people are buying my books, and I have another one close to being finished."

The kids were silent on the way home.

"I heard Denise and Ophelia squabbling about something before they left," Kenny said. "Do you have any idea what that was about?"

"It might have been because they have differing opinions about how often I should release a book," Emmy replied.

"How often are you planning to release one?"

"Since this series is pretty easy to write, I was thinking at least one every six months and possibly every four. I have outlines for ten books, and I'd like to get them written as soon as possible."

"I'm going downstairs to work in the studio," Kenny said to Emmy, who was reading in the family room. He walked up behind her and kissed the top of her head. "The kids are reading, and I said they could stay up until ten."

"It is a school night," Emmy said looking back at him.

"They promised to turn out the lights on time."

"They better. I'm not letting them miss school."

"I have a melody in my head and would like to get it recorded before I forget it. I won't be working too late. Wait up for me."

Emmy read for several more minutes before getting up and heading to the kitchen. She poured a glass of water and cut another slice of banana bread. *I should have added a few more chocolate chips to it.* She noticed the roses on the island again, took a bite of the banana bread and leaned closer to the roses. *I love the smell of fresh flowers and especially roses.* She sat on one of the barstools to eat and closed her eyes. *Thank you, Lord, for allowing me to still be here...* She prayed for a moment and then listened. She opened her eyes and looked around the room. *I wonder why all I can remember from being in a coma are the dreams I had about high school. I hadn't thought of some of that stuff for twenty years or more. I'm not sure if I ever told Kenny, or anyone, about some of those events.* Her reverie was interrupted by the sound of her cell phone. She listened to it ring twice before getting up. *Did I leave you on the desk?* She walked over to the kitchen desk, moved some junk mail and found her phone. *Who could be calling this late?* She checked the caller ID and smiled.

"I hope this isn't too late to be calling. You weren't in bed, were you?" Rory asked.

"It might be late in Florida, but it's not even ten here. How are you?"

"We are doing good. You?" he asked.

"We are all good. I was just thinking about you."

Rory walked into the kitchen and grabbed a beer from the fridge. "Were they good thoughts or bad?"

She chuckled and said, "I'm not sure. For some reason I was thinking about the dreams I had in St. Bart's. Can you believe the accident was a year ago yesterday? Kenny surprised me with a dozen roses.

"I would have called then, but I thought you might be busy." He took a long drink of his beer before asking, "Are you fully recovered?"

"I suppose so. Though sometimes I find myself wandering around the house not knowing where I am or what my name is."

"For real?"

She shook her head. "No! I don't have any issues from the accident except for one."

222

"What might that be?"

"I don't drive as fast anymore." She finished her banana bread and cut another slice.

"That's good. Hey! I was online and noticed on your website you have another book available. Is it any good? Should I break down and buy a copy?"

"Why were you checking my website? I hardly ever go there."

"It's the only way I have to keep track of you since you never call or email or text me anymore," he teased.

She made a face. "I do so! I called you from London even though it cost a fortune."

"Oh, was that you? I thought it was a prank call," he said and then finished his beer.

"You are such a riot," she said. "How long do you have?"

"Two minutes, so give me the short version."

She tapped her jaw and said, "I got an idea for a book. It's gonna be a series, by the way."

"Oh, great! More books I will have to buy."

"The idea came from the dreams I had in the hospital. Did I tell you about those?"

"You might have mentioned something about some wild dreams."

"So I created a fictional city and high school and some characters that are kinda based on real people."

"Am I one of those fictional people?" he asked using air quotes.

"Kinda, but I changed everyone's names."

She told him the names and described one of the early scenes in the book.

"So, this bully used to push you around, huh? I can't see anyone ever pushing you around now."

"A few times, but then you straightened him out. Do you even remember that?"

"It appears I stood up for you on a few occasions."

"Yeah, but there were times when you got me into trouble, too," she said.

223

He waved a hand. "No way, Em. You never got into trouble on account of me."

She laughed. "We always thought my parents never knew about me sneaking out of the house, but Mom told me they did know. She said they thought I was too young to get into any real trouble."

"Had they only known," he said and then sighed.

"Shut up! What did I ever do that was so bad?"

"Do you really want me to answer that?"

"No! Not if you want to live until your next birthday. Happy birthday, by the way."

Ha! It was last month, Olivia," he replied.

"I know. But we haven't talked since then."

"So you admit you've been ignoring your best friend, huh?"

"I was kinda busy in Denver on your birthday."

"My birthday is the same day as your anniversary, so I don't want to know why you were busy. Denver, huh?"

"Kenny was on tour, remember?"

"Anything new going on?"

"Have you heard about Kristen and John?" she asked. She stood up and walked down the hall to the family room.

"I heard about them splitting up."

She plopped on the couch. "She filed for divorce."

"I'm sorry to hear that."

"Yeah, it sucks."

"I should let you go, Em. Rochelle is ready for bed," he said a few minutes later. "Say hi to everyone for me, and make sure you drive safely."

"I will. Kiss Rochelle for me."

"Yuck! Why would you want to kiss Rochelle?"

"I didn't mean it like that, you creep. Good night and thanks for calling."

She ended the call and closed her eyes. *Thank you for calling, Rory. I really needed to hear from you.*

By the time Emmy left the house to pick up the kids at school the next day, she had finished her first draft of the second book in her new series.

I need to come up with a title for this one. I used a quote from the book for the first title. Maybe something will stand out when I go through it again. She waited in line for the kids and waved at Sloane, who was helping with the younger children. *You do look a lot better since you lost all that weight.*

"Mom!" Kevin shouted as he climbed into the Odyssey. "You won't believe what happened."

"Are you going to tell me, or do I have to guess?" Emmy asked looking in the rearview mirror.

"It was no big deal," Heather said as she climbed in. "Some of the boys were caught trying to start a fire in a garbage can. They were so dumb."

Emmy made sure the kids were buckled in before she drove away. *I remember Rory doing that and even worse stuff in grade school.*

"What did you do today, Mommy?" Isabella asked.

"I finished the first draft of the next Claire and Ruby book."

"Will you let us read it?" Heather asked. "Are there things in this one like the first one?"

"What do you mean?" Emmy asked as she eased up to a red-light.

"Naughty stuff like when you and Rory stole some of Grandpa's beer."

"That was the characters in the book," Emmy said. "It's fiction. That means it's made up and not completely true."

"Sure, Mom," Heather said then she and Isabella giggled.

"I'm telling Father James to put a lock on the fridge in the garage if he wants to keep his beer in it."

"Mom! We have never stolen any of his beer," Heather said.

Kevin stared out the window without saying a word.

Chapter Twenty-Nine

"You're home early," Mama said as Tony walked into the kitchen.

"All I had to do today was hand over the keys to the new owners," he said.

Emmy opened the oven and removed a pan of muffins. "For real? Or do you mean symbolically?"

"Symbolically, and why are you here, brat? Don't you have an oven at your house?"

She set the pan on the stove, turned around and made a face at Tony. "FYI, I'm helping Mama bake muffins for the fundraiser at St. John's."

Tony walked over and started to take a muffin, but Emmy smacked his hand.

"You can have that one," Emmy said pointing to a muffin on the counter. "It fell on the floor, and we can't use it."

Tony picked it up, examined it and took a bite. "Ten second rule."

Emmy laughed and said, "Ha! It was on the floor for a whole minute before I picked it up."

"Doesn't matter. It still tastes good."

Mama leaned against the counter and sighed.

"Are you all right?" Tony asked.

Emmy moved next to her and patted her hand. "I know why you sighed."

Mama wiped her brow with a towel. "It's still hard to believe the company has been sold. Your father and Daniel started it over fifty years ago."

"It was founded in 1962," Tony said. "It says that on the front door."

Emmy placed the muffins on a platter and asked, "What are you gonna do now? Are you gonna try to get a job with the company? They might need someone with your skills to... "

Tony pointed a finger at her. "You better watch it."

"I was going to say with your extraordinary organizational skills."

"Why don't I believe you?" Tony asked after finishing the muffin.

Emmy shrugged as she grinned.

"Since it's so close to summer, I've decided to take some time off. I can't remember the last time I was home all summer long. Where's Kenny? Did he leave already?"

"They left around seven this morning. They had to fly to Seattle for a TV thing."

"What are you doing later?" Tony asked.

"Working on my book until I have to get the kids. Unless I ask Diane to do it Why? Have you got a better offer?"

"I'm going to buy a new pickup truck. Want to come with me?"

"Why are you buying a truck?" Mama asked. "You have the van and Sloane's old car."

"She never uses her car, and I hate driving it."

"Is that because you're too fat to fit in it?" Emmy asked with a straight face.

"No, I don't like it because it's old and unreliable. The van is getting old, too."

"It's a 2010 Sienna," Emmy said. "Those things last forever."

"It's got close to 150,000 miles on it. Sloane would like to buy a new one soon."

"So, you're going to beat her to the punch and buy a truck, huh?" Emmy put her hands on her hips and frowned at him.

"I think we can afford two new vehicles," he said.

"I don't think so, buddy," Emmy said. "You don't even have a job. How would you get financing?"

"Sloane has a good job."

"She teaches at the church's school. She only makes half of what she could earn if she was still at McGee Junior High."

"It called a middle school now, Emmy," Tony said.

She rolled her eyes and threw up her hands.

"We have enough money in our investment account to buy a truck. I did make some money from the sale of the company."

"What kind of account?" Emmy asked.

227

"Very funny. I can withdraw money if we need it. It was set up so we wouldn't have a penalty," Tony said.

"You have to pay income taxes on it."

Tony sighed and said, "Why did I even mention it. Do you want to go or not?"

She grinned and said, "Sure. As long as I get to drive it."

Three hours later Tony and Emmy left Anderson Ganley Ford in his new truck.

"Why on earth did you buy the most expensive one they had?" Emmy asked while checking out the interior.

"It had all the features I wanted, and they lowered the price by nearly ten grand," he answered.

"Are you going to use this as a work truck, or a fancy car to drive around?"

Tony pressed the accelerator to the floor to test the engine and transmission. "Maybe both."

"Sloane is going to kill you when she finds out how much you spent," Emmy said hanging on as Tony took a corner too fast.

"She knows what I paid."

"You better not complain if she wants a new minivan."

"Em, we do know how to manage our money," he said.

Tony shook his head as he watched Emmy flipping through different radio stations.

"I thought all trucks had eight cylinder engines. This is a six cylinder, right?" she asked a few minutes later.

"It's a turbocharged engine, Em. It gets better gas mileage," he explained.

She turned to look out the rear window. "Mama will need a ladder to get in this thing."

"I doubt she will go anywhere in it. She has her own car, and Sloane has the van."

"Do I get to drive it sometime?"

"Maybe. Are you sure you want to?" he asked.

She shrugged. "The boys will be happy you got a truck, but I can't see Dotty or Noemi liking it."

"They might surprise you," he said.

"Emmy, could you grab that bag, please?" Dad Colwell asked. "It slipped past me while I was lifting this one."

Emmy grabbed the handle of the blue suitcase with the Fridays At Five logo stitched on the side. "Is that all of them?" She asked setting the fourth suitcase on the cart.

"Me-maw, is that all the suitcases you have?" Kevin asked watching the baggage carousel go round and round. "You were gone a really long time."

"We didn't need to take a lot of clothes with us, or bring a lot back, because we have wardrobes in both places," Mom Colwell explained. She hugged the kids and added, "I missed you all so much."

"Kevin, can you help me push the cart, please?" Emmy asked.

He scooted behind the cart and began pushing. After straining for a moment, he got it moving.

"Do try not to run into anyone or anything," Emmy said. "Girls, help your brother."

"How!" Heather asked.

"Stand on each side and help him guide it," Emmy said.

"What time will Kenny get home?" his father asked after the van was loaded.

"He should arrive around three."

Dad Colwell checked his watch. "It's just after noon now. Would anyone like to stop at Darby's for lunch?"

Kevin shouted in the affirmative.

"Dad, we don't have to stop," Emmy said.

"But I'm starving, Mom," Kevin shouted from the back of the van.

Emmy relented and they stopped at Darby's but decided to take the food to the Colwell house to eat.

"If we get the luggage inside, I can take it upstairs after we eat," Dad Colwell said.

Minutes later they sat at the table. Emmy prayed and then passed out the food.

"Grandpa, who was watching the house while you were in Florida?" Isabella asked.

"One of our neighbors would come by and check on it every few days. They would walk around the house to make sure no one had broken in."

"What about mail? We get some every day," Kevin said.

"Most of our mail was sent to Florida," Grandpa explained.

Grandma added, "We had someone come in once a month to clean."

"Mom said we could stay in the carriage house this summer," Heather mentioned.

Emmy waved a finger and shook her head. "I said you could if your grandparents agree. You need to ask them first."

"Can we stay, please?" Heather asked using a facial expression she knew would work on them.

"Of course you can, dear," Grandma said.

Emmy rolled her eyes. "I told them they would have to do chores and not be a bother."

"They won't be a bother, Emmy."

"Mom, I really think they should stay with Me-maw and Gra," Kevin said. "It will be a good experience for them. They will learn how to be responsible people."

"Thanks, Kevin," Heather said.

Emmy stared at her son. "You're only saying that because you think you will have the house and pool to yourself."

Heather and Isabella looked at each other.

"Ha!" Emmy exclaimed after seeing the look. "You forgot about the pool, huh? If you're staying here, you won't have a pool to use all the time."

The girls whispered to each other for a moment.

"We would still like to stay here," Heather said and Isabella nodded her agreement.

"It's settled then," Grandma said. "We just have to work out what time is best."

Chapter Thirty

"I'm sorry I haven't come over lately," Emmy said as she poured a cup of coffee for herself and Kristen. "How are things going? Have you talked to John at all?"

Kristen added creamer and sugar to her coffee. "I talked to him for a few minutes the last day of school. He wanted to see the kids before they left for Florida."

"I didn't know they were going to Florida. The kids didn't say anything," Emmy said.

Kevin ran into the kitchen, opened the fridge and grabbed a bottle of water. He saw his mother and Kristen sitting in the breakfast nook and shouted, "Bye, Mom, I'm going to play with Ben. I might not be back for a long time."

"Come back here, young man," Emmy hollered.

He stopped just before reaching the mudroom door and walked back to the table. "What? I was kidding about being gone a long time. Can I go play?"

"Yes, but why didn't you tell me Zach and Grace were in Florida?" Emmy asked.

"I guess I forgot," he answered with a shrug. "Why are they in Florida?"

"Their grandparents are taking them to Disney World and a few other places," Kristen said.

"That sounds like fun. Can I go now?" Kevin asked. "Ben wants to play football."

"Okay, but come home for lunch, please," Emmy said. She waited until Kevin left and asked, "What else is going on?"

"I've been interviewed three times by Glenn Rosenthal."

"Interviewed for what?"

"A job, Emmy. Why else would I be interviewed?" Kristen asked. She looked at Emmy and understood. "Oh, you and Kenny are interviewed quite often."

"Who's Glenn Rosenthal?" Emmy asked and then drained her coffee. "Should I know that name?"

"He runs Liberty Manufacturing now. His father started the company, and Glenn began working there after he graduated from

Roosevelt. He was one of those kids everyone thought wasn't all that bright."

"How old is he?" Emmy asked. "I don't remember the name."

"He's older than us. I think he's a few years older than Christopher, but he had a sister the same age as Derrick."

Emmy looked up at the mention of an old friend. "How is he? Christopher, I mean. Are he and Maddy still in Pittsburgh? I've kinda lost touch with them."

"Christopher manages the Pittsburgh plant."

"I know they have a son, but I think I remember Randy telling me they had another baby."

"They had a daughter. I think she's two now," Kristen said. "Maddy is only working part-time."

"Randy's got four kids."

"I know, Em. We see them at church every week," Kristen said.

"There's a little coffee left."

Kristen put her hand over her cup. "I'm good."

Emmy got up, refilled her cup and then sat down. "What will you be doing if they hire you?"

"The lady who manages their office is retiring at the end of the year. I would be replacing her."

"You would be like Gladys Posey, right?" Emmy asked. "Is she still working, or did she retire when you guys sold the company?"

"The new owners asked her to stay for a few months to help with the transition."

"Good move. She's been running the place from the beginning," Emmy said.

"Not quite, but for close to forty years if I remember correctly. Where are the girls?" Kristen asked.

"Over at Diane's," Emmy replied. "They're helping her with Lily and Conor while Brady and the boys are on vacation."

"Where did they go, and why didn't Diane go with?"

Emmy laughed and said, "Brady decided since his company is going so well he needed a new hobby in addition to

232

photography. He chose to take up fishing. He bought all this gear and took Carson and Caden somewhere in Minnesota. Somehow he convinced Bennett to go along." Emmy laughed and added, "Bennett wouldn't know how to catch a fish even if one jumped into the boat."

Kristen ran a hand through her long hair. "John tried to get me to go fishing in Canada with him and his brothers one year."

"I don't remember that," Emmy said.

"That's because I didn't go. They were staying in this primitive cabin with no water or electricity. Not exactly my idea of a good time. I can't see Caden fishing. He is too sensitive."

"He's becoming more like Carson the older he gets. He's still more sensitive if you want to call it that, but he's certainly not a wimp. He stands up for himself when he needs to."

"I finished reading your latest book. Is the next one written?" Kristen asked.

"Close," Emmy answered. "I revised it for the millionth time last night. I was going to let Kenny and the girls read it before I send it to Denise. The girls can be tougher critics than anyone. They tell me if some parts are boring or unrealistic."

"What did they think of the first one? Did they say anything about what you and Rory did. They do know those characters are you and Rory, right?"

Emmy bit her lip.

Kristen stared at Emmy for a time. "Okay, I will pretend the book is total fiction."

"If you don't spend all your time in the pool or on your phone, I have something you might want to read," Emmy said Tuesday morning from the doorway of the girls' bedroom.

Isabella sat on the edge of her bed and stretched her arms over her head. She looked over her shoulder and saw that Heather was still asleep.

"How late were you up last night?" Emmy asked.

"Later than we should have been. I finished the Jenny M. Russ book and Heather might have finished another Harry Potter. Why? Are we in trouble?" Isabella asked.

233

Emmy shook her head and then smiled.

"Did you finish your next book?" Isabella asked. "Can we read it, or do we have to wait until we're older?"

"You can read it if you want. There's nothing in it that you... never mind. I'll send you the file. I want your opinion before I send it to Denise."

"Don't editors get paid," Isabella said holding out a hand.

"They do, and they also pay for room and board."

After dinner Isabella helped Emmy clear the table and said, "I finished your book, Mommy. I made a few suggestions and sent it back to you. Overall, I would say it's pretty good. You can tell it's written by an older person."

"How can you tell?" Emmy asked.

"Because of the old-fashioned language, but you might sell a few copies."

Emmy stood still with a plate in her hands and stared at Isabella.

"What?" Isabella asked. "You asked for my opinion."

"How long did it take you to read it?"

"Almost three hours. I would have finished it sooner, but I had to clean our room. Kevin said it smelled funny."

"He probably said that to embarrass you. I doubt if it really smelled."

"Heather's side smelled," Isabella said with a grin.

After driving Kenny to the airport Wednesday morning, Emmy got a call from Teresa Joseph.

"I just dropped him off," Emmy said. "I waited until they were in the air, and I'm on my way home. I must have just missed you."

"Paul got a ride from Dave, so I didn't have to take him." She added three drops of lemon oil to her tea, stirred it and took a sip.

"I'm happy the guys are touring. Kenny gets so lost if he can't play in front of people."

"Paul is the same. He could never survive the hours I work."

"I don't think I could either. Twelve hour shifts are too long."

"I have some sad news, Emmy," Teresa said. "Amanda Lenhart called me earlier. Jennifer is back in the hospital."

"Oh, no! Why? What happened? She's been doing so good."

Teresa sighed and said, "The leukemia is back. They took her to Chicago to see that specialist."

"I thought her leukemia was in remission."

"It flared up again. Amanda wanted the wives to know, but she didn't want the guys to hear about it yet. She didn't want to disrupt the tour or anything."

Emmy didn't respond for a moment.

"Are you still there, Emmy?"

Emmy wiped her nose and asked, "Are we not supposed to tell them? They should know. Jennifer is like a daughter to all of them."

"I think maybe Jeremy wanted to wait until the weekend."

"Should I not tell the girls?" Emmy asked. "The girls are pretty close to Jennifer. She's only a few months older."

"I wasn't going to tell the boys until Paul gets home, but you should do what you feel is right."

"Thanks for calling, Teresa. We will be praying for Jennifer and all the Lenharts."

Chapter Thirty-One

Kenny came to a stop in front of the carriage house, looked over his shoulder and said, "All ashore who's going ashore."

Emmy rolled her eyes and whispered, "Such a dork."

"Daddy, you're so funny," Isabella said.

"Arrgh! That's because I'm the captain of this mighty vessel." Kenny opened his door and walked to the back of the van.

Kevin, who had been sitting in the back row, squeezed past Heather, opened the sliding door and jumped out. He ran toward the house shouting, "Yeah! No sisters for a whole month!"

"Kevin Michael! Get back here. You can help your sisters carry their suitcases upstairs," Emmy ordered pointing to the carriage house.

"Do I have to?"

"You have to," Emmy answered.

Kevin kicked at the driveway and pouted.

"Kevin Michael, please do as your mother asks," Kenny said. He opened the back of the van and set the four suitcases on the asphalt driveway.

Kenny's parents stepped onto the back porch and waved.

Emmy waved back. "Are you sure you don't mind them staying for a whole month?"

"We don't mind at all," Mom Colwell answered.

"The service door is unlocked," Mr. Colwell said. "Do you need some help?"

"Thanks, Dad, but we got it. I want to show the girls how to set the alarm and adjust the thermostat. We'll come inside in a few minutes."

Several minutes later everyone sat at the breakfast table.

"I made two pies," Grandma said. "We have cherry and apple."

"Can we have ice cream, too?" Kevin asked.

"It's in the freezer. Will you get it out for me?" Grandma asked.

Kevin returned with vanilla and chocolate ice cream.

"Now, who would like some dessert?"

236

Emmy helped her mother-in-law cut the pie and scoop out the ice cream.

Heather looked at her brother's plate and made a face.

"What's wrong with this?" he asked.

"Yuck. Who likes chocolate ice cream on cherry pie?" Heather asked. "It's gross."

Grandpa Colwell chuckled, pointed at Emmy and said to the kids, "I recall an occasion when your mother was about eight or nine. Your grandmother made a cherry pie, and your mom insisted on having chocolate ice cream on her pie."

"Mom! Wasn't it yucky?" Heather asked.

"I didn't often get to have chocolate ice cream. If my parents bought ice cream at all, Daddy usually insisted it be spumoni."

"Is that the kind with the green ice cream?" Kevin asked.

"It's pistachio," Kenny said. "It usually has chocolate and cherry, too."

"Didn't you get some of the chocolate part of the spumoni?" Isabella asked.

"Daddy would eat the pistachio, Mom would eat the chocolate, and Diane and I would be stuck with the cherry," Emmy explained. "That's why I never buy desserts like Ben & Jerry's Cherry Garcia."

"Emmy, you don't have to do the dishes," Mom Colwell said later. "I can put them in the dishwasher."

"I don't mind," Emmy replied. "How do you really feel about the girls staying here? I think they're too young to sleep in the carriage house."

"Carter and I talked about that. I certainly think Kevin is too young."

"He wants to camp out in the woods with Ben and Caden, but I quashed that idea. They would try to stay up all night, and at the first spooky noise, they would come back inside."

"We could let the girls spend one night out there to see how they like it. You certainly don't need to worry about their safety. All the windows and doors are alarmed, and the place is built like a fortress."

237

"I'm not too concerned about that, but they've never slept on their own not even while we were on tour," Emmy said.

"Let's not worry about it now. They might decide on their own later," Mom Colwell said.

"Kenny, would you tell the girls we're ready to leave?" Emmy asked as he walked into the kitchen.

He rounded up the kids, and everyone went outside.

"Do I get a kiss and a hug before we go?" Kenny asked.

Heather and Isabella kissed and hugged both parents.

"Kevin, you can at least tell your sisters goodbye," Emmy said. "You might not see them for a long time."

He grinned at his sisters and said, "I'm gonna sneak into your room and read your diaries while you're gone."

"No chance of that," Heather said. "We brought them with us. We're not stupid like you and your friends."

"Heather! We don't call people by that name," Emmy said. "Kevin will not disturb your room, right, Kevin?" She stared at him. "Right?"

"Fine, I won't go in their room, but I bet they get scared and sleep in the house," he replied as he walked slowly back to the van.

"We are not going to get scared," Heather insisted.

"There's a ghost living in the carriage house," Kevin said.

Isabella looked at her father. "Is there?"

He shook his head. "No, Isa, there's no such things as ghosts."

Kevin grinned at Isabella, raised his arms and said, "Woooo. I'm going to haunt you."

"You are such a creep," Heather said. "We aren't afraid of ghosts."

"Kevin Michael, get in the van," Emmy insisted. She hugged the girls. "You don't have to sleep out here, and your brother never needs to know if you don't."

"We will be fine, Mom," Heather said.

"Isa, what was that?" Heather asked shortly after midnight. "Did you hear that noise?" Heather shook her sister hard enough to wake her up. "Isa! Listen to that. What is it?"

Isabella turned onto her back, looked around the room and listened for a time. "It sounds like something walking across the roof."

"You mean like an animal or something?" Heather asked.

The exposed wooden beams creaked as the strong wind whistled through the trees. The girls heard a thud as something landed on the roof.

"What was that?" Heather screamed. She scooted as close to her sister as possible.

"It was probably just a squirrel running across the roof," Isabella said.

"That sounded more like a wolf. Squirrels aren't that big."

They stared at the exposed rafters for a minute, but the noise didn't return.

"Maybe you should turn on the bathroom light," Isabella suggested.

"I'm not getting out of bed. You do it," Heather replied.

"We can both do it."

"Okay," Heather said.

They held hands, got out of bed, scurried across the bedroom to the bathroom and flipped on the switch. They dashed back to the bed and borrowed deep under the covers. Isabella wrapped her arms around her sister.

"Are you scared, Heather? You're shaking."

"A little. Are you?"

"Not as much with the light on," Isabella said. She poked her head out from under the comforter.

"Should we wake up Grandma and Grandpa?" Heather asked.

Isabella thought about it. "No, I don't hear it anymore. I think it was the wind. Maybe a tree branch broke off."

"We can't ever tell Mom or Kevin that we got scared," Heather said.

"Can we tell Daddy?"

"Maybe, but he would have to swear to keep it a secret for life."

"Carter, maybe you should check on the girls. It's after nine and Emmy said we shouldn't let them stay in bed all day."

He set down his paper, took another sip of coffee and said, "Elly, I think Emmy meant not to let them sleep past noon. Don't you remember how late Kenny would sleep at times?"

"If you won't do it, I will."

"Okay, let me finish my coffee then I'll check on them." He held up a finger. "On the other hand, they might already be up and are getting dressed. They wouldn't want me..."

"Is anyone up?" Isabella asked as she and Heather walked into the kitchen. "We're ready to help with chores."

"I was just going to check on you," Grandpa said.

"What would you like for breakfast?" Me-maw asked.

"Mom told us not to request anything special. We're supposed to eat whatever you make," Isabella said.

"Good! I just had some grits and bacon grease."

"Did you really, Gra?" Heather asked.

"He's pulling your leg, sweetie. I can make eggs or pancakes or... "

"Pancakes!" the girls hollered.

As they ate their pancakes, Isabella said, "Gra, we heard some noises on the roof last night. It sounded like something walking around."

"And the rafters made noises, too," Heather added.

Grandpa and Grandma smiled at each other.

"I will check, but I think one of the tree limbs might be too close to the roof."

Heather and Isabella looked at each other.

"I told you it was a tree," Heather whispered.

"No you didn't," Isabella whispered back. "You thought it was a wild animal."

"I have an idea," Me-maw said.

The girls stopped whispering and looked at her.

Me-maw removed her white apron and said, "You could play in the carriage house during the day and sleep in the house at night. That way none of us would be scared."

The twins looked at each other and nodded.

240

"We could sleep in the house if you need us to," Heather said. "We don't want you to worry about us."

"That's a great idea," Gra said. "You can share a room, or each of you could have your own."

"Gra, is it true Mom had her own room to sleep in if she spent the night here?" Heather asked. "When she was a kid, I mean."

"Why did she sleep here if she lived just down the street?" Isabella asked.

"There were times she would stay overnight. I don't remember how many times, or the exact reasons," Gra replied.

Me-maw added, "She would sleep in the guest bedroom across the hall from your father's room."

"Did they ever sleep in the attic room?" Heather asked.

Kenny's parents looked at each other for a moment.

"I don't remember them ever sleeping up there," Me-maw said. "It would be too cold in the winter and too hot and humid in the summer."

After lunch the next day Me-maw gave the girls five dollars.

"What is this for?" Isabella asked.

"That's for helping me clean and dust the bedrooms. I hate vacuuming."

"Mom said we're supposed to help you." Isabella tried to and the money back. "We're not supposed to get paid."

"Then consider this money for a treat. You did mention ice cream, and the Robbins ice cream stand is open now if you would like some."

Heather grabbed the money. "In that case, we'll take it. Come on, Isa, we can go for a walk and get some ice cream."

"Please stay in Raynor Park," Me-maw said.

"We won't go too far," Heather replied.

The girls walked out the front door and turned right at the sidewalk.

Heather looked at the houses across the street and said, "Other than Gra and Me-maw's house, they are so small."

241

They walked a bit farther, paused in front of 16301 East Fifth Street and stared at the small home.

"Are you sure this is it?" Heather asked.

"It's the right number," Isabella said.

"It looks so small now. Was it always such a tiny house?" Heather asked.

"It looked bigger when we were kids," Isabella said. "Mom said we were only a few months old when Grandma and Grandpa moved to a new place."

"But we've walked past here before. Why does it look so different now?"

Isabella shrugged and they kept walking.

"Didn't Uncle Rory live on this street somewhere?" Heather asked.

"Yeah, but I'm not sure which house. All I know it that it had two stories. I don't see any big house," Isabella said as they kept going.

"How did Mom and Daddy live in such a crowded neighborhood? The house are so close together," Heather said. She pointed to a house in obvious need of repair. "That one has two stories. Maybe that's where the Porters lived."

"It needs to be painted a different color. That green is ugly, and the front steps look ready to collapse," Isabella added.

They bought cones with two scoops of ice cream and headed home.

"Let's go by the grade school," Isabella suggested.

"Do you remember where it is?" Heather asked.

"It's by the park. We've been there before."

A few minutes later they walked through the park, admired the new equipment and stood in front of Robert T. Colwell Elementary School.

"It's certainly not as nice as our school," Heather said.

"It's a lot older, Heather. You do realize it's named for Daddy's grandfather, right?"

"I'm not stupid, Isa. He's in one of the pictures on the stairway at Me-maw's house."

242

"I will pick you up after church," Emmy told Heather. "Are you sure you're ready to come home? It's only the first day of July. You did plan to stay a whole month."

"Mom, I can tell you're teasing me. Don't you want us to come home? Didn't you miss us?" Heather asked.

"Of course I missed you, and don't say anything, but I think Kevin missed you, too."

"He better not have been in our room," Heather said.

"I don't think he has. He and your father went to a baseball game with Tony and Ben instead of going to church today."

"Me-maw made us go to their old church again. There aren't many kids who go there, and none that we know."

"I'm glad you went, sweetie. I'll see you soon."

"Did they help with chores, Dad?" Emmy asked later.

Grandpa Colwell chuckled and answered, "Isabella helped without complaining, but Heather would put up a fuss."

"She's like that at home, too."

On the way home Emmy asked, "How did you like sleeping in the carriage house?"

The girls looked at each other without answering.

Emmy stopped at a red light and turned to look at the girls. "Aren't you going to tell me?"

Isabella sighed and said, "We only slept out there three nights, and each time the noises kept us awake all night."

"That's all right. I used to get scared when I slept out there, too."

"Didn't Daddy keep you from being scared?" Isabella asked.

"There were times he wasn't with me," Emmy said accelerating through the intersection.

"Why not?" Heather asked. "Was he on tour all the time?"

"Not always, but... never mind. You'll have to read about it in one of the Claire and Ruby books."

Chapter Thirty-Two

"Do I have to go to your show, or can I spend the night with Ben?" Kevin asked the morning of the Fourth of July.

Emmy looked at Kenny, who was sitting in the breakfast nook drinking coffee. "Ask your father."

Kevin repeated his request to his father.

"Don't you want to see the fireworks?" Kenny asked.

"Not really. Fireworks are boring. Ian has some bottle rockets and a few firecrackers, but I'd rather play with Ben."

"It's all right with me if it's all right with your mother."

"She said to ask you," Kevin said with exasperation. "Mom! Dad won't decide."

"The girls are going with me," Emmy said.

"That's because they get to sing one of your songs." Kevin shuffled his weight back and forth as he inspected the four bananas in a basket on the island. "I'll be so bored."

"Okay, if Sloane says it's all right, you can stay with Ben."

"She said it was all right. You can text her if you want."

"I will," Emmy said. She texted Tony and he replied right away. "Okay, you can stay with Ben tonight, but you need to take a shower before you go to bed."

"I will," Kevin promised.

Emmy walked over and stood behind Kenny. She ran her hands through his hair. "You need a haircut."

"I meant to go yesterday, but I got busy."

"I know you guys usually have a large crowd for your Fourth of July shows, but how have the other shows been going. Are you still selling a few tickets?"

He turned around, grabbed her around the waist and pulled her onto his lap. "FYI, we have been selling plenty of tickets. I do believe we've even sold out a few venues."

"Oh, I didn't realize you guys were playing at corner bars."

"Ha! Ha! You are such a laugh riot."

She put her arms around him and said, "Actually, the only reason the stadium will be full tonight is because of one of the opening acts."

"You are referring to Hucky Eichelmann, right?"

"Who?" she asked while squirming to get up.

He held on tight and said, "Don't you remember the guy who opened for the Lonesome Cowboy Band?"

"Vaguely, is he on the bill?"

"No, I think he passed away. We're stuck with some other local singer and her band of amateurs."

She jumped up and said, "My guys are not amateurs. They are some of the best musicians in the country."

"Which country? Albania?"

"Is that a real country?" she asked.

"Use to be. I think it still is. Are we riding together?"

"We can if you want. I need to be there by three if I want to do a soundcheck. The first band goes on at four thirty."

He chuckled and said, "We've done so many of these shows at the stadium we could skip the soundchecks. Will and the sound guys have all the settings saved on flash drives. I love the new digital boards."

"You used to say you thought they didn't sound as good as the old analog mixers."

"They've made a lot of improvements to them over the years," he said.

Emmy texted Barry Newton after lunch, and he replied an hour later.

"Is he coming?" Kenny asked while Emmy was taking a shower.

She wrapped a towel around her and picked out some clothes. "He and Fender are coming. I texted Nelson and told him to make sure to add their names to the list and give them backstage passes."

Do you remember the last time you saw Barry?" Kenny asked.

"Not really, and will you quit staring at me. I need to get ready and make sure the girls are getting cleaned up."

"But I like staring at you, m'lady."

"Such a dork. I bet I haven't seen Fender or even Barry since the 2015 show," Emmy said.

After a quick soundcheck, Emmy and the girls wandered around backstage while Kenny and the other guys did a few interviews.

Heather tapped her mother's shoulder and said, "Mom, there's a guy over there waving at us."

Emmy turned around and saw Barry Newton approaching.

"Emmy, you may not remember me, but my name is Barry."

"Oh, Barry, you don't have to be such a nerd. How could I ever forget you and believe me I've tried." She looked up at the tall young man beside him and offered a hand. "Fender, you're taller than your father now. Of course, he's a shrimp."

Fender shook Emmy's hand and smiled at Heather and Isabella.

"He goes by Isaac now," Barry said.

"Really? Isaac Newton, huh? Now where have I heard that name before?"

Barry waved a hand. "Yes, I know that's not much better than Fender, and he gets teased at times."

Emmy grinned and said, "He could always go by Fig."

"You were the only one who called him that," Barry said.

"Kristen called him Fig a few times, too," Emmy replied.

Barry smiled at the twins. "I can't believe how grownup and pretty you have become. You look so much like your mother."

"Barry, did you just compliment me?" Emmy asked.

"If I did, it was purely unintentional," he said.

Heather and Isabella smiled at Isaac, and he asked where they went to school. The girls answered and pulled him a few feet away to talk more privately.

"You are still living in Mama's old house, right?" Emmy asked as she and Barry caught up on family news for a moment.

He nodded. "I don't ever plan to move. It's still a great house, and we've kept it updated. Last year I did the upstairs hall bath."

"By yourself?" Emmy asked.

"I do know how to fix more than computers," Barry said.

"How long have you lived there now?"

"Since the beginning of December 2010."

"It doesn't seem like that long, but in another way it seems like Mama has been living at Tony and Sloane's house forever."

"Did I mention Linda is working at the new hospital?"

"No, you didn't. She's working at Mercy, huh?"

"For a couple of years now, and I'm still at Sennco."

"I knew that. I heard you're one of the big shots now."

"I actually have my own office and a secretary. Can you believe it?"

"It's been the perfect job for you. Please tell Linda and the girls I said hi."

"I will. I do have some photos of Hattie and Zooey."

Emmy looked at the photos on his cell phone.

"Did you see where the girls and Isaac went?" she asked. She looked around and spotted them standing a few feet away from an older couple. *Ah! I see Rosco and Teresa are here. That must mean Mr. Robertson and Mona are in the crowd somewhere.*

"They're over there, Emmy," Barry said. "They seem to be getting along all right."

"Yes, I do believe you're right," Emmy said. "I should head inside. It's been good to see you, Barry. We should invite you over sometime."

"You have my number," he said.

Heather and Isabella waved goodbye to Isaac as he and Barry left the area.

"Mom, why didn't you tell us Isaac was so hot?" Heather asked when they walked into the green room.

"Oh, there you are," Bobby O'Connor said to Emmy and the girls. "I was afraid you would get lost."

"Bobby, do you know Barry?" Heather asked.

"I do," he answered.

"Do you know Isaac?"

"I met him a few years ago. Why?"

"Heather thinks he's hot," Isabella teased.

Heather poked Isabella in the side. "You said the same thing, Isa."

"Isaac Newton is way too old for you," Emmy said.

Bobby nodded. "I totally agree with your mother. I think he was born in the 1600s and got bonked on the head by an apple."

"Not that Isaac Newton," Heather said and then giggled.

"Both Isaac Newtons are too old for you and Isabella," Emmy said. "He's already fifteen, and you're only twelve."

Bobby tapped his jaw for a moment before saying, "Em, if I do my math correctly, that would be three years."

"Yeah, so what? What is your point?" Emmy asked.

"How much older is Kenny than you? Is it about three and a half years?" Bobby asked.

"That's beside the point. Things were a lot different when we were kids."

"How were things different, Mommy?" Isabella asked with a straight face.

"Yes, Emmy, please explain the differences in today's culture versus twenty years ago," Bobby said smugly.

"I am your mother. I don't have to explain anything." She pointed at the girls and then smacked Bobby's arm. "You might have a daughter one of these days, and you will want to keep her away from boys, too."

"Yeah, I'm not buying it, Em. I think the girls should be allowed to date older boys... "

"I'm gonna set fire to your drums if you ever repeat that."

Later, Heather and Isabella waited at the side of the stage.

"Can you see him, Isa?" Heather asked.

Isabella peered around the backdrop at the crowd. "I think that might be him about twenty rows back near the middle."

"Let me see," Heather said. She moved past Isabella and stared at the audience, but then she quickly ducked behind the backdrop. "He saw me and waved."

They giggled and peeked again while waiting for Emmy to introduce them. They walked onstage, sang one song, waved to the crowd and raced back to the side of the stage.

"Was he watching us, Isa?" Heather asked.

"He was and I think he whistled."

248

Chapter Thirty-Three

"Em, you need to wake up." He touched her hip and she woke up with a start. "I have some bad news."

"What is it? Is everything all right?" she asked turning onto her back.

"Jeremy called me earlier, Em. It's over," he whispered.

She bit her lip and didn't try to stop the tears from flowing. She turned and placed her head on his chest. He held her for several minutes, and then she moved onto her back again. He grabbed some tissues from the nightstand and wiped her face. She took one and blew her nose, then handed it back to him.

"I told him to just ask if he needed anything. He asked if we could sing something for the funeral."

"What did you tell him?" Emmy asked.

"I told him we would. Whatever songs he chose, and he mentioned a couple."

"We have to tell the girls, don't we?" she asked.

He nodded. "We told them this would probably happen, but that won't make it any easier." He ran a hand through Emmy's hair. "Should we wait until the girls are up, or should we wake them up now?"

"Let's wait until we hear them. They've never had anyone close to their age die before. It will be difficult for them to comprehend. It might take them a while to process everything."

"They might try to hide their feelings from us, Em. They might decide to act like it doesn't bother them."

"A couple days ago Isa asked me why God would let Jennifer get sick."

"What did you tell her, Em?"

Emmy took a deep breath and covered her forehead with her arm. "I can't remember my exact words, but it was something along the lines of what Pastor Tyler said when he did the funeral for that girl who was killed in that motorcycle crash."

"Her family seemed so desperate for some comforting words from Tyler. It's so hard to accept the death of a young person."

Shortly after nine Emmy and Kenny knocked on the girls' bedroom door and pushed it open. They sat on the edge of Heather's bed and Isabella joined them.

"You've been crying, Mommy," Isabella said. "I can tell. Does your head hurt?"

"Did something bad happen?" Heather asked. "Something bad to Jennifer? We know she's been really sick. We haven't been able to text her for a week or more."

Emmy looked at Kenny.

He understood she didn't want to be the messenger. He closed his eyes for a moment and then said, "She lost her battle early this morning. Her mother and father and her brother, Joshua, were with her."

Isabella put her arms around her mother, and Heather moved onto her father's lap.

"It's okay if you want to cry," Emmy whispered. "We know you liked her a lot."

Kenny pulled out his handkerchief expecting to need it to wipe away tears.

"Mom, do you think Jennifer is in heaven?" Isabella asked softly but without tears.

Emmy said, "I hope so. We aren't the judges. There's no way to answer that question."

"The only thing I can say is that a person must accept Jesus and have faith in him," Kenny added.

"When Jennifer wasn't sick, I asked her if she ever went to church. She wanted to go to church more, but her parents didn't go very often, mostly Christmas and Easter," Isabella said.

"Jeremy and Amanda used to go to church in the early days of the band," Kenny said. "All the guys did."

"I think she's in heaven. She said she believed in Jesus," Heather said and then allowed the tears to fall.

"Deborah Persching told us Jennifer was in a coma like Mommy was," Isabella said. "She and Jennifer were best friends for a while," Isabella said.

"Hey! What's going on? I was trying to sleep," Kevin said from the doorway. "Why are you all crying?"

250

Kenny looked at him and whispered, "Jennifer Lenhart passed away this morning."

"No!" Kevin screamed. "She can't die. She's too young. You're lying to me. Jesus won't let her die." He dashed into the hall, raced to his room and slammed the door behind him.

Emmy and Kenny heard him sobbing, looked at each other and then the girls.

"I never expected that," Emmy said.

Isabella got up and stood in front of her parents. "A few days ago we found him on the computer looking for information about leukemia. He closed his laptop when he saw me and pretended to be watching his bug videos."

"He didn't know her all that well," Emmy said. "Why would he react so intensely?"

"I better go find out," Kenny said.

"I will stay with the girls while you talk to him. Oh, does Father James know?" Emmy asked.

Kenny nodded. "I called him before I woke you up. He said he would head over to St. Bart's."

"Do you want me to talk to Kevin with you?" Isabella asked.

Kenny waited for a second, but then shook his head. "I will do it by myself."

He entered his son's room and found Kevin on the floor in the corner with his knees drawn to his chest and rocking back and forth. Kenny sat on the floor beside him and Kevin moved into his father's arms. Kenny held him close and rubbed his back until the sobs subsided.

"How can Jesus let her die? He can make her well like He did in the Bible."

Kenny closed his eyes and prayed for wisdom.

"Didn't He love Jennifer or that boy at church who had cancer?"

Kenny suddenly realized Kevin was not crying just because of Jennifer and whispered, "You were friends with Lonan Binns, weren't you? I had forgotten he was in your Sunday School class. I'm sorry."

"Why do some kids get sick and die and others get well?" Kevin asked. "It's not fair."

"I wish I knew, buddy."

"Pastor Tyler said that Lonan knew Jesus at his funeral. Did Jennifer know Him?"

"I'm not sure," Kenny answered. "Her parents used to go to church. Maybe this has brought them back to a relationship with God."

"Did Heather and Isa hear me crying?" he asked wiping his nose on his pajamas.

"They were crying, too."

"Yeah, but they're girls."

Kenny squeezed his son and whispered, "Can I tell you a secret?"

Kevin nodded.

"There are times that men are allowed to cry. I've seen Andy Walker and Tony and even Mr. Robertson cry."

"For real?"

"Yes," Kenny thought about a time when he saw Jennifer walk up to Andy and get on his case. He closed his eyes and recalled the scene. "I remember when Jennifer was about seven, I think. We were on tour and it was the last show with her father as part of the band. Anyway, she walked up to Andy, put her hands on her hips, frowned and said, "'Mr. Walker! You might try to sound mean, but I know better. You are a big teddy bear. You always send me a card and a present for my birthday. I'm not afraid of you.'" Kenny paused for a moment. "Andy tried to scowl and look intimidating, but it didn't work on Jennifer. She was a very bright child. After a few seconds he reached down and lifted her off of her feet. He hugged her close and whispered. "'You are a very brave princess, and I love you so much.'" Then he set her down and glanced away so no one could see the tears filling his eyes, but I saw them. This was back when no one outside of the band knew Jennifer had leukemia."

"When did you see Uncle Tony cry?" Kevin asked.

Kenny whispered, "You shouldn't tell her, but the last time I saw him cry was when your mother had that accident."

"He did?"

"Yes, and I've seen him cry when one of his kids would be sick or get hurt. You shouldn't tell anyone, but your uncle Tony can get emotional like a girl at times."

Kevin grinned and said, "I'm going to tell Ben sometime. Have you really seen Grandpa Robertson cry?"

"I've only actually witnessed it myself on a couple of occasions, but the story is that he cried when Lily and Conor were born."

"I won't ever tell anyone," Kevin said solemnly.

Kenny thought about a story and decided to tell Kevin. "When your mother was a baby, she got sick and had to be in the hospital for two weeks."

"What was wrong with her?"

"It was something to do with her heart. Anyway, Mr. Robertson was a very good friend of her grandfather, and he and Lily used to take care of your mother."

"Little Lily?" Kevin asked.

Kenny shook his head. "No, Mr. Robertson's first wife was named Lily. She was Brady and Bennett's mother."

"Oh, I remember now. Mommy told me how she died from cancer a long time ago before any of us kids were born."

"Yes, anyway, when your mother was sick, her grandpa Colasanti and Mr. Robertson would stay at the hospital all night long. That way your grandpa and grandma could go home and get some sleep."

"Does Mommy know he did that?" Kevin asked.

"She didn't know about it for years, but she does now."

"So, you're telling me it's okay for big strong men like me and Ben to cry sometimes, right?"

"I guess I am."

Kevin stood up and said, "Then it's okay if Heather and Isa know I was crying."

"Stephanie, we have decided to cancel all three shows next week and make them up later," Andy said over the phone. "Could you draw up the press release for me. I need to contact the promoters and rework the contracts."

"Do you think any of them will give you a problem?" she asked.

Andy laughed and said, "Not if they ever want to book another Fridays At Five show."

"I will get on it right away," she replied.

Stephanie Grachan thought of her four young sons and tried to imagine how she would feel if one of them ever passed away. She gathered her staff in one of the Fridays At Five offices in the Walker Management building and went to work. She emailed the release to Andy an hour later.

"I don't think you need to make any changes," Andy said. "I guess this is why we pay you the big bucks. I would never be able to write about Jennifer the way you did."

"Thank you. Should I call the florist and send flowers to the family?" she asked.

"That's not part of your job, but I would appreciate it if you handled that."

"Consider it done," she said.

Kenny continued to stare out the windows of Andy's office.

"That's done," Andy said. "Have you talked to Jeremy yet?"

"I haven't. I can't decide if I should call him, or go to the house. I'm sure they have plenty of stuff to do, and their families are already there."

"I could go with you if you want to stop by the house later. I have to make a few calls before I can get out of here."

"I know Emmy and the other wives were going to stop by the house this morning," Kenny said.

Kenny waited two hours. Then he and Andy drove to the Lenhart residence.

Joshua Lenhart answered the door and waved them inside. "Come on in. Mom and Dad are out back. You just missed Emmy and Mrs. Joseph. Mrs. Rawlings might still be here somewhere, but I know Mrs. Persching left earlier."

Kenny listened to Joshua rambling about family rather without emotion.

254

They followed Joshua outside, walked up to Jeremy and offered some words of consolation.

"I know that doesn't help, but I don't know what else to say," Kenny whispered.

"There's nothing anyone can say right now." Jeremy choked back a sob. "I'm grateful she lived long enough to become a teenager. That was important to her."

Soon the other members of Fridays At Five and some of the key members of the organization arrived to offer condolences. They whispered among themselves and stayed longer than they expected.

"I can't imagine what they're going through," Jeff Rawlings said on the way back to the cars. "She was doing so good, and then she's gone."

"How did your kids react?" Kenny asked.

"Frances told them after breakfast, and they didn't show much emotion," Jeff said.

Kenny listened as the other guys talked about their kids' reactions. He commented to Andy when they were back in the car, "I guess my kids were the only ones who cried a lot."

Andy started his 2019 Acura RDX and they drove away. "I caught that, too."

Kenny stared out the window for a moment and then said, "I guess we aren't as close as when we started the band."

"It happens. You have lives and they don't always intersect. It doesn't mean you guys aren't still friends."

"I suppose you're right."

"Kenny, are you awake?" Emmy asked Sunday morning while running a finger through his hair.

"I'm awake, Em. How are you? Did you sleep okay?"

"It took a while to get to sleep. You?"

"I woke up around five and couldn't get back to sleep."

She turned on her side and scooted closer. "What were you thinking about?"

"The songs Jeremy and Amanda want us to sing," he answered.

"You never told me what they requested. It can't be 'Yolanda's Song', can it?"

"No, no. They asked if we could sing 'I Will Be True To You' and 'Sweet Girl.'"

Emmy thought about the lyrics for a moment. "I can see how they would ask for 'I Will Be True' but 'Sweet Girl'? It doesn't really fit."

"That's why I was thinking about it. I think we could write some new lyrics for the second verse. We could make it about Jennifer."

"Do you have anything in mind?"

He got out of bed and picked up a notebook from the nightstand. "I wrote some thoughts down." He read them to her and looked for her reaction.

"Not bad, but I think we can do better. Maybe we can work on the lyrics after church," she suggested.

"What time should we get to the funeral home?" Jeff asked Tuesday morning. "Frances suggested we get there early and leave so we don't create a distraction."

"I was thinking the same thing," Dave said. "We aren't bringing the kids, are we?"

"We weren't planning to bring the boys to the wake," Jeff said. "Have you talked to Kenny or Adam or P.J.?"

"Just P.J. He agreed with getting there early."

"I'll call Kenny and Adam and tell them what we're thinking and get back to you."

"Sounds like a plan. Macy did say Danny and Deborah were interested in going. They knew Jennifer better than the younger kids."

Calls were made and the members of Fridays At Five met at the Linton-Sullivan Funeral Home shortly after one o'clock.

Isabella and Heather held Emmy's hands, and Kevin walked beside his father.

"Aren't any of the other kids coming?" Kevin asked. "The only ones I see are them." He pointed to Danny and Deborah Persching.

"They might be here tomorrow," Kenny said. "We aren't going to stay long today. We just need to talk to Jennifer's parents for a few minutes."

The funeral directors ushered the group into the room and closed the door.

Each of the men shook hands with Jeremy while the wives talked with Amanda. Joshua stayed close to the casket shifting his weight from one foot to the other while wringing his hands and trying to stretch out the collar of his white dress shirt. He glanced often at his sister.

"Kevin, maybe you should say something to Joshua," Kenny suggested.

"Like what?" Kevin asked.

"You are smart. I'm sure you will think of something."

Kevin took a deep breath and walked slowly toward Joshua. "I don't know if you remember me or not. I'm Kevin Colwell. I'm sorry that Jennifer got sick again."

Joshua nodded and looked at his sister.

Kevin looked at Jennifer for a moment. He turned to Joshua and whispered, "I always thought she was so pretty, and she always treated me better than my sisters."

"She was always nice to everyone. I'm going to miss her a lot," Joshua admitted.

Kevin looked at his sisters, who were standing behind their mother. "Don't tell them, but I would miss them if something ever happened. How old are you?"

"I'll be sixteen in August. You?"

"I'm ten."

They talked about school and where they lived for a moment.

"My mom almost died in a car crash. Did you know that?" Kevin asked.

"Yeah, my father told me. That was a bad scene. Dad was pretty shook up when he heard about her accident. He used to play in Fridays At Five until Jennifer got sick the first time. He sometimes plays in your mother's band. I'm not sure what he will do now."

Kevin saw Danny and Deborah Persching talking to each other at the back of the room. He looked at Joshua and asked, "Do you know them very much? I know who they are, but they don't talk to me or my sisters much."

"They don't talk to me either. Deborah and Jennifer used to be friends, but something happened. Jennifer never told me what."

"What about Danny?"

Joshua shrugged. "We're not exactly friends. It's like other families where the father's work together. I really haven't seen any of those kids much since the divorce."

"I asked Mom why they got divorced, but she wouldn't tell me anything."

"I don't know why either. Jennifer thought maybe Mr. Persching had a girlfriend, but who knows?"

"Mom and Dad are supposed to sing tomorrow. I heard them practicing yesterday."

Joshua nodded, glanced at his sister and almost smiled. "She always said 'Sweet Girl' was her favorite song of all time. She used to drive me nuts because she would sing it all the time."

"They're going to sing that one. Dad said he wrote it a real long time ago and it's about Mom. I'll tell them Jennifer liked it." Kevin saw his father motioning to him. He turned to Joshua. "I guess I'll see you tomorrow. I'm really sorry about your sister." He waited for a few seconds and then hugged Joshua.

On the way home Emmy asked Kevin what he and Joshua were talking about.

"All kinds of stuff. He's pretty cool even though his sister just died. He told me that song was her favorite."

"Which one?" Emmy asked.

"Sweet Girl."

"Really?" Kenny asked.

"Yeah. He said she used to drive him crazy because she always sang it."

As they got ready for bed, Emmy asked, "What did you think about 'Sweet Girl' being her favorite song?"

"I've always liked that song," he said with a grin. "It's about one of my favorite girls."

258

"One of them, huh?" Emmy teased as she put her arms around his waist.

"Maybe one in particular."

"I was thinking about the new lyrics," Emmy said.

"Don't you like them?"

"I do, but I was thinking maybe we should sing it the original way since Joshua said it was her favorite song. How do you feel about that?"

"It never mentions you by name, Em. I suppose we could sing it the original way. I've never thought of it as a duet though."

"Me either, but I'm just adding harmony. I'm not singing lead at all."

"Let's pray about it, and God will tell us what to do."

"Thank you for singing," Jeremy said after the service the next day. He shook hands with Kenny and hugged Emmy.

Emmy whispered, "We weren't sure why you requested 'Sweet Girl,' but then Joshua told Kevin it was Jennifer's favorite song."

"She used to sing it all the time. It would drive Joshua up a wall, but he's going to miss hearing it now."

"Before we knew... the reason... Emmy and I wrote some new verses that made it more about Jennifer. We were going to sing them until this morning. Emmy felt the Holy Spirit telling her we needed to sing the original for Jennifer." Kenny reached into his pocket and pulled out a single piece of paper. "We thought you and Amanda might want to read the new lyrics sometime." He handed the handwritten lyrics to Jeremy.

Jeremy took out his reading glasses and read the lyrics. "Thank you, guys," he said softly as his voice cracked. "This means a lot." He held out his arms for a hug.

Kenny and Emmy obeyed.

Chapter Thirty-Four

"Some of you may have heard about the recent loss in the Fridays At Five family," Kenny said to the crowd in Boston a week after the funeral. He peered into the audience and could see some cell phones light up. "We usually sing this song much later in the show, but tonight we're not going to do it as an encore or as a song to get everyone dancing and waving your hands." He paused for a moment. "Some of you might know I wrote this for Emmy when she was about fourteen or so. Emmy's my wife in case you don't know. Anyway, tonight we want to dedicate this song to our former keyboard player and friend. Jeremy Lenhart was one of the original guys in the band. He was in the band before I was. He and Jeff and Dave knew each other and were looking for another musician to join the band." Kenny pointed to the guys and said, "Unfortunately, they found me."

Jeff shook his head and grinned at Dave.

"This was one of the first songs I ever wrote that they considered good enough to make the set list. We recorded it for the *Transition* album and have played it at every show since them. Well, maybe not every show. Tonight we want to do 'Sweet Girl' and dedicate it to Jeremy in memory of Jennifer."

Dave softly counted off the song as Kenny turned his back to the crowd and fought back tears.

"I thought you were gonna lose it," Jeff said after the show. He put an arm around Kenny's shoulders and squeezed them. "Everyone would have understood if you had."

"I couldn't let Jeremy or Jennifer down," Kenny said.

Frankie Hanna approached with Kenny's cell phone and handed it to him. "It's Emmy," Frankie said and walked away.

"Hi, Em. Everything okay?"

"We're okay. I just wanted to see how you did. I know you were doing 'Sweet Girl' for Jennifer."

Kenny walked into his dressing room and closed the door. "It was rough. I talked for a minute about Jeremy and Jennifer, but I had to turn around when Dave started the song. I asked God for strength to do the song without breaking down."

"I wouldn't have been able to do it," Emmy said. "I still struggle when I sing 'Yolanda's Song.'"

"Does it get easier?"

"It will after a while. You have to give it time."

"Kiss the kids for me, and I'll be back Saturday," he said.

"Have I told you lately how much I love you?"

"Maybe."

"I love you, m'lord."

Kenny ended the call and sat down. He placed a towel over his head and wept.

"Daddy! You're home!" Kevin shouted when he saw Andy Walker park in front of the garage. He ran up to the SUV and waited for his father to open the door. "How was your trip?"

Kenny set his briefcase on the ground, opened his arms, lifted his son up and hugged him. "It was a good trip, but I'm glad to be home. Did you miss me?"

Kevin grinned and said, "Oh, were you gone?"

Kenny set him down and ruffled his hair. "Your mother sets a bad example for you." He saw Emmy and the girls approaching from the back of the house.

"Daddy! We were swimming. Do you want to swim with us?" Heather asked.

He picked up both girls even though they were soaking wet. "Can I talk to your mother first?"

"Okay, but if she tells you I yelled at Kevin it was because he deserved it."

He set the girls down, smiled at Emmy and surprised everyone by picking her up like a baby and kissing her. "Did you miss me?" he asked while looking at her bikini.

She looked at the girls, and they giggled.

"I might have missed you a little," she said and then smiled.

"Did anyone miss me?" Andy asked.

"We missed you, Uncle Andy," Isabella said. "You should change clothes and go swimming with us."

Andy wiped his forehead. "I might just take you up on that.

261

It has to be close to a hundred in the shade."

"You should go home and put on your trunks and come back," Kevin said. "We're going to make hot dogs on the grill for dinner. I asked Mom to make baked beans, too."

"I should see if I have any steaks at the house," Andy said. "I'm not eating hot dogs."

Kenny set Emmy on the ground and kissed her.

"We're going to make burgers and I do have four steaks," Emmy said.

"You've talked me into coming back. Should I bring anything other than some tasty beverages?" he asked.

"Father James stocked the fridge in the garage, so you don't need to bring anything," Emmy said. "He's coming over later."

Andy closed the tailgate and asked, "What time are you planning to eat?"

"Around five, but you can come over anytime and use the pool."

"That was a fine piece of meat," Father James said later while rubbing his stomach. "You grilled it to perfection, Andy."

"Thank you." Andy drained his beer and leaned back in his deck chair.

"The hot dogs were great," Kevin said. "You burned them just the way I like them."

"There are some baked beans left," Emmy said. "Do you want to finish them?"

Kevin shook his head. "I'm too full. Can I eat them later?"

"Okay," Emmy said. "I need help clearing the picnic table."

The kids pitched in to help while the men sat at one of the round deck tables. Emmy joined them a few minutes later. The kids came back outside just as Dany and Darian appeared pushing a baby carriage.

Kenny spotted them first, stood up, waved and said, "Come and join us. We just finished eating dinner. Are you hungry or thirsty?"

"We're good," Darian said.

The twins sprinted across the deck, down the stairs and slid to a stop beside the carriage.

262

"He's sleeping now, but you can watch him," Dany said.

"Can we push him around?" Heather asked.

Dany looked up at Darian.

"It's okay as long as your mother agrees," Darian answered.

The girls looked at Emmy, who had joined them.

"It's okay with me, but you have to go slow. Stay on the driveway and take turns."

The girls departed with Patrick Cullen sleeping in his baby buggy.

"Come up to the deck," Emmy said. "Are you sure you wouldn't like something to drink?"

They declined and followed Emmy back to the table.

"How was your trip to Maine? Where exactly do you go?" Emmy asked.

"The closest town is Belfast Springs, but the cabins are on Pierce Lake. It's a few miles out of town," Dany explained. "Two of Mom's aunts live in Maine, and the family owns four cabins."

"How did Patrick do with all his cousins?"

"He loves to watch everyone."

"Liz texted me after they got back. She said David got carsick on the way home."

"I heard that," Dany said. "We were lucky. Patrick slept most of the time."

"Did you drive straight through like Tyler?" Kenny asked.

"Yes, but we stopped more often, I think," Darian answered.

After several minutes of casual conversation, Darian looked at Kenny and said, "We need to talk to you about something."

Father James stood up. "I need to get back. I want to talk to Father Mathias about his sermons."

"I should go, too," Andy said and left for home.

"Thanks for coming over," Emmy said.

"Is it something serious? Did something break at the house?" Kenny asked.

Darian shook his head and waved a hand. "No, the guesthouse is perfect. That's why this is rather difficult to say."

"Oh, no," Emmy said and then put a hand to her mouth.

"After much prayer and discussion, Dany and I have decided to explore the possibility of finding a home of our own."

"We don't want to sound ungrateful," Dany said. "We love living out here."

"We love having you guys as neighbors, but we understand. Renting is not the same as owning your own place Have you started looking?" Kenny asked and then looked at Emmy.

"We have done some searching online, but nothing else," Dany said. "Do you hate us, Emmy?"

"Yes! You have to live with us forever," she answered just to see their reactions.

"I think Emmy is kidding," Kenny said.

"Of course I am," Emmy said. "I totally understand wanting your own place. Years ago when Lindsey and Cameron lived there she told me they were afraid to make any changes because it wasn't their house."

"We haven't really felt like that, but we haven't made any changes," Dany said looking at Darian.

"We did paint the bedrooms, but you knew that, right?" Darian asked.

Kenny nodded.

"Have you guys figured out how much you can afford?" Emmy asked.

Darian replied, "We have gotten preapproved for a loan and have an idea where we want to start our search."

"Do you think the girls will understand?" Dany asked. "I hate to disappoint them."

"They will be disappointed because they love you guys, but they will adjust."

"Do you want me to tell them?" Dany asked.

"No, I will do that, but I might wait until you find a house," Emmy said just as they heard a baby crying.

Chapter Thirty-Five

"I just left the courthouse," Kristen said. "Do you want to grab lunch or something?"

Emmy saved her work on her laptop. "How can you be hungry? You just got divorced."

"I still have to eat, Em. I have a craving for Chinese," Kristen said.

"I could do Chinese," Emmy replied. "Are you going to pick it up and come over here?"

"I could. What would you like?"

"Where are you stopping?"

"The Pagoda House is on the way," Kristen answered.

"I like that place. Let me grab my menu. We are ordering the lunch specials, right?"

"Yes, and I want the number two. Sweet and sour chicken."

"You are so predictable, Krissy," Emmy said walking down the hallway to the kitchen. She grabbed her menu and flipped it to the back. "Hmmmm, I think I'll get either fifteen or sixteen. Do you remember what the difference between Empress and General Tso's chicken is?"

"Not really, but they're both spicy, I think."

Emmy thought about it and made up her mind. "I'll take number fifteen. Empress chicken. Can we order Crab Rangoon, too?"

"Anything else, your highness?"

"Ask for extra packets of the hot mustard, please. I'll pay you when you get here."

"I can still afford to buy lunch," Kristen said. "I will be there as soon as I can."

Kristen set the paper bag on the counter forty-five minutes later.

"I'll get the plates and stuff," Emmy said.

They sat in the breakfast nook to eat.

"We used to take the kids to Pagoda House, but we haven't done that for several years," Emmy said. "It's so much more convenient to order out."

"They even deliver. We do that," Kristen said.

"I used to get their tea. They would give you those little cups without a handle," Emmy said as she squeezed some hot mustard onto her fried rice.

"How can you stand that stuff?" Kristen asked as she watched. "I prefer the sweet and sour sauce."

Emmy grinned and said, "That shows how much different we are."

Kristen stared at Emmy. "I'm waiting."

"You are all sweet and nice and everything, and I'm hot and spicy," Emmy said. "Do you ever read the fortune cookies?"

"No so much."

"I do, but I always add 'in bed' to the end."

"So does that mean you are hot and spicy in bed?"

"Kenny thinks so," she answered, took a bite of rice and made a face.

"Too much mustard?"

"Just a little," Emmy said.

"Are you going to tell me how it went at the courthouse?" Emmy asked a few minutes later. "I know you're keeping the house. What else did you guys decide?"

Kristen explained more about the settlement.

"He better keep his promise," Emmy said. "You should send the kids to the most expensive college in the country."

"Why would I do that?" Kristen asked as she scooped up the last of the rice on her plate. "I think it would be more important to send them to a Christian college."

"I was just joking. He is going to help with house payments, right? Do you want more rice or anything?" Emmy asked. She stood up, walked over to the counter, filled her plate and looked at Kristen.

"I'm good."

"How much do you owe on the house?"

"It's under fifty thousand, and I can handle the payments since I'm working again, or I could use money from the sale."

"Did you take the whole day off?" Emmy sat back down and opened another hot mustard packet.

266

"Yes, and don't you dare offer to help."

Emmy chuckled and said, "And just how do you plan to stop me if you get in financial trouble?"

"I am sure it won't come to that."

"Did John find a place in Columbus yet?" Emmy asked while rinsing off the plates and placing them in the dishwasher. "Do you know how much assistant coaches make at Ohio State?"

"He found a three bedroom house to rent for now," Kristen replied. "I don't know exactly how much his will earn, but I think it's more than either of his brothers."

"Isn't Kirk the head coach for some college in Tennessee?" Emmy asked.

"Southern Tennessee State, but it's a small university and the pay isn't great."

"Are you going to let the kids visit him soon?"

Kristen shrugged. "Not before school starts."

"He did what?" Emmy screamed into her phone a week later.

"He got married," Kristen repeated.

"To who? How could he do that? He had to have been seeing this woman before you guys divorced." Emmy made the word woman sound vulgar.

"Obviously, Emmy. He wouldn't marry someone he just met."

"I hate him for doing that," Emmy said.

"You aren't supposed to hate him."

"Okay, maybe I don't hate him, but I absolutely hate what he did. Do Zach and Grace know?"

Kristen walked into her office, sat down and turned on the computer monitor. "I have not told them yet. I am waiting for a proper time."

"Ha! There won't ever be the right time, Kristen. How could he do this? Doesn't he know how devastated the kids will be? Have you talked to his parents at all?"

"They called yesterday evening to talk to the kids. That's how I learned about the wedding."

267

"Did they get married in a church?" Emmy asked.

Kristen shook her head. "Em, he's Catholic. They were married at his in-laws' house. I guess his new wife goes to a Presbyterian or Episcopal church or something like that."

"What is her name?" Emmy asked.

"Why? Are you going to track her down?"

"Maybe. What is it?"

"Helena Stampley, and she's not changing it to Randolph."

"Why not?" Emmy asked. "Is she ashamed of it?"

"Her family insisted. They are old money if you know what I mean."

"Did she want John to change his name?" Emmy asked sarcastically.

"Don't be silly."

"Where did he meet this person?"

"I do not know for sure, but the Stampley family owns one of the largest construction supply companies in Ohio. They might have met through work," Kristen said.

"I'm going over to Tony's later. I'll ask him if he knows," Emmy said. "I'll talk to you later."

"Don't make a big fuss about this, Em," Kristen said.

"I need to talk to you," Emmy said as she walked onto the deck.

"What about?" Tony asked flipping some burgers over. "Are you staying for dinner?"

"No, and it's about John and Helena," she answered and pointed to one of the burgers. "That is going to taste like charcoal if you leave it in the center like that.

"John and Helena who?" he asked while moving the small burger to the edge.

She smacked his arm. "Don't give me that. You know exactly who I mean."

He closed the lid to his Webber Summitt and faced her. "John and I met her a few years ago at a convention in Chicago."

Emmy looked at the grill and asked, "Is this new? It's bigger than ours. How much did it set you back?"

268

"I bought it in June, and it was on sale," he answered.

"How much?"

"I paid $2500 and tax."

"So, did you know he and that woman were having an affair?" she asked. ""You could have bought a smaller one and saved a grand, or picked a different brand."

"I have more family members than you. We need a bigger grill, and no."

"No. Are you telling me the truth?" she asked and immediately waved a hand. "Forget that. You never lie to me."

"I swear I did not know. I only met her that one time. I didn't know John was seeing her occasionally." Tony reopened the lid and moved the burgers around.

"What is she like? Why on earth would he abandon his family for another woman?"

"Well, it certainly wasn't for her beauty," Tony answered with a chuckle.

"Why do you say that?"

"She wasn't nearly as pretty as Kristen, and I think she's older than John."

"Get out!" She smacked Tony's arm again. "How much older?"

He shrugged and said, "I don't know for sure, but I would guess she might be five or ten years older. She's taller and kinda skinny."

"They're done," she said.

"Would you grab that for me, please?" He pointed to a platter on the table behind them.

She held the platter and he placed the burgers on it.

"Why did you make so many?"

"Peter, Ben, Taylor, Coby and myself."

"What about Mama and Sloane and the girls? Don't they get to eat, too?" She set the platter back on the table.

He turned down the grill. "It's just the guys tonight. All the females are in Ohio visiting Sloane's parents."

"Yeah, I forgot. Sloane did mention it at church yesterday. Do you think you can handle them by yourself?"

"Are you volunteering to assist?"

"Nope! I got my own. I hope you're feeding them more than just hamburgers."

"Mama made a huge bowl of potato salad, and I picked up chips at the store," he answered. Then he waved a finger at her. "No way! You cannot have any of the potato salad. I know how much you like it."

"I use the same recipe, but mine never tastes as good," she said looking up at him.

He waved his hand. "No! No! No! And that look is not going to work. I don't fall for that anymore."

"Please, for the sake of my children?" she begged.

He shook his head and crossed his arms over his chest.

She spun around and kicked the table. "Then you can't ever raid my fridge for leftovers ever again, creep."

Tony laughed and said, "Mama left a smaller bowl for you, brat. It's in the fridge."

She grinned without turning around and walked into the house. *I knew Mama wouldn't forget how much I like hers.*

"It's just a half day today, Mom," Kevin said as Emmy tried to comb his unruly hair. "We don't need a lunch."

"You better behave for Mrs. Patton," Emmy warned. "Wash your hands again. They're still sticky from the pancakes."

He marched to the bathroom and Emmy turned and walked back to the breakfast nook.

"Mom, do we have to call Sloane Mrs. Bertucci, or can we call her Aunt Sloane?" Heather asked.

Emmy rolled her eyes. "You know the answer to that. You have to be respectful."

"It will be so weird if Noemi calls her Mrs. Bertucci instead of Mommy," Isabella said and then carried her empty plate to the sink.

"It doesn't matter what Noemi calls her. You and Heather will address her as Mrs. Bertucci. Would you call Mr. Ruiz by his first name?"

"We don't even know his name," Heather said. She gulped

down the rest of her milk and left the glass and plate on the table.

Emmy pointed at the table and Heather rolled her eyes but she did what her mother wanted.

"Who's taking us to school?" Kevin asked coming out of the bathroom and holding up his hands.

"I'm taking you," Kenny said. "We are leaving in five minutes, and we have to pick up Caden and Lily."

"I can't believe she's in first grade already," Emmy said.

"We will be in high school in two years, Mommy," Isabella said with a grin. "Dotty is going to The Barclay Academy this year. Carson is a junior and Peter is a sophomore."

"Stop it. You're making me feel old," Emmy replied.

Kenny and the kids left for school.

Father James returned from his morning walk around the St. John's neighborhood and called Emmy. "Did I miss the kids?"

"They left five minutes ago. How was your walk? I need to start running again."

"It's rather humid and warm already."

"It is August," she answered and sat on a barstool at the island. "Did I tell you about Dany and Darian buying a house?"

"You did mention it."

"Kenny doesn't want the guesthouse to sit empty."

"Have they started their search?"

"I know they are using a real estate agent from church, but I don't know if they've seen any houses yet."

"So, you have time to come up with a plan."

"I thought we could ask Pastor Tyler if he knows of a family that needs a place to live."

"That's admirable, but you need to be careful before you allow someone to move in."

"I know that. I suppose I could use it as my office and do all my writing there."

"Good idea," he said. "You certainly don't have enough room at the house."

Chapter Thirty-Six

Sloane returned home after school with the kids. She walked into the kitchen and saw Tony grabbing a carton of Ben & Jerry's ice cream from the freezer.

He turned around, saw her and said, "I'll share if you want."

"I would love some, but it goes right to my hips," Sloane said setting her purse and schoolbag on the island. "I'll just take one bite."

Tony grabbed two spoons and they sat next to each other.

"How did the interview go?" Sloane asked. "Did they offer you the position?"

"They did and I accepted it. I start next Tuesday."

"Exactly what do you know about human resources?" Sloane asked and then took a scoop of ice cream.

"I had to deal with the HR department a lot."

Sloane took another bite and asked, "How many people are in the department? Are you going to have to travel to Pittsburgh very often?"

"I'm not sure how many people work in my office. I've only met two of them."

"Oh, excuse me. It's your office already."

"You know what I meant." He watched as she took another bite. "I thought you just wanted one scoop."

"This is my favorite flavor. How many plants does Liberty Manufacturing have now?"

"SoHam, Pittsburgh and Knoxville. I shouldn't have to travel too often."

"Does Kristen know you're going to be working there?"

"I talked to her before I left," he answered. He walked to the fridge, chose another flavor and sat down.

"Did she resign?"

"No, she thinks it will be fun to work together again."

"Are you her boss, or is she higher up then you?"

"We are in different departments, but I suppose I am higher up the ladder."

272

Sloane chuckled and said, "Don't tell her that. You do remember that Gladys Posey ran B & K, right?"

"I bet I make more money than Kristen," he said.

Sloane shook her head. "Not for long if you ever mention it. She will have you terminated in an instant."

"Mom, when will Dad be home?" Ben asked on the way home from school. "Does he have to work late every day?"

"He should be home before dinner," Sloane answered as she made sure Coby was buckled tightly in his car seat. "Why do you want to know?"

"Well, it's his first day of work, and I want to ask how it went."

Sloane stared at Ben for a moment before closing the van door.

When Tony arrived home, Ben raced into the kitchen and asked, "How was work? Did you see Aunt Kristen?"

"It wasn't too bad, and I saw her numerous times. The office area isn't all that big. How was school? Anything special happen?"

"It was okay, but I need to ask you something." Ben looked at his mother and grandmother, who had just entered the kitchen. He hesitated then said, "I want to tryout for the football team."

All three adults froze and then looked at Ben.

"What football team?" Sloane asked. "There's no team at Crest Ridge."

"This is at the Y. They have a league for kids my age," Ben explained.

"They play tackle football at the Y?" Tony asked. "I didn't know that."

Mama looked at Ben and sighed.

"I don't know, Ben," Sloane said. "With your father working again, there might not be anyone to take you to practice. When does the team practice?" she asked.

"I think it's Saturday mornings."

"There goes that excuse," Sloane whispered. "I will have to discuss this with your father."

"Okay, but I really want to play, and the tryouts are this Saturday. You have to sign a form." He grabbed the consent form from the counter and handed it to Sloane. "It doesn't cost too much, and Billy Lomas is going to be on the team." Ben raced out of the room and sprinted upstairs.

Tony looked at Sloane. "Who?"

"He's a student in Ben's class, I think."

"What do you think, Mama?" Tony asked.

She waved a hand. "This is your decision. You won't use me as an excuse to say no."

"So, you'd rather he didn't play, huh?" Tony asked.

"I'm getting too old to worry about anyone getting hurt playing football or any other sport."

"Well, what do you think?" Sloane asked as she climbed into bed that night.

"I was even younger when I started playing," Tony said.

"Is he talented?"

"He can catch and throw the ball better than most kids his age," Tony said. "He's improved quite a lot this summer. He can run faster than any other boy his age."

"It sounds like you've made up your mind."

"I don't want to be one of those parents who push their kid into doing something because they wanted to do it. Do you know what I mean?"

"I get your point. If we agree to let him play, and he doesn't like it, will you be upset?"

"I don't think so. It would be nice if he participated in athletics, but I'm not going to force it on him."

The next morning Sloane handed Ben the signed consent form.

"Does this mean I can tryout?" Ben asked.

"Yes, and we will make sure you have a ride to practice."

"All right!" Ben hollered and pretended to tackle his youngest brother.

That evening Tony gets a call from Mitch Baylan, who introduced himself as a former college player and Ben's coach.

274

"Would you be interested in assisting me with the team?" Mitch asked after a short conversation. "I know the kids would be excited to have another former player as a coach. It's strictly volunteer at this point, but I'm hoping to use this experience to get hired by a high school or a small college." Mitch spoke for a time about his experience as a college player for Sterling Tabor College in Kansas.

When Tony could finally answer, he declined. "I'm not sure if I could commit to being available every Saturday morning because of my job."

"Well, if you change your mind, give me a call. I can always make room for you on the staff," Mitch said and hung up.

Tony stared at the phone and muttered, "You make it sound like you're Nick Saban or somebody who has dozens of assistants. It's YMCA football for little kids, and I've never heard of that college in my life."

"Are you going to have to work every Saturday?" Ben asked his father at breakfast.

"No, but I really need to be there this morning, buddy. I'm sorry about missing your tryout. You can tell me all about it when I get home."

Sloane took Ben, Taylor and Coby to the tryout later that morning.

"When you get older, you can tryout, too," Ben told his younger brothers. "I will help you practice if you want."

Though Taylor showed some interest in watching, Coby spent his time on the playground equipment. Sloane sat on lawn chairs with some of the other parents and watched the tryouts.

"These are tryouts in name only," one of the parents said. "The coaches have to keep anyone who wants to play on the team."

"Sometimes there aren't enough players to field a complete team," another parent said.

Sloane watched Coach Baylan showing the youngsters basic football skills for longer than she thought necessary. She listened to his gruff tone and lack of patience with the less skillful players at times. She crossed her arms over her chest at one point.

"Bertucci! How many times do I have to tell you how to catch the football?" the coach yelled when Ben dropped the ball. "It's not that hard to do. You just place your hands like this and grab it. Didn't your father ever teach you anything? I expect more out of you." He looked at the other players, which included three girls, and asked, "Is there anyone here who can catch the football and run toward the end zone?"

Sloane saw Ben turn his back to the other players and wipe his face. She stood up and was about to storm after the coach when she felt a hand on her shoulder. She turned to see who it was.

"Let me handle this," Mr. Lomas said. "I think I can talk some sense into Coach Baylan."

Sloane nodded and sat down.

"Did the coach upset you, Ben?" Sloane asked on the way home. "I saw you wipe your face after he yelled at everyone."

"I wasn't crying, Mom," Ben insisted. "I got some dirt in my eyes. That's all."

Sloane didn't press the issue until Tony got home.

"He was really yelling at the kids?" Tony asked. "They're just little kids. Why would he yell?"

Sloane shrugged.

"Did any of the other parents say anything?"

"One mother said something about the Y having trouble finding volunteers."

"I'll talk to Ben and see if he still wants to play." He went upstairs and knocked on Ben's door. "Can I come in, Ben?"

"You can come in, Dad."

Tony entered and found Ben on the bed playing with his latest electronic gadget.

"Is that one of those shoot-'em-up games?" Tony asked.

"Yeah," he answered.

"How did practice go?" Tony asked.

"It was all right," Ben answered without taking his eyes off the game.

"Your mother said the coach might have yelled at you and the other players. Did he?"

276

"He yelled a lot. Billy said the coach they had last year didn't yell, and everyone liked him."

"Do you think you will like Coach... What is his name?"

"Coach Baylan. I'm not sure yet."

"Do you still want to play on the team? You don't have to if you don't want to."

"I thought it would be fun, but he made us do the same stupid stuff over and over. Is that what coaches do?"

Tony chuckled and said, "Different coaches use different techniques on their players. When I played for the Bears we had this coach who liked to get in our faces and yell."

"Was that Coach Shackleton?" Ben asked.

"Yes, but it was just his way of getting us to improve. He would yell and scream, but he cared a lot for the players and would bend over backward to help us if we worked hard."

"I don't think our coach likes us," Ben whispered. "If you were our coach, would you yell at us?"

Tony rubbed his jaw for a moment. He looked at his son and said, "No, I think I would be patient and try to coach without raising my voice."

"Can you be our coach, please?" Ben asked.

Tony hugged Ben and whispered, "I can call your coach and see if he needs some help."

Chapter Thirty-Seven

"I'd rather come out on stage with everyone else," Jeremy said moments before the Fridays At Five show in San Diego.

"We know, but this is a special night, and we want to introduce you properly," Jeff said. "We want you to hear the crowd's reaction."

"What if they don't react?" Jeremy asked. "I will look rather foolish."

Dave put an arm around his friend. "Not a bloody chance."

Jeremy looked at Kenny, Adam and P.J.

"I agree with Jeff and Dave," Kenny said.

Adam and P.J. nodded.

"Fine. You guys win," Jeremy said.

"We will do two songs, and then introduce you," Jeff said. "You can come out and say something if you want."

Jeremy shook his head. "I don't want to say anything."

The house lights went out, and the crowd roared.

"We're ready to go," Will Consoli said from his position behind the FOH console.

The band's intro music filled the auditorium.

"Are you ready, boss?" Frankie Hanna asked.

"Let's do this," Kenny answered

Frankie handed him his Gibson ES-5 Switchmaster and made sure the strap was adjusted correctly.

Frankie and the other techs turned on their flashlights and led Kenny and the guys onto the stage. Dave moved into position and counted off the first song as the intro music ended.

Jeremy Lenhart watched from the side of the stage as the lights flashed and moved in time with the music. He waited for the pyrotechnics to explode and smiled. He waited till the end of the first song and then closed his eyes. *Lord, I want to thank you for your many blessings. Thank you for allowing Jennifer to be part of our family for thirteen years. Now she is part of your family for eternity. Please help me get through tonight, and thank you for showing me this is where I need to be.* He opened his eyes and looked at the lights overhead.

Kenny waited for the crowd to settle down after the second song and then motioned for them to sit down. "Thank you for that energetic greeting. That was 'Do You Wanna Hear My Heartbreak' from our second album. For those of you who don't know, albums are those big round discs that go on your turntable."

Jeff glanced at P.J. and whispered, "If Emmy was here she would call him a dork about now."

Kenny continued after the crowd stopped laughing. "Before we do our next tune, I want to welcome one of the original members of Fridays At Five back to the stage..."

As Jeremy walked out and waved, the crowd rose to their feet and created the loudest racket the band had heard in a long time.

"And you were worried about a reaction," Jeff said though Jeremy couldn't hear him.

"Give it up for Jeremy Lenhart!" Kenny shouted. He watched as Jeremy took his position behind his rack of keyboards. He waited until Jeremy smiled and nodded. He twirled a finger and the band started playing again.

"Well, how does it feel to have the first show under your belt?" Jeff asked on the way back to the hotel.

"I was nervous until the third or fourth song. I was tentative with my playing and didn't want to step on Adam's toes," Jeremy answered.

"If the crowd reaction was any indication of how we sounded, I think you did all right," Jeff said. "It's like you never left."

"Hi, Emmy. I'm sorry I didn't call before the show, but the meet and greet lasted longer than scheduled."

"That's okay. How did it go? Have Adam and Jeremy adjusted to playing together?" Emmy asked while staring at the ceiling fan above the bed. *I really need to get that dusted.*

"They sound like they've been together for years. Somehow, they just know what the other is going to play."

"How was the crowd?" she asked.

"Pretty rowdy tonight. Last night was more laid back."

279

"I meant how large was it," she said as she picked up the remote and adjusted the fan speed.

"Oh, I get it," he replied. "I think the place was sold out or very close to it."

"Do you think you're selling more tickets because people know Jeremy is back?"

"I don't doubt that at all. We added a section to 'Sweet Girl' after the second bridge. Jeremy plays a solo and it gets a big reaction."

"I might not be home when you get back," she said.

"Oh, where are you going?" he asked.

"Kevin wants to watch Ben play football, so I told him we would go."

"Has he expressed any interest in playing?"

"No, he just wants to watch. Oh, did I tell you what happened to the coach?" Emmy sat up on the edge of the bed. "I meant to, but I might have forgotten."

"What happened?" Kenny asked and motioned to Cole Milne to close the door to his dressing room.

"Well, last week the idiot started hollering at the kids because they let a player on the other team score a touchdown. He threw his whistle and the parents confronted him after the game and told him to put his whistle in a place it really shouldn't go."

Kenny laughed as he listened to Emmy and tried to picture the situation.

"Anyway, Tony agreed to take over. This is supposed to be a league for kids who've never played on a team before."

"It's flag football, right?" Kenny asked.

"Yeah. The players have to wear mouthguards, but they don't wear helmets or cleats. There's a rule that all players have to touch the ball at least once every game. That way one player can't dominate the game. It's supposed to be fun for the kids, but Sloane said that coach was making the kids cry. Can you believe it? They're only ten."

"He was probably a frustrated player himself. It's good the parents fired him."

"If you get home in time, you can come over to the Y and

watch with us. Ben's game starts at eleven and doesn't last an hour."

"I will try to make it, Em."

Kenny and Andy drove straight from the airport to the YMCA the next morning.

"I can see Emmy and Kevin and Sloane," Andy said as they walked toward the field. "Emmy's waving her arms like a windmill."

Kenny walked up behind Emmy and touched her shoulders. "You made it!"

"Anything happening?"

"You just missed it!" She stood up and pointed at the players. "Ben ran all the way down the field for a touchdown. He spun around and dodged the whole other team. You should have seen it. It was like Barry Sanders was running. He could be pretty good if he keeps playing."

Kenny said hi to Sloane and high-fived Taylor and Coby. Tony saw Kenny and Andy and waved.

"Why don't they wear helmets, and is that a girl?" Andy asked.

"It's flag football, Andy, and girls are allowed to play," she answered. "I wish I could have been on a team like this when I was that age. I used to play with the kids in the neighborhood a lot."

"You did, Em," Kenny said.

She grinned at the guys and said, "And I was better than almost all the boys."

They watched the teams shake hands after the game and waited for Tony and Ben to join them.

"Mom! Did you see that touchdown?" Ben asked.

"I did. Good job," Sloane said with a smile.

Emmy high-fived Ben. "It was awesome. Your father was never that good a runner. He once got caught by this fat lineman after he intercepted a pass." She looked up at Tony and made a face.

Tony sighed, rolled his eyes and said, "He had the angle on me, brat. How many times do I have to tell you."

Emmy grinned and said, "Yeah, that's a lame excuse."

Sloane asked, "Did your team win?"

Ben shrugged. "I don't know."

"Did you have fun?" Emmy asked.

"Yeah!" Ben said. "It's a lot more fun since Dad took over the team. He doesn't yell like the other coach. He tells us to help each other and have fun."

Alexa Mullins and her mother walked over.

"Good game, Ben. I really liked your touchdown," Alexa said with a smile. "I'll see you at practice."

"Thanks, Alexa. You did a good job, too," Ben said.

Emmy waited until Alexa and her mother walked away and said, "Ben, she's cute. Are you friends?"

Ben stared at Alexa for a moment, looked up at his mother and father and then Emmy and muttered, "She's just a girl on the team."

"Uh-huh, and I think she likes you," Emmy said.

Ben hung his head and kicked at the grass.

"Mom! How can you say that? Girls shouldn't be playing football," Kevin said.

"Your mother was a pretty good player when she was young," Tony said.

"Was she really?" Kevin asked.

"She was really good... for a shrimp," Tony said and then backed away.

Emmy stuck out her tongue at Tony, but then she smiled and said, "I could outrun him, but then he was always pretty slow."

282

Chapter Thirty-Eight

"I am not going on a blind date, Emily. I don't care how much you beg," Kristen said emphatically.

"It's not exactly a blind date, Krissy. You know Wyatt, and you did say he was nice," Emmy said.

Kristen sat at her kitchen island with her chin in her hands and her elbows on the granite countertop. "He is nice, but I am not ready for a relationship."

Emmy laughed while walking around the first floor looking for Kenny. *Where did you go?* "Going out for dinner does not constitute a relationship."

"Ha! I know you. In your mind we are already engaged."

Emmy giggled and said, "Maybe just going steady."

"This is 2018, Em. No one goes steady anymore. If I did agree to this, and I am not saying I will, but if I do, then you and Kenny have to go with us."

"If I can find him, I'll ask if we have any plans for tonight."

"Tonight! I can't go out tonight," Kristen insisted.

"Why not? Zach and Grace can come over here. Father James is here, and he's not doing anything."

Father James heard his name as he passed Emmy in the hallway. He looked at her, tilted his head and said, "I might be playing cards tonight. I just stopped by to return a book I borrowed."

Emmy put a hand over her cell phone and shook her head. "Not tonight. You owe me for covering for you with Father Dennis. I might need you to watch the kids and Zach and Grace."

"Not a chance. I'm on call," he replied and continued to the kitchen.

"I'll get a sitter," Emmy promised.

"My hair is a wreck, and I haven't had my nails done all month," Kristen said. "I don't want him to see me like this."

"Get out! You look gorgeous as soon as you get out of bed." Emmy walked through the mudroom, into the garage and found Kenny pumping up the tires on his mountain bike. She held up a finger and waved it at him.

He finished putting air in the tires, placed the pump back in the cabinet and waited by his bike.

"Just a second, Krissy. I found Kenny in the garage." She checked him out.

He glanced at his biking shorts and shrugged.

"Are we busy tonight?"

"Not that I know of. Why?" he asked tilting his head and putting on his helmet.

"Kristen wants us to go to Ciao Bella with her and Wyatt."

"This is your idea, Emily!" Kristen shouted into her phone. "Don't give Kenny the impression it was mine."

"What time?" Kenny asked.

"Eight," Emmy answered. "I have to find a babysitter."

"It's okay with me."

If you give me ten minutes, I'll go biking with you," Emmy said. "Krissy, it's all set. We'll pick you up at seven."

"Does Wyatt know about this?" Kristen asked.

"I'll call him. I'm sure he will want to go. Talk to you later and wear a nice dress."

"Are you going to wear a dress?" Kristen asked.

Emmy giggled and said, "No way! I'm going to wear my old jeans. I'm not the one who's going on a romantic date."

"You are such a stinker, and I don't know why I let you talk me into things. You better call me back if he can't or doesn't want to go."

"He will want to go. I promise," Emmy said and ended the call.

"What are you doing, Em?" Kenny asked.

"Doing a favor for Kristen. She needs a nice dinner and someone to talk to besides her kids. I'll be back in a minute. Would you check my bike, please?"

Kenny shook his head as Emmy raced into the house. He got her bike down and checked it over.

"Yes, this is Emmy Colwell, and I would like to make a reservation for this evening at eight. There will be four of us. Would that be possible?" Emmy asked as she changed clothes. "I'm sorry for the late notice."

284

Mr. Sabatino smiled and pretended to check. "I might be able to reserve a table, but only if you bring me a copy of your book and sign it for me."

"Oh, Mr. Sabatino, you don't have to pretend to like my books."

"Nonsense! Florentina and I love reading about you."

"Please don't believe everything I write about," she said.

"Should I reserve your usual table?"

"Yes, please. It's for Kristen. I'm setting her up with one of the pastors from church," she said gleefully.

"I thought Kristen was the matchmaker."

"She used to be, but now it's my turn. We'll see you later."

She changed into her biking clothes and raced downstairs, passing Father James in the hallway again.

He turned and watched as she disappeared through the mudroom. He shook his head and muttered, "I don't think she will ever grow up."

"You need to wear your helmet," Kenny said. He brushed her hair out of her face and placed it on her head. He buckled the straps and grinned.

"What? Why are you looking at me like that?" she asked.

"Have I told you lately how cute you are?" He touched the tip of her nose. "You still look like a teenager, Em."

She laughed and said, "I'm gonna make you an appointment to see Dr. Larson. You obviously need glasses."

They returned to the house an hour later just as the girls were getting back from a visit with Dany and Patrick Cullen.

"Mom! What happened to you?" Isabella asked.

Heather laughed and said, "You're covered in mud. Did you crash your bike?"

"It wasn't my fault," Emmy said handing her helmet to Kenny. "He cut me off, and I had to swerve to avoid a crash."

Kenny held up three fingers and grinned at the girls.

"How many times did you crash, Mommy?" Isabella asked.

Emmy turned to look at Kenny, but by this time he was hanging up the bikes. "Too many times." She sat down and took off her shoes.

Kevin heard the commotion, opened the door and stood on the top step leading into the mudroom. He pointed at his mother, laughed and said, "Way to go, Mom. It's more fun if you get all muddy."

"Should I hose you off, Em?" Kenny asked and then winked at the kids.

"No, but you could run upstairs and grab some clothes. I can't go inside like this, and I can't take these off until I have something to wear."

"Can me and Ben go biking and get all muddy?" Kevin asked.

"No!" Emmy said. "The trails are way too muddy and wet."

"But you got to have fun," Kevin said.

"That's different. I am an adult," Emmy said and marched past Kevin into the mudroom. "Kenny, will you grab some clothes, please?"

"Do you need clean underwear, too, Em?" he asked knowing it would make the kids laugh.

Heather and Isabella grinned at each other, and Isabella asked, "Should we take a photo and post it on Instagram or Facebook, Mommy?"

"Don't you dare!" Emmy hollered.

Father James stood in the mudroom room door and stared at Emmy. "Where do you think you're going, young lady? You are not coming into the house covered in mud."

Heather used her cell phone and took a photo anyway.

"Where am I supposed to go, and why are you still here?"

"I decided to watch the kids tonight." He pointed to the garage. "There is a shower in the basement utility room."

"But it's filthy and totally open. There's no shower curtain," Emmy said.

He shook his head and folded his arms across his chest. "Not happening. Basement. Now!"

"I hate you all," she said and stuck out her tongue as Heather took another photo.

"Didn't you ever ride a bike when you were a kid?" Emmy asked Father James.

"Yes, but I... never mind." He laughed and walked away.

She marched to the basement and soon Kenny appeared with clean clothes. He set the clean clothes on a shelf above the rinse tub and watched as she stripped out of her biking clothes.

"Should we throw those away?" he asked holding up her clothes with his fingertips. "They might clog up the washer."

"You can rinse them off in the tub in the laundry room or use this one. Did you bring a towel, or am I supposed to air dry?"

"It's under your clothes," he said with a grin.

She saw the look and said, "No way, buster! Go away and leave me alone."

"You have some mud right here," he said and wiped her cheek. "You're still cute even covered in mud."

"Kristen is here, Em. Are you ready?" Kenny asked later that evening.

"Just a minute. I'm trying to decide what top to wear."

He walked into her closet.

She held up two tops.

"The blue one," he said. "Kristen's wearing a dress. Are you sure you want to wear jeans?"

"Yes, because I haven't shaved my legs all week." She put on the blue top. "I'm ready. Wyatt said he would meet us there. Maybe he will offer to bring Kristen home."

"Em, if it's meant to happen, it will."

"I just want Kristen to be happy."

They walked into Ciao Bella just before eight and Kristen spotted Wyatt waiting, but he didn't see her.

Kenny walked up to Wyatt and shook his hand. "Have you been here before?"

"I came with Tyler and Liz for dinner. The food is great," Wyatt said.

"The ladies are waiting over there."

"Do I look all right?" Kristen asked flipping her hair over her shoulder.

"As beautiful as ever," Emmy said. She smiled as Mr. Sabatino approached.

"Good evening, ladies. I must say you look as beautiful as ever, Mrs. Randolph." He smiled at her and then looked at Emmy and sighed. "This way, please."

"I told her to wear a dress, Mr. Sabatino," Kenny said.

They were seated in the new addition, and quickly placed their food and drink orders.

"So, Emmy, I saw a couple photos earlier today," Wyatt said.

"Really?" Emmy asked.

Wyatt grinned and explained, "You appeared to have been playing in some mud."

"Kenny, please remind me to ground Heather for life when we get home."

Kristen tried not to get caught staring at Wyatt, but he saw her looking and smiled.

"How is your ravioli, Em?" Kenny asked.

"It's good. Can I have a bite of your lasagna?" She reached out with her fork and snagged a bite. "This is almost as good as Mama's." She looked at Kristen, who was engaged in conversation with Wyatt. *I knew you guys would get along.* She smiled at Kenny and whispered, "I think you should take me home early."

"Why? Don't you feel good?" he asked loudly enough for Kristen and Wyatt to hear.

"Are you okay, Em?" Kristen asked.

"I'm fine, but it's been a long week, and I'm kinda tired," she answered.

Kristen stared at Emmy for a moment. "I need to powder my nose. Would you come with me, please?"

Emmy set her napkin on the table and followed Kristen to the ladies' room.

"What are you doing?" Kristen asked.

"Nothing," Emmy said.

"How long have we known each other?" Kristen asked.

Emmy shrugged and said, "Forever?"

"Not quite but long enough for me to know what you're doing. You don't have to pretend to be sick and leave me with Wyatt."

288

"I just thought since you were getting along, you might want him to take you home," Emmy said.

"FYI, he did ask if I wanted to grab some coffee."

"Really!?" Emmy's eyes sparkled as she looked up at Kristen. "Then I feel a lot better. Should we skip dessert so he can take you home early?"

"I think it would be better if we go to your house," Kristen said.

"Why?"

"Well for one thing, my kids are there."

"They can spend the night," Emmy said.

"Do you have any coffee at home?" Kristen asked.

Emmy sighed in surrender. "Yes, and we have ice cream, and I could make some brownies."

"Ice cream would be okay, and we won't stay too late."

"Everything was scrumptious, Mr. Sabatino," Emmy said on the way out. "We're going back to our house so Kristen and Wyatt can get to know each other better. That's why we didn't order dessert."

"Would you like some to take home?" he asked.

Emmy bit her lip before whispering, "I love your tiramasu."

"If you have a moment, I will bring some out."

Kenny gave Wyatt the directions to Bristol Ridge."

"I know where it's located, but I think I'll follow you."

They arrived the house, and Wyatt parked in front of the garage and followed them inside.

"Maybe you should sit in the living room while I make the coffee," Emmy suggested.

"I could show Wyatt my studio," Kenny said.

"Don't you dare," Emmy whispered. "He is here to talk to Kristen."

"Okay, Em." Kenny held up his hands in surrender. "Should I go to my room?"

"Let me think about that. Let them talk for a while."

Emmy heard Father James in the kitchen. She started the coffee and asked, "Have they been good?"

"As the purest of angels," he said. "I'm making popcorn, and we're going to watch *Invasion of the Zombie Clowns*.

"You are joking, right?" Emmy asked.

"Of course," he answered. "We watched that earlier."

"Why did I even ask. I'm going to make coffee, and we brought back some tiramasu. Would you like some?"

"I appreciate the offer, but no thanks. I will pop in another movie for the kids so you can finish your matchmaking, but then I'm leaving."

She stuck out her tongue.

"If it's God's will..."

"I'm just giving Him a little nudge," she replied.

Kristen walked into the kitchen a couple of minutes later. "We should drink the coffee in the breakfast nook. I would be afraid to spill anything in your pristine living room."

"We've only used the living room a handful of times. I always tell the kids it belongs to another family, and we're not supposed to use it."

"Do they believe you?" Kristen asked.

Emmy stared at her for a moment.

"Is the coffee ready, Em?" Kenny asked as he and Wyatt entered the kitchen.

"Almost. Wyatt, this is my brother, Father James," Emmy said.

"I believe we met at a birthday party." Wyatt shook Father James' hand.

"Either that or at a baseball game," Father James replied.

"Where are the kids?" Kristen asked. "The house is much too quiet."

"They are downstairs in the media room." Father James looked at Wyatt. "It's soundproof. No one can hear them screaming."

Emmy rolled her eyes and said, "He's letting them watch scary movies."

"I'll send you my bill for watching the kids. I'm leaving."

"Thanks for staying, and I'll send you the bill for their therapy. They are too young for those movies."

290

Kenny helped Emmy with the coffee and dessert, and they took seats in the breakfast nook.

"It must be very private out here," Wyatt said looking out the window. "I don't see any lights."

"We're in the middle of the woods," Kevin said.

"What are you doing up here?" Emmy asked. "You're supposed to be watching movies with Father James."

"Heather, Isa and Grace told me to come up here and see if Aunt Kristen and Pastor Wyatt were having fun."

"Tell them it's none of their business, and you better stay downstairs until I tell you to come up."

"Can we crash in the basement tonight? Are Zach and Gracie staying over?" he asked eyeing the dessert. "What is that?"

"It's our dessert, and it's not for kids."

"Does it have booze in it?" he asked. "It smells like coffee."

"No, it does not," Kenny said. "Get yourself downstairs, young man."

"You're no fun," Kevin said as he left.

While Wyatt and Kristen were talking about the church, Emmy stared at him. *Your eyes look green tonight, but that's probably because of that green shirt. You aren't as tall as John, but that's a good thing. I wonder if you have any tattoos. Probably not, but it wouldn't matter. Liz said you haven't dated anyone since your wife passed away. I guess that means you haven't had sex either.* She jumped as Kenny touched her hand.

"Em, Kristen asked you a question."

"Oh, sorry, I was thinking about... about... Do we have enough cereal for the week, Kenny?"

"Maybe," he answered.

"What was your question, Kristen?"

"I asked if you had given any thought to changing Sunday School classes since Pastor Williams will be gone for several months."

"Who's taking over his class?" Emmy asked.

"Dennis Orman," she answered.

"Then I'm switching. I didn't care for him when he subbed

291

before," Emmy said. She put a hand to her mouth after looking at Wyatt. "Oh, no. Please, don't tell anyone I said that."

Wyatt grinned and said, "It will be our secret, and between you and me, there have been other people decide to switch."

"Em, there are six or seven adult classes," Kenny said. "People often switch depending on the subject."

"Are you going to lead a class?" Kristen asked Wyatt.

"I'm going to lead a discussion about different ways to eliminate stress in a Christian home."

"That sounds interesting," Emmy said. "Kristen, you should check it out."

"Are you saying there's a lot of stress at my house?"

"Not now," Emmy whispered.

Would anyone like a refill?" Kenny asked.

"I would," Wyatt said. He followed Kenny to the kitchen.

"Why did you say that? He knows about the divorce," Kristen whispered.

"Sorry, Krissy. I didn't mean it like that. I was just trying to help."

The men sat down.

"Should we play a board game?" Emmy asked. "We have several."

"Maybe another time, Em," Kristen said.

Wyatt glanced at the clock and stood up. "I really should go. I need to study for my class again."

"I should get the kids home," Kristen said.

Kenny called the kids on the house intercom, and a moment later they raced upstairs.

"Do we have to go already?" Zach asked his mother. He stared at Wyatt for a moment before turning around and running away.

Kevin followed Zach to the family room. "Are you all right?"

Zach sat on the couch with his arms across his chest. "Why did he go to dinner with Mom? She needs to get back with Dad."

"It's kinda weird, huh?" Kevin said. "Pastor Wyatt is pretty cool, but he's not your dad."

"I don't want her to see anyone else."

"Thanks for dinner," Wyatt said as Kenny walked outside with him.

"Not a problem," Kenny said. "I hope you enjoyed your evening."

"I did. Tell Emmy thanks for setting me up with Kristen."

"She will be thrilled," Kenny said. He waited until Wyatt got in his car and left before coming inside.

"Well, what did he say?" Emmy asked. "Tell me quickly before Kristen comes back."

"Where is she?" Kenny asked.

"In the family room talking to Zach. He's upset, and it's my fault. I didn't mean to upset him."

Kristen returned before Kenny could relay Wyatt's message.

"Thank you for dinner and making Father James watch the kids. Would you mind if Grace spends the night?"

"Of course not. Zach is welcome to stay, too."

Kristen shook her head. "He wants to go home. I think he needs some special attention tonight," Kristen said.

"I'm sorry I upset him. I guess I didn't think about his feelings. I'm really sorry."

Kristen hugged Emmy. "It's not your fault, Em, and I appreciate what you did."

Later, after getting the girls to quiet down and go to sleep, Emmy crawled into bed and nudged Kenny. "You never told me what Wyatt said."

Kenny turned on his side to face Emmy. "He said..."

"Tell me the truth," Emmy insisted.

"Fine, he said to tell you thanks for setting him up with Kristen."

Emmy grinned and moved on top of Kenny. "I knew they would hit it off. They are perfect for each other."

"Are you going to show me how much you enjoyed the ravioli?"

"It was delicious, m'lord," she said before kissing him.

Chapter Thirty-Nine

"Tell me about the house you found," Emmy said as she held Patrick on the couch in the guesthouse. "I won't ask how much you paid."

Dany opened her laptop and turned it so Emmy could see it. "I have photos, and I don't mind telling you the price."

"It looks nice," Emmy said as she shifted Patrick. "How much?"

"We got the sellers to lower the price to $245,900. That was $20,000 below list price."

"That sounds like a deal, but it's a lot of money," Emmy said.

Dany grinned and asked, "Is that more than you paid for your house?"

"Point taken."

"We have over a third of the price to use as a down payment," Dany said.

Patrick turned his head, looked at Emmy and smiled. Then he spit up all over her.

"Oh, Emmy, I'm so sorry. Let me take him. There are paper towels on the counter." Dany pointed toward the kitchen.

She took Patrick to his bedroom while Emmy cleaned her shirt as best she could.

Dany returned alone, "He's sleeping for now. Let me show you more photos."

Emmy looked at the photos and commented on a few.

"It was built in the 90s, but the roof is fairly new and so is the furnace. Darian and his father were there for the inspection," Dany said.

"Are you going to change the carpeting?" Emmy asked.

"Darian wants to put in a laminate floor everywhere other than the bedrooms. There are three bedrooms and two and a half baths."

"What about the basement? It has a basement, right?" Emmy asked.

"It's a full basement, but it's not finished. Darian said the

294

rough plumbing is already there for a full bath though."

"There's a two-car garage," Emmy said.

"Yes, but right now it's full of stuff."

"Make sure they empty it and clean everything before you close," Emmy suggested.

They talked for a few more minutes before Emmy stood up.

"I'm happy for you, but we will miss you a lot." She reached into her purse, pulled out an envelope and handed it to Dany.

"What is this?"

"You could call it a rent refund," Emmy said with a grin.

"Emmy!" Dany tried to hand it back.

"You can open it later when Darian gets home."

Dany looked at Emmy for a moment. "No, I better open it now." She did and looked at the check. "What?" Dany looked again to make sure she saw it correctly. "No way, Emmy," Dany said. "You can't write us a check for," Dany looked at it again. "This is for $45,000."

Emmy hugged Dany and whispered, "We did the same thing for Cameron and Lindsey when they bought a house. We put your rent in an account and let it earn some interest. You've been paying into your own account for nearly six years. We rounded up a bit." Emmy let go of Dany and used a tissue to dry her eyes. "We could have let you live here for free, but this way you get a nice surprise."

"Emmy, we can't take this." Dany tried to hand the check back again.

Emmy shook her head. "You can use it for new furniture or whatever the house needs. Tell Darian to talk to Kenny. He will let you guys use one of the trucks and a bunch of the road crew to move everything."

"You guys are too generous," Dany said and then remembered something. "You better not pay off our mortgage like you did for Lizzie and Tyler."

"I would but Kenny said I couldn't because you might get upset. He said Darian can be rather stubborn about his independence."

295

"That's right, so don't you forget it," Dany said. She hugged Emmy again.

"Dany, I can't breath," Emmy whispered.

"Can we watch the guys loading the truck?" Kevin asked. "We won't get in the way."

Kenny looked at Emmy. She nodded.

Kevin and Ben raced out of the house and ran all the way to the guesthouse.

"Hey, guys," Darian said when he spotted the boys.

"Dad said we could watch if we stay out of the way."

"Maybe I should put you to work," Levi Sayer said as he pushed a large container up the ramp into the truck.

Kevin and Ben watched as the members of the Fridays At Five road crew emptied the house and loaded everything into the truck.

Kevin pointed at Levi and told Ben, "Mr. Sayer is in charge of all these guys and even more. He makes sure all the band gear gets set up right."

"They sure work fast," Ben said. "How did they get this truck back here? It's really big."

"That guy over there is the driver." Kevin pointed at Larry Twilley. "He's one of the drivers for Dad's band, and those guys are Jess and Joe Zawaski."

"I've seen them at church. Dad said they are from some foreign country and used to be in the circus."

Kevin nodded. "They used to work for Mom, but now they work all the time for Dad. He said they work harder than ten men."

An hour later Larry Twilley headed for Darian and Dany's new house.

Kevin and Ben ran up the front porch steps and knocked on the door.

Dany opened it holding Patrick. "Did you watch those guys?"

"Yeah, but we stayed out of the way," Kevin said. "They work fast, huh?"

"They sure do."

"We can help clean if you want. We have to do chores at home, so we both know how to do stuff," Kevin said.

"That's really sweet, but I think it's all done. As soon as a room was emptied, two men started cleaning. They just finished the great room."

"Mom said you guys should come over for dinner if you want. She said you might not have time to cook anything at the new house."

Darian walked in the back door in time to hear the offer of dinner. "Would you tell your mother we would like to have dinner, but we are going to order pizzas for everyone."

"I like everything on my pizza," Kevin said.

"What do you like, Ben?" Darian asked and then chuckled.

"I don't like pineapple pizza, but I'll eat everything else."

"Would you tell your mother we'll be back around six, and don't let her complain about us buying the pizza," Darian said.

"I'll tell her. See you later."

Dany and Darian returned just before six.

"You didn't have to order the pizza. I would have done that," Emmy said. "You can set them on the island."

"It's the least we could do after all you've done," Darian said. "There are different kinds." He saw Kevin and Ben race each other into the room. "I ordered one with pineapple and extra anchovies."

"Yuck!" Kevin said.

"I'm kidding," Darian said and then laughed.

Heather and Isabella dashed down the stairs and rushed up to Dany.

"Can we hold Patrick if we're careful?" Heather asked.

"Okay, but he might get fussy," Dany said while handing him to Isabella. "I haven't fed him since three o'clock."

"We'll bring him back if he starts fussing," Isabella said.

"Take him into the family room, but don't run," Emmy said. "You can set him on the rug if you want. He won't want to be held."

He's been trying to scoot around, and he's good at sitting up," Dany said. "Oh, I didn't think to bring a high chair."

Emmy waved a hand. "No matter. We've kept one around. I'll have Kenny get it."

Dany watched the twins walk slowly down the hall while talking to Patrick. "They will be old enough to babysit in a couple of years."

"Don't remind me, Dany. They like to tease me about how old they are. They enjoy making me feel old."

"Can I help with anything?" Dany asked.

"We're about ready. I do have a salad if anybody wants some. There are different kinds of dressing in the fridge."

A few minute later everyone gathered in the kitchen to eat.

"I'll pray for us, and we can eat." Emmy closed her eyes. "Lord, we thank you for this food. Amen."

"Mom! That's the shortest prayer you've ever done," Kevin said with wide open eyes.

"I know everyone is hungry," Emmy said. She counted the chairs around the breakfast nook. "Kevin, would you and Ben mind eating at the island?"

"Can we eat in the family room and watch a movie?"

"Not a chance. You know the rules," Emmy said.

Kenny brought the high chair up from the basement.

"Could you put it on the end," Emmy said pointing to where she meant.

"Can we sit by Patrick?" Isabella asked.

"You better ask Dany."

They did and she agreed. He began hollering for food as soon as she buckled him in.

"Does anyone want salad?" Emmy asked.

No one took her up on the offer.

"I'll eat some. It will get wasted if I don't," Emmy said.

"Did you have time to unpack anything?" Kenny asked.

"Ha! Those guys wouldn't leave until all the furniture was set up. Tyler and Liz came over. He and Darian unpacked the clothes while Lizzie and I worked in the kitchen. I'm glad we closed Wednesday. That gave us two days to work on the place."

"Did the guys do a good job installing the laminate floors?" Kenny asked.

"They ripped out all the carpeting, cleaned up and had the new floors done before seven o'clock," Darian answered.

"Did you paint anything?" Isabella asked.

"Just the bedrooms," Darian answered. "Could you pass the dried peppers, please?"

Dany handed the jar to him. "It looks like we've lived there for years, and other than deciding what we want to do with the basement and maybe putting on a new deck, we're set for now," Dany said.

"What kind of pizza did you get?" Kevin asked Ben.

Ben looked at his pizza and shrugged. "Don't know, but it's got lots of stuff on it."

"You can have my olives if you want."

Ben took the olives and gave Kevin some Canadian bacon.

"Does anyone need more to drink?" Emmy asked.

"I'll take another glass of tea," Kenny said.

Emmy brought the pitcher to the table and refilled his glass. "Anyone else?"

"I'll take some more," Dany said and then looked at Kenny. "Have you made a decision about the guesthouse?"

"Not yet. It's okay if it remains empty for a short time."

"You should take the rest of this home," Emmy said as she combined the leftover pizza into one box.

"Do you mind if we do?" Darian asked.

"Not at all," Emmy answered looking up at him. "Girls, it's time to say good night to Dany and Patrick. They're going home."

The twins hugged Dany and kissed Patrick.

"I might need a couple babysitters in a few years," Dany said.

Kenny walked outside with Darian, who carried Patrick." Let us know if you need anything."

"You've already done enough, Kenny. We'll never be able to repay you."

"No need to," Kenny said and shook hands. "I'll send Dany out as soon as I can break her away from Emmy."

"I'll start the car," Darian said.

Kenny walked inside and found Emmy and Dany embraced

in a hug. He went to the powder room and brought back a box of tissues.

"I am gonna miss you so much." Emmy said.

"I'm going to miss you more," Dany said.

Kenny smiled and handed each of them several tissues. And then some more. And a few more.

"I better go before Darian wonders what happened to me," Dany said.

Emmy hugged her one more time and then let go.

The plane carrying the Fridays At Five entourage departed from Tampa International Airport shortly after ten Saturday morning. The guys relaxed and talked about their plans.

"That's another tour in the books," Jeff said. "I'm going to take some time off and work on the house."

"What are you remodeling now?" Jeremy asked.

"Frances wants to remove the wall between the kitchen and dining room to open things up."

"I'm going to spend a month in Montana," Dave said. "I haven't been to the ranch since February."

Kenny looked at Adam and P.J. "What are your plans?"

"I'm supposed to help Teresa get ready for Thanksgiving. She wants the house cleaned from top to bottom. Her family is coming this year. After that, I'm going to chill."

Adam smiled and said, "I wasn't supposed to say anything earlier, but Juliana and I are expecting. She's due at the end of April."

The guys congratulated Adam.

"Emmy would say it's about time," Kenny said as he shook Adam's hand. "She will be thrilled to hear it."

"What are your plans, Kenny?" Jeff asked.

"I'm going to be lazy through the holidays. I'm not going to touch my guitar or write any songs until next year."

Andy shook his head. "Unlike you bums, I will be busy planning next summer's tour. I don't make any money unless you're working, and I need some extra cash."

The guys laughed.

300

"Are you planning to buy another house or something?" Jeff asked. "I have two in Timberline Heights that have been completely remodeled."

"And you're asking a small fortune for them," Jeremy said.

"I put a lot of money into those projects," Jeff countered.

"I'm sure by the summer we will we ready to hit the road again," Kenny said.

Dave looked out the window at the clouds below him and said, "Next year we might actually be on the road instead of flying above everything."

"Do you mean we might be back to traveling in buses?" P.J. asked.

"It's a possibility," Dave said.

"I'd rather travel in a bus than give up touring all together," Kenny said.

"We did have some good times back in the bus days," Jeff said.

"One of us should write a book about some of the stuff that happened," Dave said.

Everyone stared at Kenny.

He shook his head. "No way! I'll stick to writing songs, and there's not a chance I'm letting Emmy write it."

"She doesn't know everything about those early tours, does she?" Jeff asked.

"We're still alive, aren't we?" Kenny answered.

Chapter Forty

"Can you believe it's already eight, and the kids haven't demanded we get up to open presents," Emmy said as she ran her fingers through Kenny's hair.

"I can't remember being in bed this late on a Christmas morning since the girls were born," Kenny said. He smiled at Emmy and touched the tip of her nose. "Did it feel like this year went faster than ever before?"

"All of it except last winter."

"Winters always seem to take longer than when we were kids."

"Speaking of kids, should we try to be like Juliana and Adam?"

"How do you mean?" Kenny asked.

Emmy grinned and moved on top of him.

An hour later Kenny heard a knock on the door.

"Are you and Mom ready to get up?" Heather asked. "It is Christmas."

Emmy was drying her hair as she walked out of her bathroom. "Why didn't you get up early?"

"We thought we'd let you guys sleep in. It's not like we're little kids anymore," Heather said.

"Hey! It's about time you got up," Kevin shouted as he dashed past Heather in the bedroom. "I checked the family room and Santa Claus was here."

Heather rolled her eyes and headed downstairs.

"Did he leave some presents?" Emmy asked.

Kevin looked at his mother, grinned and said, "Mom, I know Santa isn't real, but I'll keep pretending he is if it will make you feel better."

Kenny's parents and Father James arrived, and a few minutes later Andy Walker appeared.

"Look who decided to show up for Christmas," Andy hollered as he walked into the kitchen.

Emmy smiled as Charles La Rosse removed his coat and hat and handed them to Andy.

"What am I supposed to do with these?" Andy asked. "Kevin, will you take care of these, please?" He removed his own coat and hat.

Kevin hung the coats and hats in the mudroom. "Uncle Charles, have you been in Germany all year?"

"Most of it, but I did a bit of traveling."

"Where did you go?" Heather asked.

"I visited New Zealand and Australia again. I spent two months on the Cook Islands and some of the other ones close by. I really enjoyed Fiji and Samoa. I spent two weeks on a safari in Africa."

"Did you see any elephants or lions or rhinos or giraffes?" Kevin asked.

"I saw lots of wild animals and I shot all of them," Charles said with a grin.

Isabella walked up to him with her hands on her hips. "You better tell me you're joking."

"I shot them all with my camera," he said. "I can show you the photos later if you'd like. Are you enjoying the snow?"

"Ben and I built a gigantic snowman yesterday," Kevin said lifting his arms over his head. "It's snowing again today so we might so sledding. We found this big hill in the woods and made a path to slide down."

"I'm starving," Andy hollered. "What's for breakfast? Or should I say lunch?"

"We have everything we need for a fry-up," Kenny said.

"Good! I'll let you do the cooking while I entertain these kids, who are growing up way too fast."

After the late breakfast everyone gathered in the family room. Emmy read the Christmas story from the Book of Luke as the kids sat on the floor and listened without complaining.

"We like hearing that story now, Mommy," Isabella said. "We used to be in such a rush to open our presents."

"Aren't there usually more couches in here?" Charles asked as he held out his hands to the fireplace. "That feels nice and warm."

"We moved one downstairs and rearranged things so we

303

could put the tree in the corner and have all the seating face that way," Kenny said. "It's a Christmas tradition."

"Who is going to play Santa?" Emmy asked.

"We will," Isabella said. She and Heather passed out the gifts.

"This one is for you, Gra," Isabella said. "It's from Kevin. I can tell by the handwriting. His is so sloppy."

The girls made sure everyone had a gift to open. They even found one for Charles.

"How did that get under the tree?" Kevin asked. "No one knew he was here."

Emmy grinned and answered, "Maybe there really is a Santa Claus."

Kevin looked up at his mother with wide eyes.

"Is anyone hungry?" Emmy asked later that afternoon. "I made sloppy joes, cheesy potatoes and Kevin requested baked beans. There's pie and ice cream for later, too."

"It sounds delicious, Emmy, but Carter and I promised to spend some time with James and Nora this evening. Thomas and Sherry flew in from Virginia yesterday, and we haven't seen them yet."

"That's okay, Mom," Emmy said. "Let me get your coats, and say hello to everyone for us."

"They are staying for a few days. You should stop by the house to see them."

"We will make an effort to do that. The girls love to talk about their horses, and Kevin likes getting guitar lessons from Frankie."

"Now that the band is finished touring Frankie mentioned going up to Minnesota and staying in his cabin for the winter," Mom Colwell said.

"Most people head south for the winter. Frankie does the opposite," Emmy said.

"He enjoys the solitude," Dad Colwell said. He hugged Emmy and put on his coat and hat. "Thanks for everything."

"You're welcome, Dad."

"I'm ready for some real food," Andy said. He opened the

fridge, looked through it and asked, "Where's the beer? Don't tell me you drank it all."

"If we have any, it's out in the garage and FYI, I haven't had a beer since the accident."

"I'll take one, too," Charles said.

"I second that," Father James said.

Andy grumbled and headed out to the garage after he couldn't find any of the kids.

"Do you miss it?" Charles asked.

"Not really. I have had a few glasses of wine, but we don't even keep that in the house anymore. Tony gave up beer when he was elected to the church board. He doesn't miss it either, and he's lost weight."

"I do enjoy a tasty beverage," Charles said.

"Emmy used to buy whatever cheap swill was on sale," Father James said. "I prefer something better."

"Daddy used to buy Budweiser," Emmy said. "He preferred quantity over quality."

"Should we eat in the breakfast nook, or the dining room?" Kenny asked.

"We don't use the dining room enough," Emmy said. "Let's eat in there since it's Christmas. The girls can help you set the table while I get everything out of the oven and warm up the sloppy joe stuff."

"Do you need any help?" Charles asked a few minutes later.

"You and Andy can take the beans and potatoes to the dining room. There are hot pads in that drawer." She counted the sloppy joes on the plate. "There's twelve. That's enough to get started. Kenny, would you carry these to the dining room."

Isabella volunteered to pray for the meal, and Emmy smiled and nodded.

"Jesus, we thank you for everything we have. We want to thank you on your birthday for everything you have done for us. Please help us share our things with children who aren't as fortunate. Amen," Isabella said.

"Do I have to give up my new guitar?" Kevin asked. "It's

the only one I have."

"No, but maybe you could donate some things you don't use anymore," Kenny said.

"You can give all my old baby toys away."

"We already did," Emmy said. "Kevin, you have to eat more than beans. Take one sloppy joe."

"Okay, but I want more beans after I eat these." He grinned at his sisters, who ignored him.

"How long will you be in town?" Emmy asked while handing the salt to Charles.

"At least through New Year's. My mother wants me to come to Knoxville before I head back oversees."

"Oh, speaking of Knoxville, we got a Christmas card from Jennifer and Ryan Sinclaire. She included a short letter about their year."

"How are they doing?" Kenny asked. "How old is their daughter now?"

"She turned four back in May," Emmy answered. She turned to Charles and said, "They named their daughter Emmy Rose, and she's a real cutie."

"Why would they give her such a name?" Andy asked.

Emmy made a face at him.

"Is she touring?" Kenny asked. "I haven't heard a new CD from her lately."

"When Klaus took over from his father, he dropped a bunch of artists. Jennifer was one of those. She isn't touring as much, and she mentioned they are trying to add to the family."

"Could I have another scoop of potatoes, please?" Charles asked. He handed his plate to Emmy.

"Is that enough?"

"Yes, thank you."

Andy pushed back his chair a few minutes later and patted his stomach. "I can't eat another bite. Everything was delicious."

"We have pie and ice cream if anyone has room," Emmy said.

Only the kids were ready for dessert.

"We're going to head home," Andy said. "Thank you for

dinner and breakfast." He stopped at the bottom of the stairs and hollered, "Merry Christmas! Charles and I are leaving."

Heather and Isabella stood at the top of the stairs to say good night. Kevin raced down them and hugged Andy and Charles.

"Thank you for the guitar strap. I will practice a lot."

"That's good because we might need a new player for the band," Andy said.

"Take this pie home," Emmy said handing it to him. "We have another whole one and half of the cherry pie."

"I don't need it, cuz."

"Speak for yourself, Andy," Charles said. "I happen to like Emmy's pies."

She got their hats and coats and held the pie while Charles put his on.

"Thank you, Emmy, and Merry Christmas," Charles said.

"You, too. Let me turn on the lights for you." She waited until they were in Andy's Acura and waved as he drove away. She looked up at the falling snow and allowed some to fall on her face and tongue. She headed inside after hearing the landline ring. She heard Kenny answer it, and checked the garage fridge. *I don't know why we even keep this. It's empty most of the time.* She went inside, saw Kenny staring out the kitchen window and headed to the family room to join Father James.

"I'll let everyone know," Kenny said and hung up.

"Who was on the phone?" Emmy asked as Kenny returned to the family room. She watched as he plopped down on the couch and sighed.

Father James set his magazine down and looked at Kenny. "Are you all right? You look pale."

"That was Amanda Lenhart on the phone," Kenny said looking at Emmy first and then Father James.

"Is she okay?" Emmy asked sitting next to Kenny. "Nothing happened to Joshua, did it?"

Kenny shook his head. "No, but Jeff is in St. Bart's. It seems he was shoveling the driveway earlier and had a heart attack. Amanda said he's in bad shape."

Chapter Forty-One

"We should be thankful he even survived," Dave said as the members of Fridays At Five met at their office Saturday morning.

"Amanda stayed with Frances again last night. She spent most of the day at St. Bart's, but came home around ten. She said Jeff was able to talk to her," Jeremy said.

"Why was he even shoveling snow in the first place?" Andy Walker asked raising his voice. "He could certainly afford a snowblower if he didn't want to pay someone to do the job. He's got three sons who could shovel snow. He had no reason to be out there in the first place."

Charles La Rosse patted his lifelong friend's back. "Settle down. We don't need you having another heart attack."

"Did he ever have any trouble with his heart before?" Adam asked.

Kenny looked at the guys. Dave shrugged and P.J. shook his head.

"I should make all you guys have physicals every year," Andy said sitting down at the conference table.

"How could we ever know he would have such a massive heart attack? Jeff has always been active around the house. He's always remodeling something or other," Dave said.

Kenny added, "He's lucky Frank was helping him and called for an ambulance right away."

"I don't want any of you guys to ever lift a snow shovel again," Andy ordered.

"I don't own one to the best of my knowledge," Dave said.

"We have a company that takes care of most of the homes in Bristol Ridge. Emmy used to like to shovel snow, but she won't do it if it's too cold. What was the temperature on Christmas, anyway?"

"In the teens," Charles answered. "I checked the thermometer on Andy's deck."

Jeremy cleared his throat and asked, "Do we need to think about canceling the summer tour? I understand that's several months away, but will Jeff be recovered enough for the rigors of a tour?"

"It's too early to tell," Kenny said. "It took Andy a long time to fully recover from his heart attack."

"That's because I was old and fat and out of shape," Andy said patting his stomach.

"At least Jeff gave up smoking years ago," Dave added. "He doesn't drink much. Maybe an occasional beer."

"Personally, I can't imagine performing without him," Kenny said. "I don't think he's ever missed a show before."

"He missed a couple when his father passed away," Jeremy said.

"We certainly don't need to decide anything today, but I could switch to bass since we have Tommy available to play guitar," P.J. said.

"Your son could play bass," Kenny replied. "He's pretty good, and you're still better on guitar than he is. Tommy likes to remain in the background. He might feel more comfortable playing bass since he could stay by Dave."

"Does anyone know how long Jeff will be at St. Bart's?" Charles asked.

Everyone had a different idea about the length of his hospital stay.

"No matter when he gets out, he will need time to recover and regain his strength. He might even need a heart transplant like that blues guy," Andy said looking at Kenny.

"I know who you mean, and he needed a new liver," Kenny replied. "He survived that and is back to touring all over the world. I don't think this is the end of Fridays At Five. We survived when Jeremy needed time away, and if we need to replace Jeff for a year or two, we will survive that."

"Yeah! You guys are still young compared to some of the bands I followed when I was a young man," Andy said.

"Who do you mean?" Charles asked. "Benny Goodman, Glenn Miller, The Dorsey Brothers?"

"You're a real riot, Charles," Andy said pointing a finger.

Check out these other titles by the author. Visit the website:
kennethleemcgee.com

<u>The Emmy's Story Series</u>

1. We Were 'posed to Get Married
2. One Of The Guys
3. A New Friend
4. Did You Like the Ravioli Tonight?
5. Completely and Forever: A Wedding
6. It's Time To Go!
7. How Difficult Can It Be?
8. Forever... Isabella... Forever
9. The Forgettable Year
10. Turning Thirty
11. Hello, I'm James
12. Remember The Struggle
13. But God! I Write Songs
14. A Lifelong Dream
15. Gideon's Tree

<u>The Annie Mercer O'Dell Series</u>

1. Roosevelt High
2. North Park College
3. Smoky Mountain Summer

<u>Stand Alone Books</u>

1. Growing Up In Kinmundy Junction
2. Grandpa, Lions and Kitty Cats: A Collection Of Short Stories For Children Of All Ages